SUNDIAL

SUNDIAL

CATRIONA WARD

NIGHTFIRE

A TOM DOHERTY ASSOCIATES BOOK

NEW YORK

This is a work of fiction. All of the characters, organizations, and events portrayed in this novel are either products of the author's imagination or are used fictitiously.

SUNDIAL

Copyright © 2022 by Catriona Ward

A Nightfire Book
Published by Tom Doherty Associates
120 Broadway
New York, NY 10271

www.tornightfire.com

Nightfire™ is a trademark of Macmillan Publishing Group, LLC.

Library of Congress Cataloging-in-Publication Data

Names: Ward, Catriona, author.
Title: Sundial / Catriona Ward.
Description: First edition. | New York : Nightfire, 2022. | "A Tom Doherty
    Associates book."
Identifiers: LCCN 2021041755 (print) | LCCN 2021041756 (ebook) | ISBN 9781250812681
    (hardcover) | ISBN 9781250852601 (international, sold outside the U.S., subject to
    rights availability) | ISBN 9781250812698 (ebook)
Subjects: LCGFT: Novels.
Classification: LCC PS3623.A7315 S86 2022 (print) | LCC PS3623.A7315 (ebook) |
    DDC 813/.6—dc23
LC record available at https://lccn.loc.gov/2021041755
LC ebook record available at https://lccn.loc.gov/2021041756

Our books may be purchased in bulk for promotional, educational, or business use. Please
contact your local bookseller or the Macmillan Corporate and Premium Sales Department at
1-800-221-7945, extension 5442, or by email at MacmillanSpecialMarkets@macmillan.com.

First U.S. Edition: 2022
First International Edition: 2022

Printed in the United States of America

0 9 8 7 6 5 4 3 2 1

For Agnes Matilda Cavendish Gibbons and Jackson Blair Miller,
who are the brightest, most shining godchildren I could wish for

SUNDIAL

ROB

IT'S THE CHICKEN pox that makes me sure—my husband is having another affair.

I find the first blister on Annie the morning of the Goodwins' party. She is in the bath and the window is a blue square of winter sky. The shadows of bare sycamore branches lie sharp across the white tile. Annie sits cross-legged in the tepid water. Her lips move, some secret song only for the plastic animals that bob around her. Annie won't bathe at a temperature warmer than blood. She doesn't like things too salty or sweet or sour, and her favorite stories are ones in which nothing happens. She is wary of extremes. I worry about her physically, my fragile second child, in a way I don't about Callie. Annie is small for nine and people often assume she is younger. Callie worries me in other ways.

The party is the Goodwins' January tradition. They call it their "blues banishing bash." They're a perky family who live next door on the left. Their two smart sons Sam and Nathan are near Callie's age; they have interesting friends as well as great taste in wine and food and art. It's the one occasion in the year our whole family looks forward to. We always have *the best time* at the Goodwins'.

Annie bends over and whispers to the rubber duck in her lap. The sight of her vulnerable spine, the dark paint-licks of hair clinging to her neck—these things make my throat close up hot. I don't know what it's like for other people but love and nausea are often indistinguishable to me.

"Arms up," I say. Annie obeys and as she does I see it: a red mark on her upper arm. I recognize it instantly. I put my hand on her forehead, on her back. Both are warm—too warm.

Annie scratches at the rash and I enclose her hand in mine. "Stop," I say gently. "That will make it worse, my little beet."

She makes a small sound of dismay. "I'm not a beet," she says.

"A cauliflower, then."

"No!"

"A rutabaga?"

"No, Mom!" But she stops scratching. She is a docile child.

I find that I am scratching my own arm in sympathy. I sometimes confuse my children's bodies with my own.

I PUT ANNIE to bed and go to the bathroom cabinet. Here are the crowded shelves of a busy family with two children. I push aside old cough syrup, disposable razors, nail scissors, Irving's diabetes medicine, my birth control pills, a water pick we never use, painkillers, a broken powder compact. I must clean this out when I have a minute. At the very back I find what I'm looking for: a full bottle of calamine, neck all crusted up but still good. I bought it a few months ago for Callie's eczema.

Annie's temperature is 101.5 and her eyes are even more unfocused than usual. I should have caught this earlier, I really should have. The stinging reflux of guilt washes over me. She scratches at her arm.

"No, sweetie," I say. I get her mittens from the dresser, fetch duct tape from Irving's toolbox, and fasten the mittens to her pajama-top sleeves. I give her Tylenol and cover her in calamine.

"Rob," Irving calls up the stairs. His voice is rough with morning. "Oatmeal's ready." He clears his throat, coughs. "And coffee," he adds.

I sit by Annie and let the exhaustion take me for a moment. I always find my younger daughter's presence soothing and conducive to thought. We have been on this merry-go-round for so long, Irving and I.

I make a decision tree in my head. Then I go downstairs to break the news.

CALLIE IS TALKING high and feverish in the kitchen. "And they caught him," she says, "because of the gas station surveillance footage. That's where he bought the cement."

"Where did you hear that, sweetie?" Irving says with an edge in his voice. I almost feel sorry for him. Callie likes to talk about murder at breakfast. "What have you been reading?"

"Just stuff," says Callie. "Just around. The woman was acquitted. It's difficult to prove. They had injected him with air, just air! It causes a pulmonary em-bo-lism. Emblamism? No, embolism."

I join Irving at the coffee maker. "Annie has chicken pox," I say quietly. "I don't understand how it's possible. When was she exposed? And she's vaccinated."

"It's not a hundred percent effective." Irving's eyes are sunk deep in dark pouches, gleaming like secrets. Last night was a bad one.

"Trust us to be in the unlucky percent," I say.

He smiles tightly and spoons oatmeal into Callie's bowl. Cartoon deer run around the inner rim, just above the mealy grounds. He adds four slices of strawberry and begins to pour on that sickly syrup Callie likes. I place a warning hand on his shoulder. *Not too much.* Callie's body seems to refuse to tell her when she's full. If she is not gently checked, she will eat until she is in agony, until she throws up. I can't handle two sick children today.

Irving shrugs me off like a horse flicking away a fly and keeps pouring syrup. Irving loves sweet things but cannot have them. He stuffs his daughter with the food he longs to eat. But he's not the one who stays up with her at night.

Callie sits at the table, watching us. She saw me trying to stop him pouring her too much syrup, I know she did. Unease bubbles up. I can never tell what Callie is thinking.

"Poor Annie," she says, nibbling a nail. "Sad face." A recent habit of hers, talking like those little pictures you get in a text message. I find it alternately enraging and amusing.

Irving puts the oatmeal down in front of Callie. She is large for her age, golden-skinned, with a broad angular face and fervent green eyes. When she speaks it is pinched and effortful, as if she's being squeezed like an accordion.

"Mom can look after Annie," Callie says. "Dad, me and you will go to the Goodwins' on our own." She scoops up oatmeal with her finger and puts it in her mouth, eyes on me. "Party hat, wineglass." Irving and Callie have a little club, all their own.

Irving looks at me, one eyebrow raised. It's the look he gave me in the bar, the first time we met. It used to make my heart beat fast and splashy. The intimacy of it. His silent question, to which only I have the answer.

"Use a spoon, please," I say to Callie. "No, sorry, hon. We all have to stay home. You can carry the chicken pox on your clothing. There will be lots of little kids at the party and we don't want to risk making them sick."

"Rob," says Irving. "Let her go."

Irving wants to put on his party self, be the handsome science professor, raise his eyebrow at people who haven't seen it a hundred times. Most of all he wants to be in a crowd with her, eyes meeting at a distance as they talk to other people, hands leaving moist prints on their wineglasses, the longing between them stretching across the room like fine gold wire. I've seen it before and will again, no doubt.

"I want to see Nathan and Sam," Callie says.

"You can see them any time," I say. "They're next door."

"Not if I break my ribs," Callie says. "Not if I get hepatitis. Not if I drink bleach and die."

"Callie, please. There will be babies, pregnant women, old people there. Maybe unvaccinated children. Do you want to be responsible for them getting sick? I mean it. We're staying home. I know how fast these things spread—if even one of my fourth graders gets flu, they're all sick within the week."

Callie's scream starts low in her abdomen, like the growl of a big cat. Then it rises like a launched rocket, ear-shattering. It is so loud I feel it like a punch, see it in the air like stars. Irving bends over her, speaks in her ear. Callie screams higher and higher. I meet Irving's eyes. I allow the corner of my mouth to turn up, the merest fraction. *Contradict me again,* I think at him. *I dare you. Tell Callie that you and she can go to the party.*

He lowers his gaze and strokes Callie's shoulder, murmuring about pancakes. Her screaming stops. It gives way to little giggles. She and Irving stare at me. The same little smile plays about both their mouths. They have the same lips. And it sets me off, even though I know it shouldn't.

"That's it!" I shout. "You go and clean your room. Change your sheets. Maybe that will get rid of the weird smell in there."

Callie covers her mouth and laughs into her palm. Irving gets up and starts doing dishes, like it's nothing to do with him. I stare at the back of his head, the red place where the barber went too close, and I wish I could throw something, like he does. But I've got no power here.

I take Callie's abandoned bowl of oatmeal and carry it upstairs. I put it on Annie's rash in cooling handfuls. She puts her hot little cheek against my hand, and that helps some.

I TEXT HANNAH Goodwin. *Sorry! We have a case of chicken pox. Safest to stay home. Sad face.* I delete the last in irritation. Callie's habit is catching. *Have fun, come over for drinks on the deck next week. R.*

I read it over carefully and replace *R* with *Rob x.* That's better. That looks normal.

"THIS WILL BE fun," I tell Irving and Callie. "We'll have a family day. Movies, games, Chinese food . . ."

Each of us has strong objections to the others' movie choices. Following the path of least resistance we end up putting on something no one wants to watch, about a man followed around by a giant rabbit that might or might not be only in his mind. Irving sits between me and Callie, an arm around each. I check on Annie every half hour. We hear the music start next door just after eleven a.m. The laughter begins, high, excited conversation that soon builds to a feverish pitch. Once or twice there comes the sound of breaking glass. Irving turns up the volume but the movie is so stupid it can't hold anyone's attention.

"I'll go to the store for oatmeal and calamine," he says. I know what that means; I can see it in the tiny, repeated tensing of his jaw. He'll go to the store and on the way home it will be natural to stop by the party for a drink. Just one, of course; at least that's how it will start. I feel so angry that it's difficult to see. Little black spots drift over my vision.

I say, "We already have oatmeal and calamine."

"You might be infectious like Mom said," Callie says, seriously. "You might make a little kid sick." I feel a rare rush of love and gratitude toward her, even though I suspect it's just because she doesn't want to be left alone with me.

Beside me I feel Irving's mood narrow to a point. No one speaks. On-screen, the imaginary rabbit follows the man. Next door, jazz plays through shouts of joy.

Eventually I say, "Enough," and turn the movie off. This is family life, in my experience. Always trying to do things like the families in magazines or on TV, followed by the abrupt plummet of failure.

I'm not really a TV person. The first time I saw an action movie I nearly died of excitement, or at least that's how it felt. These days I don't understand why anyone bothers to watch soap operas or go to movies. I don't even read or watch the news. Living is enough. It is so intense and painful.

IT TOOK MONTHS of pleading and blackmail to wear Irving down each time, but I won the battle to finish college, to get a teaching job, and after Annie, to go back to work. Irving is very big on traditional values. The only thing that swung it for me was that there was an opening at the kids' school, which meant I could be in the same building as them all day. That and the fact that we needed the money. Irving's father lost a lot in the big crash.

I love my job. At school I am known as the child whisperer. The name is a joke but it's also a fact that with my students, I am magical. The withdrawn children blossom shyly under my care. The hyperactive, the manic, become calm and docile in my presence. A fourth grader known in the staff room as the terrapin, because of her tendency to bite when she is bored, writes me passionate book reports on Maya Angelou. I have no such powers at home.

I love my house too, a boxy Cape Cod set on a rational eighth of an acre of green, sloping lawn. It's the woman who gives the house its energy, its style—isn't that what people say? Two live oaks stand on either side of the door. The backyard has a pine deck shaded by the tall maples that line the alley. I built the deck over the course of three weekends, following a design I found in a library book. It really wasn't difficult. I ordered the lumber and then I put it together like a puzzle. (One rare way in which Callie and I are alike—we both get most of our knowledge of life from library books.) Anyway, it's lovely to sit out there at sunset or on a hot day, with the maples leaning over all green. I feel like I'm sitting in the treetops. It's so easy to sweep clean, too. The neighborhood association never has to tell us to cut our grass or keep our two flower beds mulched, or sweep the limestone path that curves up to the white front porch. I keep it all in order. I love the yard, for its simplicity, its containment. It's so different from where I grew up—hot dead sand and rock stretching on in every direction. Stare at all that space, day after day, and it begins to feel like a trap.

I feel safe here, among the neat rows of family homes. There is the odd gesture toward individuality—this yard has a birdbath or even a small pool. That clapboard is painted a daring shade of pink. Stained-glass windows, different styles of knockers, different kinds of stone for paving the path—these are the greatest extremes to which choice can go. But they are meaningful. They're the marks people put on the world.

I said I felt safe here. Maybe what I meant was that my children are safe. Those two things don't always go together. Maybe at some point everyone has to choose between one and the other. It's better to be part of a unit—"The Cussens"—than individuals. You get noticed less, that way.

IRVING GOES INTO his study and shuts the door. Callie gets out her drawing pencils. She never has a problem entertaining herself, and I never have to nag her about schoolwork. There are startling, unexpected patches of relief in her personality. She sits at the rolltop desk in the living room, bent very close to the page. The pencil makes its drowsy sounds. She starts to hum tunelessly. It's annoying, and I want to tell her to put on her glasses, but I thrust down both these impulses. I learned tactics early on. I pick my battles.

BY ONE P.M. Annie's rash has spread. Her mittened hands are clutched under her chin; dark hair lies across her cheek, fluttering with her breath.

I check the tape on the mittens, which is secure, and move the hair away from her mouth.

"Too bright," she murmurs, so I draw the curtains, plunging the room into vague silver dark.

"Do you want the star lit?" I whisper.

"Yes," she whispers back without opening her eyes. I go to the window-sill and turn on her night-light. The lamp is the shape of a star and it glows luminous in the dim room; the softest pink, the color of cotton candy, or the depths of a pale peony, the color little girls dream in. I always feel that Annie is safer when the lamp is lit. I know that doesn't make any sense.

When I look up, Irving is standing in the doorway. I hadn't heard him approach. He has always had the ability to stand perfectly still, as though no breath moves in him. It's unnerving in a living thing.

"How is she?"

"She's sleeping."

"Don't take your stuff out on the children, Rob," he says. "Callie really wants to go to the party. Let her. You can't keep her home because of Annie."

Annie stirs, opens one eye. "Water," she says in a small voice.

"Sure, sweetheart. Mommy will get it. Out of my way," I say to him through rigid lips as I pass. "You did this."

He turns a furious back on me and goes to the bathroom to take his diabetes pills. It will take him a couple of minutes to find his meds. I moved them to the back of the bathroom cabinet, hid them behind an old tub of Vaseline. A petty gesture but that's the kind of thing that's available to me, these days.

THE FIGHTS ALWAYS start differently and they always end the same, with us arguing like snakes, hissing as I load the dishwasher or fold laundry and he grades papers, his pen stabbing the air, both wary of our children sleeping above. We have been doing it for years. Eventually we fall into bed exhausted, weakened by the venom that consumes us.

Last night it started with our electric toothbrushes, which were out of power. Both were connected to their chargers but someone threw the switch that controls the bathroom wall sockets, so they went flat. Callie has a bad habit of playing with switches.

It began with the toothbrushes but it wasn't long until we started on Katherine the lab technician. Irving works late hours. This doesn't bother me. The lab technician works late, too. Katie, as he calls her, wears a perfume called Sentient. I know this because it is all over his suits. His closet reeks of it.

I hissed with clenched fists, throat closed up so tight that the words squeezed out like bile, eyes burning.

Irving started pointing. He never touches me—he points instead. His stabbing finger trembled an inch from my face, jabbing in time with his words. "You wanted this," he said. "It's all you wanted when we met. Now you've got it, all you can do is whine."

The mess of adult life, where you've both dug in so deep, where blame is a tapestry so tightly woven that it cannot ever be unpicked.

I AM TRYING to read when I hear Annie crying upstairs. "No," she sobs. "No, no!" I open her door. She and Callie are struggling over something, wrestling it back and forth. It is the pink star lamp. Annie's head is thrown back, her mouth a black *o* of sorrow. Callie is as expressionless as ever, but her lower lip is caught between her teeth. "Give it to me," she says in her tight voice. "Or someone will die."

"I hate you, Callie," Annie says. "God hates you." She lunges with a mittened fist.

I thrust them apart. Somehow the pink lamp is still intact. I take it from Callie's damp grasping hands, stow it safely out of reach on the windowsill. Goodness knows why Callie wants it.

"Mom," says Callie, "don't let her keep it!"

"She's being mean to me!"

"For goodness' sake," I shout. "Both of you! Be quiet. Read a book!"

IRVING SITS AT the kitchen island with his feet up on a chair. I repress a leap of irritation. He knows I hate that—dirty feet on my nice chairs.

I love my kitchen most of all. I agonized over the wood for the island and I never forget to oil it on Sundays. I designed the pattern of the floor tiles, the spirals of soft blue-gray glazed terra-cotta. I built the overhead rack myself, like I did the deck. Carpentry's not too difficult if you take your time. I hung the copper-bottom pans just so, in order of ascending size.

There's a bowl of something mealy in the center of the island. Pride of place. "What's that?" I go to the cupboards to hunt for aspirin. Not for Annie, for me.

"I'm making a spotted dick," Irving says. He doesn't cook but he takes pride in his cakes and puddings, starchy tasteless English things you have to steam. He thinks they're classy. "Hey, Rob," he says. "Taste and tell me if it needs more currants."

There's nothing I want less, but once more I pick my battles and get a spoon, thinking of Annie and Callie with sorrow. They used to be such good friends and play together all the time. I would chalk it up to Callie reaching a difficult age, but every age has been difficult for Callie.

I dip a spoon in the bowl before I see what's actually there. I scream, I can't help it, even though I know that's exactly what he wants.

He's laughing, bent over and breathless. "Your face!"

"That's horrible." My voice shakes. "What a horrible thing to do to someone."

"I have to warm them," he says patiently. "I'm going fishing with John tomorrow." I can smell the maggots now, the acid, the ammonia rot of them. Irving keeps these big blocks of bait in the refrigerator in the garage. I should have known there would be retribution for me denying him his party. In the bowl, the warming maggots stir little blunt heads. Their bodies are red as blood.

I BELIEVE THAT everyone has one story that explains them completely. This is mine.

Callie was two, a difficult toddler, late to speak and full of silent fury. Even then, a grim scowl covered her face at all times—except when she looked at her father. Then a timid smile crept over her features and I saw that she really was just a baby.

She was also an escapologist. She could open doors, cupboards, drawers, manipulate handles and locks that should have defied her tiny hands.

Irving was due home from a conference that afternoon. Callie had been up all night. She never, ever slept when her father was away. I was exhausted; the air was thick and fuzzy like I felt. I put her in her high chair to go to the bathroom. I was gone for, I swear, no more than thirty seconds. When I came back into the room she was half out of the chair, half in the sink, one tiny arm plunged shoulder-deep down the garbage disposal. Her eyes were intent, her small hand strained toward the switch on the wall.

I ran and seized her to me tightly. "Never, never do that again," I shouted. She looked up at me in wonder, and then opened her mouth wide. She began to scream, a needle in my head.

It was hours before I finally got her down in her crib. The world seemed to tremble around me like Jell-O. I sank onto the couch and was asleep in a moment.

I woke to his hand on my head. Irving was looking down at me, dark eyes still.

"Callie's been a nightmare," I said.

"I'm fine, thank you," he said, acid. "The conference was great."

"I didn't know it would be like this. I don't think she likes me." I heard my whiny tone and a part of me hated myself.

"She's just a child. Try and have some perspective." There was an unfamiliar cadence to his sentences. My heart sank. *Another one.* During the honeymoon period of Irving's crush on a woman he will fall into her speech patterns.

I sat up and leaned in as if to kiss him. There was whiskey on his breath. "Was there even a conference?" I asked, surprised by my own directness.

He took a pinch of my hair between forefinger and thumb and pulled until my eyes watered. "Go check on your daughter," he said. "Christ." He let go of my hair and brushed his hands off, as if ridding them of something unpleasant.

I got up off the couch, but I didn't go up to Callie. I was filled with something fierce and effervescent, ready to spill over. "I can't do this anymore," I said, surprised to hear how reasonable I sounded. "I'm leaving. We don't have to be married, Irving!" It felt like a revelation, like a bolt of light. But when I saw what was in his face, I ran.

After a beat of surprise Irving came after me. I ran through the house, doorframes slipping in my grasp. As I went a terrible thing happened. My body remembered this—running, fear, danger panting close behind. It came up suddenly, memory, and took me by the throat. I have to believe that's why I did what I did next. I opened the front door. The afternoon air was the breath of freedom. But I didn't run. I waited until Irving came up behind, then I stepped out onto the porch and slammed the door behind me, right on his reaching hand. I actually heard the crunch, followed by his cry of pain. I turned away. I thought, *No one can make me do this anymore.*

I went across the front yard, which was bare dirt right down to the street; we hadn't had time to do anything with it. *What will I do?* I thought. I didn't have a job, or friends.

Something sat at the bottom of the earthy slope, on the curb. I thought it was a cushion or a footstool dumped there for freecycling. It happens sometimes, even in a nice neighborhood like ours. But it was Callie, squatting almost in the road in her gray sleepsuit with pink elephants on it.

I ran to her, my body made of fear.

She looked up at me with her big eyes, still swollen with crying. "Pale," she said. She was stroking a brown, dry weed, which had sprung up between the gaps in the concrete. It had a little husk of a flower on the end. I sat down next to her, suddenly exhausted. "Sorry, honey," I said. "I'm sorry." I knew then I wouldn't leave. It wasn't her fault, any of it.

I picked her up. For once she didn't fight me, but laid her head on my shoulder. We went slowly back to the house. I put Callie back in her crib. "I'm going to make you a garden," I told her, and kissed her head. Maybe she wouldn't let me love her, but I could still take care of her.

Irving's hand was badly bruised but not broken so I put ice on it and we sat at the crooked Formica kitchen island, both silent and exhausted in the lee of the fight. *I should do something with this room,* I thought. It was very bare and cheaply finished; the linoleum was cracked underfoot and the faucet leaked badly. I pictured it hung with good copper-bottomed pans, pots of herbs on the sill, maybe even a spice rack.

"No more late nights," I said to Irving. I didn't mean late nights, I meant no more coming home in the mornings, speaking in other women's voices. "Deal?"

He looked at me, measuring. "You don't get to ask for favors," he said, nodding at his bruised hand.

I had to try to make it right somehow—make it tolerable between us. I put my hand hesitantly on top of his good one.

"Callie learned a new word." I told him the story, laughing and crying a little bit, too. He smiled and I almost sagged with relief at being forgiven. And a fierce spike of pride—she said it to me, not him. Then I saw what we had to do.

"Let's have another one," I said. "A baby."

"Yes," he said. I almost wept at being back in the warmth of his approval. And if there were two of them, maybe he'd let me have some of their love.

I have wondered since why he agreed. His father hadn't lost everything yet. I think Irving was hoping for a boy. He thought the old man might be more generous if we had his grandson. As for me, heaven help me, I wanted one all my own. Callie has always belonged to Irving. You're supposed to have less selfish reasons for wanting a child.

I got my wish. When Annie was born, I felt it right away—a warm beam washed over me when she opened her deep blue eyes. She was an easy child from the first, and she was mine. She and I fit together, part of each other in a way that Callie and I have never managed.

It didn't work completely. The children have pushed Irving further and further from the center. He doesn't relish the edge of the spotlight. And there was no boy for Irving's father to write checks for. But I hold on, because this way I can give my children two parents to take care of them, a house filled with light and flowers, a scented garden with grass to walk on. Even when Irving's late nights start up again, as they always do, I hold on.

It's for them, but it's for me, too. Sundial, Falcon, Mia, the stuff with Jack—all of it set me aside from others and I still have that burning need to blend in. I long to disappear into the unremarkable mess of women with families and houses in the suburbs and teaching jobs and small ambition. As for Callie, she's my daughter and I love her. I will never, ever let her know that sometimes I don't like her. How hard I have to work sometimes to love her.

So, that's the person I am. Now, anyway. There are other, older stories, but they are about a Rob who is years dead and gone. I walled her up, sealed her off in the dark. Maybe she starved and died down there. A hopeful child, buried beneath the desert sand. Maybe that's a good thing. There's no place for her in this family.

It occurred to me much later how strange a word it was, for a two-year-old: *pale*. I have puzzled over it.

THE DOORBELL CUTS through my reverie, high and harsh. I'm on the couch in the living room. A notebook lies open in my lap. I was supposed to be making notes for next week's lesson on Mark Twain (oh, the terrible things we teach our children) but I see that I've been writing Arrowood instead. Callie is drawing in the corner. How long have we been sitting here like this? Dissociation, June the therapist calls it. I call it a welcome break. The doorbell rings again.

"Are you going to answer that?" Callie, acid. She doesn't look up from the page.

I get up, flustered. The notebook drops to the floor; I pick it up quickly and put it in my pocket. As I hurry toward the hall I hear the creak of the mail slot. Those hinges need oil. Someone calls through, "Hello?"

My insides curl up like baby mice but I put a smile on, even though she can't see me yet. People can hear it in your voice if you don't smile.

"Hannah," I call back, "how's the party?"

Hannah Goodwin's eyes are two blue moons fringed with auburn lashes. When she sees me they narrow at the edges. I'm not the only one doing fake smiles today.

I stop a couple of feet away from the front door. "I won't come any closer," I say. "Better safe than sorry." I realize that I'm still in my robe. With everything going on this morning I haven't had time to dress.

She says, "How are you feeling?"

"Oh, I'm well," I say. "It's only Annie who has it, but we thought better safe than sorry."

"Poor Annie! We're really missing you all. Listen, there was something lying in the middle of your path when I came up. Dead. A gopher, I think. A cat must have got it. I put it in the trash but it left such a mess behind. Maybe get Irving to turn the hose on it later, huh, princess?" It's a joke we share, calling one another fond names in old-fashioned accents, like forties movie stars.

"Thanks," I say.

"You OK?" Her eyes hold concern. "You and I are due a big cocktail and a catch-up, Rob." A screech of jazz trombone from next door punctuates her words. "Let's make a date to go away for a weekend sometime. The boys never stop talking about that Memorial Day we had in the desert . . ."

I allow myself a little inward smirk. We had them stay over once at Sundial, and Hannah can't stop angling for another invitation. The Goodwins have a time-share in Florida. That's the kind of thing Nick Goodwin likes, but Hannah has more refined ideas. She would much prefer to tell her yoga class about the desert. *So spiritual, the Mojave. You can really connect with yourself there.*

"Rob?"

"Sorry," I say. "I spaced out there."

"Do you need anything? I can run out to the store . . ."

"You're an angel," I say. "We're OK. I had a grocery delivery yesterday so we're stocked up."

Hannah's eyes crinkle again. "Well, you have my number—just say the word. Sam had it last month, it was a nightmare."

"I remember." Last month, twenty-two days ago to be exact, the Goodwins came back from Australia. The following day Sam Goodwin came down with chicken pox. So we haven't seen Hannah for a while. *I* haven't, anyway.

"I brought a little treat for you all. I'll just leave it on the step. You're a doll!"

"You're a treasure," I say.

"Call me later."

Hannah and I usually speak once or twice a week in the evenings. I doubt we'd be friends if not for the fact we live next door, and our children are similar ages. We're very different. But there is something bonding about the grinding exhaustion of parenthood, the constant teetering between laughter and tears, about that weary love for your children, planted so deep it is everything you are. Hannah and I have grown close. I like her. She's the kind of person I imagined having as a friend when I was young, before I understood what friends were.

When we're on the porch swing and she looks at me in that wry sideways glance and the night is warm and the kids are asleep, I can almost believe that this is all of who I am; Rob the teacher who lives in the suburbs with my handsome sciencey professor husband, who has at last found a good woman friend who understands me.

I don't know if she deserves those mean thoughts I had about her. She seemed to love it out at Sundial. The place has a grip. Many people feel it, few understand it. That's a good thing.

WHEN I'M SURE she's gone I open the door cautiously. Party streamers flutter in the tree in the Goodwins' front yard. From the back, the party is building to the roar of a good drunk. The cold air is faintly laced with cigar smoke.

On the step at my feet is a lemon meringue pie. Beyond it, halfway down the path, is a slick viscous patch left by the gopher's body. I feel like I can smell the dead flesh where it lies in the trash.

It took me months to find black limestone for the path at a price we could afford. I love its texture, the rough way it holds the warmth of the sun and gives it back to your bare feet. I had the landscaper lay it, not straight, but running in a soft curve up to the front door. In the summer it is hemmed by rosemary bushes, thyme, lavender, and blue sage, punctuated by odd stabs of red lobelia. I took a lot of trouble with the colors.

Now when I look at my beautiful path all I see is death and shining blood.

I feel someone standing behind me. I don't need to look to know it's Callie. She has a sixth sense for sugar. I bend and take the pie off the step. "Not 'til tonight, after dinner," I say, closing the door.

"Dad just went out the back," she says.

Of course he did. It's too much suddenly. I sit with a *thump*, back against the front door. Hot tears worm their way down my face. Soon I am gasping for breath. My nose is plugged as if with concrete. My face is swollen and tight as a plastic doll's. Still the tears come.

"Mom?"

Oh god, Callie. I've got to get it together. I try to steady my breathing, to make this a little less scary for her. Although—I don't know if Callie does get scared. Not like other people. Strange, the thoughts that arise while you're sprawled in your hallway like a baby deer, weeping in front of your preteen daughter.

"Don't cry, Mom," Callie says. "Wait—uh, just a sec." She gets up and I hear rummaging from the kitchen. My head feels very heavy in my hands.

"Here." Something hovers into view. I stare at it for a moment. A forkful of lemon meringue pie. A noise comes from my throat; high, loud, and brief. It's an unnerving sound, even to my own ears. Callie doesn't flinch. She looks at me, steady. "It will help," she says.

So I take it. The lemon clings to my tongue, tart, the meringue melts in a sugary fountain in my mouth. It does help, a little. "Thanks," I say. I am half laughing because it's so touching, her giving me pie to cheer me up, but part of me wants to cry all over again, because this is what comfort means in my daughter's poor emotional vocabulary—egg white and lemon curd and sugar made by her father's . . . well, never mind that.

"I'm OK now. Thank you so much, sweetheart." I take another mouthful of lemon meringue to reassure her.

Callie looks at me with her head tipped to one side for a moment, then she nods in satisfaction. I can almost see the tick appear by my name, taking me off her list of things to do. I'm fixed, she no longer has to worry about me. She goes back to her drawing. The humming resumes.

I keep eating. It's good pie.

I HAVE HAD my suspicions about Hannah and Irving for a while; there were signs. On a couple of nights I was pulled from the soft depths of sleep by the gentle click of the back door. The long showers he took, the exhaustion. The wine on his breath in the middle of the day. And he seemed happy, which I knew had to come from something outside our marriage.

When I saw the chicken pox blister on Annie's arm it felt like tumblers falling into place on an old-fashioned safe, or a golf ball drifting gently across a green, to fall perfectly into the hole. I just knew. No one went between our house and the Goodwins' while Sam was sick. Or no one was supposed to, anyway. I guess they couldn't help themselves. Did he take Annie over there with him, while he was supposed to be watching her? It doesn't matter exactly how it happened. My husband infected my little girl. For that I can never forgive him. I think of gopher guts spilling out on the hot cement.

Irving knows the game is up. I saw it in his eyes, earlier, when I told him about Annie's chicken pox. I look at the pie where it sits beside me on the floor, craters gouged out of it, fork standing upright in the layers of lemon curd, meringue, and pastry. I wonder if they arranged it between them; her distracting me at the front door while he slipped out the back. So they could meet and go—where? Into that clutch of undergrowth on the next block, the one that's always full of brown snakes in the summer? Do they drive somewhere?

I've noticed that Nick Goodwin never looks at Irving or says his name. It's always *sport,* or *big guy,* or *pal*—friendly sounding, but it's how you'd address a child. His gaze is always focused somewhere over Irving's shoulder. Nick knows, though he may not be conscious of it yet.

I don't think he'll be able to ignore it much longer. Is Nick the type to live in denial, or the kind to force a confrontation? Denial, I guess. He's a Realtor, they're pretty good at adjusting reality. I go the third way: I burn with rage inside while presenting a smooth exterior. Not recommended.

What I can't stop thinking is: *I like Hannah.* I like her way more than I like Irving, some days. The loss of our friendship feels like physical pain. A dull ache. Period pain, maybe. I want to say to her, *Pick me, you don't know what he's really like.* I can't seem to feel anything appropriate, even about my husband's affair.

ANNIE EATS THE pie delicately with her fingers. She will often follow Callie's lead, but with twice the intensity. Callie refused a fork a couple of times, and now Annie won't use cutlery at all. "Sweetheart," I say, and then I leave it. Let her do what she wants.

"Are you and Daddy fighting?" she asks.

"Why do you ask me that?" The guilt is a squeeze on my heart.

"When you look at each other you go all black and fuzzy."

Kids understand so much. It can be terrifying, sometimes. "Well, it's healthy for grown-ups to fight," I say. "To get out what's on the inside, so they can be friends again."

"Are you and Daddy friends?" Her eyes are as big as a bush baby's.

"Your father and I are best friends. Like you and Maria."

Annie plays with a fragment of meringue between her fingers. "Maria doesn't like me anymore," she says. Her lips purse in an unnervingly adult expression of sorrow. "She's mean to me at school. We don't eat lunch together. It makes me so sad. It makes me want to *die*."

"Don't say that, honey." I take her in my arms.

I am dismayed. Maria is a beautiful little girl with satin-sleek dark hair. She looks like a doll and she always speaks in complete sentences. "Please, Mrs. Cussen, I have finished my cake." She and Annie always played gravely and quietly together. I thought she was the perfect friend for my daughter.

"I think Maria's having a hard time at the moment," I say. "You know it's just her and her mom right now. Her mommy and daddy are getting a divorce." I can't help but feel a grim little thrill of pride. No matter how bad things get, Irving and I haven't put the kids through that. We have clung on to that much. I am ashamed at the spurt of malice I feel toward little Maria, who has wounded my daughter's gentle soul. I hold Annie and breathe the scent of her hair.

THE JET OF water leaps off the paving stones, loosening the blackened dried guts. If I waited for Irving to come home to clean this up, there would be gopher all over the path until goodness knows when. What makes this a man's job, anyway? The blood, the smell? Anyone who has been through childbirth has seen worse. It's funny how you forget so much about labor—the pain and sound of splitting flesh. It's self-defense. The body's kindly editing, to protect the mind.

I get this taste in my mouth sometimes when I'm afraid or angry—like days-old soda, sickly sweet. It comes to me in dreams, even. It's here now and I want to spit, but of course I can't, anyone might see.

It's not the first dead animal I've come across. Hannah said a cat must have killed the gopher, but people around here keep their cats indoors. I think a predator is passing through the neighborhood. A coyote or a fox, maybe. A badger or a racoon, perhaps. I've heard they all kill for pleasure. Whatever it is seems to be using my black limestone as a dinner table. I often find these telltale smears on the path. In other parts of the neighborhood I come across the corpses—eviscerated, spread-eagled across stoops and sidewalks and porches. Loops of intestine gleaming in the early sun. Small paws curled up in death, half-closed eyes showing a crescent of blue sclera. So very dead. It's terrible when everything around you seems like a metaphor for your life.

I AM WAITING by the back door in the tall January shadows when Irving comes in.

"Rob," he says when he sees me. He is more than a little drunk. "Just been out to the grocery store." He swings the bag at his side.

"Did you get everything you needed?"

He smiles at my tone. "I did," he says.

"Good. Go inside."

I flick the dead bolt on the back door behind him. "No more grocery shopping," I say. "I've got your keys. You go out again, you stay out."

"Are you crazy?" he asks slowly. I keep my nerve.

"Better go find Callie, she was asking for you."

He stops, a hunch of embarrassment on him. I know that look. He needs something. Asking me for anything sticks in his craw. "I couldn't see my medicine earlier," he says. "You know I need to take it at the same time each day. Have you . . . ?"

"I hid it behind the big tub of Vaseline in the bathroom cabinet," I say. "Hope you find it."

He comes from behind, is on me before I realize. His forearm snakes around, rests lightly against my throat, not restraining me, flesh barely kissing flesh, like a promise. His other hand blocks out the light. For a second I think he's going to cover my eyes, like children do when they sneak up behind. Then I'm afraid he'll slide his fingers into the socket, take my eyeball between forefinger and thumb and gently pull it out. I gasp and bat at his hands. The scream in my throat comes out as a muffled rasp. But Irving's cupped hand just hovers before my face. He breathes into my ear, filling it with the stink of liquor.

"Hope I find it, too," he says. He doesn't touch me, hasn't done so since that day, but he likes to come close.

CALLIE WAS NINE and Annie six. Irving and I were having the mother of all fights. It had already lasted days. We hissed at each other whenever we thought the girls couldn't hear. At night when the kids were in bed we yelled and sobbed and threw things. We woke them up sometimes; Annie would cry. She got back to sleep easily; she was too young to really understand. Callie has always been quick. I know she understood. But Callie never cried and she never said anything.

One evening when Callie was watching TV in the living room I went into the kitchen and he was waiting for me behind the door, still as a post. I started to whisper something hurtful, to let out some of the stored-up bile. Irving reached out and pinched the bridge of my nose so hard I heard the cartilage squeak. Pain rushed through in a fiery flood. I opened my mouth to scream. But I remembered Callie in the next room and thought, *I mustn't,* so I stopped my throat. I stood there, eyes watering, screaming in silence. There was very little blood but for a couple of days after my nose was swollen and tender as a ripe plum. Annie kept reaching for it, saying *boo-boo.*

The following afternoon was a Saturday. We were setting off for bowling with the Goodwins as usual. It was Hannah and Nick's turn to drink so Irving and I took two cars, room enough for both families. I started to get into the jeep with Annie. Callie watched from the step, waiting for Irving to finish whatever he was doing indoors. Whenever we leave the house at the last minute, Irving finds something he has to do: unload the dishwasher, hang a picture, make a call. It's an exercise of power, making me wait, anxiety rocketing higher and higher as we grow later and later for whatever it is we have planned. Also I think he needs the adrenaline of urgency to do anything at all.

Annie always rode with me, Callie with Irving; it was the natural configuration. But now I stopped and called Callie to me.

By the time Irving came out I had both girls settled in the jeep, Annie in the child seat, and Callie belted into the back. "Bye, Irving," I said, and backed out of the drive. His face had horror in it. He thought I was taking his daughters. *Good,* I thought. *See how it feels?*

"Why aren't I riding with Dad?" Callie asked.

"I wanted some Callie time," I said.

The SUV followed us closely all the way to the bowling alley. I could see him in the rearview mirror, hunched over the steering wheel. His eyes were pinpricks of rage. Around him, the Goodwins were laughing.

The bowling alley was loud with the happy clamor of a family Saturday. I waited until the Goodwins were all busy putting on their shoes. Then I said into Irving's ear, "Don't you ever touch me again, ever." He nodded once, face blank. I realized in amazement that I had won.

After we got home and the kids were in bed, I lay listening to Irving's sounds from the bathroom. I never use the en suite. I don't understand them. Why would you defecate so close to where you sleep? I want at least two doors between those activities. It's one of the reasons I love suburbia so much. It barely acknowledges that we have bodies.

When Irving came out I sat up. I wished I hadn't gotten into bed, I didn't like looking up at him.

He smiled, rueful, and raised an eyebrow at me. I smiled back, relieved. "I'm going to wait," he said. "For when this fighting is over, and we're happy again. We'll go to French restaurants like we used to. We'll fall back in love. So deeply in love that it burns us to be apart. Then, one day—maybe we'll be having breakfast, maybe we'll be watching a movie. Something normal. But you'll look over at me to make a joke, ask a question, and I'll be gone. Then you'll look for Callie, and she'll be gone, too. I'm going to leave you when you least expect it, and I'm taking her with me." He loomed over me and planted a kiss on my forehead, light as a dry leaf. "I'm smarter than you," he said. "I've got endurance. I can wait long enough to make it really hurt." He picked up his glass of water from beside the night table and hurled it at the wall. The sound was like the world opening. Glass flew like diamonds. Irving smiled. Then he got into bed and a moment later he was asleep.

I lay awake beside him, watching the water drip down the ochre bedroom walls. I had chosen that paint color to be soothing. *Like a Tuscan villa under the evening sun,* I thought.

Irving kept his promise—he has not touched me in anger since that day. He takes it out on glasses, dishes. Every day I wonder, will it be today? My head shattering against the wall, instead of a plate, or a glass.

ANNIE WON'T TOUCH the soup I made, or the orange, or the sandwich. So, what the hell, I give her a cookie left over from Christmas. It's a violent pink color, frosting and all. Annie shouldn't have any more sugar after that lemon meringue pie, I know, but to hell with it. She eats hungrily, then goes to sleep.

Now for some Rob time.

I go to my study, which is just off the living room. Before I start anything I always sit down in my chair and take several deep breaths. *Be where you are. You can't write with chicken pox and adultery and worry about your eldest daughter all whirling around in your brain.* I write longhand; it's the only way I can think.

I started writing the Arrowood School series a couple of years ago, at night, while Irving was working late. It was a chef at a restaurant in Escondido, that time. She must have been good; he gained a lot of weight that year. It's about a fancy boarding school on the New England coast. I must have read *Summer Term at Bingley Hall* a hundred times when I was a teenager. Books sink their hooks deep into your mind at that age. When I first decided to become a teacher I had a secret hope that the school would feel like Bingley Hall. It only took one seminar of teacher certification to put an end to any such misconceptions. Maybe there are Bingley Halls in the world—in England, maybe—but I haven't seen them. Maybe they existed once and now they're all gone. Maybe it's a good thing they only live in our imagination now.

But thoughts are free, as they say. This one's told from the point of view of the sporty girl. She has secrets. I think I'll make her a thief in this one. There's a scandal in each of the Arrowood books. They're a very troubled set of teens.

It's a good distraction. More than that, really. A place to go. There are four Arrowood stories, now. I suppose they're long enough to be called novels. I've never shown them to anyone. Why would I? They are a private thing.

I write in pencil because the last thing I do right at the end when I finish each one is go back through and change all the character names. I use the names of people I know while I'm writing. My family, mainly. Book after book, Rob, Irving, Callie, Annie, Jack, Mia, and Falcon betray each other and make friends and whisper secrets. They walk the halls of Arrowood, arm in arm, carrying their books to class and quarreling over who's going to take who to the Spring Formal with the neighboring boys' school.

None of these things happened of course, but it's an act of remembrance, nonetheless. Call it therapy if you like.

EVENTUALLY THE PARTY next door winds down. The music stops and the talking dies. Car doors slam and someone falls over, I think. I hear the sick smack of flesh on concrete. I shake my head in irritation. They'll wake the kids up. Plus, the head girl was about to do something particularly dastardly and now I've lost the thread.

I take my deep breaths and pick up the pencil again. Everything clicks off. It's wonderful, like vanishing.

ARROWOOD

Callie made her way down the cliff path toward the sea with her cuneiform grammar books under her arm. She was behind in class and planned to study in the shade of the cliffs, with her toes buried in the sand. Miss Grainger would be so proud of her when she realized she had caught up, despite having focused too much on field hockey the previous semester. Callie had a little crush on Miss Grainger; she was so smart and her hair was so chic in that little bob.

But when Callie reached the beach she realized she wasn't alone. Voices were raised over the sound of the wind. Not wishing to appear intrusive, Callie instinctively crouched down, so she was concealed behind a screen of nodding cattails. Right away she wished she hadn't hidden—it would look so low if she was found, as if she had been listening.

She could hear a familiar voice. It was Callie's best friend Jack talking to someone. Jack's real name was Jacqueline but Jack hated it. Not even the teachers used her full name. Callie and Jack were always together. They told each other everything. Well, almost everything.

"Thank you for meeting me here," Jack said. "I didn't want to make gossip."

"What is it, Jack? I have to teach a glassblowing class in twenty minutes," another voice said. Callie almost gasped aloud. It was Miss Grainger. How peculiar. Callie had been thinking of her just a moment before!

"I have to talk to you about something very serious."

"Oh dear, Jack. Please go on."

"Callie's the one who has been stealing from the other girls," Jack said. "I had forty dollars in my bedside locker, a present from my aunt. It was supposed to buy me new soccer cleats! But this morning it was gone."

"Did you look underneath everything in your locker?" Miss Grainger asked. "Often if you look underneath, you find unexpected things."

"I did, Miss Grainger, I did! But the forty dollars is really gone. It has to be Callie. She's the only one who knows the combination."

Callie gasped silently. She went bright red, even though there was no one to see her, hidden as she was in the long grass. How humiliating that Jack thought she was a thief—and now Miss Grainger did, too!

"It's good you brought this to my attention. Theft is a terrible thing," Miss Grainger said. "We've suspected for a while, in the teacher's lounge, that it might be Callie. Now we have to act."

"If you suspected, why didn't you do anything?" Jack asked angrily.

"I should have done something," Miss Grainger said sadly. "I hoped it wasn't true. You see, I made her mother a promise many years ago, before she died. I swore to Rob that I would protect Callie. She and I were close once, as close as you two. But this has gone too far now. Callie will have to be expelled. It's affecting the other students. Her mother, Rob, was a witch, you know. I think Callie might be a witch, too. Witches steal, that's the first sign. Soon after that they go bad and mustn't be allowed near other girls."

"Witches aren't real," Jack said.

"Lunch is almost over. You'd better get back to school." Miss Grainger's tone had changed. She was cold, no longer friendly. "And, Jack?"

"Yes, Miss Grainger?"

"Promise not to say anything about Callie to the other girls. Or to any teachers. I'd like to deal with it myself."

"OK, Miss Grainger."

Callie's heart was beating fast. How had Miss Grainger known her mother? But there was no time to puzzle over it. She mustn't be expelled, not now—her father would never forgive her.

She slid the razor from her sock and flipped it open. She ran her finger lightly down the blade, leaving a paper-fine crimson cut across the tip. She would make it quick. She owed Miss Grainger that much.

But when she pushed her way out of the long grass, the beach was empty except for the gulls. Miss Grainger was nowhere to be seen. Callie turned and watched Jack's ponytail bobbing in the distance, as she made her way up the path toward Arrowood School on the clifftop, green pennants flying from its nine stone towers.

ROB

I'M FINALLY GETTING ready for bed when Irving yells my name. There is something sticky in his voice. It sends a cold finger down my spine. I run.

Annie is a white slip between the covers. Her whole body shakes. There is a pool of vomit on the floor. Irving's hands hover above her. He seems afraid to touch her. "There's something wrong."

I hunt in the bedclothes for Annie's small hands. The mittens are still firmly taped to her wrists. Something else meets my fingertips. I hold the bottle up in the lamplight.

Irving says, "For God's sake, Rob." He thinks I hid his pills here, that this is my fault.

The empty bottle of diabetes medicine is missing its cap. Several realizations come at once, now.

"I'll call an ambulance," Irving says.

"No," I say. "Don't touch the phone." Irving stops. I feel his eyes on me but I don't have time for him right now. I ask Annie, "Did you eat these a long time ago, sweetheart? How long?"

"Just now," Annie says.

I pick Annie up and take her to the bathroom. I thrust my fingers briskly down her throat. I make her throw up again and again. I see a lot of blue—the pills. It's followed by pink frosting. I don't stop until I'm sure her stomach is empty, until she dry heaves.

I sit her up on the bathroom floor. "How do you feel, darling?"

"Better," Annie says. And she does look better. "Bad candy."

"Very bad. Who gave it to you, sweetheart? You can tell me."

"I gave it to myself," she says and starts to cry.

But Annie couldn't have taken the lid off the pills herself. Her hands are still covered with the mittens and the childproof cap takes both strength and dexterity. And where did the cap go? Someone took the safety cap off the bottle and fed her the pills.

I put Annie back to bed and search her room. I turn the closets inside out and do a fingertip search of the bed linen, despite her drowsy protests. But the cap of the pill bottle is nowhere to be found.

IRVING SITS AT the kitchen table with his head in his hands. Hangover's starting. "You've got to keep a better eye on her, Rob," he says.

In the center of the table, the maggots stir busily. Some of them reach tentatively up the side of the glass bowl like tiny fingers. They're waking up, getting lively. Maybe it's my imagination, but their fat red bodies seem to be making a sound as they rub together—a dry rustling. The stink gets stronger as they warm up. "How did she get the pills, Irving?"

"Beats me. I took one and then I put them back in the cabinet. Top shelf, like usual. How could she get up there? I mean she could drag a stool into the bathroom to stand on, I guess . . ."

The words are out before I can think. "Did you give them to her? The pills?" It's an almost impossible thought, here in my soft-lit kitchen, which is hung with wine racks and expensive handmade copper-bottomed pans. Almost.

Irving's pupils contract almost to nothing. I feel the feather-light touch of fear. "I mean, to play with or something." I make sure to sound hesitant, like I'm seeking approval. But it's too late. The question lies between us like a wound. There are things that cannot be said in a marriage without changing it forever.

Irving gives a coughing bark. The tendons of his neck stand out in cords. "Don't be nuts, Rob," he says. "You know how you get."

"Swear it on Callie's life."

He shrugs. "OK, I swear."

My muscles give with relief. I sink down onto the kitchen floor. The world is spinning too fast. I believe him. You can't be married for twelve years to a compulsively unfaithful man without developing a fine instinct for the truth. "Thank god," I say. "Thank god."

"Wow, Rob," says Irving, weakly. "You need help."

"I really do," I say. How could I have thought that my husband had poisoned my child to score points? "What do you think June the therapist will say when we tell her I accused you of attempted murder?"

We stare at each other for a second before I say, "And how do you feel about that?" At the same time he says, "How does that make you feel?" and we both giggle a little and the tightness inside us eases, just a touch.

But a cool, mad voice inside me says, *Maybe it would have been better if he'd done it.* The seed of something even more terrible is growing in my mind.

"Where's Callie, Irving?"

"In her room."

The seed pushes forth sick tendrils.

"What's she doing in her room?"

"Sleeping, what else?" he says with overt patience. I had been wondering how Irving could be so blind, but I am beginning to realize that he's not. I can see that, under the patronizing manner, he's unnerved.

Callie is a light sleeper. We must have woken her. But my elder daughter, who is drawn to commotion, who turns her curious gaze on arguments and car wrecks with equal fascination, is not here. Normally she would make sure she had a front-row seat for the drama. She is nowhere to be seen.

When people say something is "unthinkable," what they usually mean is that they don't want to think it. They are resistant to an idea. But that is not what *unthinkable* means. I understand that, now. It means to be confronted with a thought so vast, dark, and monstrous that it will not fit into any known shapes in your mind. It is poison and madness flowering behind your eyes. I clear my throat to free it from the taste of old soda. The worst part is that I'm not as surprised as I should be.

I usually try not to make too big a deal of it. I know how difficult the relationship between sisters can be, especially if they're close in age. Passionate to the point of fury. *Girls grow out of it,* I told myself.

Callie holding a hank of Annie's hair, mouth pressed to her ear, whispering. Annie's head pulled back, mouth gaping, her eyes watering with pain. The red imprint of fingers on Annie's little arm. A couple of bruises Annie couldn't explain. *Don't play too rough, girls.*

Did I hold back because I was desperate to hide the fact that Annie is my favorite? And, if I did, how will I get through the rest of my life knowing it?

CALLIE IS NOT asleep. She is sitting at the desk in her room. There are paper and pencils in front of her but she isn't drawing. She is just sitting. Anatomical sketches cover the walls; beautiful pencil diagrams of skeletons. Birds, something that looks like a squirrel, something else that might be a newborn puppy. They are precise, to scale. She mounts them herself on gray box frames. The effect is attractive. Callie is so gifted, but she has no talent for life. Her shelves are stacked with books about psychology and serial killers. They have little Dewey decimal labels across the spines—library books. Most of them, as I know from experience, will be long overdue.

"Get up from the desk, please," I say. She does as I ask with no questions. My bad feeling builds. I start to riffle through the contents. It is very neat, organized. Drawing pencils, chalks, erasers, paper, X-ACTO knife. Some dented dog-eared anatomy books.

"What are you doing, Mom?" Her tone is curious rather than angry.

"I'm looking for something. Do you know what I'm looking for, Callie?"

She keeps her eyes on the floor, but she can't keep her gaze from sliding to the corner of the room where her big beanbag sits.

I handle the beanbag carefully, palpating it for foreign objects. Nothing. Under it, the corner of the carpet curls up somewhat, like the edge of an old sandwich. I lift it and there it is, the loose board. I lever with my fingertips and it comes up easily. Beneath it is a sizable space, about two feet by two feet. The hidey-hole is almost completely filled by a weathered blue backpack. It's Callie's, an old one from fourth grade. I lift it out and unzip it. I reach my hand in carefully, cautious of sharp objects. I set the contents out on the floor beside me. A bottle of hydrogen peroxide, a plastic Tupperware tub. When I open the Tupperware, a cloud of rot bursts forth. Inside it is the corpse of a squirrel, sealed in a sandwich bag. I can see pale glimpses of maggots through the fur. I've seen more maggots today than I care to ever again. The urge to retch comes like a tide. I cover my mouth and it passes, or recedes a little, anyway. There are a couple other things. A tube of superglue. In a plastic protective sleeve, a heavy, creamy piece of paper, with a drawing of some bones on it. No, not a drawing. Actual bones, glued to the paper.

I look at the bone collage for a time. Then I get up. I go to the wall, to a drawing of a small snake. I turn the frame over.

The snake bones are glued to the back of the drawing, perfectly mirroring it. Each rib is there, correctly placed. I turn over a picture of a mouse. There it is on the back, mirrored in bleached bone. However many dead animals we found lying around the neighborhood, there were many more we never found.

"They were like this when I found them," Callie says, unconvincing. Then she says, "I didn't want it to happen."

"Callie." I can't think of what to say next. "Why?"

"I don't know, Mom," Callie whispers. "Everything gets all flat and shiny."

The rucksack contains one last thing, zipped into the little pocket at the front. It is the childproof cap of Irving's medicine bottle. I stand up. My breath comes short and my vision goes gray at the edges. I steady myself on Callie's desk. I see the drawing she has been working on today. It is of the bones of a child's hand—roughly the size of Annie's hand.

My hand meets her cheek with a crack. It leaves a red mark across her golden skin. She puts her hand to the place, touches it tentatively, as if it were hot. The expression in her eyes doesn't change; remains vague, as if she's having another conversation that I can't hear.

I have never before laid a hand on my children in anger. It's me who cries, not Callie. It is like physical pain, the tear that is opening in my heart.

"Mom." Callie's hand is light as driftwood on my back. It's the second time she has comforted me today.

I get myself under control, or as close to it as I can. "You've been doing this for a long time. There are so many." I'm surprised to hear that my voice sounds regular, mom-like. I might as well be discussing a school art project. I dry my eyes and blow my nose. I always keep Kleenex in my pocket.

Callie looks down at the floor and twists her fingers. She speaks so quietly that I almost don't hear her answer. "I've always been doing it."

"What's this for?" I ask, holding up the hydrogen peroxide.

"It makes the bones white," she says. Things are beginning to make sense now, in that way they do during a crisis; with a slow, deadly roll. The bad smell in her room, the bleach, the plastic tub.

I take a shuddering breath. But I am not revolted or afraid anymore. Instead, I feel strangely close to her. We're being honest with one another for the first time in years.

"I've always done it with the bones. Even before I actually did it, I wanted to. I know who I am. Just like I know that people don't like me," Callie says. "Even you."

"I like you, sweetheart," I say. "I'm your mother. I love you." But do I?

"I know it's bad," Callie says, flat. "I don't know what to do. I'm so zzzzzzzz, sleepy face."

"I know what you mean," I say truthfully. I hold out my arms. She nestles into me. Her arms snake around my waist. I think about those strong little fingers and a wave of cold rolls through my belly. But I don't flinch. I hold her. I can do that much.

"I'm scared," she says into my shirt.

I stroke her back. "We're going to figure this out, OK?"

She looks at me with those deep green eyes, my eyes, and says, "I'm sorry, Mom."

I feel a rare, all-consuming rush of love for her. It flows in, now, filling the deep places and everything that's missing.

I SIT BY Annie. Her breath comes regular and slow. Even in sleep her presence is infinitely soothing. My thoughts dart to and fro like fish in a pond. I reason desperately. Maybe Callie is suffering from nothing worse than an excess of curiosity. Didn't nineteenth-century naturalists do precisely what she is doing? Is her treatment of these animals any more callous than our everyday consumption of meat? I mean, I try to buy pasture-raised, free-range, and organic, I really do, but it's so difficult when you're busy and—

I take a deep breath. I have to focus.

Annie is awake and watching me quietly. "I want to pray," she says. "Will you pray with me, Mama?"

I don't know where she got God. The first I knew of it was one night a few months ago, when I found her saying her prayers, kneeling by her bed, hands clasped like a child in an illustration. We are an entirely secular family. In my opinion you can't be a scientist or teach in a school without abandoning all faith in a benign creator.

"Sure," I say. "But pray lying down this time, OK, sweetheart? I don't want you getting out of bed."

She closes her eyes. Her lips move fervently. I watch her with a deepening sense of mystery and of failure. Both my children are impenetrable to me. Outside in the hall I stop. That gash in my heart is deepening, opening into a bloody crack. The sensation is so vivid that I am genuinely surprised, when I look down, to see my gray cashmere cardigan with its horn buttons covering my chest.

MY KITCHEN LOOKS strange to me. What did I think I was doing with all this artisanal wood and handmade this and copper and chrome that—the crafty expensive things on the counters, in the sink, on the shelves, hanging above the butcher block in rows? The fifty-spice rack on the counter. I asked Irving for it as a present on my last birthday. Who needs this many spices?

Irving sweats. Ice tinkles in his glass as he raises his glass of Scotch and even with everything else going on, I feel an acid spurt of irritation. He couldn't sober up, even for this. His dark hair falls over his brow and sticks to it. "The girls were probably just playing with the bottle and the cap came off," he says.

"Don't be ridiculous," I say.

"What did you say to me?" Red squirming things in his voice. Normally I would take heed of that tone. But there's no time.

"Giving Annie those pills was not a game. I need to get Callie away from here."

Irving just shakes his head slowly, looking at me. My heart goes cold. He's in that mood.

Quickly, I make a decision tree in my head. *How can I get Callie away from Annie, and where would we go?*

This is something I do with my fourth graders to help them with logic and problem-solving. I visualize my questions and the possible answers branching out and out. I follow each branch until I reach a conclusion. I can do it in a split second, my mind racing like brush fire.

I have it—where to go with Callie. I'll have to get around Irving, though. I feel him watching, so I take the cardamom from the spice rack and turn it in my hands, as if that's what I'm thinking about.

Irving says, patient, "You're not taking my daughter anywhere. Callie isn't Jack, no matter how hard you push all that stuff onto her. I think you do it to get to me."

"That's kind of narcissistic," I say without thinking.

He plucks the jar of cardamom gently from my hand and whistles it, overarm, at the wall. It explodes, glittering. The air is filled with the rich scent. I feel my pulse throughout my body. Irving reaches out his delicate fingers and takes the jar of dried sage from the rack. His eyes are deep shadows. I wonder, as I always do in these moments, whether it will be the sage and then me.

Sometimes he can be headed off but I have to do something decisive, and quickly. Kill or cure, as they say.

I take the dried sage from Irving's hands. I do it firmly with no fuss. "I'm going to take Callie to Sundial. We need a girls' break. You and she are such good pals. Maybe she's acting out because of me, you know? I get tense. Girls sense that from their mothers."

He hesitates. I see him wavering on the edge. He's appeased, but the mention of Sundial is a risk. It can go either way. "OK," Irving says, holding his hands up. He switches to the role of defeated husband. "I can't argue with you when you're like this. I'll just take care of your sick daughter. Maybe Hannah can pitch in."

I know I should walk away. But this one drives a hot spear of anger through my gut. I wish I could have affairs and drink too, but I can't, because someone has to take care of these fragile beings who've been put in our care, and it's me, it always is, and the wash of resentment rolls over me; it burns like acid on my skin and even though I've just won a huge victory, I still can't help myself. I grab the bowl of maggots off the table. They are thoroughly warmed up now and they writhe like a little sea in the bowl. I march across the kitchen holding it at arm's length. I unlock the window, throw up the sash, and dump them into the night, onto the flower bed below. I flinch and gasp as a maggot grazes my wrist. It isn't wet, as I had expected, but dry, almost scaly.

"How does that help?" Irving suppresses the ghost of a smirk. "You're being completely irrational."

My rage vanishes. I feel very cold and alone. That was stupid. I could have undone all my good work with my temper. And he's right, it doesn't help.

"One of our children just tried to kill the other," I say. The reality of it sends cold fingers down my spine.

"Mothers pass things down, don't they?" Irving's voice is soft. "The secrets I keep for you, Rob."

"Callie and I leave first thing in the morning," I say. I watch him consider his options. He doesn't want to let us go, but this way he gets our house to himself. And so does she.

I CALL HANNAH. There's surprise in her voice. It's past two a.m. "Hey, Rob, I'm just cleaning up after the party, let me—"

"I'm going away for a few days," I say. "Maybe longer, I don't know. I'm taking Callie with me. I just want you to know. Irving might need help because Annie's got chicken pox. Plus, she ate something she . . . never mind. She'll be fine, but if there's a problem, you'll be there? I need you to say it."

The receiver feeds back fear and silence. "Does, does Irving know that you're . . . ?"

"Jesus, Hannah. Would I tell you, of all people, if I was leaving my husband? We are coming back. I'm not making you party to an abduction or anything."

"OK," she says after a moment. Her lips are numb, I can hear it. "Rob, what is this? Do *you* need help?"

"You don't get to ask me questions like that anymore," I say. "Friends do that. You and I are not friends."

I STOP ON the threshold of Callie's room. I don't want to go in, to be surrounded by all those bones. She's still up, sitting on her bed, hands in lap. Her eyes are fixed on a point on the blank wall in front of her. She's waiting for me. What does she think will happen? I look at my daughter, and the distance between us feels like miles; we are perched on the edge of a great crevasse, and it will take everything I have to hold us back from the brink. "Pack a bag—we leave first thing in the morning. Stuff you'd take for a weekend trip. We're going to the desert. Just you and me."

"Annie and Dad aren't coming?"

"No. Annie's sick."

"I only want to go if Annie goes."

I stride into the room and take her face in my hands. She flinches and I loosen my grip. "Look at me. You are not going anywhere near your sister again until we have a very serious talk."

"I'm not going anywhere with you," Callie screams. Her scream rises and rises. *Keep her calm,* the cold voice inside me says. *You need her calm for this.*

"Shhhh," I say manically, petting her back. "Shh, sweetie. Don't be scared. Mommy didn't mean to scare you. It's a little special trip for us, OK? We're going to have *the best time* together."

Callie stops screaming. Her breath comes in little huffs. "Well," she says in her squeezed voice. "I guess it's OK if Dad takes care of Annie while I'm gone. Maybe a trip would be nice. I get very stressed around here. I have a lot on my mind. Exploding head."

"Good girl," I say, squeezing her shoulder.

I can manage her until we get out there. Then what?

IN THE MORNING Annie's still asleep, curtains drawn, when I go in to say good-bye. That's good. I don't think I could take her expression when she realizes I'm leaving. The pink star shines soft on her hair, her eyelashes cast long shadows on her cheek. *This is for you, my love,* I think. *For all of us.*

CALLIE

WE STOP FOR gas and Mom gets out. I see her blond hair like a waterfall, breathe the rich metal reek that leaks from the pumps. I love smells that are supposed to be bad for you. Glue, gas, bug killer. When she gets back in the car, her mouth is tense.

Dumpster Puppy whines and pushes his head against my hand. I see the seat belt through his transparent ears. *She's taking us somewhere secret,* Dumpster Puppy says. *Better watch out for trouble.*

"She's taking us to Sundial," I say scornfully. "You've never been there but I have. Calm down." Dumpster Puppy is a pessimist. That means someone who knows how things are. But he's good company because we can talk to each other without words. He's right, though, something's up. The air has a crackly feeling.

It's good that Mom let me bring Dumpster Puppy's bones, but I wish I could have brought all the pale ones. They will be sad without me, my little animals. Usually they nestle in my pockets, sleep in the hollows of my body at night. Now they'll have to wander the house, lonely. Dad and Annie don't know how to talk to them.

Pale Callie sits beside me, humming and looking out the window. She knows about Sundial. She's been there. I don't have Pale Callie's bones. I don't know what Pale Callie is, really. Just that she goes where I go and always has.

I watch the back of Mom's head. I think of what Dad said while he was hugging me good-bye. Mom was putting the bags in the car so she didn't hear.

"Be careful out there, bud," Dad said, warm in my ear. Dad and I are best buds. "If you get scared out there, you call me."

"Why would I get scared?"

"Your mom . . . she can be a little unstable."

I felt a little thrill of fear. I knew what he meant. The crying, the screaming late at night. Always yelling at Dad. She lies, too. I can always tell, even if she doesn't know it herself. For example, Mom doesn't like me, even though she swears she does.

I could see her wondering if I would tell him about the slap she gave me. I don't know why I didn't. Maybe it's because it made Mom seem a little more like me, just for a second. And it's a powerful thing, to keep a secret.

It's a long ride to Sundial and we're not even out of town yet. Pale Callie and I play "warm or pale." This is where I guess whether the people we see through the window are ghosts or not, and Callie tells me the answer.

I point to a kid on roller skates holding her mom's hand. *Warm,* Pale Callie says. A man sleeping under the freeway is pale. But that was an easy one. He looks pale.

The lights hold us here for a few moments on red. In the front seat, Mom pushes her hair away. I look at the back of her slim neck. It's strange how beautiful she is. It's like she's nothing to do with me. Pale Callie yawns and points to a guy on the crosswalk in front of us. *Nearly pale,* she says. *Cancer. He won't last the year.*

"Sad face," I whisper.

ROB

We pull over to look at the biggest ball of string in the world. It's not as big as I expected. It's dirty, too. Once green, it is now faded to khaki by sun and rain. The split rail fence is low and when I lean over to look closely, I see that the surface is peppered with little patches of black mold. You'd think they'd keep it indoors or at least under a roof of some kind. I suppose string doesn't last that long, anyway. They probably make up a new ball every couple of years. Not everything is meant to be forever. I try not to think, *twenty bucks each,* because it is an absurd price, but I've paid it now and there's nothing to be done about it.

These thoughts slide around and over one another in my head like live eels. It is difficult not to say anything but I stay silent because Callie is wide-eyed, almost trembling with pleasure. "It's like a giant head," she whispers, not to me but to herself. She takes my hand; she has forgotten that she doesn't do that anymore. The contact is a warm shock, it sends the peculiar electricity of love throughout my body. *This isn't about me,* I remind myself again. *None of it is. This is for Annie—and for Callie.* I try to ride her excitement, to enter into her pleasure in the day, in the big dirty ball of twine listing on the dry ground before us, in being alive.

We stand there, hand in hand, and after about ten minutes I say, "OK?" When I look down Callie is watching a ladybug that has landed on her sleeve. It marches confidently toward the bare flesh of her arm. Callie is transfixed. She can't seem to move or blink. "Come on, sweetheart," I say. I coax the ladybug onto my fingertips and blow it gently away, into the world.

"Why did you do that?" she says, turning those big eyes up at me. "I wanted to keep it."

"Time to go," I say after a moment. "For pie!"

There is a moment where everything hangs in the balance, but then she smiles and says, "Waffles?"

"Sure," I say, trying not to think about all that sugar.

As we walk back toward the car I ask, "Are we having *the best time* yet?"

"We're having the best time!" Even with everything, I feel a warm swell at her words. Usually she only has *the best time* with Irving.

That's important. I need her to be relaxed and to trust me. Trust doesn't sit naturally between us, so just this once she can eat anything. Pine cones with peanut butter, if that's what she wants. I want her to enjoy these last hours of the journey. Although nothing can make what I might have to do any easier.

SHE EATS THE waffles in fist-size bites. Whipped cream and syrup run down her chin. My cup of hot water with lemon steams in front of me. "There's no hurry," I say. "We're making good time. We'll be at the house by dark." She nods but does not slow her pace. She chews hard, mouth open. Dark cavern, white cream, masticated waffle.

The waitress was pretty once, I'm sure. Now she has that lined, dark leather face you see all over southern California, the face of someone who grew up in the sun but didn't hear about sunscreen until it was too late. She smiles at Callie and says, "You want some more?"

"No," I say. I promised myself she could have anything and I will stick to that promise. But her body has no stop signal, so I have to monitor the amounts.

The waitress looks at me, and I see myself for a moment in her eyes. Smooth hair, sensible cut, loafers, slacks, dainty silver chain showing at the neck of my white, pearl-button shirt. Makeup subtle, skin good, body taut with years of self-control.

She hates me and for a moment I hate myself, too; am filled with loathing for this mask, which I have so carefully constructed, year by year, until it has grown into me and I no longer know who the person under it is, really; whether I can take it all the way off, or whether I should.

Then I feel a surge of anger. *Back off,* I feel like saying to the waitress.

You don't know what it cost me to get here. But I don't say anything. Instead I smile and tip 20 percent.

I CRANK THE AC—the big bag of cheap cuts I bought earlier in the supermarket is starting to sweat. The plastic is sealed but I still feel like I can smell the purpling meat, just about to turn.

From the back seat, Callie hums and mutters. I worry about this too, her recent habit of holding lengthy conversations with herself. Sometimes I catch the odd phrase. She seems to have an imaginary friend. At twelve she's much too old for that, but it makes sense—emotionally she has always been cautious, even backward. In typical Callie fashion, her imaginary friend seems to be called Callie. How I could raise a daughter like Callie is a mystery to me. But even these draining thoughts can't distract from the feeling that comes over me as we approach Sundial.

The highway fades in the sinking sun. The sky above the mountains is littered with early stars. The air grows cold, the world darkens. We roll up the windows and put the heat on but even so the desert cold makes its way into our flesh. This is the Mojave's other weapon, the cold that will kill you, if the day doesn't. It always gives me a thrill. The knowledge of safety drawing near, of warmth and walls, even as death strokes the back of your neck with a chilly finger. It can't get us. Across the desert, we approach home.

THE HOUSE ISN'T really named Sundial. On the deeds it's listed as a street number in the high ten thousands. But Sundial is the name my father gave it when he built it. I grew up here.

We tried renting it out one summer, to a group of girls in short, fringed skirts. They came here for music festivals, sound baths, maybe a little peyote, and were willing to pay a sum that seemed criminal to me. They left early. It's too far from everything and creepy, they said, all those abandoned buildings, the high fences. At night some desert animal stole their laundry from the line, their shoes from the porch. They heard it breathing around the windows, the doors. Were we sure Sundial wasn't haunted?

The house is so near to that Grainger place, out toward the Cottonwoods—the puppy farm, isn't that what they call it? Anyway we kept their deposit.

Pawel told us scary stories about the puppy farmers, Lina and Burt, when we were growing up. They're one of the more unpleasant local legends. Callie knows about the puppy farm of course. I tried to convince myself these interests of hers were a phase. *Kids like scary stories,* I thought. *I did once.* True crime and gory news items have always repelled me, but stories are different.

I don't think what Callie's going through is a phase.

We only come out here occasionally. Irving says the desert makes him weird. *What's wrong with weird?* I ask, to annoy him. (He's right. The desert does that.) I suppose I could get a TV for the house but the idea seems ludicrous, like mascara on a tiger. Anyway, I know why he doesn't like Sundial, and it's not because of the lack of TV. It's because he doesn't like remembering.

He wants to sell it and it's one of the few points on which I risk opposing him absolutely. It was mine before we married and it's my name on the title so he can *sit and spin,* as Callie would say.

Sundial first comes into view from a couple of miles away. The house is hidden now and then by bends and stacks of rock but always reappearing, each time closer, like the house is coming toward us, not the other way around.

CALLIE TUGS MY sleeve. "Don't do that, it's silk," I snap.

"Stop!" Callie is outraged and pinched. "We're in Honesty. You *forgot.*"

"I didn't," I say, but she's right. I was lost somewhere in the past, or maybe the future, it's hard to tell.

The skeletal remains of Honesty rise around us on either side of the empty highway. We always stop here on the way to Sundial. It's tradition. So I pull over and we get out. Rusted buildings and machinery rise from the land, casting long shadows in the short winter dusk. The air is cold. Slanting light falls on scabbed metal.

The town of Honesty was established in 1870. Three thousand people lived here once. When the railroad changed its desert route and diverted toward Palm Springs, it died. Now all that's left of Honesty is the old high-way that runs through it. Piles of cracked beams, dented tin roofs. Joists and girders form emaciated silhouettes against the rosy dusk.

"Don't touch anything," I say, as I always do. Callie lacks any sense of self-preservation. "And stay clear of the buildings." Most are collapsed, the others not far off. Callie shrieks something at me and runs into the ruins. She loves it here.

CALLIE

"Do you like it here?" I whisper to Pale Callie.

It's OK, she says. But I know she loves it. Her outline pulses and gleams with pleasure. I can see a star shining through her head.

Dumpster Puppy sniffs and wags his tail. He bounds toward the ruined buildings in the failing light. I whistle for him to stay close—I don't want him to get left behind here. I have his bones in my backpack, but what are the rules if Mom makes me drive off without him? I can't risk it.

I look back to make sure that Mom didn't see me whistling for an imaginary dog. She's watching me pretty close these days. But right now she's biting her lip and staring into nothing.

I wander on through Honesty. Here's a fireplace with no walls, half buried in sand. Here's what looks like a fallen telegraph pole, the bole cracked in two and silvered with weather. Here's a staircase rising to nowhere, the wooden slats rotted into delicate lace. But the thing that fascinates me most is behind a big stand of desert holly.

I creep around, quiet, as if it can hear me, and there it is. The mine shaft yawns wide in the ground. It's not big, maybe six feet by six feet. The dark mouth is at the bottom of a little crater shaped like a funnel. It looks like the mine is sucking the surrounding gravel and rocks right into it. The scree is steep and loose; you don't want to get near, you'll slide right in. I kick a little rock. It bounces and slides down the slope, falls into the shaft, and vanishes into the dark. Mine shafts like this are called portals. That is a good word.

There are portals scattered throughout Honesty, but there's lots of fresh poop around this one. Something lives in there. Warm or pale? Do pale things poop? Dumpster Puppy doesn't seem to.

"One more minute, it's getting dark," Mom calls. And it is. When I look around me, I can't even see Dumpster Puppy or Pale Callie anymore. They have faded into the land, as if they belong here. Horror seizes me. What if they decide to stay? What if this was what they wanted all along? This is a perfect home for them, even I can see that. What if they went down into the portal and are now somewhere else entirely?

Pale Callie, Pale Callie, I say silently. No answer. "Pale Callie," I whisper.

"Callie," Mom calls. "I want to get there before dark."

"Just a minute!" My feelings all come up in a spike. I am nearly crying now, because if Pale Callie and Dumpster Puppy don't come back, I'll be all alone.

Mom comes striding toward me across the sand. Night is falling and her face doesn't look normal. It looks like a bad drawing with bones behind.

"No!" I scream. "Not yet, not yet!" I run from her, duck behind a big pile of metal that looks like an exploded spider. I search the fading land, hunting to and fro for a glimpse of silver. I can't leave them behind. I circle back quietly, to the stand of desert holly. I can hear Mom stumbling in the dim air, calling my name. But I won't go without Pale Callie and Dumpster Puppy.

The portal looms black in the darkening air. I go toward it. Its mouth looks solid, like black velvet. I shuffle forward on my toes. I'm at the lip of the crater, but the portal looks much closer. I feel I could reach out and touch it. Somewhere I hear Mom screaming my name. The dark breathes at me. Soft, in, out, velvet blown in and out by the wind, or maybe the breath of something big, sleeping deep down in the earth. If Pale Callie and Dumpster Puppy have gone, I want to go, too. The warm world is too lonely, all on my own. Is there a noise coming from it, too? My hands itch. What does darkness feel like, to the touch?

I reach for the dark portal with both hands. There is sound coming from it. Music, but not music like any I've ever heard. Like cold stones striking each other, and long shafts of ice cracking . . .

I feel a sharp pain in my ankle. Dumpster Puppy pants up at me, his tongue a silver spoon between his little razor teeth. *Ow,* I say, resentful. I didn't know he could bite.

Pale Callie says, *Come back. You're not supposed to be here yet.*

Mom comes around a pile of tumbled stone; the air is jagged and spiky with her rage. She drags me away from the mine shaft. I can see the marks my heels leave in the shale.

She holds me tightly by the shoulders and looks at me. Her hands are like steel. "You could have died. Do you understand?" There's something yellow and gleaming in her eyes for a second. It looks like regret. She looks *unstable.* Like she's sorry I didn't fall down into the dark and leave her in peace. Which is more dangerous, the portal or my mother?

"Let me go!" I yell.

Instead she takes me tightly in her arms. I'm enclosed in her warmth, her breath hot on my neck. "Get in the damn car," she says and releases me. "Don't you ever do that again. I'm not kidding, Callie." Her face is normal and tired, her voice is just stressed like usual.

I'M SO GLAD to be back in the warm humming box of the car, and even the seat belt feels good, strong across my chest. *Where did you go?* I ask Pale Callie and Dumpster Puppy. *I was so scared.*

There were tons of other dogs there, Dumpster Puppy says. *I went to say hi.*

So there are pale things in Honesty. Dogs. I wonder if I'll see them one day. I think about that for a while as the sun goes down through the car window, a finger of orange on the sky. All the ghosts of pioneer dogs, and later the wild ghosts of the ones who were left behind when the town was abandoned.

I had to go get him because it isn't time yet, Pale Callie says.

I know that self-important tone and I roll my eyes. Pale Callie is being weird again. Once, for about a week, Pale Callie just hung there in the closet like an old shirt. All she would say was *embolism, embolism, embolism.* Then she just went back to normal, trailing me to school in the morning, hiding in my backpack, saying salty things about the teachers.

Pale Callie sings, *Cross my heart, hope to die, stick a needle in my eye.* She's even made up a tune for it.

They used to do that to make sure you were dead, in the olden days . . . It's fun to tell her something new for once. Pale Callie can be such a know-it-all. But she doesn't even let me finish the story, which is typical.

Look, she says, *we're here.*

ROB

My heart is still pounding from the scare Callie gave me. I looked down at my phone for an *instant* and she was gone. She's still so good at vanishing—as if she has slipped out of the world. I found her by an old mine shaft, for heaven's sakes. She was reaching for it like it was a pony to pet. It was very dangerous and exactly what I told her not to do. She so easily could have slid down the scree and fallen in. I lost my cool and screamed at her—I can still see her startled eyes, filled with some kind of knowledge. Her foot slipped, just a little, with a scrunch, and she staggered. I caught her and pulled her away from the dark. Horror still fills my mouth with its stale, sweet taste. But there's that other thought too, worming its way up to the surface no matter how hard I try to push it down. Sooner or later Callie will try to hurt Annie again.

What if I can only keep one of my children? What if I have to choose?

"Mom," says Callie, and I swear and correct the car, which has been listing across the road. *Focus.* I come to a halt.

"We're here," Callie says, pleased. The tall five-bar gate is black against the dusk.

"Get it, will you, hon?" Good to hear that my voice sounds normal. I don't feel normal.

Callie hops back in after closing the gate. As soon as we're inside the fence my heart lifts a little. Somehow getting out of the open desert makes things seem better. All that space gets in your head, makes your thoughts go crazy. That's all those were, I'm sure. Desert thoughts.

Sundial is enclosed by miles of high chain-link fence. From the outside it looks like a government facility on one of those TV shows. There are even big red signs saying KEEP OUT. Or there were. Most of them have probably rusted and fallen off by now. We pass the toolsheds, old greenhouses, storage barns, generator huts that litter the outskirts. As we come closer to the center, there are bigger silhouettes: outbuildings, stables long ago converted into guesthouses, no longer in use. I can see a triangle of vivid blue dusk through a long dark roof. That's the pavilion where you can sit on big chairs, each hewn of a single piece of redwood, and look across the desert to the mountains in the distance. It's a cool place to think and work, even in the heat of the day. Mia and Falcon wanted Sundial to be a place of inspiration.

I took the dog pens down, but the deep posts that formed the corners were sunk in concrete and impossible to move. They are just visible from the road, lonely sentinels against the dusk. The laboratories are mercifully hidden from view, huddling in their stand of cacti. I would have razed them to the ground if I could, but it's surprisingly expensive to demolish a building, especially out here. So I gutted them, hung the door with big chains, padlocked them, and left them to rot. Their green walls are flaking, now, showing the red adobe beneath. Sometimes I go to look at them. I don't go in. I'm just making sure no ghosts linger there.

The human sundial for which the house is named lies far from the road, in a cool cairn of rock. That's a private place. It's not for casual eyes driving by.

We round the last curve in the road, and suddenly the house is there, racing toward us in the evening light. Here we are, in the heart of it.

At a casual glance Sundial looks derelict, even ruined—loose rock is piled up against the blank concrete face. The top of the façade is uneven, broken-looking, like a medieval castle decimated by ordnance. All around is windswept scrub and cacti shaped like old men, bent by the gale that races across the plains. The house is round, a perfect circle two stories high, built of massive blocks of desert rock, a cool shelter from the heat.

I struggle with the locks while Callie traces the old sign with her fingers. It's carved in wood, fixed to the wall to the left of the front door. It says NO DOGS IN THE HOUSE.

"You didn't have pets when you were a kid," she says. "Why does the sign say that?"

"We had dogs," I remind her. "But they weren't pets. We should get you a pet," I say without thinking. "A kitten, or—"

Callie says, bored, "I have a puppy already, Mom. Can we go in the house now?" I open the door and the familiar scent of warm wood and stale air greets us. But I can't move. My gorge rises as I think of what I found in her bag. That little bone portrait. She screamed when I told her to leave it. "I have to take Dumpster Puppy!"

I thought, *Just get her in the car.* I didn't want to touch the thing. I let her put the bone picture carefully back into her rucksack. I thought, *Is this what happens when you teach your children how to scream in silence?*

It comes home to me in a flesh-and-blood way—what she has done. My daughter killed a living thing. She took a warm, wriggling puppy and she—what? Raised its little body high above her head, and brought it crashing down, to break on the concrete and rotting leaves of the alley behind the house? Put her hands around its baby neck and squeezed as it yelped and wriggled, potbelly exposed and pale, oversized potato paws, which it will never grow into, scrabbling the air? Perhaps she slipped some poison into a bowl of bread and milk and coaxed it out from under a dumpster. I imagine the puppy eating greedily, milk slopping over the side of the bowl as its tail wags, no bigger than a pinkie finger. I picture Callie's still face—those green, almond-shaped eyes watching as it starts to sicken and paw at its stomach. And this last scenario is the best I can hope for.

Dimly I hear Callie saying, "Uh, Mom? The *door?*"

Jack's voice in my head. *There's a dog in the house.*

Black spots swim before my eyes. I lean against the wall of Sundial and take deep breaths.

ENTERING SUNDIAL IS like going into the mouth of a cave and finding a cathedral inside. The open-plan ground floor is high-ceilinged, soaring to the roof. Wooden stairs lead up to a gallery of red cedar, which runs around the second story, the bedrooms leading off like spokes. It's the shape of a wheel, my father used to say, because we are all connected here. I love this place but I know its power. Memories lie in the smooth stone floors, shimmer in the heat haze. Falcon, Jack, Mia, Pawel. Me too, I guess. The part of me that died here long ago.

"I'm hungry," Callie says.

"Why don't you go say hi to Grandpa and Mia?" I say. I'm shaky. I need to get out from under her eye. "I'll make pizza." She lingers a moment, looking at me.

"I'm OK," I tell her. "Honestly, sweetie. It must have been something I ate."

"But you didn't eat anything at lunch," Callie says. Her brow creases in worry. She is still a child. It's important to remember this, whatever else she may be.

I get pizza from the deep freeze and add peppers and mushrooms, some taleggio cheese I got at the market. I am determined to get vegetables into her somehow. The cork comes out of the wine with a festive pop. I bought a couple of bottles of red. I'm going to need a drink in the days to come.

I put the pizza in the oven and text Irving. *We're here. Get a trash bag, go to Callie's room and throw out everything that's hanging on the walls.* I imagine his face as he turns over the first drawing and sees the little bones. I should warn him what he's about to find. But he has to feel the shock. I want—no, need—him to be as scared as I am.

I open the screen doors at the back of the house and go out onto the patio.

My mother's grave used to be marked by a rose tree, out by the sundial. You aren't allowed to bury people on private property in California without the proper permit. My father never did the paperwork. He wasn't that kind of man. I took care of all that years later. It was easy. You write to the zoning commission and voilà. Technically the whole property is a family cemetery now. I put up two headstones closer to the house, under the jacaranda tree, so I could just see them from the kitchen window. Irving hates that. Maybe that's why I did it. My mother isn't really under there, but I don't think that matters.

I can just see Callie standing by the grave markers in the starlit night. She is as still as they are. They look like three silhouettes of stone, no distinction between the living and the dead. I wonder what they mean to

Callie, these memorials to two people she never met. I opted for two rough obelisks, hewn by a sculptor in Ojai. I think, even then, I was already preparing to varnish us with normality. Or at least, eccentricity.

"Come in now, sweetheart," I call to Callie and one of the three shadows detaches from the others and moves toward me, seeming to drift lightly across the shale and sand. For a moment I think, *Which one of them is coming?* Then Callie's face is visible in the dim. She looks very young. It pierces me. She pushes away my welcoming arms.

"Pizza," she says.

AT DINNER PARTIES when the reminiscences of childhood begin, usually as coffee is being served, I stay quiet. The names of hamsters, which days the ice-cream truck came through the neighborhood, third-grade enemies, TV shows about aliens, some game about the Oregon Trail, being kept inside as punishment on summer days. None of those things happened to me.

If someone asks me directly, I say, droll, "I can't relate there. I was brought up in the desert, homeschooled by my dad—whose name, by the way, was Falcon. We grew our own vegetables, had chickens for eggs and cows for milk."

Then people say, "How interesting." Sometimes they make a polite comment or two. "Must have been amazing, growing up in a self-sufficient community." "Wow, that's great, raised close to nature." Back in college, when I still thought I was interesting, I would respond eagerly. I would talk about how we adopted a coyote pup. I'd tell them about my hippie scientist parents and the rattlesnake den in the painted caves to the east. I liked finding ways to make it sound more normal. I converted Sacrifice into "weekly family storytelling around the fire." I never mentioned Jack. I thought I was fitting in.

It took me a while to understand that the nods and bright looks I got in response were forced. That's not what people wanted to talk about. The point of those conversations is to pretend that everyone has a lot in common. I was different—I ruined the fun.

This compulsion to seek childhood similarities is mystifying. What does it matter if two people had the same favorite cartoon turtle as a child? The differences are more important. One child was hit by their father, the other wasn't. One child was dyslexic, the other wasn't. One child had a serial killer for a parent, the other didn't.

Nowadays I let the talk move on. Memory is a noose around the neck. Sometimes it tightens on me so strongly that I can't breathe. It's hard to tell what will wake it. The scent of patchouli, sunshine, a woman's voice, firelight. Dogs panting in the sun. Long brown legs in cargo shorts, gun oil, the stink of bloody meat straight from the fridge, the taste of eggplant and slightly burned tofu. One tiny sensory impression and I'm here again, at Sundial, walking with my father at dusk or watching a rattlesnake lying across the path in spring, heavy with winter cold, straight as a length of drainpipe. The empty highway in the midday heat as it swims under the sun, the *ping* of the guardrails. Curtains of billowing dust, which leave a fine deposit of grit on the skin and tongue.

I feel her, the old Rob, when I come to Sundial, hiding in the dawn and at the edges of things; the ghost of who I once was. Could I find her again? Do I want to? It's a terrifying feeling, to be caught between two selves.

God, I miss Annie. The sensation of being apart from your child is unique. It's like being hollow. But this is the only place where Callie and I can work things out. I buried my old self at Sundial. We need to leave parts of Callie here, too.

I CALL IRVING.

"Hey," he says, sounding relaxed.

"We just got in."

"Great. All unpacked?" He's trying—he doesn't usually take an interest in things like that.

"I'm beat, I'll do it in the morning. How's Annie? Can I talk to her?"

"She's asleep."

"OK, don't wake her. Did you do what I told you to do in Callie's room?"

"Sure," he says, sounding easy. "I did it. All gone."

I grimace. He definitely hasn't. His voice is relaxed. He's maybe drunk. He hasn't seen the little bones.

I hear a slight noise in the background. It's nothing, really, hardly a rustle, could just be static on the line.

"What's that?" I ask, but I realize as soon as the question is out what—or rather who—it must be.

Irving says, suddenly loud and furious, "Rob. I've been patient with this nonsense but I think I have a right to know what you think you're doing, taking my daughter—"

"Put Hannah on," I say.

He starts on a long, garbled sentence about how she came over to see if they needed anything.

"Yes," I say. "I asked her to look in on you, just in case."

He takes a moment to think about how he should react to that. I guess he can't figure out how to turn it around on me so in the end he just says, "OK. Here she is."

"Rob?" Hannah is slightly breathless. What have they been doing? No. No point in such thoughts.

"How is she?"

"Temperature of one-oh-one this morning," she says. "She had some soup, and some strawberries this morning. I gave her Tylenol. She's getting lots of rest."

"Thanks." It's a mother's account. Strange that it's Hannah who brings me comfort, who eases the fear that is wrapped like barbwire around my heart.

I think about asking Hannah to clean out Callie's room. She'd do it. She would do anything for me, right now. But in the end I can't. She doesn't deserve it. That punishment is reserved for my husband.

"How are the boys?" I owe her one civil question, just one, for looking after my daughter.

"Good. Nick's taking them camping this weekend."

There's a pause while we think about that—Irving and Hannah alone in their houses, husband and wife both conveniently clear from the field.

"Do you want Irving back?" Hannah asks.

"Not really."

I wait, but neither of us says anything else, so after a moment I hang up.

Sometimes while we're sitting on the porch on a hot evening, drinking cold Chardonnay or, if we're feeling daring, margaritas, I look at Hannah's beautiful face and try to see her through Jack's eyes. It's a little habit I've developed over the years—trying to imagine what she'd think of things.

"Eyebrows too thin," Jack's voice says inside my head. "One of those stupid fads when we were younger—everyone wearing chokers and plucking their eyebrows until they looked like pencil lines. I bet Hannah had a goth phase. Nick definitely had a wild year or two; I've read between the lines of his Tijuana stories. Her blouse is cream, her spray tan good. Her arms and legs are toned but that blouse is loose—forgiving. Hiding a tummy, perhaps? Two kids will do that. The blouse must be new; you can't keep that color clean in a house with kids. Her nails are bitten down to the quick."

I tell myself that this is my way of keeping my razor-tongued sister near me, in my head. But Jack would never have said or thought those things about Hannah. She never knew anything about chokers or fads or having children. It's just a way of giving myself permission to be mean.

I GO TO say good night to Callie.

She doesn't hear me come into her darkened room. She kneels by the window, humming. She points through the glass at the desert night and whispers to herself. I realize that she is counting the stars, just as any child might.

CALLIE

PALE CALLIE WAKES me up. She likes to talk at night when most things are asleep in warm beds or in the earth, in the trees, or underwater. *Warm Callie, listen, it's important.*

I groan up into being awake. "What is it?" Sometimes Pale Callie tells me the good stuff. She told me where to find Dumpster Puppy for instance. She knew I would make him our friend. And I did, I took his bones. Now he wriggles beside me, snapping at invisible mosquitoes. He wags his tail at dark corners and whines and strains at the stars in the window. Dumpster Puppy can see things that even Pale Callie can't. He has secrets in his dark eyes.

"What do you want?" I whisper again.

Your mother, she says. *I know why she brought us here. It's because of the bones.*

"Well, duh," I say. "I knew she'd freak out when she saw them. She's probably trying to figure out which reform school to send me to."

Something else is going on. Something weird.

"You think everything is weird." This is true. Pale Callie doesn't really understand warm people.

She's letting you eat whatever you want, Pale Callie says.

"So?"

Ever heard of a last meal? They give prisoners whatever they want to eat before they kill them.

My heart does a strange double tap. She has a point. Mom has never done that before. The only answer that makes sense is that she doesn't care anymore. It doesn't matter what I eat because she's given up. I never thought I would miss those battles but now I feel like I might cry.

You better watch her, Pale Callie says. *I know she's your mom but she's not normal. You know what we found in her office.*

"I know." Pale Callie and I make sure we know everything that goes on in our house. (Detective. Magnifying glass!) At night we look through checkbook stubs, diaries, medicine cabinets. We know that Mom sometimes buys contact lens solution, even though neither she nor Dad wears contacts. She is a strange woman. We always know when Dad starts making the bad monkey with a lady. There are always signs. I am on his side obviously. We are best buds, me and Dad. Mom is red angry face.

It's good she writes longhand; there's no computer or passwords. Reading her private stories makes me feel funny. I would never have expected it from my mother. Blood and torn-open stomachs and knives in hearts. She looks small and golden and neat, but she has weird stuff inside her.

Pale Callie says, *In the car on the way here, she was thinking that she has to make a choice between you and Annie. She was thinking of you dying.*

My skin goes chilly. I think of what Dad said, about Mom being unstable. "You didn't understand right," I say, trying to sound confident. Pale Callie gets carried away.

It could be fun if you were pale, too.

"Maybe," I say cautiously. "I don't think I want to die. I really have to sleep now." One of the things Pale Callie doesn't understand is sleep. If I let her, she'll go on until morning, or until I cry. She can be quite exhausting to be around. But she's always been here, I don't have a choice.

"I'll be near, watching," she says. "Do you want a nice dream?"

"Sure," I say cautiously. Pale Callie doesn't always understand what nice is; she has quite particular tastes. I don't want to offend her. That's not fun, either.

This time she gets it right. I float in a dark pool. Drifts of apple blossom cover the surface, wet white petals. There is the scent of pears warmed in a bowl on a sunny window ledge. A shining steer the color of hot copper gallops through the sea, legs throwing up waves and diamonds of water in the clear air. It's not my memory—whose is it? For a moment I wonder where I've heard about a cow the color of bright pennies, then the dream folds over me and I'm gone.

———

I'M AWAKE EARLY, so I get up to look at the clocks. Clocks are everywhere if you know how to recognize them. A dandelion is a clock, obviously. Rice pouring into a bowl is a clock, each grain marking the passage of time. A school assignment, an apple as it withers, a tree waiting for spring. Each of these things measures living moments, what remains before death. *Tick, tock.*

I think about what Pale Callie said last night. She can get things wrong, but it is definitely unusual that we're here. It is definitely unusual how nice Mom is being to me. Usually she has this look in her eye, like I'm a rug she wants to straighten. Or worse, a little gleam of surprise like she just this second remembered I exist.

I go outside in the red dawn. Here in the desert the clocks are made of sand and wind. They pile up like little waves against the walls of the house, form in dunes as far as the eye can see. What these desert clocks measure is how far I could get, in the heat or the bone-cold night, before I died. Not very far, is the answer. We're twenty miles from the nearest gas station. My bones would lie in the desert and my lonely ghost would only have vultures and snakes for friends. Maybe it wouldn't be so bad. Or maybe Mom would bury me next to Falcon and Mia, and say I wandered off into the night. Maybe she'd say I jumped out of the car at a gas station and ran away into the nothing.

What's clear is that there is nowhere to go from here. I watch the sun bleed red over the sand, over the two graves. I don't want to lie cold and pale in a sand hole next to Falcon and Mia.

The west is still dark behind the Cottonwood Mountains. That's where the puppy farm was. One time I asked Mom if we could go and look at it, but she went white, her mouth pinchy. The Graingers. I shiver; the hot bursting feeling comes in me when I think about what they did. At the end Burt murdered Lina then died of an overdose. I think if you get used to killing, you can do it to anyone, even your husband or whatever. It was years ago but everyone knows about that place; it's like living near a celebrity.

The hand is cool on the back of my neck. I scream. I start to run but she grabs my arm with a hand like steel.

Mom's face is a slice of dark. Red dawn plays in her fall of yellow hair. "What do you want for breakfast, early bird?"

THE PANCAKES ARE so good, crispy at the edges and golden in the middle, and Mom lets me have syrup and even ice cream on them. That gives me a little shiver, like *uh oh*. But it's only syrup and ice cream, for criminy's sake (*criminy* is a good word, a secret swear). Pale Callie made me think weird thoughts. Now, in the warm kitchen with sunlight pouring in through the glass doors, I see that Mom looks really tired.

I decide to make a test. "Can I have a cup of coffee?"

She doesn't give that short laugh and say something mean, with her eyebrow arched high. That's what she would usually do. She doesn't say anything. She gets a mug from the dresser and half fills it. She puts a lot of milk in on top but she lets me drink it.

"Mom," I ask, "are you OK?"

"Yes," she says. "We don't spend enough time together, do we, honey? We should have done this long ago. Got away, really talked to each other, just us."

"Eye roll," I say, also rolling my eyes. But relief is flooding through me. I should have known. This is another episode in the *Great Mom Show*. Every so often she tries to bond with me as if she likes me. It doesn't work, but she gets to feel it's not her fault, and tell people how difficult I am.

I can't believe I nearly took Pale Callie seriously. She is wrong about *so* much stuff. One time she tried to persuade me that moose were related to mice and that's why their names sound almost the same. I mean, come on. Clown face.

ROB

I GET UP in the gray time before dawn. I have a pilgrimage to make. It's not for Callie to see.

I'll do the meat on my way there. I take a flashlight from the kitchen drawer, get rubber gloves and the big trash bag full of cheap cuts from the refrigerator, which I sling over my shoulder. The desert is making its music—the clicks and whispers of night are about to yield to day. When I reach the west fence I put a gloved hand into the bag and bring out a handful of meat. I throw it hard over the fence where it lands with a cold slap. I do this every hundred yards or so. Call it an offering.

When the bag is empty I scrunch it up and put it in my pocket. I turn toward the faint sound of running water, keeping the flashlight beam trained on the ground ahead. Scorpions and snakes get active in the desert at night.

The cairn of stone looms before me, the water pattering invisible on rock inside it. The spring rarely dries up, even in the worst heat or the driest winter. You can always hear it echoing in its rocky chamber. Before the great pile of rock is a semicircle of stones. Each bears the name of a month. It is enclosed by an outer semicircle, carved with numbers. One single stone sits at what would be the center of the circle. This stone marks where a person stands—they become the needle, casting a shadow over time. This is the sundial, for which the house and the land were named. Falcon made it. He wanted us to be part of this place, the earth and the passage of time. Here at the sundial we become a meeting point between these things.

As the sun rises pink over the mountains, I step gently onto the central marker. My shadow is gradually revealed in the growing light, a skeletally thin, dark, other Rob stretching across the numbers. It's January 23, the skeletal shadow-Rob tells me. I gasp a little as I always do at this small miracle. I am part of the movement of the stars, a precise fixed point in the orbiting solar system. This is what the first people must have felt each time the sun came again to break up the dark. Wonder.

It's not what I came here for.

"I'm sorry," I whisper. "I miss you. I love you." And the grief that I keep battened down with all the aspects of my new life—spice racks and my daughters and herbaceous borders, cocktails with neighbors, and PTA meetings—bursts loose. I give myself over to sorrow. I cry until my throat is hoarse and my eyes are small and dry with salty weeping.

I APPROACH THE house in the red light. Callie is staring at Mia and Falcon's graves. Her shadow is long in the dawn. Her lips are moving but too fast, like video that's been sped up. Her gaze is blank.

After a moment, when I've rearranged my face, I go toward her.

"What do you want for breakfast, early bird?"

I love both my daughters, I tell myself. *I can keep them both safe.* I repeat it over and over again like a spell.

ARROWOOD

The barn was quiet. Callie put a hand on the cow's sleek neck, which was the color of hot copper. The cow lowered her long eyelashes and leaned into Callie's touch. *You don't know what I am*, Callie thought. The cow thought she was a good person so it was comforting to be in her presence, even if only for a while.

When Callie looked up she saw Miss Grainger watching her. "Your friends aren't talking to you," the teacher said. "I remember how hard that can be."

"How did you know my mother?"

"Rob? We were best friends. We were in the Elegant Upper Fifth together, here at Arrowood when we were your age. In fact, I was thinking of her, which is why I came to the barn. It was almost on this very spot that we first met. Rob and Irv, always together. Irving Grainger—that's my name, you see."

How strange, Callie thought, trying to imagine Miss Grainger as a young girl. She didn't remember her mother, who had disappeared long ago and was no longer spoken of at home. In particular the word "witch" was never uttered.

"Often if you look underneath," Miss Grainger said, "you find unexpected things." The cow shifted. Under her right forehoof was a wad of something. Callie bent to look. It was a stack of dollar bills.

"Looks like the cow had the money all along," Miss Grainger said. But her face was serious. "Or were you trying to hide it here, Callie?"

"I didn't put it there," Callie whispered. She bent down to grab the money. "We have to take it back to Jack right away."

Miss Grainger put her silk-slippered foot on the back of Callie's neck. No matter how Callie strained, she couldn't get up. Something else was happening too—she felt a cold wind sweep through the barn. The cow lowed and bolted. Callie heard the sound of her ramming her horned head against the wooden walls, desperate to escape.

"You're lying," Miss Grainger said sadly. "It's a terrible thing in a young lady—deceit. Your mother is so disappointed. Look at her face." She took her foot off Callie's neck and put her toe under her chin, tipping it upward, so Callie saw what had brought that terrible cold wind whistling through.

In the center of the barn, something hung suspended from a chain. It looked like a long, gray cocoon, roughly the height of a person. Its edges flashed silver and pewter gray. It rotated slowly. Callie whimpered. The cocoon turned slowly in the barred barn light, and Callie saw what she had dreaded, that it had a face, faintly etched on its blurry gray surface. It was the face of a screaming woman. It was the face of her mother.

"She found a way to keep herself alive," Miss Grainger said grimly. "You better believe she's watching you. Rob and Irv, we're still together forever."

The cocoon face opened its line-drawing mouth to speak. Callie screamed and the barn went dark. The cocoon glowed, turning slowly in the air like a hanged man.

"It's time to run," said Miss Grainger and Callie seized her hand.

CALLIE

MOM THINKS ANNIE and I don't get along but she doesn't understand. Pale Callie and I would do anything to protect Annie. When we scream at her and hit her it's for her own good. Really, Annie is quite bad. She needs discipline. Mom won't do it because Annie's the baby, so I do it. Mom doesn't know about my discipline, obviously. She would freak.

Annie is a dreamy, dozy kid. Pale Callie and I are realists. We know the world is a tough place and you can't just wander around hoping people will forgive you if you look at them all cute or cry a little. She tries that with me sometimes and she is *very* surprised when it doesn't work. Still, we get on OK, or we did until the Maria thing. Ugh, Maria.

Annie and I have lunch together. It's our thing. I like to see her in the middle of the day. I don't check in on her, exactly, but I like to know where she is, when I can. I don't have many friends, I guess. It's nice for both of us. There's this bench at the edge of the playground, which is almost hidden in a hedge. No one can see you from the main building if you sit there. We like it because it lets us avoid Mom. She teaches at the school—not our classes, but it's annoying, anyway. She tries to check up on us during the day. So embarrassing. Sometimes she's waiting when I come out of math class. So we like the bench because she can't see us.

One day Annie didn't show up at our bench. Ten minutes went by, twenty, then lunch was nearly over. I was going out of my mind with worry. Maybe she had got sick? Maybe a teacher wanted to talk to her. I started to think about that, about what she might say to a teacher, and I got really worried. Gritted-teeth face!

Then I heard her giggle. She has a cute little giggle, it's quite unmistakable. I looked up and there she was, sitting on a wall ten yards away, sharing a sandwich with a little girl who looked like one of those old dolls made of china. Actually, they both look like that. Perfect skin, shiny hair, heart-shaped faces. Two little perfect dolls sitting on a wall, swinging their legs.

"Hey!" I yelled.

Annie smiled when she saw me. "Hey, Callie." Then she waved at me like nothing was wrong, like she hadn't given me the fright of my life, like we hadn't been eating lunch at this bench together all year. I couldn't believe my eyes.

I waved back.

After that Annie started spending every recess and lunchtime with Maria. They did braids on each other and made those friendship bracelets out of colored string. It seemed harmless. If Annie is dreamy, Maria is like, comatose. Maria started coming over to our house and they would sit and whisper in Annie's room. They never seemed to notice anyone else. If I spoke to Annie while she was with Maria, Annie looked at me with a gaga expression, like she had just woken up. It was like they were in their own personal snow globe. Their two heads were always together. Dark shiny hair. They looked sort of like sisters, I guess. They traded clothes all the time; Annie even started wearing Maria's underwear.

The only thing Maria wouldn't share was her purple hair band; I noticed that. It was only a plastic headband, the kind you can get in any drugstore. I was curious as to why this piece of junk was so important to her. I listened in on some of those whispering sessions. They didn't notice, not even that I was nearby, I think. That was the good thing about them being so involved in one another.

"My daddy gave it to me," I heard Maria saying in her reedy little voice. "He gave it to me so even when he's not there I know he's thinking of me."

It was getting intense between Annie and Maria, I could see that. And I know from personal experience that when people get intense they sometimes do unwise things. Pale Callie and I talked about it all night and figured out what to do.

Maria came over on Saturday morning as usual. Her mom dropped her off. Maria's mom always looks bug-eyed. She must have a lot on her plate, with the divorce and everything. No wonder she's too exhausted to keep her dumb daughter under control.

It was hot so Mom set up a slip-and-slide on the little square of lawn out back, in view of the kitchen window. Maria and Annie left their clothes and school stuff in Annie's room. When they came in hours later they were wrinkled and wet, big-eyed like baby mice. They left damp footprints on the carpet when they went up to Annie's room to change. Mom told them off about that so it was a little while before Maria noticed that her head-band was missing. Mom hates anything getting lost, even a hair band, so she turned the house upside down. "You must have forgotten to take it off before you went out," Mom kept saying. "It's probably on the lawn somewhere."

"I didn't!" Even Maria's tears were pretty.

It wasn't on the lawn. Eventually someone thought to check the girls' backpacks; Mom again of course, she's always the problem-solver.

"You must have put it in Annie's backpack by mistake," Mom told Maria. "Look, a little superglue will fix it."

"Thank you," Maria said, but when she looked at Annie, I knew it was the end of that. Mom didn't even notice. Thank god grown-ups are so dumb.

"I'LL TELL." ANNIE was a silhouette in the doorway of my room. I turned on the light. She must have been really mad because she hates getting out of bed after lights-out. Her face was red and miserable, covered with snot and tears. It was interesting to see her looking human for a change. "You're so mean, Callie. You don't want me to have any friends. I'm sick of it. I'm telling, telling, telling! Then Mom will make Maria hang out with me again and she'll send you away to a special school, or a kid prison."

"She won't," I said but my heart had begun that slow *thrum* which means danger on the horizon.

"She will," Annie wept. "I'll show her what you do with the animals."

The punishment should always fit the crime, that's good sense, so I had to get creative. And I had to be quick, before Annie realized what I meant to do. I took the X-ACTO knife from the desk. I had been using it earlier to cut out figures for a pioneer diorama for school.

"Don't!" she said. "Don't do that!" Then she couldn't say anything else because I had caught her tongue with my fingertips. The X-ACTO knife was very fine and sharp; I am always careful to keep them sharp enough to part flesh at a touch. I put the point to Annie's tongue. I knew it was a good punishment because it gave me the bursting colorful feeling all over my body. That's what happens when I get it right. It's an intense feeling, like being eaten alive. I can't tell whether it's horrible or nice but it tells me I've done a good job.

I really didn't want to do it but I knew she had to learn. "Why do you make me hurt you?" I asked.

She started to cry, and I did, too. I moved the X-ACTO knife away from her tongue and put it down carefully. I was a bad sister, I knew that. Someone who loved her would have had the courage to discipline her. Plus, the flowery bursting feeling was receding and I felt all flat again.

"Go," I told her. She ran. I wondered if she would tell, but she never did. I guess she understood, deep down, that she deserved it.

It's complicated, looking at your little sister and seeing a smaller version of your mother. I mean, Annie's not blond but they're pretty alike. But I never let that stop me from loving her. It's not Annie's fault, any of it. She's the baby and you look after the baby in the family, even if you have to be stern with her sometimes.

Dad is with Annie now, that's good. I always worry that she's going to get up to mischief when I'm not around. It's exhausting trying to keep her in line and clean up her messes, but that's what being a big sister is all about, I suppose. Red heart.

ROB

I walk some of the west boundary after breakfast, retracing the route I took this morning. The meat is gone. I never see what takes it, so I can pretend it's them, even if it's only to myself.

I go upstairs to unpack as I was too tired to do it last night. I tell Callie to do the same. She goes to her room at least, though what she's actually doing in there I don't know. What am I going to do? We can't stay at Sundial forever. We can't even stay a week. Irving won't allow us to be gone that long.

I love unpacking. It's a way of making a place mine, of taking control of the universe. I had a hanging rail put up in this room, behind a white curtain. I don't like wardrobes. I hang my chinos, my red cotton blouse, the oversize T-shirt that I wear on Sundays. I brought my favorite things: the copy of *Pride and Prejudice* I bought with my first teacher's paycheck, my cream silk robe, my bath oil that smells like a spring afternoon. I love sunlit spring afternoons, prefer them to those showier spring mornings, which everyone likes. I lay out my makeup on the dresser. We won't see anyone else out here, but it's not for other people.

My mind drifts, plotting more scenes for Arrowood. If Callie has a showdown with Miss Grainger, I need to make sure she cleans up her mess effectively. Maybe she leaves the remains in a sea cave. Maybe she burns the dead flesh in a bonfire. Black smoke spiraling up, against the clear blue sea sky . . . But better if Miss Grainger isn't dead at all, perhaps. Perhaps she escapes. No. That's not realistic. No one escapes.

I enjoy considering the exploits of my fictional schoolgirl. It helps me to stop thinking about what needs to be done here in the real world, if I am right about Callie. I should get started, but I can't bear to.

I could draw a bath right now, and change into my robe, read my book. My entire body trembles with pleasure at the thought of forgetting about it all for an hour.

I put socks and underwear in the dresser, put my shoes neatly on the little ramp in the curtained alcove. I arrange my toothbrush, creams, lotion, scented soap, floss, neatly on the ceramic shelf above the basin in the bathroom. With each item I feel a little sense return to the world. I miss my house. The desert doesn't care about me.

Last, at the bottom of the case, is my silk robe. I always pack it in tissue paper, to save it from creases. *I will have that bath,* I think. Hot water, clean robe, an herbal tea—

I pick up the robe and they spill out from the folds, hundreds of them, red and blind. They fall over the floor, my hands, onto my upturned face. Fat maggot bodies red as flesh. The stink of ammonia fills my nostrils. They writhe in the tissue paper, blunt heads butting against the white silk. All I can picture is Irving's face, his slight smile. It's so vivid, it's as if he's in the room. This is why he asked me about unpacking, last night.

"Cheese," someone says. I look up. Callie is in the doorway. There's a blinding flash and the sound of the camera being wound on. It's one of those little disposables you buy at the drugstore.

"What are you doing?"

"Dad said to take a picture of your face. It's part of the joke."

"How can you?" I ask, genuinely wanting to know. "How can you be so cruel?"

"It's funny." There's disappointment in Callie's squeezed voice. I'm not funny enough.

I grab the camera from her. It cracks and splinters under the blows of my heel. Before I know what I'm doing, I have her by the shoulders and I'm shaking.

Callie makes a small fearful sound. "No!" she says, teeth clicking. "Stop, Mom."

I stop. I am horrified at myself. I want to hurt her. My hand tingles with the recall of the slap I gave her back home, when I found those bones.

Callie runs downstairs and I should go after her but I'm angry, still so angry. My throat is filled with that cloying taste, sweet, sweet. Flat soda and rage.

I turn my handbag upside down and everything in it clatters to the floor. I grab my cell phone and dial with trembling fingers. This is a mistake, I know it is, this phone call. I'm not in control of myself, I'm giving Irving what he wants.

It only rings once before he answers, as if he's been waiting. "Hey, how's it going, desert dwellers?"

"How could you do that?" My voice shakes.

"Do what?" So that's the way he's playing it.

"There were maggots in my suitcase." I can't help it, a tear runs burning down my cheek. "They got all over my nice things."

"Oh, that's too bad." There is warmth and concern in his voice. "Callie must have been playing a joke or something. I shouldn't have shown her where I kept the bait. I saw her looking at it, you know that look she gets . . . Rob, I've been thinking, maybe you were right. A break will be good for the two of you. Time to bond."

"You did this," I say carefully. "Or you made her do it. I don't know which and I don't care. You won't let me have anything—"

"Hey, Rob. Will you watch your tone, please?" He is cool and polite.

"I want a divorce." I am shaking. I didn't know I was going to say that.

"Don't threaten me. You know what we agreed."

I am silent.

"Answer me, Rob. No divorce. Tell me you understand."

"You heard." I hang up. *I'll pay for this,* I think, *he'll make me pay.* What have I done?

I RECALL THAT weekend break in Monterey. I went for a walk on the beach with Callie. Later she cut hanks of my hair off while I slept. It was Irving who gave her the scissors. He always finds a way to drive a wedge between us.

MY BEAUTIFUL ROBE is gummy with the path of thousands of bodies. There are thin patches in the silk. I think they've been eating it. I put it in the trash and draw the neck of the bag tight. I feel a kind of grief. It was only a robe I suppose but it meant more than that. It was mine.

It takes an hour to clean up all the maggots. I bleach the floor and the inside of the suitcase. I shower and scrub myself with disinfectant.

Here are the questions that burn before me as I scrub the stink of them away:

1. *How much longer can I stay in my marriage without going mad?*
2. *Has it already happened?*
3. *Is Irving going to kill me?*

And the last, the question I ask myself each morning that he and I wake up together:

4. *Will it be today?*

I feel it, Irving's need to hurt, writhing inside him. Someday he'll open up that place again and let the maggots out. I'll make a smart remark that goes too far, his temper will burst at a well-timed gibe. It won't be the cardamom that shatters, then. His fist, so often shaken in front of my face, will land the blow that ends my life. He'll shatter my brains against the wall.

Sometimes I think that. Other times I think we'll dwindle into yellowed poisonous age together—the waiting will eat me slowly until I am nothing but strung-together bone. Maybe that's his plan.

Whatever Callie is, Irving is making it worse.

I STAND IN front of the toolshed. The shovel gleams bright, the handle a shout of red. It's new, never used.

Callie's in her room. She won't answer my knock, but I felt her presence behind the door. My little ghost. She's been stealing candy from my purse again. She doesn't know I know she does that. Cinnamon candy, my one indulgence.

I stare at the shovel. There's a little paint flaked off on that bright red handle. It's damaged, how annoying. I should have noticed earlier; it's too late to take it back to the hardware store and get a refund. I bought it over the summer; yes, it's far too late now. I still have the receipt of course, I have a special folder for them, with dated tabs, should be easy to find. Maybe I could argue them into an exchange; they shouldn't be selling damaged shovels. July, I think it was . . . With an effort, I bring these thoughts to a halt. I'm not taking the shovel back, am I?

It's no good, I can't do it.

I'll tell her everything. *That could work,* I tell myself. She might understand, and stop, and there'll be no need for that shiny shovel with its bright red handle.

The thought of reliving all that again makes me want to burst into tears. Sweet soda rises in my throat. But I have to try.

If the truth doesn't work—then it's back to the shiny shovel and the other thing, the worst thing.

I'll bring Callie outside to talk. These walls are full of ghosts. The hike to the stone garden, maybe. Wind, air, clean stone. Yes. A clean place, older than the past that lies all over Sundial.

CALLIE

Mom makes us hike. "Before the sun goes," she says.

Exercise is terrible. It's like whenever my heart goes fast my body thinks of sadness and danger. But I don't really have a choice, she went all screaming face this morning. Mouth a big black hole.

"Let's go up to the stone garden," she says. I groan inside because the stone garden is far and steep and even though it's winter it's hot out there in the sun.

Pale Callie goes, *Uh oh. Maybe she's going to leave you out there.*

Mom fills the backpack. Two bottles of water. PowerBars. Sunscreen.

It's OK, she's taking enough stuff for two, I tell Pale Callie. *Why would she take a PowerBar for me if she was going to leave me in the desert?*

She might be doing it to trick you.

"Come on," Mom says. "We'll have *the best time.*" I just look at her.

The land around here looks like a starving animal with the bones showing through. Ribs, spine, patella, all poking out of thin flesh. The hungry desert. We go up behind the house, to the east, down the canyon that's dyed in red streaks like a marble. The rocks sit in stacks above like they're judging us.

"Be careful," Mom says. There are no snakes around right now, it's too cold, but there's always coyotes."

The staircase is hidden in a narrow crack between two big red hills. It's old. The people who cut it out of the hill went pale long ago. The steps are shallow and slippery with use. Once you're high enough, you can see out over the plain, past the house, the highway lying straight like a dead eel in the sun. The fall is long. We climb on all fours using our hands and feet, like goats.

By the time we get to the top, the sun is a burning ball. The wind chills me right through my jacket but I can feel my nose burning, too. Mom notices and hands me the sunscreen. We make our way along the ridge toward the stone garden.

"Garden" makes it sound cute. It's not a garden at all. It's a place where wind or whatever has carved the rock into swooping tunnels and twisted shapes. The wind makes whistles and screams through the holes. I'd forgotten how horrible it is.

Sometimes we find shards of pottery in the earth around here, left by people who went pale long ago. Old Chemehuevi people maybe or Mohave. They're not here now. I don't know where the pale go when they're done with things.

If you dig in the earth at the bottom of the cliff, you would find bones, Pale Callie whispers. The wind has blown her edges wide; she's stretched across the sky in scatters of glittering light. *They used to throw warm things off the rock, as offerings.*

Like what?

Jackrabbits, buffalo. Callies.

Ha. Ha. I try to sound sarcastic but I'm scared. I really don't like Pale Callie's jokes sometimes.

Mom sits on a rock and pats the space beside her. We're supposed to enjoy the view, because we've come all the way up.

"Is that where the puppy farm was?" I point west. There's a shadow in the arroyo. *Arroyo* is another word for canyon. The shadow is the remains of the old Grainger place. Lina and Burt's place.

Mom looks nauseous. "Callie, if you can't talk about something nice—" Mom doesn't like to hear about murder, or anything fun. She doesn't read anything interesting like the news or about murders. I don't think she even knows what the puppy farm *was,* she just likes everything to be *nice.*

"Fine," I say.

We drink water and I count the minutes until I can say, "Let's go."

"Do you remember coming here when you were little?" she asks.

"Sure," I say.

"You never knew your grandfather," she says. "Or Mia. Your dad and I . . . well. Maybe I shouldn't have tried so hard to make us a normal family. It's not how I grew up, so maybe I'm doing it wrong."

I've heard all about how it used to be at Sundial, with the cows and the vegetable picking and the tambourines and the campfires and the tame coyote puppy and the long table under the tree in the front yard where they all ate together. Hippie stuff. Now the table is gone, the greenhouse is gone, the cows are gone.

She says, "We need to discuss what you've been doing with the animals, Callie. The bones."

There's a balloon inside me, filling quickly with air. "No," I say. "That's private."

"It can't be, sweetheart."

"You don't want to help." I look her in the eyes, which I don't do often. "You want an excuse for liking Annie better. You want everyone to think you're perfect. But you're *mean*."

She takes my hand and puts it on her chest, over her heart. "You have to stop." I try to wriggle free but she holds fast; it's scary all of a sudden.

"Let me go!"

"I can't," she says, sad. Her hand tightens to an iron grip, and it's there again in her eyes, that yellow look. The look she had when she pulled me out of the mine shaft. Like she wanted to let me go into the dark. Dad's voice in my head—*Your mom . . . she can be a little unstable.* I see why we came up here, to this high and lonely rock. I'm an offering.

I swear, I don't know how it happens. I swear I don't push her. But Mom flies backward off the rock, falls hard, rolling down the scree. She comes to rest on her back, arms and legs flung out like a star. It makes me think of the pink star in Annie's room and now I feel sick. I watch her for a moment but she doesn't move and she doesn't make any noise.

I wonder if I have killed my mother. I imagine the huge picture I would draw of her, exactly to scale, each bone in its right place. She would make such a beautiful picture. She would stay with me then, because she'd be pale and I would have her bones. Maybe she'd even be nice to me, if she was pale. Pale Callie says it can change people. But there's wet on my face, running down over my cheeks and mouth. I lick my lips and it's salt. Tears. So I guess I don't really want that after all.

I go to her and touch her—she's warm. Not pale yet. Her heart is beating. When I pull her eyelid up the eyeball is white. A pale rim of iris peeps over her lower eyelid, like a little green moon coming over a hill. She's not there.

"Come back, Mom." The wind takes away my whisper, and the crying noises I'm making. "I didn't mean to."

Mom's eyelids flutter. She makes a little noise, a sigh like she's having a good dream. Her hand opens and closes like a flower. She says, "Callie?" and I feel a glow, in spite of everything, because she didn't say, "Annie?"

"I'm here, Momushka." I am surprised. I haven't used that stupid name in a long time.

"I hit my head." Her voice is dreamy. "I guess that's what comes of skipping lunch."

"Yes," I say firmly, because this is definitely true and also it makes everything less my fault.

But memory is seeping into her eyes. "You pushed me," she says.

I want to say *I didn't mean to,* but what comes out is, "I was scared."

She closes her eyes and she's so still that for a moment I think she's gone pale.

"Mom? Mom? Where's your phone?" In this second it doesn't matter that I'm scared of her. I can't let my Mom die.

"No," she says. "We settle this, us two." Where are Pale Callie and Dumpster Puppy now? Gone. Even the ghosts are afraid of my mother. "We came here because of what you tried to do to Annie," Mom says. I stay silent. There's nothing to say.

"You look so like her," Mom says, "especially when you're angry. Sometimes I think if I'm strict enough with you, it can change what happened with Jack. I know it doesn't make sense. The past always has its hands around your neck, doesn't it?"

"I don't know," I whisper, because I'm twelve; I don't even have a past yet. She reaches up and brushes a strand of hair from my cheek. "Who's Jack?"

"She was my sister," Mom says.

"You don't have a sister," I say.

"I did."

"Were you friends?"

"We were the closest two people can be, without being one person."

This is a weird idea. I have always thought of Mom as the most solitary person in the universe. "What was she like?"

Mom looks confused. "I don't really know," she says. "Especially toward the end, we lost each other."

"What happened to her?"

"Sundial happened."

I nod because Sundial is a big clock that tells out lives and time and days. It can be dangerous to live in a place that understands life and death like that.

"I don't know what to do," Mom says. "What you did to Annie . . . It's like a part of you is already dead, in a way."

"Yes," I say, almost gratefully, because that's kind of what I feel all the time.

"Maybe daughters don't always like their mothers," she says. "I don't know. I never knew mine." She pauses. "But it's what we do that matters. You were actually going to hurt Annie. Your *sister*."

"I wasn't."

If Annie were here, she would be so mad with me for saying that. Her eyes would well up and she'd be like, "Mom, don't be mad, Callie doesn't mean to lie to you like that," in her whispery baby voice. God, she's such a pain, but I miss her when she's not around.

"You must always, always protect your sister." Mom is almost crying.

"I know." I feel terrible because she's right, and I haven't done a good job.

"Tell me this, Callie." Mom sounds thoughtful, not mad, which is scarier. "What happened with the pill bottle . . . will it happen again?"

I squeeze my eyes tight closed. The tears come anyway, stinging and glittery on my cheeks. We're talking about the deep buried things. It's like she's reached a hand inside me.

"Yes," I whisper. "It will happen again."

She nods. "Thank you for being honest. Good girl."

"What happens now, Mom?"

"You help me up," she says. "We're going to have a talk."

MOM'S NETTLE TEA steams. I have hot chocolate with marshmallows. The lights are dim. We sit on the couch together, looking out at the cold desert night, safe behind glass. Anyone looking at us would think we were a regular mother and daughter. No one would guess I nearly murdered her this afternoon.

"Mom," I say. "Please will you eat something?"

Mom says, "I'm going to tell you the truth, Callie. I'm going to explain why you have to be careful of how you feel, and what you do. Much more careful than other people."

Pale Callie whispers, *Stick a needle . . .*

Shut up. "I'm ready," I say. Sometimes it feels like everything is happening right now, in my skin, the past and the present and the future all mixed together, and that is what it's like as she talks.

ROB

THEN

THE COWS HEAR the ghost before we do. We've nearly finished milking and I'm leaning into the side of my favorite, Nimue, in the hay-scented dusk of the shed. She's a pretty cow, with big deer eyes and milk that smells rich like almonds. Her coat is a copper penny. She's a rare breed, from very cold climates. Sometimes I think she shines extra bright in the sun because she's so glad to see it. We put a bell on her because she wanders, and it rings softly now as she turns her head to look at me.

Jack cusses Elsie softly as she stamps and shifts. Milk shushes peacefully against metal. Elsie kicks. She doesn't do it hard—it's more like a brisk shove. But it makes me jump and spill the bucket, so Jack always milks her.

We're both seventeen. Jack is only a couple of minutes older than me but she's more *mature* and is kind of the boss, so sometimes it seems like years.

Suddenly Nimue throws her head up, and the bell chimes its alarm. Beside us Elsie shies and strains at her rope, neck taut.

"Stay still, dummy." Jack thumps the cow in her side. She loves Elsie, really. Elsie shifts again, picking up her feet like a high-stepping pony, and Jack grabs the bucket to save it from spilling. But Elsie doesn't stay still. She dances to and fro, as though that will free her.

"Why so spooked?" Jack is saying, when the sound cuts through the air, a high, lonely note. It makes me think of shipwrecks and cold mist and oceans. *Mermaid*, I think, lines of poetry running through my head, and then I feel stupid. What would a mermaid be doing in the desert? Or anywhere, they're not real.

The song comes again, longer, higher, though that doesn't seem possible. It's a sound of terrible sorrow.

"Is it a ghost?" Jack's voice is barely a breath.

"Shut up." I'm so glad I didn't say the mermaid thing out loud. Then I see how scared she is, her face bloodless in the hot dim of the shed.

"That would be cool," I say, determined, because we're obsessed with ghosts—*obsessed*! We really work ourselves up, whispering stories after lights-out, stroking each other's arms so the flesh rises in cold thrills. Headless women, doomed lovers, cold mists, hands that seize the steering wheel on dark highways. We're sure we're both the special kind of sensitive person who can see ghosts, and we think that we probably would see them, like, all the time, if there were any around here. It doesn't feel good to be right.

Outside, the brush rustles. Something is coming. I picture it out there in the late, burning light, ricegrass parting under its dead gray stride, rotten tattered remains of its skirt trailing in the dust, mouth opening in a ragged *o* to produce that long and terrible note. It's a woman, I just know it.

The wail comes again as if in response to my thoughts. I put my hands over my ears so all I can hear is my heart pounding. It's no better so I take them away again.

"It's coming closer," I whisper to Jack. "Do you think it's coming for us?"

"I won't let anything get you," she says. But her knuckles are white on Elsie's halter rope. The cows are both freaking out now, tossing their heads. Elsie's hoof hits the bucket with a dull *thunk*; a creamy river of milk runs across the cement floor, down into the slurry channel. Jack growls and sets the bucket upright. We didn't lose too much.

The high ghost song ends abruptly in a little sobbing sound. Then a whine.

"It sounds like a dog," Jack says.

"It can't be; Mia took the pack to the west run." Dogs aren't allowed to wander at Sundial. But the whine comes again, and it does sound like a dog, but no kind of dog I know.

The ghost dog howls again, high, followed by a growl. It's impossible to tell whether the dog is big or small, angry or afraid. It might be ten yards away or three. The desert can play with sound. Something moves, rustling the brush against the wall of the shed. A breeze maybe, or maybe a great body stalking in a circle around the building. Wind whistles through the slats, or is it heavy breath, big jaws breathing our scent?

"I'll go look." Jack motions me to stay. I shake my head and she makes a gesture of frustration and picks up the rake that leans against the wall. We edge out into the silent heat, so strong that even the cicadas are stunned into silence.

I see it first, a sandy patch of yellow hidden in a clutch of thorn behind the shed. I tug Jack's sleeve and she spins so fast I nearly fall over. Her face is white, jaw set. She's ready to fight whatever it is. She puts herself between me and the bush, pushing me gently behind her. It makes me feel safer, though I don't know what even Jack can do against a howling ghost dog. "Stay," she says. "I mean it." She creeps closer to the piercing sound.

"Only a puppy." The rake rattles against the ground as Jack lowers it; the tines carry her trembling. "What's a coyote doing in here?"

"It must have smelled the milk." Relief makes my voice loud.

"Don't get too close," she warns again. But it's so little.

The coyote throws its head back and releases that heartrending song. I edge closer. I can see the differences now, to a dog. The thick, shirred fur, the gleam of a wide eye, which is too golden. The big ears set like petals on its head, the tan muzzle. Its coat is short enough to see that it is covered in ticks. The coyote snarls at me, baring teeth like ivory needles.

Jack pulls me back gently.

"I just want to look." I'm lying. I want to pick the little fuzzy coyote up in my arms and cuddle it. So cute!

"The mother might be near, Rob." But I can see Jack wants to touch it too; her expression has gone all witchlike and pointy as it does when she's intensely interested. "Let's fetch the milk and get inside," she says.

It seems a long way back to the house. We imagine big paws pounding behind us, hot breath, jaws that can crack bone. Fear rises in thrilling spines on the backs of our necks, milk sloshes up the sides of the pails as we hurry.

Falcon is in the kitchen stirring soup. The pot is big enough to hold a small child. There are always lots of people here at Sundial. We cook in barrels, gallons, in quarts and pounds. It's not until years later that I realize it's possible to prepare food for one or two people.

Jack and I both start talking at once. Falcon waits, listening with his head tipped, regarding us brightly.

"So its mother must have abandoned it or maybe she *died*—"

"It's all alone—"

"It needs us!"

Falcon holds up his hands. "Patience," he says. "If it's still there tomorrow at five p.m. and there's no sign of the mother, well . . . we can fit one more in. Deal?"

Jack and I say, "Deal." We don't argue with Falcon.

Mia comes into the kitchen. Mia wears soft clothes that she dyes herself, and she smells amazing, like flowers and earth. Her eyebrows are like birds on a winter sky and her eyes are brilliant, dark and deep. Everywhere she goes she leaves behind a shine. She touches my head gently and I feel it long after.

When Mia comes in Jack turns her back. She stares at the wall, mouth set.

"Pawel needs you," Mia tells my father. "He's in the round room."

Falcon looks pained.

"He's having one of his days," Mia says. "Memories. You know he won't talk to me. A coyote got in?"

Jack keeps staring at the wall so I say, awkwardly, "A puppy."

"There must be a hole in the fence somewhere. We better fix it by nightfall. You send Pawel out when he's had his cry." She goes out into the sun.

Jack and I each take one of Falcon's hands. We tug in turn, like we did when we were little. Falcon turns this way and that like a spinning top.

We're too old for it, this game. But sometimes it's nice to step back over the line into kid things.

"Can we come with you and see Pawel?" Jack asks. "Can we?" I join in and we chorus, "Can we, can we, can we?" yanking Falcon around until he breaks free, holding up his hands in defeat.

"Yes!" he says. "Enough torture. Maybe you'll cheer him up."

I follow Falcon and Jack down the hall toward the sound of Pawel's weeping. He cries all the time. I don't get it. He's a grown-up; he gets to make his own choices. He doesn't have to be here if he doesn't want to.

Sunshine pours in through the glass cupola roof, which makes the round room look like a circus, with the ring made of light (I've never seen a circus). Pawel sits, face to the wall. It's like he's looking for a corner to hide his face in, but there are no corners here. Jack shivers. Her eyes are very wide. It sounds a little too like the ghost coyote.

Falcon touches his shoulder and Pawel throws himself into Falcon's arms. "I cannot forgive myself!" he says. "I cannot." His face is a mess of shiny stuff. We all hold Pawel and make soothing noises, until he stops crying.

SUNDIAL IS LIKE a little village, designed in concentric rings. Guest lodges circle the main house, like wagons in an old pioneer tale. The cowsheds and the greenhouses lie beyond that. The laboratories form the farthest circle, all tucked away behind stands of cacti, as though to say "keep out." Beyond, alone and outside all the circles, are the dog runs.

To be *curious* is the most meaningful compliment Falcon can give. There's a constant rolling stream of people through the ranch at all times. They come to talk to Falcon and Mia. Falcon runs residency programs at Sundial throughout the year. Students from Yale, Harvard, Brown, Princeton, and MIT come to work in the greenhouses, or work on electronics for the dogs. They're adult wallpaper, uninteresting. Jack and I don't bother to learn their names. In the past these visitors used to pet us on the head and exclaim at how cute we were. They don't do that anymore. I noticed that they stopped a couple of summers ago.

The guys in particular give us a wide berth now. This suits us fine. It was annoying.

Falcon worked for the government back east for a long time, and it made him sad, how much sadness there was in the world. So he came out here to the sunshine and built Sundial with our mother. They made it a place for people who have big ideas and want time to work on them. Mother died but that's OK; she's still here, Jack says. Her name was Lily and she smelled of lilies. She's in the stones of the house, in everything we grow and eat and raise.

TONIGHT IS SACRIFICE, which is our favorite night of the week. Especially because right now we are fascinated by stuff involving fire. The interns and grad students aren't allowed at Sacrifice, it's the one thing at Sundial that is only for family. Jack and I agree that it's wrong that Mia is allowed to come; it should just be Falcon and Pawel and us. Even so, it's still fun.

The firepit is a great charred circle, six feet across, ringed with stones. The area is enclosed by a high stone wall. Only the stars look down on us, here. It's a place for us to say private things to each other and the fire.

We huddle on the stone benches, under blankets. We are allowed hot milk with honey. We warm our hands on the earthenware mugs. Jack and I share an apple. I take three small bites in a triangle shape and pass it to her. It's a code. Three small bites in a triangle shape mean Mia's clothes are really, really stupid today. Actually I kind of like her skirt, a long, dark, soft material that clings and flutters around her legs, fascinating, as she moves. But Jack smiles when she sees my bites in the apple so it doesn't matter if it's true or not.

Jack takes a big bite and then a little one to the left. That means Mia's butt looks big. I giggle and apple juice runs down my chin. Jack and I pass the apple back and forth, biting messages to each other about what a loser Mia is, mouths crimping with the tart juice, firelight warm on our faces. We watch Mia expectantly over the green globe of the fruit. There's no point in it unless she kind of suspects we're talking about her. Mia feeds the firepit and smiles at us, friendly. I feel uncomfortable when she does that. It's as if she knows what we're doing and doesn't care. Or maybe forgives us, which is worse.

Mia builds the fire into a great pyramid of flame. Falcon asks us about our week. How is Jack's clarinet practice coming? How am I getting along with my painting of Pawel? OK, I say. OK, Jack says.

Falcon stands. It's starting. "You know we want you to be your own people," he says. "Our parents told us who and what to be. They shut us down, froze us. We want you to be free to feel, to choose. I want you to be able to tell us anything. We should be friends who love and guide you, not stern parents. So use this time to share your anger and your sorrow. Share it, empty it, and throw it into the fire."

There is a silence. No one stirs for a couple moments. Then Pawel gets up and throws something into the fire. It flies, silhouetted, into the flame. It's a chess piece—a king. "I throw entirely my old self in," he says, serious. He starts crying again; deep, aching sobs. Jack and I hug him. We love Pawel. He's crazy and recently he has started crying all the time, but he always shows us interesting things, like walking cacti and that giant rattler skin he found on the west ridge. For a while we just sit and watch as the chess piece is eaten away into a glowing ember.

Falcon rises. "I'm sacrificing the fireflies," he says. We settle in, eyes wide. It's sad every time Falcon sacrifices the fireflies, but it's also amazing.

"When I was a child we were very hungry," Falcon says, "but we were never allowed to show it. That would have been weak. Believe me, you didn't want to seem weak in front of my father. My brother and I were so hungry at night, we'd sit on the back porch and pretend we were eating all the things we could see. The moon, the clouds. We talked about what they would taste like. The moon like lemons and milk, the clouds like frosting. We tried tree bark a couple of times.

"One night there were fireflies. Utah's full of them at certain times of year. Don't grow up poor in the Utah mountains. The lights danced in the dark, golden. I said to Fred, 'Do you think they taste like honey? Or like candy?' They had a sort of greenish tinge, like the sherbet in the jars at the store.

"Fred said like candy, he thought, so we caught handfuls and handfuls in a jar. Close up, they didn't look so great. They were just little bugs crawling around. We ate them quickly because they tasted bad. Our mouths went numb and too late we realized they were poisonous. Fred screamed and retched. When Father came in from hunting in the morning, I had to tell him what we'd done. I'll stop there, no need to tell you what came next.

"I don't want that part of me. So burn, fireflies. Burn."

Falcon throws a handful of something powdery in the fire. We've never been able to make him tell us what it is. But it makes the fire leap up in sparks that drift slowly down around us in the night air, golden. For a moment, they do look exactly like little bobbing lights, borne on wings. Then they sink back into the flames.

"Now the dark is just dark," Falcon says softly. "No little lights in the air. Here we're at peace." Jack and I squeeze each other's hands. On one level I know it's *symbolic* or whatever, but another, deeper part of me understands that there are no fireflies in California because every so often Falcon burns them all out of existence.

No one else is moved to speak tonight so we sit for a time in contented silence. The stars wheel overhead and the fire hisses and eats the logs.

I never throw anything in, at Sacrifice. There's nothing I want to change.

IN BED, I stroke the Jack doll, and put her safely beneath my pillow. Jack turns on the night-light. It's shaped like a star and casts a pink glow. Falcon doesn't approve of night-lights. He wants us to maintain our natural circadian rhythms. *No need to fear. Don't use the crutches that other people lean on. Be bold.* We want to be bold, we really do, but Jack can't sleep without the light.

Across from me Jack settles herself upright against her pillows. "Ghost story, or *Bingley Hall*?"

"*Bingley Hall*." I'm totally over ghosts.

Jack reaches carefully under her mattress. The book is fragile with much handling. The cover is faded, creased with time. It shows a brown-haired girl in a short skirt running across a green field. Her lacrosse stick is raised to catch the ball that whistles through the air, her face up-turned, red lips parted. Other girls in the distance stare, their mouths in similar red *o*'s. *Summer Term at Bingley Hall*, reads the title in block capitals.

We found the book in some tangled bedclothes when we were clean-ing out the guest lodge after a big exodus of summer grad students. We had never seen anything like it. All the books at Sundial are beautiful or informative. The only novels on the shelves are worthwhile ones. Jack and I looked at each other for a moment and then she pulled up her sweatshirt and tucked it into the waistband of her jeans. We knew Falcon and Mia would throw it in the trash. They wouldn't do it to be mean but they wouldn't see the point in it. I could almost hear Falcon's voice, raised in surprise and disappointment. "We have hundreds of wonderful books to read, kiddos. Don't waste your brains."

The night Jack and I were introduced to the world of Bingley Hall for the first time, we fell instantly in love. It is a cold, blustering, jolly, very physical world, where strict rules and an even stricter code of honor prevail. At one point Jack paused midsentence and looked up at me. "Wouldn't it be wonderful," she said, longing, "to have rules? You'd always know what was right or wrong."

I knew just what she meant. "If there were rules, no one would ever be disappointed in you."

Now, as Jack finds the place where we left off, I ask: "What do you think Marjorie will do about Felicity cheating in French class?"

"I think she's got to take it to the headmistress," Jack says seriously. "It's a big deal."

We like to guess, even though we have read the book over and over and we know that Marjorie tries to fix things herself by encouraging Felicity to come forward. To gain Felicity's confidence, Marjorie opens up about her own shameful secret, the time she cheated in third year. Felicity then tattles on her to the headmistress and Marjorie is disci-plined instead, for her old offense. Marjorie accepts her punishment willingly because rules are rules.

Jack reads on. It's after lights-out in the dorm at Bingley. The girls lie in rows in their beds, in heavy white nightgowns. They whisper secrets to one another. I try to see it, feel what it would be like. It's a strange idea. Jack and I don't have secrets from one another.

Jack barely glances at the page as she reads. She knows the book almost by heart. But each time we devour the story as if we have never heard it before. By the end of the chapter we are hectic with excitement, our hearts are racing and we grip the blankets in white tight fingers.

"I won't be able to sleep," I say. "I feel like there are ants in my blood."

"I'll tell you a story about Mom," Jack says. Jack always knows how to help me sleep.

"Tell me about the rosebush," I say. "How it came here."

So Jack climbs in with me and strokes my head. She tells me about England, which is where our mother, Lily, was from. She grew up in a big house with gardens and streams and hedges cut into animal shapes. She probably went to a school like Bingley Hall. She loved roses. When she met Falcon and left her home behind, the only thing she took with her was a single cutting of an English rose. It still grows out by the sundial, marking her grave. I drift to the sound of Jack's voice, her fingers gentle in my hair.

JACK AND I go out behind the house, as we do each Tuesday morning, to the rippling fountain by the sundial, where the rosebush is in a blue pot in the shade of a pile of rock. Every week we water it and tend it. In the real summer heat we take the pot inside and keep it safe in the cool vault of the house. When the weather is right we put it out again, in the same spot. It's thriving.

If you didn't know, the sundial would just look like a bunch of flat stones in two semicircles. Falcon taught us how to use it. I recall his hands on my shoulders, guiding me to stand on the right stone in the central dial, marked February. "It's ten o'clock," he whispered. "See?" My shadow sliced right across the stone marked 10. It was further proof of Falcon's ability to command everything, even the sun. The sundial is special for lots of reasons. This was Mama's favorite place, Jack says, and that is why she is buried here.

She died when we were four, in a lightning storm. She had a bad heart.

Mia was Falcon's assistant back then. I don't remember when things changed between them. Jack says it was no more than two months after Mom died. Too soon. *So gross, revoltingly soon,* Jack says. *His wife barely in her grave.* It gives us a thrill to say mean, judgy stuff about Mia. But sometimes I wonder, what does a four-year-old really remember?

Jack takes my hand and says, "She loved us so much. I want you to remember it always, Rob, how it felt to be loved like that. How she kissed us good night, how she smelled like lilies, and how gentle she was. Can you feel her?"

I close my eyes and I feel Mother—soft lips brushing against my brow, the ghost of a kiss, the cold scent of lilies. But it's Jack's hand that's solid and warm in mine, holding me safe.

THE COYOTE IS still there by the milking shed at five p.m. I can't see it but I hear it where it huddles in the bush. Its song has dropped to a high whine, like a needle in the ear. It's getting weaker.

Mia's in the kitchen with the *New York Times* crossword. Her hair is held back by a red scarf. In the hot summer she cuts it short or goes to Santa Fe to have it braided tightly to her head. In these cooler months she lets it do what it wants. I suppose she must be nearly forty but right now she looks like a kid, no older than me or Jack.

"Hey," Mia says. "How's your day been?" She keeps her tone neutral and watches me carefully for signs of withdrawing. She is always careful not to force us to love her.

"He's still there," I tell her. "Falcon said if he was still there at five, we could take him in. Where is he? Where's Jack?"

"Gone to Bone," Mia says. "They all went with Pawel to pick up the feed." The dogs take a lot of feeding. Each week Pawel and Falcon return from the abattoir with a truckload of reeking offal. They dump it down the ramp into bins and we take it to the walk-in refrigerator. It's a horrible job. But I feel a little twinge that Jack gets to ride to Bone and back in the truck with Falcon. Why didn't she come get me?

"They'll be back soon," Mia says.

"It's just that—" I stop there, because Jack and I do not ask Mia for things. That puts us in her debt. But the coyote might be gone by the time Falcon gets back. And Jack forgot. She rode to Bone in the truck without me, instead.

"Falcon said five p.m. and he's still there," I say. "The coyote."

"Deal's a deal," Mia says, getting up. "Let's do it."

"No! We should wait for them!" I am suddenly frightened. Mia and me, just us two—Jack wouldn't like it.

"I understand," Mia says. "If we go get the coyote now, we'll be busy when they get back—so I guess we wouldn't be able to help them unpack the meat. You wouldn't want to miss that." She looks at me with only the slightest gleam in her eye. I've never seen that before. Mia is always careful and serious with us.

I think of the meat and the sloshing sound it makes as it pours in a stinky stream into the metal bins. I think of how our aprons and masks are spattered with blood and how sometimes there is blood in our hair.

I say, "It *would* be bad if we were too busy to help when they get back."

Mia grins. She goes to the safe in the hall and takes out the tranquilizer gun.

Mia's a *really* good shot and she hits it the first time, even in the dimming light, even through the thorn brake. The coyote hangs loose as a dead snake in Mia's arms. One of his legs is bent at an odd angle.

SOMETIMES, AT THOSE dinner parties, I also say: "On the ranch we had thirty dogs and a pet coyote." People always like that part, because who doesn't like dogs?

I used to tease men with it. I thought it made me more interesting (though the evidence never bore that theory out). I didn't use the line on Irving, however. I didn't need to.

WE PUT THE puppy in the intake pen. That's the first place all the dogs go when they arrive. Mia says we don't know if the pack will even take the coyote. Maybe they're too different.

"But you can make them," I say.

"They have their own opinions, believe me."

The dogs in the main pen smell him right away. They crowd into the corner nearest us, tails waving like a sea, bright eyes and eager muzzles straining through the chain-link.

First Mia splints his leg. Then she and I detick him, which is disgusting. We pull the gray bodies off, bloody. Some are dug in so deep we can't get a purchase on them. Mia pulls a pack of cigarettes from her back pocket and lights one. She takes a quick drag. "Don't tell your father." The smoke perfumes the evening air, mingling with the scent of sagebrush. Mia presses the glowing end lightly to the tick's back. It sizzles and stinks, and after that it slides out easily. She lets me hold the cigarette for the next one.

At some point I think I hear the truck pull up. I hear Pawel calling out and in the distance, the clang of the metal doors to the walk-in freezer. I smile a little at Mia, and she smiles back, then I catch myself and frown and look away.

"Bath time." Mia's voice has no hint of hurt but somehow I know it's there. She rinses the sleeping puppy in a diluted solution of insecticide. He growls lightly when she submerges him in the water, but he doesn't wake. He's very thin when wet. Then she puts a white collar on him to stop him licking and worrying his hurts. Last, she dresses the wounds with antiseptic.

"He'll try to lick it all away when he wakes up," she says. "Let's hope he can't get the cuff off."

She slides needles into his shoulder with practiced ease. Distemper, parvo, hepatitis, rabies. He cries out again in his sleep, a little startled *whuff*. He hasn't been in the world very long so I guess pain is still a surprise to him. He cries out again when Mia takes blood. "If he doesn't have the correct genes, we can't use him," she says. "You know that, right, Rob?"

"We can let him go if he doesn't have it," I say. "But I bet he will."

"I doubt he can hunt for himself with that leg."

I feel cold at that but then I think, *No, he will have the right things inside him, he must*. He's a wild creature but he came close to the house. He's braver than other coyotes.

We leave him sleeping in the little shed in the corner of the pen with a blanket, water, and food.

"We've done what we can," Mia says. "Now he has to make sense of all this on his own. Good timing, huh? It sounds like they've finished unloading."

I'm looking forward to telling Jack all about the coyote after lights-out, and then she'll tell me all about Bone. It's so exciting to have new things to talk about; we'll dole the news out in precious little spoonfuls.

"WHERE WERE YOU?" Falcon asks me. "Only good old Jack showed up for unloading, and only as we pulled in."

Jack makes a face. I look at her, puzzled, because I thought Jack had gone to Bone with Falcon.

"We had to get the coyote," I say. "He's in the pen now. I looked for you," I say to Jack. "Where did you go?"

"We don't have to do everything together, kid."

"Don't call me that." I feel stupid and annoyed. Four minutes older, is all. And she never answered my question. A hot flush of irritation goes through me.

We carry the tubs of meat out to the run. I slide a piece of liver in my fingers as we go. So gross. What must it be like to eat another thing's flesh? Everyone at Sundial is vegetarian except the dogs.

The dog run is in a scrub of thorn trees a couple of hundred yards from the house. The dogs live together because Mia studies their group responses and behaviors. Or something.

The pack are mostly mutts but there are some corgis, rottweilers, even a labradoodle. They're all different ages and personalities and sizes. The only thing they all have in common when they come to Sundial is that they are mad, bad dogs. Mia goes up and down the country looking for angry dogs. What she really wants is to find a very specific genetic combination.

Mia looks for what she calls the *psycho murderer gene,* though of course it's not that exactly. She's joking. And there's another gene that has a

C and an H, maybe? The other name for the psycho murderer gene is the "warrior gene." Mia thinks it helped people fight each other, back when fighting was all that mattered. That's how I prefer to think of the little coyote—as a warrior. Falcon likes us to ask Mia questions, but I only do it to make him happy. I tend to tune out during the answer, which usually involves long strings of numbers and letters. Anyway, this one genetic combination makes angry dogs much angrier.

When they arrive, they're mean and dangerous. They have had bad things done to them. Some have an eye, an ear, even a leg missing. It's suffering that seals the dogs' fate. That's why I hope the coyote has bad stuff in him, and that his short life has been hard. Then he can stay at Sundial.

I read about a town once where a coal fire had been burning underneath it for twenty years. All it took was a minor explosion in a tunnel to set off an inferno that will burn for the next hundred years. Pain and fear are like that, an explosion that sets the genes alight. I imagine the flames racing along inside the dogs, like coal seams catching fire.

I know these are just words, really. What happens to the dogs at Sundial bears no relation to warriors or coal fires. Those are just pictures our minds light on, to try to make sense of what's inside us.

We let ourselves into the run. Mia stays outside the fence with the controller. I think she tries as much as possible to make us forget she's there. Anyway she has her own job to do, apart from babysitting us. She makes notes on the feeding, even records it on her old movie camera sometimes.

The pack is a riot of grinning teeth and friendly eyes. The dogs surge around our knees. Kelvin lies apart in a corner, panting.

"Hey, boy," I call. He smiles at us as he gets up. I know dogs aren't supposed to smile like we do but anyone who's met Kelvin would disagree. He limps over slowly. The fur around Kelvin's eyes and nose is white as if with recent snowfall. Kelvin's old. He has been here a long time. He has a name. We used to let him in the house sometimes, before Falcon put his foot down and carved the sign for the front door. The little mound of dental cement on Kelvin's skull looks like a toy bowler hat.

All the dogs have one. Mia had a big battle, teaching us not to pet the dogs on the head when we were little. It looks peculiar but they don't seem to mind.

"Such a good boy." Kelvin closes his eyes as Jack and I hug him. He grins and licks our faces. I never remember to call him by his pack number, which is Seven. We are allowed to play with Kelvin, and only Kelvin.

"Sit," Jack says. Kelvin must have been a pet once, because he knows some basics like *sit*, and *stay*, and *come*. Then something else must have happened, because it was a human who did that stuff to his ears and legs.

"Play dead," I say, and Kelvin lies down carefully. It seems like a kind of magic to Jack and me. Not many of the Sundial dogs respond to voice commands. Maybe what Mia and Falcon do to them pushes their training out of their heads. Maybe no one ever taught them anything.

"It's OK, we love you now," I whisper. Kelvin's tail sweeps back and forth across the dirt. It is golden brown, rich and full as a banner.

"I think you have a hungry audience." Mia sounds amused. The dogs are sitting in a group in the center of the yard. All their eyes are on us. They whine and yelp. They're hungry, all right.

"Just let them come over if they want to," Jack calls, irritable. "God."

Mia does something with the controller. The dogs all trot over and crowd around us. There are so many mouths open, panting at me. I can smell their breath, meaty on the evening air. Twenty-Three, a rottweiler cross with thick slabs of muscle on her shoulders and hindquarters, shoves to the front. She snarls and snaps at Seventeen, a sleepy-eyed mongrel. The click of Twenty-Three's jaws is loud. She's the biggest dog in the pack, enormous even for her breed. Jack is patting flanks and pulling ears in a sea of waving tails. But I feel the feather stroke of fear. I think of the coyote's golden eye, his little murderous jaws. Suddenly the dogs don't seem very different. And there are so many open mouths. I raise both my arms above my head; the signal to Mia.

"Don't ask her for help," Jack hisses.

"Why not? I'm just some dumb *kid*." I am trying to sound brave in front of Jack but I'm relieved when the dogs pull back into their polite knot in the center of the pen. My pulsing adrenaline recedes. When Jack turns away I flutter my fingers at Mia slightly. She's frowning at the controls in her hand and doesn't seem to see my tiny thank-you.

Jack and I fill the dog bowls with food as the dogs tremble in their tight-knit group. We check their water, scoop the mess they've made into a yellow plastic bag with biohazard warnings all over it. This job is almost worse than unloading the meat. We leave the pen, locking the gate behind us.

Mia releases the pack and they dart like a volley of arrows, each to the bowl with their number on it. Kelvin goes slower than the rest and I feel a twinge of sorrow. Kelvin is such a good dog, it's unfair that he should get old.

The dogs eat. The air is filled with the wet lap of meat and tongue.

I give Mia the plastic bag full of dog turds. She takes it absently, still looking at the controller with a frown. I don't know what she does with all that poop.

Hating Mia seems to take up so much of our energy. Sometimes I wish we could lay it down for a while, like a heavy backpack.

In his pen, the coyote staggers to his feet. He must be confused and sleepy, but he stands anyway, watching us like a little king granting an audience.

I RECALL A long conversation when we were seven or so, when Mia explained the genetics that made our skin a different color from hers, and what that might mean for her and for us beyond Sundial. I don't think Jack and I understood, then, what *African American* meant. I understand a little better now. And I think I understand why the lonely sweeping desert might have appealed to her. There is peace here, far from the broken filthy heart of the world.

I DON'T SPEAK to Jack at dinner. It's still there, the little sting of resentment like a burr under a saddle, every time I look at her or hear her voice—*kid*. At dessert Jack puts all her strawberries in my bowl. She loves strawberries.

"I'm not hungry," I say.

"You know, earlier . . . I only meant 'kid' like a cool nickname. Like the Sundance Kid."

I catch my breath in an *ooooh*. I can't help it; that's what happens when I think of Robert Redford.

One summer a departing grad student left a poster for *Butch Cassidy and the Sundance Kid* on her wall. We've never seen the movie and Falcon threw the poster away soon after, because he doesn't believe in things like that. But it was too late. We had seen HIM.

"OK," I say. I know she's lying—she did mean *dumb kid*. But she's trying to say sorry. "Thanks, Cassidy."

Jack takes an apple from the bowl and bites one huge chunk and stares at me, chewing with her mouth open. It's gross and I laugh so hard that Pawel looks up, startled. It looks funny but underneath, it's the most secret, most important message, the one she only does at special times. *I'll always look after you.* Jack takes my hand under the table, and it really is OK then.

IT's THAT DAY again. Once a month it comes around, and we never stop dreading it. The MRI, followed by blood tests.

The MRI lab is the smallest building in the complex. The cacti seems to grow particularly thick around it, reaching out spines to brush our arms and bare legs as we make our way down the narrow path. Falcon flicks on the lights. The room is always brutally white-lit under the neon strips in the ceiling. I've noticed that scientists don't do good lighting. They only seem to want extremes: blinding, so that every detail stands out in relief, or pitch-black.

The needle doesn't hurt anymore, or at least we're accustomed to it. As long as I don't look and I think about puppies, it's OK. The gadolinium is cold as it slides into my veins. It lights up a certain part of our minds like a flaming torch, so Falcon can see what's going on.

It's cold inside the MRI machine. Narrow, cold, and full of noise like ghosts knocking on your coffin. It's hard to breathe in here but I always make sure I'm smiling when I come out, because Jack goes second.

"Hop up, Jackfruit," Falcon says. Jack plays with the star-shaped scar on her neck, which she does when she's frightened. The thought of being seen from the inside is horrible for her.

When we're finished, Falcon will sit and stare at the maps of our brains for hours, the patterns of dark and light like an aerial view of a city at night. We are most interesting to our father when we are not present.

The loud drumming of the machine is broken by a deafening *crack*. It comes again and again and I can hear her screaming, now. Falcon gets Jack out as fast as he can, but it's not quick enough. Her forehead is bloody where she hit it, over and over. She's always been scared of the dark but I've never seen her look like this; white, and gone somehow, behind the eyes.

"No more MRIs," Mia says. "We promise." Cocoa steams in mugs before us on the kitchen table. Jack is still shaking.

Falcon stands apart, leaning against the counter, arms folded, watching Jack with his head to one side. "But we'll keep going with the blood tests," he says. "Come on, Jackfruit." He takes her gently by the arm. "Come for a walk under the stars. No, Rob," he says to me. "You can skip this one."

Falcon and Mia have put the bedroom light out and gone, at last. Mia wanted to sit with us but one look from Jack put an end to that idea. "Uhh, we're seventeen?" Downstairs the record player starts and under it, the low murmur of voices. Pawel, Mia, Falcon.

Jack turns on the little lamp. In the pink light, I see she's holding her Rob doll tight to her chest. Falcon made us the dollies out of straw when we were little. Corn dollies, I guess you might call them. They are ugly little things, with poker burns for eyes and witch-wild straw hair. But we love them—or need them. Those two things can get mixed up. The dolls are worn smooth of expression or features now, just dirty husks. Jack named hers Rob, and I called mine Jack. When we fight, we punish the dolls, not one another. When I won't share my strawberries the Rob doll gets a twisted arm, a stabbed eye. When Jack cut off a long strand of my hair in the night, I carved a great scar across the blank face of the Jack doll. But we don't say anything to each other. The dolls are our way of feeling things without having to fight. Because we couldn't possibly fight. Who do we have but each other?

"Are you OK?" I ask. "What happened?" I see she has cotton wool taped to her arm. "Did Falcon take you back to the MRI lab?"

Jack's hand strokes mine. "He took some blood. He's worried. Sorry I scared you."

"At least we never have to do the MRIs again." I try to sound brave but she's right, I'm scared.

Jack plays with her doll's arm. "Have you ever seen anything while we were in there?"

"Like what?" Fear creeps cold fingers through my veins.

"Nothing! Darkness makes me imagine things, is all." Jack puts her Rob doll under her pillow. "Don't be scared, Rob," she whispers to the doll. "It's OK."

I do the same. I put my Jack doll under the sheets, enfold her in the warmth of my body, and whisper, "You're safe now, Jack." The dolls' worn faces are comforting and familiar against our cheeks. "Is Mom watching?"

"She's always watching over us," Jack says firmly. "She loves you so much, Rob."

I know it's just pretend but when Jack says it, she feels so real; Mother. I feel her touch on my head at night sometimes.

THE EARTHQUAKE COMES in the night, shaking the room with tiny judders. Hairbrushes and lotion rattle on the dresser, as if shaken by a delicate poltergeist. In the distance, a dog howls. Jack leaps up, gleeful. "Oh wow."

"The house is falling down!" The earth gives another little shiver and I gasp.

Jack's face falls when she sees how scared I am. She climbs into bed beside me. Her arms are warm. I close my eyes and imagine they are Mother's arms. I am still in the wake of last night—images of Jack's bloody face, talk of ghosts. The world seems very unreliable right now. Even the ground won't stay still.

"You're OK, Sundance," Jack says. "You're OK."

"Sure am, Cassidy." But I'm not. "I hate earthquakes."

"They make me shiver in a good way," Jack says. "Like the ground is dancing. I think it's over now, anyway. Try and sleep some more?" She pulls a leaf from her hair. Jack never brushes it out properly before bed.

I shake my head. My heart is still going too fast, in uneven splashy beats. Jack strokes my head.

"Shh," she says, "or Mia will come *git* you with the choo choo." She says it in Mia's rolling southern drawl. It always makes me collapse with laughter, I don't know why.

The *choo choo* is what Jack always used to call Mia's .22 rifle. When Jack was little she couldn't say her *t*'s very well. *Today* became "choday," *tacos* became "chacos." She didn't realize you called that kind of gun a twenty-two. She kept saying *two two*, no matter how often we corrected her. That was a long time ago, and she says it properly now. But every time I hear the word .22, I hear an echo in my mind like a little steam train. *Choo choo.*

THE LITTLE COYOTE has the right genes, both sets. Falcon tested the blood Mia took. So he is suitable for the pack. I am really relieved and a little proud. I told Mia so! But I'm worried, too. This next part is the test. The click.

"I want to come," I tell Mia. I have this idea that if I'm there, I can protect him, though I know this doesn't make sense.

The dog lab is next to the MRI lab, a rough cinder block structure, hidden in a grove of tall saguaro cacti. It's an ugly building like a prison or something industrial. This is where the dogs get clicked, in preparation for going into the pack.

Inside it is cool and green and humming. The air smells bitter like hot electric cables. Several grad students in lab coats stare, bored, at the centrifuges. More of them will be in the darkrooms beyond. At a certain stage, the dog medicine has to be made in the dark. At a workstation, a girl and a guy are whispering, doing something with a pipette and a beaker.

"You get some?" he says.

"Yeah," she says. "Whoa, nearly dropped it . . ."

"It's all good," says the man, slow and easy. They both laugh. They stiffen up when they see Mia, but the guy can't stifle a smirk. It seems to linger a little too long on his face. His eyes are shiny.

"Hey," Mia says, sharp. "You two should be back out on rotation."

"Sorry," the girl says. As they leave she gives a shriek of laughter and is hushed by the man. Ugh, so *annoying*. The students seem to think Sundial is all about them and we're just some kids who live here.

Mia and I go down the green corridor to the little room at the end, which is like a prison cell. The coyote is already out, breathing gently on the table. Mia takes the syringe from the bright yellow case. It's not a big deal, the click, to look at. It's an injection, containing instructions encoded in bacteria. Mia has taught the bacteria to copy DNA. When it goes into the coyote, the bacteria will cut out the bad sections of the coyote's DNA, like the psycho murderer gene, and replace them with copies of good things, like Mia taught it to. I imagine the click like millions of tiny little scissors, too small for the eye to see, busily cutting out shapes like a kid with paper chains, and slotting its own, good version into place to fill the holes. *Click click click.* After that, his brain will be ready and Mia will put his little cement bowler hat on him, and he can join the pack. If it all goes well, that is.

Mia slides the needle into the muscle of his shoulder, and it's done. The little scissors are starting their work inside him. *Click click click click.* The coyote will have all his anger and fear taken away. He will become a good dog. By the time he wakes up everything will be different and he'll join the pack. The golden flanks heave. His legs twitch. He's dreaming.

The sun is bright after the dim lab. I start to follow Mia as she heads out, but she turns around and touches my cheek. "No more science. Go do something beautiful with your time, Rob." But I don't know what that would be. I want something to take away the bad feeling.

I go to the kitchen. Someone is in the pantry, talking about microbes. Silently, I make a jelly sandwich. I wrap it in wax paper and slip out.

THE GREENHOUSE IS full of rainbow mist. Overhead, lengths of pipe give out fine water droplets that look like jewels hanging in the air. The cool and the damp feel beautiful on my skin.

This eastern corner of the greenhouse is for vegetables, filled with leafy tomatoes and tall scraggly beans. Most of the greenhouse is sealed off by thick plastic sheeting. The poisonous crops are grown in there, and everyone who goes in has to wear protective gear. Right now through the hazy plastic wall two students move slowly down the tall rows, swathed in protective suits and masks, like spacemen. The plants don't seem dangerous; they're small plantings of regular-looking grain; rye, I guess. But that's the whole point about poison—you can't tell it's there. Later, when the nodding golden heads turn black, Falcon will harvest the grain and they'll disappear into the labs, where the next thing happens to them.

Someone taps my head lightly with their knuckles and I jump, heart thrilling.

"Come back to earth, Rob." It's only Pawel.

I hug him. "I was looking for you."

"OK. Help me dig carrots."

"Or you could tell me a story." I love Pawel's stories.

"Too many carrots to get. I don't have time for stories. You know what Mia will do if I don't get these to the kitchen?" I giggle, because Pawel loves telling stories, and Mia would never do anything.

"Tell the one about how we got the first Sundial dogs from the Graingers."

"Carrots!"

"Maybe this will change your mind." I pull the jelly sandwich out of my pocket.

"Oh, man, you kids. You never give me any peace." Pawel pulls over a couple of empty crates and flips them so we can sit. It's nice in the cool greenhouse, water misting over us. He unwraps the jelly sandwich and eats it in two bites.

"OK," he says, chewing. "Long ago, before the Sundial dogs were here—before you were here—Mia, Falcon, and I lived alone."

"And Lily," I remind him. "My mother."

"Of course. The four of us, all alone. There were dogs somewhere in the distance, though. We heard them at night, crying, '*Hau, hau, hau!*'"

"That's not how dogs bark here," I remind Pawel.

"OK fine. Americans. '*Bow, bow, bow.*'"

"Bow *wow*, Pawel."

"Makes no sense. You going to listen or argue?"

"Argue!"

Pawel rubs my head hard until it goes all hot and I scream. "In the night, across the desert, we could hear all the dogs crying from the place in the canyon where the puppy farm was."

"Under the Cottonwood Mountains," I say.

"Yes. Lina and Burt Grainger locked up all the puppies in dark cages. They starved the dogs, forced them to have more and more puppies for Lina and Burt to sell. Expensive dogs, pedigree dogs—and also cheap dogs for labs. Hundreds of puppies, to sell for drugs. They liked drugs. They made the dogs fight each other for food. If they couldn't sell a dog, they hung them to see them die. It was fun for them. They say some puppies jumped in the well rather than live anymore.

"Every night, all night, we heard the crying dogs—your mom, Falcon, Mia, and me—and we said to ourselves, "No, it's not right to treat dogs like that." So we made a plan. After dark we took guns and knives and painted our faces black so we would be invisible in the dark. We walked toward the canyon. As we came near, the crying of the dogs got louder. Little ones whining. Big ones barking. They were in pain.

"We looked through the window, and we saw terrible things. A room lined with cages. Lina and Burt were watching TV. Falcon broke the door with the butt of his gun. We ran in and they jumped up. They had guns, too. We fought! Lina, she screamed and tried to strangle Mia. *Boom, boom boom!* The guns went off. When the smoke cleared, we saw Lina and Burt had killed each other by mistake.

"We opened all the cages. The dogs came out, slowly like old people. They had never seen the sky. But they started sniffing around and breathed the air. Slowly their tails came up, and their eyes got bright. They licked our hands. And we all went back to Sundial together, all the dogs bounding ahead under the desert moon, barking, but in joy this time. 'Hau hau!' And now we all live together at Sundial and everyone is happy."

I've heard about how Mia and Falcon got the first Sundial dogs from the infamous puppy farm nearby. Obviously, I know Falcon, Mia, Pawel, and Lily never broke in, attacked the Graingers, and stole all the dogs. But I needed to hear Pawel's story after watching the little coyote. That story means we're the good guys, which makes me feel better about what's done to the dogs at Sundial. They have food and air and sun. Their lives are better than they would be in a lab or somewhere like the puppy farm.

Pawel and I dig carrots. I just tear them up but Pawel lifts them carefully from the ground, as if persuading. His hands don't work so well. His fingers remember hunger, the tendons and muscles are starving. But he can fill a basket with carrots. A runner bean has broken gaily from its bonds and is listing away from the cane that held it upright. Pawel takes it gently in his hands and binds it up once more, careful to not so much as bruise a leaf. He ties the twine with the same knot he always uses. He says it's called a bowline. Jack and I have tried to learn it. "You have to believe the string is in love," he would tell us, as we screamed in frustration. Something doesn't translate from his native Polish. "The string wants to be a knot more than anything in the world."

"Your head is still up in space, Rob?" Pawel says, shaking earth from a long rooty shape. It's very difficult to fool Pawel. He doesn't have the layers other people have. He sometimes seems to know what you're feeling even before you do.

"I was trying to figure out why you seem different from family," I say. "Even though you've lived here since I can remember."

"Thanks a bunch," Pawel says. "What do you think?"

"You seem grateful to be here," I say. "You don't expect it."

"I have a lot to be grateful for," he says. "You have all given me a home. My first home since I went to jail."

"That must have been weird."

"It was. I had to earn their trust at first. But soon they saw that I am reliable. Tame. And I am very good with dogs."

As Pawel puts another carrot in the basket I glimpse the faded end of a blue tattoo emerging from his shirt. "What's that?" Pawel always wears long sleeves. I've never thought to ask why, or wondered what might be underneath them.

"The past," he says.

"Can I see?"

He looks at me for a moment. "Yes," he says. "Why not?" He rolls up his sleeve. On his forearm, in bluish ink, are nine figures in a row. I think the ink was once black. At first I think they're people, but when I look closer I see that they are chess pawns.

"You must, like, really like chess?"

"My mother and father taught me to play. They taught all of us, all my sisters and brothers. We played many games, my family, when I was growing up. That is why I chose a pawn to represent each of them."

"Where are your family now?"

"Gone," Pawel says. "I miss them every day. When first I arrived nineteen years ago, Mia hugged me. She was your father's assistant, then, of course. But she was so kind. It was the first time another person had touched me in many years. I don't count fighting or beatings. I was very alone."

"That's sad. I'm never alone, because of Jack." I try to imagine it. But there's just a hole there, a blank space. That reality doesn't exist—me without my sister.

"I understand Jack," Pawel says. "She suffers." His tone is mild so I don't know why I feel a thin seam of cold open up in my chest.

"No, she doesn't."

"Maybe you don't want to see it."

"No one understands her like me." Fury is rising in me. How dare Pawel say that? When I look I see that the sprinklers have made his face all wet and shiny, as if it were glazed. Then I realize that he is crying. Pawel cries sometimes because of the past. He did bad things and everyone he cared about abandoned him after that. Or maybe they were dead. He went to jail for a long time and when he came out he was alone. Newborn. We are his family now. But even though he has been free for twenty years a part of Pawel will always be in jail.

THAT NIGHT I hold Jack's hand extra tight across the beds. *Pawel doesn't know anything,* I think. Jack's mine and I'm hers. That's how it is. No one knows us like we know one another. Pawel can suck it. He's a *dumbass.*

"Jack." She doesn't answer right away, and I feel, not for the first time, that her attention is elsewhere. She's silent, not lost in thought but focused on something. No, watching something. I follow her gaze to the blank wall, the curtained window opposite.

"Jack," I say again.

She takes a moment too long to turn her head. "What's up, Sundance?" Her eyes are gone. For a horrified moment I think it's the Jack doll looking at me. Blank corn dolly face. Poker burn eyes. There's something wrong with her.

I have to be brave. I try to imagine what she'd do to help me. I take her in my arms. "What are you looking at?"

She turns a little toward me, but keeps her gaze fixed straight ahead. "They're everywhere, Rob," she says. She speaks quietly, out of the corner of her mouth, as though whatever's in the room with us might hear. "They're coming through the walls."

"What are?"

"The ghost dogs."

"Don't be weird," I say, but it's me who feels weird. Little chills running all up and down the length of me.

"Look," she whispers with such force that I do look, though all I can see is the curtained window, the wall, with its scratch from when we tried to play squash on it one time.

"There's nothing here, Cassidy," I say. "Nothing at all."

"They're *here.*" Jack reaches out a hand. "Cinnamon," she whispers. "Here, girl. Here, Jinx; here, Jethro—remember them, Rob? They were only puppies but Mia gave them the choo choo because she said they were too sick to live. Here's Arthur. He was my favorite too, but Mia let him get tick fever. She didn't check him carefully enough. And there are all these other ones, Rob, so many I don't know. All the dead dogs. All killed by Mia the murderer." Jack shakes and sobs. I am so freaked out I actually consider getting Mia.

"Look at me," I say. "Hold my hand. There's nothing."

"There are so many fireflies." Jack turns to me and I see she's not crying after all. Her eyes are wide and lidless with fear. She takes my hand. I think she's going to hold it over her heart like usual but instead she starts to twist it as if wringing a neck.

"Ow, Jack, you're hurting me."

"I don't want to go back." She stares, blank, pulling each of my fingers as if she wants to pluck them off.

"You're hurting me!" I say again with rising panic.

She lowers her head. With relief, I see she's going to kiss my fingers better, like she used to when we were little. "Don't make me," Jack says. Too late I realize what she intends. I scream and slap her hard, as her teeth sink into my thumb.

Jack looks at me blankly, then starts to cry properly. She picks up the Rob doll and hugs it. A little line of blood spills from the corner of her mouth, down her chin onto the doll's head. It's my blood. "Why did I do that?" she whispers to the place where the doll's ear would be. "Why?"

CALLIE

Mom stops. She looks thin and empty—like the story's been inside her, keeping her upright all this time. Now it's coming out she's deflating like a balloon. "I think I have to take a break, Callie."

"OK." I wonder what I'll do? There's no TV.

She goes to the refrigerator. I can smell the big plastic bag of meat. "Sorry, honey," she whispers, touching my cheek. "This must all be very weird for you."

"I'll do it," I say. "The meat." She must be really tired, or she wouldn't let me.

I bet I can see it if I climb the west ridge.

The sunset is red like insides. I throw handfuls of meat over the fence. Ground chuck, steaks that are the browny-purple color that means they're bad. I watch them splat on the ground. A big piece of meat on the bone, lamb leg, I think. It's heavy; I can't get it over the fence. In the end I leave it where it is, resting against the inside of the fence. I'll pick it up on the way back.

I climb the west ridge, where the sun still lights the tips of the Cotton-woods. And I can just see it in the arroyo. The puppy farm. That is a dumb name for it. I know all about that place. I read up on all the stuff Lina and Burt did.

Maybe she brought you out here to put you in the puppy farm, Pale Callie says and I jump. She's been pretty quiet recently. Does she sleep?

Shut up, I say. *It's not there anymore.* I know that. I like the library, the quiet sound of microfiche.

As I'm going back to the house I feel rather than hear something stir behind me. When I turn there's nothing but long shadows thrown by the juniper. The meat I threw over to the other side is gone. So is the big lamb bone I left inside the fence.

Huh, Pale Callie says. *I guess there's a hole somewhere.*

I run through the dusk, my flesh crawling.

Mom is looking out the window for me. Her face is crinkled. She looks worried. She hugs me when I get back inside and I let her. I don't want to make her mad again.

"Something's coming through the fence," I say.

She goes pale. "No more going outside alone, Callie." Then she goes around the house locking doors and windows, closing shutters. "The desert seems empty, but it's not." Mom shakes her head. "It's a neighborhood. Just a really big one. Pawel used to scare us with those stories . . ." She closes her eyes and swallows. "Never mind."

She seems tired and harmless. But I remember how her face went all red and her mouth opened like a yowling cat. She hit me the night before we left for Sundial and since we got here she has shaken me, yelled, and broken my camera. She's unstable, for sure.

You can only do three things with danger: run away from it, fight it, or make friends with it. I don't know which one to do.

I GO TO Mom's bedroom and open her door. She is sleeping. I watch her breathe, her mouth, her cheek, one hand curled there just so, the other arm flung up above her head. Mom's breath is a clock, too. In, out. I listen to it for a time.

Her cell phone vibrates on the dresser, purring with text messages.

I tiptoe over and pick it up. *Prrrr,* it goes in my hand. Dad again. I take it down to the living room, tiptoeing like a fairy on the corners of the stairs.

I call Dad. He answers right away. "Rob." I nearly don't recognize his voice because it is all thin with anger. Coiled snake!

"Dad?" I say.

"Callie?" Right away his tone changes. It gets warm. "Hey, bud, are you OK?"

"I think so," I say.

"Where's your mother?"

"Zzzzz," I say. "Sleeping face."

"What did she do?" It's that careful blank voice he uses to hide it when he's mad. "Tell me."

"She shook me, Dad, when she found the stuff in her suitcase." Why did he say it would be funny?

"Did you get the joke picture like I asked?"

"Yes, Dad," I whisper.

"That's good."

"But it wasn't funny like I thought it would be. Then Mom stamped on the camera and broke it."

Dad takes a deep breath. "Well, that sucks. You couldn't stop her, a big girl like you?" Tightness in his voice. I am wary. I know how he gets. I feel like crying.

"Why are you and Mom fighting again?"

"It's grown-up stuff, bud."

"Can I speak to Annie?"

"OK," he says heavily, after a moment.

"Callie?" I feel a burst of love when she says my name.

"Hey," I say. "How are you feeling?"

"OK," she says. "Itchy. Why did you and Mommy leave me?"

She sounds so little and sad, it wrings my heart like a flannel.

"Mom and I have to have a talk," I tell Annie. "Mom's—she's sick, Annie."

"Like me?"

"Kind of."

"Can you make her better, Callie?"

"I'll try." My heart sinks, though. How do you fix unstable? "Until then, can you be good for Dad?"

"Yes," she says. But I'm worried. She has that whiny tone in her voice that means there's mischief brewing. She's going to cause trouble.

"You better not say anything to Dad," I tell her. "You understand? If you tell, I'll have to punish you."

"OK, Callie," she says in her little frightened voice. But there are no guarantees. Annie is unpredictable.

On the phone I hear someone say faintly, "Irv?" There's a tight sound and then a gasp.

"Hi, Mrs. Goodwin," I say. Maybe Dad has started pulling Mrs. Goodwin's hair, too. That would make sense. He does it with everyone sooner or later. "How is Mr. Goodwin? And Sam and Nathan?"

"She just stopped by to check on us." Dad's back on the phone.

"You know what," I say, "I'm fine here with Mom. You better stay where you are. Stay with Annie."

He starts to talk but I push the little red button and his voice disappears. I put the phone down gently on the counter. I probably shouldn't have hung up while he was talking, he doesn't like that. But I don't want him to come get me. He shouldn't leave Annie alone. I don't know if Mom is the right person to be around Annie right now.

Pale Callie says, *Maybe we'll get a new mom soon.*

I'm so worried and when I'm worried everything around me turns to boiling smoke.

Calm down, Warm Callie, Pale Callie says.

Shut up. But she's right, I have to calm down. Those little bright spots are dancing before my eyes and that feeling is coming up in me, the one I can't stop.

I stand very still with my eyes closed, fists clenched tight, until the air stops swirling all hot and black.

You better find something sharp. Stick a needle in my eye!

Mom counts the knives, I say to Pale Callie.

I bet she's hidden them.

Pale Callie is very smart sometimes. The knife drawer is empty. So is the big block on the counter.

I pull the drawer out as far as it will go. *Maybe one fell down the back.*

Good thought, Pale Callie says grudgingly. Then: *There's something down there.*

I pull it out. It's an old black box, covered in buttons of different colors. It has an antenna on it like a radio.

What is it?

I dunno.

I run my fingers across the buttons like a piano. There's a panel in back—I open it. The insides of the box are all crusted and white. Whatever it was, it doesn't work anymore.

I press the little button that looks like candy. Nothing happens. I guess it's broken. But I like broken things, things other people have no use for, so I slip it in my pocket.

I PUT THE cell phone back on the dresser delicately, like it's a living thing. I stand listening to Mom's breath for a second, and when I look back her eyes are open and she's watching me.

"Do you need something, Callie?" I don't think she saw me bring the cell phone back. Or did she?

I try and make my voice cute, like Annie's. "Are you ready to carry on with the story, Momushka?"

She seems pleased. "OK," she says.

I've got no weapon and I can't run away, so I'll try making friends.

ROB
THEN

I AM HEAVY with exhaustion and chopping dogmeat seems to get more disgusting every morning. I couldn't sleep last night after Jack saw the ghost dogs. My thumb pulses gently under gauze. I told Mia that I hit it with a hammer.

"Are you OK?" Jack asks for the twelfth time. I don't know how to answer her. She looks like her normal self, if a little tired. It's hard to believe she tried to pull my fingers off last night.

"What *was* that, Jack?"

"I must have been having a dream."

"OK," I say. It didn't seem like a dream but I don't want to fight.

"It won't happen again, Sundance," she says. "I promise. It's just, I'm going crazy here. We have to put the Plan into action."

"OK," I say. *We have to put the Plan into action* is the kind of thing the girls say at Bingley Hall. I hadn't actually thought it was a real thing we were going to do. It's just an idea, like how we lie in bed at night designing our perfect boyfriends. Mine has good blond hair, and looks exactly like Robert Redford but with green eyes like me. He does something creative like choreography. He's French. Jack's is a lifeguard, dark-haired but with blue eyes like Robert Redford. (Neither of our imaginary boyfriends likes science at all.)

"You have to be the one to ask Falcon, OK?" Jack wipes her hands on her apron, leaving a bloody streak. "He might listen to you. You're the good one."

"I'll ask," I say. "But I'm *not* the good one."

"Oh, Falcon," Jack puts on a high voice. "Tell me again about *low activity monoamine oxidase A.*" Jack hides the bottom half of her face with her apron and flutters her eyelashes. "I'm the bad one. The interesting one."

"Well, you're exactly like Marjorie when she finds out about the cheating on the exams in the fourth year."

"Am not!" As Jack turns away I gently place a piece of liver on her ponytail. It rests there for a few moments before sliding down her neck and into the collar of her T-shirt while she screams. Everything is back to normal.

THE LONG BENCHES at the table under the jacaranda tree are almost empty. It's getting hot and most of the Sundial visitors have had breakfast and set to work. There are a couple of graduate students down the far end. Falcon is telling them a story about his freshman year at MIT. They listen with big eyes, nodding furiously. I think one of them is a girl and the other one a guy but they have the exact same haircut, the same big eyes. I've heard the story a hundred times before; it's about a philosophy professor and a doughnut. I didn't understand it the first time and I still don't.

"I'll take Twenty-Three out to the west run this morning," Mia says to Falcon, leaning over to pour him coffee. Steam writhes around her face like incense.

A shadow falls across my plate. "Hey."

I look up. Some youngish guy in his twenties in a dazzlingly white button-down shirt—I've never seen anything so white. Blank face, dark hair, not interesting. He leans in toward me, just a little too close. I can smell him, clean skin in the hot sun.

"Rob," Jack says. I hadn't heard her approach. "There you are." She slides herself in front of me so the guy has to move away.

"Huh, you two have different color eyes," he says. "I never noticed before."

"Not all twins are identical, dumbass," says Jack, taking my hand. "We're fraternal twins. That fancy college doesn't teach you much, does it?"

"You're smart." He seems pleased by her rudeness.

"You're not. You'll sweat through that shirt in twenty minutes. You're in the *desert*." The guy throws up his hands and turns away. Jack and I giggle. I am so relieved she arrived when she did. I never know how to get out of situations I don't like.

"Girls?" We both start and Jack flushes. Mia is right behind us. "We don't talk to guests like that." Jack just stares but Mia nods, as if Jack has agreed, and carries on toward the kitchen.

Jack takes an apple from the fruit bowl, eats three bites in a neat row and then passes it to me. That particular pattern, a line of small bites means, *Mia is a loser.*

Falcon is watching us now, from across the table. I eat the rest of the apple, uncomfortably aware of his eyes on me. Why did they both choose just now to pay attention? *Loser.* The word is wet in my mouth. I feel it travel down my throat as I swallow, down to my stomach, where it simmers like a boiled pebble.

A hummingbird thrums in a nearby clutch of desert honeysuckle. Its wings are a desperate blur, its breast a dash of crimson.

"It's like a heart that beat so hard, it burst out of a chest," I say, then immediately feel stupid.

Jack watches the bird. "Like us," she says. "We're each other's heart, outside our bodies."

Warmth floods through me. I'm usually the sentimental one.

"Falcon," Jack says, "Rob and I want to ask you something."

"Well then, let's talk." Falcon leads the way to the long wooden pavilion at the top of the nearby rise. There are slabs of tree trunks for seats, low tables, a dais. This is where the grown-ups relax in the cooler end of the day. It opens onto the desert to the west, where the mountains rise blue in the far distance.

"I'll sit," Falcon says. "If it's important. It will help me focus." He pulls up a log and sits down in one elegant movement. Jack and I stand before him.

"Falcon," I say. Then I stop and look at Jack, helpless.

"We've been thinking," she says, "that we'd like to apply to college."

"OK," Falcon says, eyebrows raised. "Well, that's certainly something we can talk about."

"But we'd like to go to regular school for a year first, so we can learn all the stuff we need to know." Jack's voice almost cracks with longing. Her eagerness spreads to me, even though I don't share it really. "If we're going to go to college, we need to graduate high school. We need to learn about things like woodshop." I don't know where she picks these things up.

"Darlings," Falcon says. "I'm so glad you came to me. We can adjust your syllabus however you like. More clarinet? Less Arabic?"

"We want to go to a real school," Jack whispers. I can almost read her thoughts. The green field, the lacrosse stick raised, the skirt flying, teammates openmouthed with admiration.

"Why would you want that?" Falcon is genuinely puzzled. "I can teach you everything you need to know."

"It's not the same," Jack says. I put a warning hand on her arm. It is hard as rock; her fists and muscles are clenched. "We want to go places. Why do we never GO anywhere? It's not fair! I want to go to regular school and have a regular life."

I don't know what Jack thinks a regular life is. I don't know what I think it is, either. As for school, the only example we know is Bingley Hall and I have my doubts about how regular *that* is.

Falcon's face falls. "I have tried to give you something better than a school," he says. "I have tried to give you an education. I am sorry you feel that's not enough."

"You like having everyone around," Jack says quietly and with venom. "Don't you? *Falcon.* Praising you, telling you how good and kind you are. Like this is a little country and you're our president or something. You don't want to let us go because we make you feel good." She picks up a rock and hurls it. The stone misses Falcon, strikes one of the pillars holding up the pavilion. A chip of pine flies into the blue sky, leaving raw pale splinters on the wood.

"Jack!" I am full of horror.

"No, Rob, let her express herself." Falcon says to Jack, "You're angry, sweetie. So be angry. Let it out."

Jack stares at him and I swear I can actually see the rage coming off her skin like a mirage hovering over sand. Then she starts to cry, big ugly sobs, her teeth bared, lips stretched in a grimace of sorrow.

Falcon puts his arms around Jack and her shoulders heave. She clings to him. "I'm sorry," she says.

"I know." He strokes her hair and gradually she quiets. "No chores this morning, OK? Go do something beautiful with your time instead." Mia and Falcon are always telling us to do that. I don't even know what it means. Falcon touches Jack's cheek. She flinches away from him. "And hey. Try and be nicer to Mia, you two."

I am so relieved that Falcon said no to school. There was always the terrible possibility that he might decide that it was our decision.

PAWEL BRINGS ARMFULS of juniper branches to Sacrifice. They pop and sizzle on the fire as the peppery scent rises into the night. He worries a piece of twine in his fingers, tying and untying the bowline. I think he's going to speak but then Mia stands up. Flame plays on her serious face. Jack squeezes my hand in dismay. Mia takes a turn maybe once a year. She always burns the same thing and it always ruins the evening. It makes us feel bad for her.

"I left Alicia in the house with him," she says. "Even though I knew what he was like, I still left her there. I wanted to leave all my old self behind."

Mia takes a white scrap of linen from her pocket. It is drenched in peppermint oil. We can smell it from clear across the fire, where we sit. The oily cloth falls into the heart of the fire and ignites, spitting like a firework.

"This is what he smelled like," she whispers.

Falcon puts his arms around Mia. "Thank you," he says. "You gave us your truth." Jack makes the tiniest noise into her blanketed knees. It is barely louder than a voiced breath. But I know it's contempt. I think Falcon knows it too, because he gives us a rare hard look. I burn with the injustice of it. I didn't do anything!

"Thank you, Mia," I murmur, and Falcon nods.

Under the blanket, Jack's hand creeps into mine. Across the fire, Mia cries. Pawel puts his hand on her back. He doesn't say anything, but his eyes are wet with tears.

We all get up and go to bed soon after that. The evening never lasts long when Mia sacrifices. It is always the last word on things. Mia has been sacrificing that handkerchief ever since I can recall, but she can never seem to burn it for good.

LATER, AS WE lie in the glowing pink light, Jack reaches across and takes my hand. She holds it to her chest with both of hers, clutching me to her heart. I think about what she did to my hand yesterday and I start to pull away but her voice is so sad when she speaks. "What do you think it's like? Handkerchief."

We know it's not called that, what happened to Mia and her sister. But the real word is too short and brutal, doesn't seem to mean anything. "Handkerchief" conjures aspects of it we can understand. Mia's sadness, her pain.

"I don't know." I shiver.

"If someone hurt you, I'd kill them," Jack says. "I wouldn't stay quiet, and I wouldn't leave you alone. We'd run away together."

"I'd never leave you, either," I say, choking on the thought of it.

"Maybe bad things happened to her, but she didn't have to come here and boss us around like she's Mother. Right?" Jack's voice takes on the familiar hectoring edge it acquires whenever she starts on this. She stares straight ahead, at the wall, as if she could see through it, out into the desert.

"It's OK, Jack," I say. "It's all good." I have been trying to work the phrase into my conversation. It seems to me the height of relaxed cool. But right now it doesn't feel *all good*.

Mia has been telling us that story for years. But I understand it in new ways now. My body and my skin hear it, imagine it, in a way they never did when I was younger.

To this day when I encounter that word I hear the word *handkerchief* in my mind, and catch the faint scent of peppermint. Maybe that's why I hate the news so much. That word is everywhere.

"Don't think about that stuff anymore, Sundance," Jack says. "OK? Think about the hummingbird we saw today."

I do, and my heart eases a little. "Tell me again about Mama," I say.

"She had soft brown hair," Jack says. "Our hair will probably go darker and be that same color when we're older. She had eyes that were blue like mine, not green like yours. She was always a little breathless because of her heart problem. It made her voice sound growly and cute. Like a teddy bear if a teddy bear could talk. She loved roses. That's why Falcon marked her grave with a rosebush, not a headstone. She was big into genetics and she wanted to help kids who are born with disabilities."

Some of this Jack must have picked up from Falcon or Mia, some of it I guess is from her own memory. The two have blended together. But I can see her in my mind, I really can. A mild, slightly shy woman with dove-soft hair and Jack's eyes, who cares about people and loves us most of all. The touch of her hand on my head at night, the scent of lilies drifting through my dreams.

"She liked tapioca. She hated the color yellow—maybe she associated it with wasps. She was stung bad when she was a child."

I fall toward sleep, carried by Jack's voice, my Jack doll held close, folded tightly to my chest in both arms. It's only as I am on the very edge of unconsciousness that I see her hand moving through the air, stroking, petting something I can't see, fondling unseen ears, her palm caressing a soft, invisible coat. For a moment I swear I hear the gentle panting of a happy, tired dog.

Sleep vanishes in an instant. I lie awake for what seems like hours, watching my sister stroke the air as if it were alive.

FOR THE THIRD day in a row Jack misses milking. So I do both cows, head buried grimly in Elsie's side as she sidles and kicks. After I take the milk to the kitchen I hang out with Nimue in the paddock for a while. She seems to like me, and I always know where to find her, which is more than I can say for some people these days. Nimue's breath smells like warm grass on a spring afternoon. She leans into my hand. I scratch her poll, which she loves, but in the end she gets bored of me too and ambles away toward the shade of the thorn trees, her bell ringing softly with her stride.

I wander the edge of the property, staring at the gray Cottonwood Mountains. Around me, the desert is busy and full of sound. Clicks and rustles and shivers, stone and scale and wind. The desert ignores me. I never seem to find anything beautiful to do with my time. Without Jack I'm just bored.

A dark streak races across my peripheral vision. I see Mia standing straight as a post outside the big wire enclosure of the west run. Twenty-Three sits at a distance from her, trembling with pleasure.

Mia walks toward the dog. She's holding down the *stay* button on the controller with her thumb. Each footstep blows up little explosions of dust. Twenty-Three pants. The brown rottweiler markings above her eyes always make it seem like she's looking at me twice.

Mia kneels before the dog, frowning in the glare. She examines the mound on the dog's skull, which looks like a lump of gray putty. It's fused to the bone and houses the wiring that runs through the bore-holes down into the dog's cranium, ending in tiny electrodes, which are lodged delicately in the important centers of the brain.

"Can I watch?"

Mia starts and turns. Her face is open and startled. Eagerness breaks on her face. It's sweet and a little pathetic, like the loser being grateful that the popular girl says hi—the kind of thing that would happen at Bingley Hall. I feel a slight whisper of guilt. Are Jack and I so mean to her?

"Sure," she says. "Take a seat. Best in the house."

I unlock the gate and step out. I'm beyond the borders of Sundial now. Desert stretches around us. It feels strange. Jack and I aren't usually allowed outside the fence. Bad people now live over in the old arroyo, where Lina and Burt's place used to be. I sit down cross-legged a couple of feet behind Mia.

"I can feel your eyes on the back of my neck," she says.

"Sorry." I shuffle backward in the dirt.

"Better," she says. "I mustn't get distracted right now."

"What's it feel like?" I ask. "Controlling her."

"Kind of like firing a gun," she says. "Women don't often get to feel powerful like this, you know?"

Twenty-Three trots away from us. When Mia presses a button on the controller, she turns a sharp left. Then again. She trots around and around in a perfect rectangle. I watch her, squinting in the noon sun.

"Good girl," Mia says, and goes to reward her with love.

I can't help thinking that maybe Twenty-Three wanted to turn in a rectangle. Or maybe she's learned that she gets cuddles when she does it.

"How does it work?" I ask, making my voice interested. I've learned how to get approval, too.

"Well, they're not robots," she says. "This sends a pulse tone of eight hundred hertz to the pleasure centers. I can make it very pleasurable for her to run in a rectangle. She wants to perform the action because it makes her feel good. But I have to train her to seek out that pleasure wave to her brain, to seek out the commands. Not every dog takes to the process, you know. There were failures."

I nod, because I remember the year we stopped giving the dogs names. We are both silent for a moment. Cinnamon. Jethro. Jinx.

"We learned from that," Mia says. "Things are different now."

The medial mammillary, the posterior hypothalamus, the campi foreli, the medial lemniscus. The names sound like flowers. Sometimes I imagine the electrodes as stamens of light, glowing deep in the dogs' minds.

Twenty-Three licks Mia's hand, then lies down.

"Did you do that?" I ask.

"I made a downward impulse pleasurable to her, which made her want to lie down. The lick? That's all her." She smiles down at Twenty-Three. The dog looks up, her tail lashing back and forth in a frenzy of love. "They've been with us so long, some of them."

Mia designed the electrode system and the little skullcaps made of dental cement. She tried different variations, over and over, until the dogs stopped getting infections and dying.

My face must be showing some feeling I'm not aware of because Mia sighs and touches my cheek.

"We don't live in a perfect world, Rob. You know where the dogs come from."

"The puppy farm," I say. Not all of Pawel's story is made up. "You rescued the puppies after the police came."

"The original dogs, yes," Mia says. "It was a bad place. We wanted to give them a chance. A couple others came from the Princeton and Langley projects when they shut down. Those people have a lot to answer for—they did a bad job placing the electrodes. We had a lot of work to do, to replace those and make the dogs safe and healthy again. And then there were others, like her." She gestures at Twenty-Three.

I try never to look at Twenty-Three's tail. It's horrible, because you can't help seeing what happened to make it that way. Her tail is not docked, and it's longer than rottweilers' tails usually are. But someone has cut it. The bare patches on the fur show where they tried first. Lots of tries.

No one, not even Mia, ever, ever touches Twenty-Three's tail.

Mia pauses. "You know," she says, "if you're really interested, you could be more involved. We could bond you with a new dog, you could be part of the training . . ."

I say cautiously, "What about the coyote?"

"Would you like that?" Mia says. "OK." We are both trying to restrain ourselves, keep calm. A barrier has been breached. Mia wipes her face, like maybe some sweat rolled into her eye.

"Mia," I say, "are you lonely here?"

She looks thoughtful, like she's really thinking about my question. She doesn't say, *How silly, there are so many people around*. Mia doesn't try to dismiss you or trick you like most adults do.

"Sometimes," she says. "But often I'm very happy. I think it's a good trade-off."

She puts the controller down on the baked earth and takes a yellow ball from the pocket of her cargo pants. "Come on, girl. You've earned some playtime."

Twenty-Three sits up, ears pricked. Mia throws the ball hard. Twenty-Three uncoils and gives chase with her ears pinned back on her head. Mia gets up and runs after her. They could be any woman and her dog running through the blue day, just for joy, for the fun of it. Twenty-Three gallops the ball back to Mia, shaking her head with happiness. She goes down on her forelegs as if praying and drops it at her feet. Mia fondles her scruff roughly and throws the ball again. I try to look at Mia, really look, not just glide over her in the way you do with things that are around you every day.

She's tall and strong. Her face is like a pretty horse, long and fine-boned with big eyes. She moves through the world like she belongs in it. Even when she's just in her regular jeans and T-shirt she always has a little hint of color somewhere on her—red laces on her sneakers, maybe, a silver comb in her hair or earrings shaped like parakeets—like a bright green shout against her dark skin. It's like a secret hint, a reminder that Sundial isn't everything about her. She has seen things, Mia, you can tell. But she gave everything up at twenty to live in the desert to look at dog poop with a couple twice her age and their resentful twin daughters.

The controller lies by my left foot. I nudge it with the toe of my sneaker. It has six buttons on it. They're basic instructions. Dogs respond best when you keep things simple. Left, right, go seek, stay, come here, and hunt.

The *hunt* button, near the top left corner, is small, striped red and green like hard candy. My finger hovers above the button. I don't touch it. It's powerful enough to be held in this moment, between doing it and not doing it. *Hunt.* Mia's never been able to get them to do that one. It's too complicated an instruction.

"Do you want to try it?" Mia is smiling. "She could use the exercise."

"OK!" Despite myself I am excited. Mia usually never lets us near when she's training the dogs to hunt.

Mia gets a rabbit from the shed. It's not a real rabbit, nor does it look at all like one. It doesn't look like a person, either. It's just an old shirt, tied to a wooden frame.

Mia sets up the rabbit in the distance, in the trees. She takes Twenty-Three up to the rabbit, and puts her nose to the shirt. When Mia goes back inside the perimeter fence the dog tries to follow, grinning and looking up at her, hoping for attention. Mia shoves her gently away and closes the gate. She always puts a fence between her and the dogs when they hunt, even though it never works. Twenty-Three puts her nose through the wire, whining.

"Come on, girl, you know you like it. OK," Mia says to me. "Ready?"

I push the red-and-green button. Twenty-Three goes rigid. All of her is alert. Then she moves, a black streak on the dun land. I feel like I can smell Twenty-Three's mouth, her fat body, her drool. I feel faint but also there's a butterfly wing of excitement beating in my chest. Mia grabs my arm. I can feel her excitement too, thrumming through her hand.

But Twenty-Three runs past the "rabbit" and bays at the foot of a thorn tree. A startled bird explodes up into the blue air. I press the green-and-red button again but Twenty-Three bounds and leaps, barking at the sparrow, already a distant dot in the aching sky.

"Dumbass," I whisper, and Mia looks at me reprovingly, fighting a grin.

"She is kind of a dumbass," she says. Her laugh is a resonant, rolling giggle, and it carries me with it; I start laughing, too.

I couldn't say what makes me look up. Jack stands a few feet away in the shade of a spreading acacia tree, watching me. She has been there awhile. She saw me having fun with Mia. Leaf shadow and feeling chase across her face. My heart thumps. *I was just being stupid, fooling around*, I want to yell. *I haven't done anything wrong. Stop looking at me like that.* Then I want to say sorry, to run and hug her, try to make it right. But I know I can't. I open my mouth but it can't seem to make any useful words.

It doesn't mean I like her, I think hard at Jack. *She's still what you said in the apple.* Jack turns and walks away. There's no way to tell whether she heard how much I love her, or not.

I look at my little purple plastic watch, which has a picture of Snoopy on the face. Falcon gave it to me for my twelfth birthday. It was during that phase when I wanted everything to have Snoopy on it. T-shirts, lunch boxes, baseball caps. I still wear the watch every day, even though the thin plastic strap cuts into my wrist, leaving a red shackle mark on my flesh.

Tuesday, says the little box by the dial, where the days of the week turn. The hands point to quarter to nine. We should be at Mother's grave, now. That's why Jack was looking for me.

Anger stirs in my throat, hot. Jack missed milking, didn't she? If she hadn't done that I never would have forgotten to go to the grave. Never. This is all her fault; it's so unfair. In the distance Twenty-Three leaps, mad and high, into the air, barking at the birds. Mia claps, watching her with delight.

THAT NIGHT JACK'S hand does not reach out between the beds. I start to be afraid. Maybe she will never forgive me. I cry a little. I really am trying to be quiet but there's no way she doesn't hear me—I have never been good at crying in silence. But still she lies there like a stone or a dead thing, and the crying doesn't make me feel any better, actually it makes me feel worse, makes me feel like I'm broken open and I can't close up again.

When I wake the next morning, this sense of dread is still there. There's no moment of relief, no split second in which I think everything is fine. I remember straightaway how I let Jack down and how she hates me. But the dawn is here through the window and the day looks to be warm and bright and I think, *She can't hate me forever.*

"Jack," I say to the dawn. "I'll do whatever you want. I'll put all her clothes down a skunk hole. I'll—I'll put her in the MRI machine. I was wrong. Please don't be mad anymore." There is silence. "Jack?" Now I can hear that it's more than a silence. It's absence. I sit up, heart slapping wet against my ribs.

Jack's bed is empty. It's even neatly made, and that's when I know things are bad. She always leaves it in a swirl of crumpled bedclothes. The smooth, tucked-in sheets, the blanket folded at the foot—they are an ending.

I tumble out of bed, legs not ready, and go to the closet. Her half is stripped, wire hangers bare. Her shoes are gone from the rack. Her drawers gape open, empty. Her underwear, jeans, and shirts are gone. And the pink star lamp is gone from the little table between the beds. The Rob doll sits on her pillow. Jack has left me behind.

I look out at the growing heat of the day and my heartbeat thrums wetter and faster. It gets so hot out there that your skin blisters within hours. There are snakes and scorpions and rockslides and coyotes. If she covered a lot of ground in the night, we'll never find her and she's already dead. *I killed her,* I think. *I killed Jack.*

Falcon has gone for supplies with Pawel and he won't be back for hours. So there is only one person to go to, and dead or not, Jack will hate me even more for it. I picture her floating through our bedroom walls at night, haunting me like the dogs, pale and forever angry. But there's nothing else to be done.

Mia is chopping liver in the kitchen. I try to speak but I can't. Mia puts her hand on my shoulder. Her eyes are inches from mine, steady. "What's wrong?" She never messes around.

"Jack's gone," I say. "She wasn't in her bed. She was mad at me . . . I think she ran into the desert. Maybe—maybe the dogs could find her?" But that's a Bingley Hall plot, not a real idea. Our dogs aren't for that kind of thing.

Mia's face is frozen; she is as still as a statue of a woman. "Think," she murmurs to herself through stiff lips. Then she takes my hand and strides out of the kitchen, not out back toward the dog pens but to the lot to the east of the house, where all the trucks and cars are parked in the shade of the salt cedars. She stands in the humming heat and runs her eyes down their ranks. "What's missing? Falcon took the pickup, right?"

"I don't know," I say. I don't understand why it's so important.

"Help me, Rob. Think. Who left late last night, or this morning?"

I dimly recall that one of the research assistants was due to leave this morning, the one who wears the blinding-white button-down shirts— the one who smells too clean. He made a big deal of his good-byes last night. His name is something unusual that made me think of old men and dusty books and civil war. "That dark-haired guy said he was leaving early," I offer. "He was the only one."

Mia scans the ranks of cars again, face drawn. I have never seen her like this before. She looks middle-aged, suddenly. "He had a white Chevy. Right?"

"I think so." But I can't focus on the departed grad student now. I don't understand why Mia is talking about him and counting the cars, when we should be getting ready to go out into the scalding heat after Jack.

"The Chevy's not here," Mia says. "I'll try to catch up to them. Go inside and wait. When your father gets back, tell him what's happened. But tell him to stay put. I'm dealing with it. Got it, Rob? Don't let him follow."

I am starting to understand that Jack is not dead in the desert. That should make me feel better, but I feel frightened in a different way. Something new is happening.

The hours after that are like scenes in a dollhouse. The memories are soundless, static. I remember them in miniature, from high above. Falcon's face, caught in horror, Pawel and me hanging onto his arms to stop him running back to the truck. Only Mia's instruction, repeated again and again by me, brings him to a halt. He always listens to Mia. I can see a tableau of solemn faces; the other interns and assistants, huddled in groups, half thrilled and half unnerved by the unaccustomed drama. I remember someone asked what would happen about lunch, but I don't remember who, or their voice, or the tone. I remember that we sat and waited. Pawel and I each held one of my father's hands.

I imagine it so often, I feel like I remember parts of it I wasn't even there for.

I watch from a great height in the blue sky as Mia sees them, twenty miles down the highway to the south with a blown tire. The dust has already coated the Chevy in tan grit. The research assistant turns, wrench in hand, as Mia's jeep roars into view. He is angry. He has been cheated. Mia helps the grad student put on the spare. Then she tells him the right turnings to head back toward Yuma. She tells him never to come back to Sundial. She wrestles Jack from the car, into her jeep. Jack screams, plants her heels, leaving drag marks in the dust behind her. Sometimes even now I think about how different everything would have been, if it weren't for that flat tire.

Jack hid it perfectly from me. They must have met in secret, snuck out at night, gone for walks in the barren rocky hills while I did my chores. But I never had a single clue. I didn't hear it in her voice when she spoke to him. Her casualness, her studied rudeness, was perfect. *Not all twins are identical, dumbass.* Even when Jack ran, it was Mia who worked out what had happened, not me.

Jack is crying as they pull up in front of the house. Her face is pink and swollen through the windshield. As Mia jumps down I glimpse the rich leather of her gun belt against her jeans, under her loose white shirt.

I wait until she's upstairs. I can hear Jack shouting and Mia pleading. Something crashes to the floor. A book maybe.

I FIND FALCON in the kitchen. "I need to talk to you," I say. I don't know how to do this, to tell a story on my own. But I try.

I tell him about Jack seeing the ghost dogs and missing chores, about her biting my hand. I feel so bad for telling on her. But I reassure myself with the knowledge I'm doing the right thing. It's for her own good, and not revenge for her leaving me behind, not at all.

Falcon nods. "She's having a hard time," he says, comforting. "She'll be OK. It's a difficult phase." He goes to the foot of the staircase. "Come down here, Jack," he calls. "We need to talk."

Falcon doesn't punish her, even though maybe I think that's what Jack really wanted. Is it what I wanted? He takes her into his office. I start to follow them but he stops me gently with a hand. I am left blinking at the closed door.

"Sure," I mutter, "go do something beautiful with my time." But I don't know what to do with myself when I'm alone. I put my ear to the door. I can't hear anything but a low murmur of voices.

I sit on the floor in the hall. I try and imagine a date with my imaginary boyfriend. Maybe we'd go to a restaurant. I've never been to a restaurant. Did the Chevy guy take Jack to a restaurant?

An hour passes before they're done. The door opens and Jack comes out. I jump up and run to her. It takes me a moment to realize that she's crying again. She looks all pink and young and there's a new slump to her shoulders. I realize that I've never seen Jack look defeated before.

I reach for her hand. "What did he say to you in there?"

She shakes her head. "I can't."

"I'm sorry I told on you. I was worried."

"It doesn't matter," she says.

"Let's get away from here." I lower my voice to a whisper. "I'll come with you, Cassidy. I'll run away, too. Let's go tonight."

"You don't understand," she says, tired. "I'm not leaving here, ever."

"It'll be different this time," I say. "Because we'll be together. We'll go find Bingley Hall maybe. We'll have friends and boyfriends—"

"You're not listening."

"I mean it," I say. "It'll be fun if we're together."

"You're a dumb kid." Jack punches me in the chest, leaving me gasping. Then she takes me by the throat and squeezes. "You don't know anything. Everything's different now but you're a dumb kid who doesn't even notice or care."

"Stop," I whisper. Her fingers are strong. Even now, I don't want Falcon to hear. I don't want her to get in even more trouble. "Please, Jack. Stop." When she lets go I wear a necklace of deep red crescents where her nails dug in.

Jack's face collapses. "I'm so sorry, Sundance." She reaches for me and I slap her hand.

"I don't care if you're sorry." I back away from her.

Her face hardens. "That's right, you only care about putting on that good-daughter act."

I gasp, tears rising, "You're crazy and I hate you."

Jack is as quick as a snake's strike. Her hands hold my head in an iron grip. Her breath is hot in my ear. "No matter how good you are, how hard you try, you're still less interesting than me."

ARROWOOD

The girls of the Uncouth Lower Fourth charged one last time against the prefects of the East Tower. Broken plates covered the floor and the air was full of screaming. Madame Salaud the French mistress seized Millicent by the braids. She swiped once with her scimitar and Millicent screamed. Madame Salaud raced off toward the Mathematics wing, holding Millicent's severed pigtails aloft.

Callie ducked low, hunting for Jack. She had to tell her the truth. Ducking behind a column in the dining hall to avoid a thrown javelin, Callie saw a little hand twitching under a nauseous pile of girls from the Polite Middle Third.

"Help," said a muffled voice. Callie began to pull the girls off the pile one by one. They groaned, rubbing their stomachs.

"I feel queer," said Iris Muddle. "The milk must have been off at breakfast." She threw a punch at Callie, who ducked easily. Iris had awful aim, on and off the net ball court.

"Help," said the little voice again, sounding desperate. "I can't breathe!" The hand waved urgently.

Callie pushed aside more groaning bodies, revealing the owner of the hand to be Little Annie, gasping for breath underneath. "Oh, thank you!" cried Annie, before she saw who her rescuer was.

Callie reached down a hand to help the younger girl up. "Don't touch me," Annie whispered. "You're the thief of the Uncouth Lower Fourth. I'm afraid of you."

"Don't be silly," Callie said. "Buck up. Get back to your dorm, it's dangerous out here." She seized Annie by the shoulder and tried to pull her to her feet. Annie screamed and hit at Callie with her little hands. "Stop it!" shouted Callie. Before she knew it she'd slapped the younger girl. Annie backed away, sobbing, holding a hand to her crimson cheek. "Wait," called Callie, "Annie, I didn't mean it—"

Jack stood nearby, eyes wide with horror. She had seen the whole thing. "I don't know what you've become," Jack said. "Stealing from my locker, now this."

"I didn't steal," Callie said. "Jack, you have to believe me! It was Miss Grainger. Maybe she's a spy from another school or something. I planned to confront her, so made sure I was the first to arrive at Home Economics class this morning— only to find her putting something from a blue bottle in the porridge. They all ate that porridge for breakfast, Jack! Then they all started going crazy and attacking one another. She must have found a way to make me take some of that stuff, too. You know I would never, ever hit a girl from the Lower Third."

Jack looked torn. Callie could see she wanted to believe her friend. But she shook her head and shouldered her pike. "I've got to put a stop to a bare-knuckle boxing match on the squash court," she said.

"Jack!" Callie seized Jack's hand and looked into her eyes. "We're best friends," she said. "I wouldn't lie to you."

"I can't take the word of a thief," Jack said. The disappointment in her eyes was more than Callie could bear.

"Please, at least give me a chance to prove it. I think I know where Miss Grainger will be—in the observation classroom above the ocean. We can't let her get away with this, Jack, we have to defend the school."

"It's no good, Callie, let me go."

Callie released her friend's hand. She watched as Jack walked away from her through the dying remains of the battle. She felt like a part of her had died, too.

She bent and wiped her straight razor clean on her knee sock. Her face wore a grim expression. Callie turned and began to push her way through the wrestling girls, toward the classroom above the ocean.

ROB
THEN

Sundial empties out. The preppy boys and girls go back to wherever they came from. I see the betrayal in Mia and Falcon's eyes. They welcomed in the clever children, the *curious*. But sometimes the curious children have white Chevys and will try to steal their princesses from the tower. Soon it's only us and Pawel left. Pawel gets even quieter. He wanders the grounds of Sundial like a ghost, carrying a coil of wire on his shoulder, a shovel, a gun, lengths of twine knotted into bowlines.

Falcon and Mia sit with us for hours, asking us about what we feel and trying to talk about growing up. It's gross and weird. But most of it is focused on Jack. So that's good, I tell myself.

We watch from the gallery window. The little coyote lies on the table. His flanks rise fast, up and down. He's unconscious but he looks like he's running. Falcon's eyes are serious above his surgical mask. The saw buzzes. I can smell bone dust even through the glass. I hate this part. I try to take Jack's hand but she moves it away, dreamily. She's by my side, an inch or two away, but it might as well be miles.

Mia prepares the putty skullcap, which will protect the coyote's brain from infection and dust. Falcon runs the electrodes into the pleasure centers of the dog's mind. Mia covers the hole in the skull with sterile putty, concealing the electrode leads. They cover him in blankets and give him an IV for fluids and some vitamins. Falcon tattoos the wide, translucent ear with blue numbers. The coyote is number Thirty-One, now. They wheel him out to the recovery room.

It's possible to feel the horror of something and to accept it all at the same time. How else could we cope with being alive?

I THINK OF the little coyote as we are eating dinner that night, under the jacaranda, beneath the desert stars. I picture him lying alone in the cold metal room, sides heaving as though he is running away from his fate, which is already upon him. *I'll make it OK for you,* I promise him, silently. *I'll keep you safe.*

"Jack," Mia says.

Jack does not look up. She plays with her rice and beans. She hasn't eaten much since she was brought back. She drifts through Sundial like one of her ghost dogs. Falcon and Mia talk about her late at night, I know it. I lie awake listening to the low murmur. I can't hear much of what they say, but her name comes up a lot.

"Jack," Mia says again. "Falcon and I start working with the coyote tomorrow morning. We're going to bond him."

Bonding is where Falcon comes into his own. He makes the dogs' brains receptive and soft, ready to accept Mia and the pack.

Mia says, "We think it's time you were more involved with things around here. Would you like to join us?" Her face is hopeful. "We can bond him to you. It'll be kind of like having a dog."

"OK," says Jack with a shrug.

The unfairness is like a blow to my throat. He's mine, my little wild puppy. "I thought," I say, "I thought . . ." I stop because no one is paying me attention. Everyone is looking at Jack, drawn in by the electrical storm that tosses about her these days.

"But he's mine," I say. "You promised." The twin thing isn't always good. Sometimes you know things you wish you didn't. Like right now, I can see that Jack knows how this hurts me. I can see she likes that.

"Come on, Rob," Mia says, smiling at me. "Jack needs something to focus on right now." I feel an acute sense of loss for something I never knew I had. But how could I have realized that I was the favorite, until I wasn't anymore?

"Where's Pawel?" asks Jack, suddenly.

"He had some stuff to do tonight," Falcon says easily. But there's a stiffness in him. *He's lying*, I think, in wonder. *He doesn't know where Pawel is.*

I PEEK FROM under the covers. Jack lies in bed staring up at the ceiling. In the pink light she looks like a photograph, she's so still. I wonder if the ghost dogs are pouring through the walls, trotting through our prone bodies, sniffing at my limbs with their shadowed, trembling noses. The thought makes me shrink. I stay still, which every child knows is the way to avoid the notice of monsters.

After a while, when she thinks I am asleep I guess, Jack starts dandling her Rob dolly, making shadow puppets with it in the dim pink light.

"Jack isn't doing so good in the pack." Jack is whispering but it doesn't sound like a regular whisper. It sounds like the sounds are being dragged out of her. "Mia has to take her out back and *git* her with the choo choo. So sad."

Her eyelids slowly droop. Her legs are flung akimbo, one hanging over the side of the bed, foot sticking out. Her sock has a hole in it and the sight of her foot so pink and vulnerable makes my heart lurch. For a second I want to get better socks out of the drawer and put them on her. Then I touch my neck, where I can still feel the faint traces of her fingernails. Her red notebook is clutched in her hands. I see her writing in it at night when she thinks I'm not looking. Some hippie thing Falcon told her to do, probably. Release her feelings or whatever.

Her eyes close and her breathing grows deep and even. Time to go.

I'VE NEVER BEEN out of the house at night on my own before. The thicket of cacti around the labs looks like people, arms reaching for the sky. I inch my way through them, hands outstretched, wary of spines. I go to the big steel door of the dog lab and punch in the key code, as I've seen Mia do a hundred times: 112263.

The coyote is still out. Mia's little scissors are working away in him, busily cutting and pasting. I put my fingertips on the glass to watch him. He's definitely asleep. The tip of a little pink tongue protrudes from between his jaws. He looks very small in the tiled green room. Green is supposed to be soothing, but for who? Dogs are color-blind. So it's meant to soothe the people who do the stuff to the dogs.

I go to the big cupboard where they keep the medicine. It's locked, but the key is just lying on top. I open it and look at the ranks of bottles. I've seen Falcon administer it enough times. He injects it but I'm not confident enough with a hypodermic to do that. I'm going to have to improvise.

I'm not stupid; I know what they're growing in the greenhouse. Ergot, on living rye. Ergot is a fungus. It makes you crazy. Those girls in Salem were tried as witches but I've read they actually had ergot poisoning. It makes you see things, it takes your mind weird places. Falcon found a way to process it into medicine to help the dogs learn. The lysergic acid makes the brain more receptive, Falcon says, makes it easier to form new neural pathways. They take a little trip, he says, and after that they love Mia forever. It seems to work.

I slip into the observation room. The coyote's rank scent fills the room. I'm suddenly aware that I'm in a confined space with a wild thing. I go close. His breathing stays steady. I drip a little medicine onto his protruding tongue, then put my hand near his nose. It wrinkles a little and he growls in his sleep. I flinch; I imagine needle teeth piercing my flesh. But I take a deep breath, and I don't take my hand away. I let my scent travel into his dreams, as the medicine works in his brain. "You're mine now," I whisper. "Not hers." I feel like a witch, casting a spell.

I EASE THE bedroom door closed behind me, lifting it slightly, so the hinges don't make that long groan. Jack lies in bed, ramrod straight, eyes closed, just as I left her. Her notebook isn't in her hands anymore, it's on the nightstand, as if she woke up to write, then went back to sleep.

There's a smell in the room now too, like metal. One of her feet still sticks out from under the covers. My heart lurches, cold. Her foot is bare, mottled with dirt, the sole dusty; there's brown dirt between her bare toes. How come I didn't notice that before? *Maybe it wasn't there before*, a voice inside me whispers. *Maybe she's been walking, like you.* I picture Jack gliding through the night like a ghost, her wide-open eyes, toes just grazing the dirt.

Holding my breath, I lean over her. She breathes evenly, one corner of her mouth pulled slightly down. Something dark stains the corner of her lips like berry juice or a shadow, maybe. I can't tell which.

I think about opening the notebook. But I'm not sure I want to know what it's like inside her mind.

JACK, FALCON, AND Mia watch the coyote through the little glass window. I peer around them. No one moves aside so I can go to the front. Thirty-One, as I suppose I have to think of him now, is awake. He staggers wearily to the water bowl. He laps and then lies down with a whine. He doesn't seem ready for training but Mia and Falcon say he is.

Falcon takes a vial out of the high cupboard, and enters the green room. He wears big gauntlets and boots. He injects the medicine into the coyote's shoulder. The coyote turns and bares his teeth but it's half-hearted. He's confused, defeated, in pain. Falcon leaves the room quickly.

I watch through the sliver of window I can see over Jack's shoulder. I know this stage, have seen it before. The coyote's eyes go black and alive. The medicine rushes through him. Mia sends him enjoyment. His posture straightens. His tail takes on the still alert posture of a dog ready to work.

Falcon comes back into the viewing chamber and confers with Mia. They talk so quietly that even a few feet back I can't hear what they're saying.

Mia asks, "Shall I try now, Jack?" She asks like Jack's opinion is really important.

Jack nods and Mia pushes a button. The coyote wanders aimlessly. His head droops. Then he happens to turn left. His ears shoot up. His too-black eyes are alert. He whines and turns left and left and left until he is describing ever tighter circles, fed buzzing happiness by the electrodes in his brain. Then Mia changes the instruction. He turns left again, but the pleasure is gone. He growls. The world is gray and painful again. He mopes, wandering until he finds that now, lying down produces this intense enjoyment. He lies and pants, until the pleasure stops, and he has to seek it out once more.

Thirty-One learns quickly. He is smart. Slowly, directed by Mia, he begins to walk in simple shapes—a square, a diamond. There is no human contact for this. He must be focused on his own sensations. I wonder if he's lonely or scared. I think the medicine helps him forget that.

For an hour we watch Thirty-One stumble in his limping circles. He looks so confused and tired. I feel like screaming at them to stop. But I can't because I have no reason to be here and if I make a sound they might realize that and tell me to go.

At last Mia stops. Thirty-One stops, too. He lowers his head and pants. "Everything's working," she says. All my organs release in relief. He's a good dog.

Jack gets up and goes to the door of his room. I can see she's scared and I am about to say something nice to her when she shoots me a look, as though she knows exactly what is on my mind. I remain silent. Jack goes into the green room. The door closes behind her with a *clang*.

Thirty-One turns like a flash to face her. "Slowly," Mia says through the intercom. Jack inches toward the coyote. He bares his teeth and snarls at her. The sound is liquid, rising.

"OK, no, get out of there, Jack," Mia says.

Jack doesn't move. At first I think she's smiling at the coyote, but then it looks more like something else. They stand and snarl at each other.

"I said get out of the room." Mia's voice is tense.

Jack shakes her head. Mia grabs the tranquilizer and lunges for the door. As she turns the handle, the coyote whines and lowers his head. His tail starts to wag. Jack fondles his ears and he licks her hand. Mia opens the door slowly. Her hand is trembling on the latch.

"You, out, right now," she says quietly to Jack. "Get."

Jack obeys. When she's gone the coyote sniffs the door and whines.

He throws back his head and sings his sorrowful ghost song. Mia grabs Jack by the arm and hustles her out. "Thank god," she mutters to Falcon. "Stupid goddamn idea. What were we thinking?"

Pawel doesn't come to dinner again. I push tofu around my plate and don't say anything. Even a coyote picked my sister over me.

NIMUE HAS GONE wandering, and Jack and I walk the perimeter fence, to see if she has broken out. We call her name and listen for the soft ring of her bell. We pass the sundial, and the spring. The rose is not in bloom. It looks like a dead piece of stick with some leaves on it. Something's caught in the wire fence, somewhere, and it keeps making a thudding *ding* as the wind swings it, again and again. It's really irritating.

My resentment is a fiery seed in my stomach, growing each day. I watch how they fuss over her, how they note how much she eats for breakfast. They try to tempt her to smile with her favorite books and food. The seed burns harder and brighter until my chest is filled with a burning star.

"I don't understand why you're here, I don't need you to look for a *cow*," Jack says.

"Mia told us to stay together."

"You do everything they say. This place is nonsense. Falcon and Mia are such fakes—look at all that stuff they do with the dogs; it's cruel."

"It's important research," I say. *Research* is a sacred word at Sundial.

"Really, Rob? You think so? That MK Ultra thing with the controller—it's not even their own idea. The CIA did the same experiment with electrodes in dog brains back in the sixties. Making them run in a square, lie down, bark . . . They gave up because it had no practical application. Falcon and Mia are just hippies who want to be important."

"Why do they do it then?"

"You just don't *think*, do you?"

The thudding carries on, regular, something hitting the fence. It seems designed to give me a headache. I find the perfect dart to wound. "Did the guy with the Chevy tell you that?"

Jack goes white and her teeth nibble her lower lip. Her escape has never been mentioned between us until now. "Shut up!" She picks up a rock and hurls it at me. It whirs by my head, sending pulses of horror through my chest.

"At least I know what's real." Jack's voice is high and uneven.

"I don't, I suppose." I mean to say this but it comes out more like yelling. "Fine. Go. Do whatever. What the hell is that sound?"

Thunk, thunk.

She's staring behind me at the fence. I turn and follow her gaze. A jackrabbit stands in the distance. After a moment, it comes down on all fours. It runs straight at the fence. *Thunk.* The rabbit picks itself up again and wanders. Then it runs at the fence again, making for the desert. It doesn't seem to understand that there's a fence between it and all that open space. *Thunk.* I see, then, that there are two red holes where its eyes should be.

I CRY AS Mia holds me; big wet sobs. "It's OK, Rob. I'm sorry you had to see that. Crows do it sometimes. Magpies, too. We've taken care of it." Somewhere a door opens. Low voices in the hallway beyond. Pawel is back.

THAT NIGHT JACK stares at her reflection in the tall pier glass. "You don't belong here," she says.

"Why don't you leave?" I say, stung. "At least I like it here. You hate everything."

Jack lashes out so quickly that I gasp and stagger. Her fist hits the corner of the mirror. The old glass shatters, cobwebbing out in tiny cracks.

"Stop it," I say. I know, in this moment, that she is going to kill me. With two delicate fingers Jack picks out a shard of glass, like a thin shining fang. She picks up the Rob doll that lies on her bed.

"Always lying to me," she says, drawing the shard of glass across the doll's face. I hear the sound of fabric tearing and white stuffing comes out of its mouth. "You're going to put me back in the dark."

I put my hands over my face and eyes, as if that could protect the doll. "Stop it, Jack."

"Liars go on pyres," she says in a croaking, aged voice. "Liars go in fires. Liars drown in mires." I feel my hot tears, my hot breath against my sweating palms. I hear Jack stabbing the doll's face over and over. "Liars are criers." The sound of punctured cloth seems to go on forever. I press the heels of my hands into my eye sockets and watch the patterns bloom in the dark. I try to focus on that, rather than on the world. It works, kind of; the noise, her voice, recedes. So I don't notice right away when the sound changes. The whispering and the taut sound of ripped cloth are replaced by a light trickling noise, a patter like spring rain.

I look up. Jack is clutching her wrist. Red wells up between her fingers. It spills onto the white fluffy comforter, pools in the seams, trickles to the wooden floor. It's fascinating, so red, too red to be real. It's beautiful like a dream or some trick being played.

"At least I didn't do it to you," Jack says. She sounds normal, relieved. "That's good, isn't it?"

I stagger to the doorway and scream for Falcon and Mia.

THE EMERGENCY ROOM is a blinding, white-lit hell. It's Saturday night and there is a man with one eye and a stick sleeping on the plastic chairs in the corner. There is a child with a pale face shiny with sweat. Some guy wearing what I realize, after a moment, are fluffy rabbit ears. There are lots of other people. Some college kid crying, a bad trip. I can't take in the scene as a whole, only odd details stand out.

Jack is seen quickly because of all the blood. Blood gets people's attention. The doctor is young, tired. He's from around here, you can tell—Mohave, maybe. He has the desert look.

Jack lies on the gurney, pale as a pencil drawing. "Don't worry," Mia says. "You'll be OK." She takes Jack's hand.

I watch Jack's still, unconscious face and realize for the first time that I'm afraid of her. I look up to find Mia's eyes on me. She smiles a little but it's not happy. It gives me the same feeling I get with the MRI, that my inside self is on public view.

"We're low on blood," the doctor says. I hadn't noticed him come in. "Any of you compatible types?"

Falcon says, like a child reciting a poem, "I'm AB positive. Jack's A positive. Rob's O negative—" Someone in the ward beyond starts crying in brief, broken sobs.

"O, universal donor," the doctor says, interrupting. It's like he doesn't have time for full sentences. "Are you seventeen?" I realize he means me.

"Yes," I say, dazed. "Is she going to be OK?"

"Come with me, please," the doctor says again.

"MOST PEOPLE LIKE to look away when we do this," the nurse says. She has acne and bad breath. "We're like horses that way. We don't like to see blood. You know, horses can smell a battle on the ground years after? Blood. My pinto won't go up that one trail out by Lina and Burt Grainger's place, you know, that puppy farm. Nothing to see but the horse can still tell. My big brother says he saw them in Bone from time to time. Lina and Burt. He says they seemed OK—quiet types. Lots of people knew them—to say hi to, anyway. How could anyone have guessed what they were doing out there at that place? So awful. Anyway, most people close their eyes when I do this." She shifts away from me, half an inch or so. The legs of her stool scrape the floor loudly. She's nervous. Something about me is making her twitchy.

I keep my eyes fixed on the nurse's wary expression. *I'm not even the interesting one,* I feel like telling her. *I'm the good one.* It makes me laugh, which turns into a dry sort of crying.

THEY DON'T KEEP Jack at the hospital. "I slipped and broke the mirror," she tells them. "That's how I cut myself." And we all nod. The doctor looks at us for a long moment, then lets us go. He's seen too much of the desert to be concerned with the problems of teenage girls.

I WATCH AS Mia gives Jack a vitamin B shot. Jack doesn't seem to notice.

"It can help with depression," Mia says. "We'll try this for a couple weeks. Could try some D supplements, too . . ." I can tell she's trying to sound cheerful. For some reason it makes me more depressed.

I resolve to watch Jack's every move to see if the vitamins help. I am going to be vigilant about Jack's well-being. I'm going to take notice of everything that happens to her from now on. Everything she does and says.

JACK AND I are digging in the dog graveyard.

Number Fifteen got an infected tick bite a couple weeks ago. He died last night. He had been sick for a while; it wasn't a shock. It took us some time to find an empty corner for him. All the dead dogs. I wonder if Jack will see Fifteen racing through the walls of our bedroom tonight. If she tries to tell me about it, I'll cover my ears and put my head under the pillow.

The digging is hot work. Jack says, "Poor dog," in her regular voice.

I never liked Fifteen. He smelled bad and he ate his poop all the time. His body is in the big, dented icebox beside us. I can't help picturing him in there, his big milky eyes staring at the dark.

The hole is finally done, four feet deep. I stop to drink from the pitcher. The well water is cool and tastes like stone. Mia has given us lunch in our favorite lunch box, an old tin one with Snoopy on the front. It used to be our favorite, anyway. I don't know what Jack likes anymore. We've stroked Snoopy so many times that his face is worn away; he's just a pair of ears. But I know he's there. Even though I know it's stupid, using the lunch box makes me feel better.

The push from behind is so gentle, Jack uses her fingertips only. I feel each of them on my back. I stagger and slip, and a moment later I am lying in the grave on my back, looking up at a rectangle of sky. Beside me a severed earthworm end waves desperately. I scramble up and pull myself out. It takes a few tries. The sides of the grave start to collapse.

I hurl myself on Jack and knock her to the ground. There is some kind of earth grub in my hair, and it lands on her face. She stares up, unmoving.

"What was that for?" Tears run into my gasping mouth. "What's with you? Why are you like this?" Part of me even wonders what that sound is, the dull retort of bone on bone. I seem to hear it before I see it, my fist striking Jack's face just below her left eye. Red steals up her cheekbone, across her chin. I hit her again, and then I stop. We stare at each other in shock. She reaches up and touches the place, wincing.

I get off her.

Jack sits up calmly. For a long moment she stares at me with her black eyes. "Fine. I'll tell you."

She takes her red notebook from her pants pocket and flips it open. The pages are covered in blue ballpoint, her neat cursive. "I always wondered if I'd give it to you. I don't think you'll like it, Sundance. But you can have it if you want." She tears out the pages and I hold my hand to take them. But she doesn't give them to me. Instead, Jack takes the Snoopy lunch box and turns it upside down. Our sandwiches fall to the dusty earth. I smell peanut butter and apple. Jack puts the pages in the box and closes it up tight, then she throws the box into the freshly dug grave. Quickly, she lifts the lid of the cooler and tosses Fifteen's body into the hole. It lands on top of the tin box, hiding Snoopy from view. The corpse makes a dull *thump* on the earth. His forepaw comes to rest by the waving earthworm. Jack grabs her shovel and hurls a storm of dirt into the hole.

"So, Rob," she says through hard breaths. "If you want to know *what's with me*, here's where the answer will be. All you got to do is come and dig up the grave. Sift through the rotting flesh with your hands—"

"I'm going to tell Falcon," I say. "You're a psycho."

"Go on then," she says, shoveling, eyes on the hole. "I'll tell him things, too. You hit me. He'll find out exactly who you are."

"Jack," I say. "Cassidy—"

"You're such a child. When are you going to grow up? What, dumbass, you're going to live here forever with Mia and Falcon, helping with their dumbass experiments?"

I turn and run—not toward Sundial but away. I run along the fence, open desert beside me, until my breath saws in and out and my skin feels like it's on fire. I pass the sundial and the spring, I pass the ramshackle sheds at the edge of the compound. I run until the beaten paths end and I'm stumbling through scrub. There's so little tree cover out here, the ground seems to throw out heat. I think of rattlers but I don't care. I want to run myself out of existence.

"I hate her, I hate her, I hate her," I gasp as I run. The "h" on *hate* gets lost on the wind. It sounds like I'm saying, *I ate her, I ate her, I ate her.*

My foot slips and I go flying. My hands skid on the shale. The rocks are hot enough that I almost feel my palms hiss on them. Blood comes. My face is pressed to the hot ground. I can see the stems of the arrow weed, and close by, a fence post. The wind is up. The desert moans. The taste of soda trickles down my throat, sickly warm.

Something lies by the fence post: burning brass. I reach out and as my fingers brush its scalding surface, the bell tips. It gives a soft little *clink.* Nimue. I stare at the bell. I know she's dead. Something killed her. I'm afraid to think what, or who. Everything I loved about Sundial is gone.

The bell is too hot to touch with bare fingers but I can't stand to look at it anymore. I kick it hard into the thicket of arrow weed. It clunks somewhere in the dust. I make my way back. My hands are scuffed and bleeding, my throat feels like sawdust and my head swims in the heat. But it's time to decide who to be.

Mia is splitting logs by the wood stacks. From a distance, the ax blows sound like gunshot. She pauses when she sees me, wipes sweat from her brow. "What is it, Rob?"

"I need your help." It's not too late for me to put my own Plan into action.

By dinnertime Jack's face is swollen and bruised, one eye almost puffed closed.

Falcon hisses when he sees her. "My Jackfruit. What happened?"

"I was jogging the boundary," she says. "I tripped on a stone and my face hit the fence post. Dumb, right?" It's unnerving how normal she can sound when she tries. That dead, grinding voice only comes out when we're alone.

"You have to be more careful out there." But he sounds pleased. He thinks she was doing something healthy, good for her body.

Jack stares at me and eats a mouthful of tomato salad. Unless you knew her really well, you couldn't be sure that she was smiling.

I should be worried that she's going to tell Falcon. But it's not fear I feel. Instead there is a thrilling wingbeat in my chest as I recall the sound of my fist on her cheekbone.

CALLIE

I ALWAYS WAKE at dawn in the desert. For a second I don't know where I am. That's OK. It's when I remember that it becomes scary.

Mom's still asleep, I can tell. The house is talking to itself in small sounds, the way houses do when no one's up. She's tired; the story is sucking her dry like a vampire. Or maybe she's the vampire.

I need a weapon, I say to Pale Callie. *Dad told me so.* It's not just him, though. I saw Mom's face when she talked about hitting. I know that look. I understand it. Whatever it is, she's got it in her, too.

Pale Callie sings, *Cross my heart, hope to die, stick a needle in my eye.*

I put my hands over my ears. *For once, just shut up.*

I play with the controller I found in the back of the drawer. I stab at the button that looks like candy. *Hunt,* I think. *Hunt.* Who's hunting, me or Mom?

Hunt me! Dumpster Puppy goes down on his forelegs, playful, ghost tail wagging. He's so cute, it's fun to chase him. He leaps away; I run and climb all over, hunting him. He always escapes, leaping into the air, running over the ceiling, disappearing into the mirror and becoming a silver reflection. That is against the rules but he does it, anyway. Cheater. I've never been bored since Pale Callie taught me how to do the animal bones. I always have friends to play with now.

We run and scream until I am panting, mouth dry as sand. Dumpster Puppy never gets tired, though. Time passes differently with the pale.

If you were pale you could run forever too, and never get tired, Pale Callie says. She hovers by the ceiling in a corner by the window. Her edges hum like a swarm of flies.

"I like being tired," I say. Being tired is a clock. But playing with Dumpster

Puppy has given me an idea. I get his bone picture from where it sits on the dresser. Mom put it under the bed and I put it up again.

What are you doing? He bounds around. *Hey, Callie! Hey, Callie?* I gently detach his fibula.

Hey, Callie, can I have that back? Can I? He runs around me in a hobbling, three-legged circle, a dark gap where his bone is now missing.

"Sorry," I whisper to him.

I go quietly down to the kitchen. The refrigerator thinks and hums. I take the grindstone out of the cupboard and put it on the counter. Carefully I break the end of the bone. I ease it back and forth on the whetstone, until it achieves a slicing edge. Now it is a knife. I slip the bone knife into my pocket and go upstairs. After that I just sit on my bed, staring, not even thinking. What can I think about that is not terrible? Above all I must not think about what will happen if Pale Callie is right and Mom brought me here to end me. I like being warm and I don't want to be pale. I imagine how the little bone knife would feel, sliding true, slipping home into flesh. The sound it would make as it punctured the skin. *Pock,* like a sucked lollipop. My head bursts with color and noise. I breathe very deeply to try and make it fade.

But I need to see if it works. I take my pillow and I stab it. The *pock* sound the knife makes as it punctures the pillowcase is just how I imagined. Bursting color. I do it again. *Pock.*

I stab and stab. My breath is coming quite fast and my tongue comes out a little between my teeth. *Pock, pock, pock,* goes the knife through the pillowcase.

When I look up, Mom is in the doorway, watching. Her face is the color of oatmeal. "Give it to me, Callie."

I give her the bone knife.

"Stay in your room." Her voice is quiet, which is scarier than yelling. She closes the door with a *click.* I think maybe she'll lock me in, but she doesn't.

She's gone for a long time. I get hungry but I don't know whether I'm allowed to go downstairs and make a sandwich. I can't hear anything; it's like she's not even in the house. But I didn't hear the car start so she hasn't gone for groceries or anything. I look out the window. There she is in the distance, just inside the perimeter fence, in the shade of a big tree. She's doing something—quick movements, sun shining on metal. But I can't see what.

I sneak down the stairs, into the silence of Sundial. The wind is high outside. But faintly, to the east, I can hear grunting, effort, something striking earth.

I slide open the patio doors, gentle as a breeze, and step out. Pale Callie and Dumpster Puppy cling to me. They're scared, and that makes me even more scared. I creep along the side of the house, treading silently.

She's leaning on the handle of a shovel by a big pile of earth. She's sweating; it must be hot even in this chilly winter sun. She's been digging for some time. It's a rectangular hole, five feet or so by three.

Huh, I say silently to Pale Callie. *Mom's digging a big hole.*

That's not a hole, Pale Callie says. *You know what that is.*

I go back to my room, heart pounding.

ROB

I TURN THE little bone knife over and over in my hands. The animal was young when it died and the bone is slightly pliant. It probably couldn't pierce flesh. I think it's from that disgusting bone portrait she insisted on bringing.

I can't get Callie's face out of my mind. The absolute focus in her eyes, the pink tongue protruding as she stabbed with this little knife. How did she make it? It doesn't matter.

The branches of the decision tree glow before me.

1. *How can I stop Irving from keeping one, or both, of my daughters?*
2. *If I have to take on more teaching work, how can I watch them all the time?*
3. *If I can't watch them all the time, how do I stop Callie from hurting Annie?*

I see the diagram in my mind's eye. It glows with irrefutable logic. The answer is there, and it's always the same, no matter how many branches I follow. I'm out of options. There's only one thing left to do if I'm to keep even one of my daughters.

The worst thing.

I go to the toolshed. The shiny shovel winks in the light like a greeting. *Hi, Rob, I've been expecting you.*

THERE ARE TWO gravestones at Sundial, one each for Falcon and Mia. But many things lie underground here, unmarked. The whole place is a graveyard. Sometimes I lie awake at night and picture it like a layer cake or a medieval painting of hell. All the hidden things, lives pressing down on one another, the weight of years, and the heat of guilt forging them diamond-hard. Indestructible secrets lie in the ground at Sundial.

The white picket fence around the dog graveyard is weathered silver now; planks have come loose and tap gently in the wind. That's the same; there's always wind out here, swooping in cold, slapping your face with rough hands.

This was the dogs' graveyard but there are other things buried here, too.

I have to find the right place; a certain grave. I dig several shallow holes, but none of them is the right spot. More than once the blade of my shovel strikes white bone. A long-fanged skull stares at me, empty-eyed. A big dog, a German shepherd maybe. I take the little bone from my pocket and lay it down gently, here. It seems the right thing to do. I find two puppies side by side. Other bones are adrift in the earth, pulled apart by time and scavengers. I keep digging, grim, searching the ground for glimpses of blue.

I need what I buried here after it all happened.

Something gleams in the dirt, showing back the burning sky. I bend down, heart pounding. It's a fragment of mirror, dull with time. The sight of it makes me feel cold. The past and now, intertwining. But I have to keep going.

I find what I'm looking for after an hour or so. Through the brown earth shows bright color. I toss the shovel aside and kneel to dig with my hands. The very soil seems to smell rotten here, moist and bad on my palms. I try not to think about dead flesh decaying, becoming one with the earth.

The box is protected by a graceful curve of bones, as if the ground itself had ribs. I claw at the earth and soon it's in my hands. The blue plastic case.

I grab the shovel to widen the hole but as I do, something else catches the light. The exposed corner of an old tin, rusted now with time. Snoopy's face is patchy white, but his ears are still there, glossy black.

No. I looked for it, back then. It wasn't here.

I dig the tin out of the earth with trembling fingers. There can be no mistake. It's our old Snoopy lunch box. I thought it was gone. The desert has given it back.

I force myself to wait. I have to finish here, first. I dig outward and upward, enlarging the hole until it's about six feet long, four deep. That should do it.

IN THE KITCHEN I wash the grave earth off my aching arms. Then I take the blue box and the rusty tin up to my bedroom. Well, what is *now* my bedroom. It belonged to Mia and Falcon, once.

I pass Callie's room. That was mine then. Ours. Callie's door is shut. It's a little different from all the other doors in the house. The ornate edges of the panels are a near but not perfect match. The wood is paler, it lacks the patina of age. But you have to look very carefully to see that it's newer than all the other doors.

I knock. "Are you OK, Callie?" I make my voice sound normal.

"Uh huh," she says.

"We need to keep going. See you downstairs in half an hour."

"Uh huh."

I take my precious burdens into my bedroom and shut the door. *Closed doors lead to closed minds,* I hear Mia say, and I shake my head in irritation. There is too much memory here. Everything drags a weight of ghosts behind it. I put the blue plastic case on the dresser. That can wait.

I open the tin lunch box with trembling hands. There are the pages, still folded neatly in half. I wait for a moment before opening them, smoothing them on my knee. There it is, her handwriting, in old blue ballpoint. How could such a messy person have such neat cursive?

I swear, I can smell her in the air. She always smelled slightly sweet, like a grapefruit. Before she began to carry around that miasma of dirt.

WHEN I HAVE read the pages I sit staring ahead, trying to take it in. The whole world is changing around me, soft and luminous. Or maybe it's me that's changing. I feel it, my edges becoming soft where they meet the air, as if I am dissolving into nothing and being remade, as if inside a chrysalid. Those names.

She's in the room with me, her hand on mine. Her voice, clear as a bell.

Kids are mirrors, reflecting back everything that happens to them. You've got to make sure they're surrounded by good things. Remember that, Sundance.

Hot tears streak down my face. There was always only one option—the only way I can save both my daughters.

I open the blue plastic case carefully. Dirt showers out from the cracks, but the syringe inside isn't broken. The liquid, that distinctive pale purple, looks the same as it always did. Do things like this go off? Expire? I touch the plunger. I imagine depressing it, pushing the needle deeper, deeper into flesh.

Too hard. I don't know if I can face it.

IRVING HAS CALLED seventeen times. I call him back.

"You should really keep your phone on you, Rob," he says smoothly. *Danger.*

"Is Annie OK?" I ask. "Just tell me that first."

"You're awfully demanding for a woman who abandoned her sick daughter to go on some vision quest in the desert."

I take a deep breath. *Here goes.* "I'm keeping Callie away from you forever," I say. "And I'll get Annie, too. I'll tell them about you, what you are."

"OK, Rob. What brought this on?" He sounds weary. Dealing with his neurotic wife. "Did I forget a parents' evening or something?"

"It's over, Irving." I hate myself for how my voice shakes. I hate how my tone goes up a little at the end of the sentence, making my statement sound like a question.

He sighs. "You sound a little worked up."

"I'm stable," I say. "I'm steady as a rock."

"Maybe I should come out there."

"Don't come anywhere near me."

"I'm really very concerned, Rob. Callie says you shook her."

Guilt tears through me. When did they talk? I take a long breath. Then I say again, in as even a tone as I can manage, "I meant what I said. I'm divorcing you and taking the children."

"You know I can't let you do that, Rob." He's using his reasonable voice.

I disconnect the call with the gentlest of touches, as if somehow that could soften the enormity of the action. You don't hang up on Irving.

"You've done it now, Sundance," I whisper to myself. The edges of the world shiver.

I PICK UP the phone and call Irving again. I am appeasing, this time. I hate the slight whine in my voice. I cry. The merry-go-round turns, again and again.

Then I go down to where Callie is waiting.

ROB
T H E N

I STAND AT the kitchen window, looking out to the east, toward the dog graveyard. I have the letter in my hand. I have waited for this moment for months, but now it's here I am strangely nervous.

I think of Fifteen, his corpse by now clean bone, lying in the earth. I picture the tin box lying in the embrace of his ribs, a metal heart in an ivory cage. I wonder if there's anything about my mother on those pages, which lie buried in the box. Lily. Maybe there's nothing meaningful at all. It would be a good, cruel joke. I can picture it. I sneak out in the dead of night, dig up the grave by flashlight, pick through the suppurating flesh to retrieve the box, only to find a limerick or a joke written on those bits of ragged paper. Perhaps the word *dumbass*, over and over again . . .

I am ready to leave Sundial's mysteries where they lie—dead beneath the earth.

I WAIT UNTIL dinner when we are all there, eating in the kitchen. The winter nights are coming in. Wind slaps the windows. It's eggplant and tofu scramble. It's Falcon's night to cook and it's the only thing he makes. The eggplant is a gray gelatinous mess. The tofu is crumbling and dry.

"It's Rob's turn to start the conversation," Falcon says. We each take turns to bring a subject of interest to the dinner table. Otherwise we eat in long silences. Falcon and Mia usually choose music or art. They are still trying to educate us.

I take a deep breath. "I wanted to tell you that I got my GED," I say. "I did it through the mail. I've been applying to colleges. I've been accepted."

Jack looks up at me slowly. Her eyes are dark pools. She's been way more normal recently, though we don't speak much. She works outside with Pawel, mostly. She sleeps at night and she has a dark tan, up to her T-shirt sleeves. She should look well but she looks thin and bitten away.

I barely glanced at the college prospectuses when I was applying. I got accepted to a couple, and chose the one that gave me a full scholarship, in Cielo. It's a grim little joke that out of all the colleges in North America, the one that gave me full tuition is no more than three hours' drive from Sundial.

"Where did you get the money?" Falcon looks at Mia's downturned eyes and says coldly, "Of course."

"She decided," Mia says almost defiantly. "And it is her choice, Falcon. She'll be OK. After all, she's eighteen."

"Not yet." Falcon sounds petulant. Wednesday is our eighteenth birthday.

"We have neither the reason nor the means to keep her here," Mia says. Her tone is formal, without her usual warmth. She is talking to Falcon like a scientist, not a partner.

Jack's face is as still as wax. "That sounds good," she says. "I wanted . . . Maybe I could still . . . ?" She looks at Falcon.

I feel a hot little rush of glad spite. I took something Jack wanted.

"It's too late for you to get the grades," Falcon says gently. "Maybe next year, Jackfruit."

Jack says sadly, "I forgot."

Suddenly my plan seems stupid, childish. I realize now that I thought something would happen to stop me going. I have a terrible dawning feeling that I am going to have to do what I said I'd do. Leave Sundial, leave Falcon, the dogs, Mia . . . and Jack. What's the point of it all without my sister? "I don't have to go," I say. "I could stay a year and then we could apply together."

Jack looks at me for a moment with her shadowed eyes. Then she turns back to Falcon. "Rob and I don't need to listen to you," she says to him, "since you're not our real father."

I roll my eyes heavenward. She's trying to make trouble again. I really did think she was doing better. Falcon has always been immune to her barbs, so now I wait, expectant, for his indulgent denial. But there is only silence. Mia's eyes are fixed on her plate.

"I am your father in every way that matters," Falcon says slowly.

That's not what he should be saying. He should touch Jack's head gently and tell her that we're all going to have hot cocoa, then we'll go outside and look at the stars. That's how Falcon deals with Jack, and it almost always works. Slowly, my chest begins to fill with cold water. "Jack?"

My sister's eyes are cold and dead, fixed on me. "Didn't you notice at the hospital? You have O type blood. Falcon has AB. You can't be Falcon's daughter. I could be, I guess; I'm type A. But we're twins so we must have the same father—not Falcon, though."

"You are the one who asked me not to tell her, Jack," Falcon says. "Remember that."

"I don't understand," I say. "Was . . . did Mom have another husband or something?"

"You're such a dumbass," Jack says. "We're adopted. Did that make you feel better about yourself?" she asks Falcon. "Did it make you and your girlfriend feel like good people?"

"But you remember her," I say. "Mom was pretty and nice."

"I made her up," Jack says.

Something drops away inside me, in a long fall. "What is she talking about?"

"We thought it was harmless when Jack first started talking about a mother named Lily," Mia says. "Who could deny two sad children a little comfort? Now I think maybe that was a mistake." Mia looks at Jack with a little tight smile.

"Well," Jack says. "It's all out in the open at last. Everything there is to tell."

Falcon says, "We tried to do right. We had no experience with children."

"No," says Jack. "You're not natural parents."

Mia's face is twisted and slippery. This is very scary. Mia never cries. "You could have done this another way, Jack."

"Tell me," I say. A dark tide rises; I feel like I'm drowning. "Now."

Falcon says, "You came to Sundial when you were five—"

"Mia and Falcon adopted us from Nebraska," Jack says.

They all look at each other for a moment. It's like they've had a club of their own, all this time, and I wasn't allowed in.

"I hate you," I say. "All of you."

Mia puts a warm, kind hand on my back. "You chose your names, Rob. Did you know that? You were very late to speak—six. I knew you were both just taking your time. Einstein didn't speak until he was five. It happened while I was bathing you. You said 'Rob,' and pointed at yourself. Then you pointed at your sister and said 'Jack.' It was the first thing you'd ever said. It's supposed to be wonderful, raising children." She smiles. "And you know? Once in a while, it was. Know what else? I wouldn't change having you two, even if things could have been different for me and Falcon." There is love in her voice, but also sadness, the answer to a question I have always been too self-absorbed to frame. Maybe I had some vague thoughts that Falcon didn't want any more children, or that Mia was above such things. Maybe I assumed that Jack and I were enough.

Before I think, I say, "I'm sorry." Mia wouldn't have been that much older than I am now when she and Falcon decided to adopt us. Once again I feel that particular double stab of guilt and resentment—the suspicion that Mia is a better person than me.

"Rob," Falcon says. "We could not have loved any biological children more than we love you. And look at you. You are both so accomplished, so educated, so curious—and entirely your own people." Falcon's tears shimmer on the brink of spilling over. "We haven't done everything right," he says. "But you have given us so many reasons to be proud."

Fury rises in me, fills me to the brim, the sweet flat taste laps against my teeth. "Trust you to turn this into a compliment to yourself," I say.

"Rob—"

"No. You always say you want me to decide who I am. Well, now I'm going to." I get up and leave the dinner table.

All this makes a kind of sense. Strange relief runs through me. I'm not a desert person, after all. I'm a prairie person. I'll leave this place and never come back. I will become who I was meant to be.

In our room I ball my fists and try to breathe. There is too much feeling and I have to let it out.

I take the Jack doll from under my pillow. Slowly, I tear the arms and legs off her. Sawdust plumes in the air. "You always have to be the center of attention." I can't even tell which part makes me the angriest— that Jack kept the truth from me for so long or that she finally told me in this moment which was supposed to be all mine.

I look up to see Jack watching in the doorway. "I did it for your own good," she says. "You should get away from here."

"You took Mother from me," I say to the ruins of the doll. I feel pretty, kind Lily with her weak heart recede into the blackness of the never-was. I rip the head. It gives with a dry dusty sound.

"I just wanted you to have something nice," Jack says. "A good memory." She sounds regretful, and for a second I believe her. "Falcon told me," she says. "The day I ran away. I told them not to tell you. I really was trying to help, Sundance."

"I guess you changed your mind. You only did it to hurt me."

"I don't know," Jack says, thoughtful. "Maybe. I can't be entirely sure why I do things, anymore."

"Who are they? Our parents."

"It was a closed adoption. Nebraska is all we know."

"Why don't I remember?" I say.

"Maybe you don't want to."

"It doesn't make sense," I say. "Doesn't the government, like, check up on adopted children? Social services?"

"They probably did. How many people used to come through here, asking weird questions with clipboards?"

I shake my head like a dog trying to clear it. "You've ruined everything. You're worse than Falcon and Mia. You think you're better than them but you're not. You're worse because you know what lying about that stuff means for us. For me." My voice cracks. I am crying, I realize. I despise myself for it, I feel like a baby. But I can't stop the tears. Jack looks on, unmoved. "You couldn't even wait for me to find out by digging up those stupid pages you wrote. You were probably looking forward to that. But I took too long."

"It's good you didn't dig it up. I shouldn't have done that." She turns to look at me. At this close distance I can see how dark her eyes are, how dilated the pupil is, how unfocused her gaze. The overblown pupil, the rim of iris, they remind me of something, but I can't think what. "Your eyes," I say. "Are you OK?"

She laughs, a mean sound. "I can see right through you, Rob. Don't use me as an excuse because you're afraid to go."

"You used to say you'd always protect me." Even to me, my voice sounds bitter. "What a crock."

I KNOW MIA and Falcon thought everything they did was for the best. I try to remember that.

ROB

THEN

I MEET IRVING at Cielo during the first year of my bachelor's.

College doesn't bring the freedom that I'd hoped. I major in English Lit because it's the furthest I can get from science. The professors are tired, no one goes to class. The dorm is generally knee-deep in a haze of weed. My roommate is a nice girl but I correct her pronunciation of the word "pneumatic" on my first night and she doesn't speak to me again after that. Nothing is familiar.

Everyone else seems to have a secret shortcut to getting on with one another. They talk about school and boyfriends and families. I have no experience of the first two, and I soon find out that my family bears no resemblance to anyone else's. College is nothing like Bingley Hall. I try to make friends but there always comes a moment when I say something about Sundial or my childhood or the dogs, and their eyes go blank and it's over.

I speak to Jack the first week.

"How's Kelvin?"

"OK."

"Everyone here is weird," I say after a long pause. I twist the cord in my fingers. I imagine her holding the clunky plastic receiver to her thin cheek with both hands. I take a deep breath. "I don't think I like college." Silence. "Jack? Jack?"

She doesn't hang up so it's a minute before I realize she's gone. Afterward I can't stop picturing it; the squawking receiver swinging from the telephone table in the central atrium, dusk falling as I say her name over and over.

After this a polite phone conversation with Mia and Falcon once a week is the extent of my contact with Sundial. Part of me kind of ignores this. The rest of me can't think about anything else.

It doesn't help that the campus is covered in rhododendrons, which attract hummingbirds. They hover, bright in the air, tiny dashes of color like bloody hearts. I think of what Jack said to me before she ran from Sundial. *We're each other's heart, outside our bodies.* I think bitterly, *She already knew she was going with that guy when she said that.*

I discover beer. It's great. I take to going to bars alone. In bars, if I seem odd, people assume I'm drunk. It's often true. I'm lonely, though I don't realize it. I've no experience of loneliness.

The Purple Shamrock has green beer on Saturdays and half-price tequila. It's always seething after five p.m., which I like. It's good to be surrounded by warm bodies. By seven I've already drunk too much but I'm still working to get to that exciting stage, where I fit into the world as perfectly as a puzzle piece. The bar is comfortably or uncomfortably full, depending on your outlook, the air bristling with heat and thought. I catch eyes and hold them as I slide between bodies. I'm yearning for something, though I don't know what.

"Jack?"

I turn, elbow first. I see a black eyebrow like a broad penstroke raised above a dark eye, a grave face, the kind of face old painters gave saints, before my elbow meets his ribs. He doubles over at the blow, which catches him in the solar plexus. He holds himself stiff and bent, as though he's about to come apart.

It's the name that shakes me. *Jack.* It's common enough, but he breathes it into my ear, in that intimate way. I feel the cilia still trembling with his breath. He means her, he means my sister.

He looks me in the eyes and sees something there—the color of my eyes or the more feeble spirit behind them, perhaps. "It's you, not her," he says. "You probably don't remember me."

"I do," I say. "You tried to run away with Jack. You took her away from Sundial. But Mia caught you. I'm the other one. My name's Rob, in case *you* don't remember." His name had escaped me, had blended so seamlessly into the other preppy faces and ironed shirts, lost among the other cumbersome East Coast Harvard boy names, the Franklins and the Jeffersons and the Logans, all sweating in the desert heat, damp with their desire for Falcon's approval. But now somehow it's right here, pulled from the depths of my mind, buzzing in my mouth like a bee. I say, "Hi again, Irving Cussen."

He stares then gives a bark of a laugh. "Seems so long ago, doesn't it? The funny thing is, I thought it was you, that first time."

"Really." I draw out the word, trying to give it Jack's edge, her skepticism. *Not all twins are identical, dumbass.* "Kind of careless to kidnap the wrong girl. Anyway, what are you doing here? I thought you were a Harvard boy."

"Princeton, actually, but I got out of there."

"Kicked out?"

"Not exactly. Yes, in a way."

"For abducting teenagers?"

"It's all politics, you know? I was made an example of. But there was an adjunct professorship open here, so—"

"Kind of a step down," I say and he smiles in rueful agreement.

The barbs fly between us without pause. I'm not usually this good at conversation. As we talk everything else drops away—the bar, the noise, the shoving—and we are enclosed in a private world, a snow globe all our own.

We get drinks and find a corner. His knee touches mine. He tells me about his rich dad, who has a ranch in Montana and oil wells in Texas.

"That's right," I say. "Rich daddies buy their sons into Princeton. And you still messed it up."

He takes a long look at me, reaches out and takes a pinch of my hair between forefinger and thumb. He yanks it so hard that my eyes water and I think the hair will come out at the roots. "Like I said, I thought she was you."

Our eyes lock, mine watering with pain. I know it isn't true—he never thought Jack was me, back then. But he can tell, somehow, that I like the idea. He senses the weak places in me, the bad places, and puts his finger on them. It feels intimate.

All of me is buzzing with the sudden violence of the moment. I want to do something irrevocable, like cut my finger off. I want to stay here forever in this now, for all time, until the end of the world, him looking at me just so, dark eyebrow raised.

"Liars get put in fires," I whisper, and he says, "What?" and leans forward, so I kiss him.

For our first date Irving picks a French restaurant. It must be the only one in Cielo. There's a red checkered tablecloth on each table, and a little silver vase with a rose and a frond of fern in it. I've never eaten dinner in a restaurant before. He picks up the menu. "I'll translate for you."

"That's OK," I say. "I speak French." A little, almost imperceptible wave of irritation crosses his face. I've spoiled it for him.

I'm not a complete idiot. I can tell that there's something practiced about it, that Irving has a routine, a ritual. This is what he does. He takes girls somewhere French or Spanish or Turkish or whatever and translates the menu. I'm not too upset. The idea that he dates lots of women makes him seem glamorous and well-traveled. Kind of Robert Redford–ish. I feel different, unique—the one girl who speaks French. It's all very exciting.

The owner is a large man with sad eyes. His name tag says "Pierre" but he introduces himself as Pete. "I own this place," he says. "Went to Paris in '72. Never forgot how that city made me feel. Romance and wine! I wanted to bring a little piece of it back with me."

"That's lovely," I say. When he's gone to fetch bread I say to Irving, "I want to remember everything about tonight." I touch the rose and the fern that sit in the center of the table in the little silver vase. They're both made of plastic.

"It's a sell," Irving says. "He wants us to get carried away and order his quesadilla de foie gras or whatever. This isn't a real French restaurant. Look at this! *Crock mesieur.*" He gestures at the menu.

"Well, I like it," I say, because I do. I order a Campari, which isn't French but seems close enough, and Irving has red wine. There's almost nothing on the menu that doesn't have meat in it, so I order a side salad and a fruit cup. I make the Campari last all through dinner. I don't want to be tipsy—don't want to miss anything about the evening. Irving goes through a bottle, which seems right to me; he's a grown-up so he's allowed.

Irving pays the check and then takes a pen from the breast pocket of his suit. At first I think he's doodling on the menu, which seems rude. But as we get up to go I see that he has corrected all the spelling and grammatical errors in red ink, like a teacher.

Pete comes to clear the table as we're putting on our jackets. He picks up the menu and I see his face fall. He looks very young for a moment. He must have written the menu out himself. I picture it—him hunched over a *Collins French Dictionary* in his apartment upstairs, painstakingly looking up each word, writing each menu over and over by hand.

The night is still warm. We walk to Irving's car through pools of streetlight. I say, "You hurt his feelings."

"I like things to be done well, and his French was bad. It offended me. Why should his feelings count more than mine?"

I'm filled with a kind of exhilaration, tinged with apprehension. What will happen when I get something wrong? He's so certain of the world and his place in it. But it also makes me feel safe, like there's a right and wrong to everything.

Irving drives us back to his apartment and we have sex. That goes better than dinner, although I'm aware of being hungry throughout.

SO WE FALL in love, or I do, or he does—I still can't be sure of the precise, tangled details of it all.

Irving likes the idea that we've been star-crossed from the start. He likes the idea of having almost done something scandalous—running away with a seventeen-year-old from her family home. In later years he persuades himself that it was in fact he and I who ran away from Sundial together. At least, I've heard him tell it that way. It seems romantic when we get together later. He likes that I am smart and educated but don't really know anything about the world, likes the idea of introducing me to things. He likes women with opinions, I will discover. Lots of women with lots of opinions.

As for me, I mistake intensity for passion, like many people, I suppose. I feel like this is real life, at last.

I TELL MIA and Falcon I'm seeing someone. I'm sitting on the bench in the hall, at the pay phone, twisting the dirty green coil of phone cord in my fingers. Three girls are waiting so I make it quick. Mia sounds happy. "Does he let you be who you are?"

"He insists on it," I say.

"That's great," Falcon says. They're sharing the receiver. "We can't wait to meet him." They're getting more comfortable in conventional parent-of-college-student mode. They could deceive a casual observer at this point.

"It's a little soon." I can't consider what might happen if I take Irving to Sundial. A kind of red haze falls over my vision. "Is Jack there?" We haven't spoken in months.

"She's out with the dogs," Mia says. "I'm sure she'll call you this week. She'll want to catch up." I hang up and cede my place to a plump girl in dinosaur pajamas. She's wearing a big metal retainer and gives me a dirty look, even though I kept the call short, well within my allotted fifteen minutes.

Jack doesn't call. I don't take Irving to meet Mia and Falcon.

IRVING AND I are walking through campus. We've been together two years. It is a gray day, which sits heavy on the gray buildings, somehow making their sharp angles look even more brutal. Ivy has been encouraged to climb the walls, to lend them assurance, the semblance of years. But it's still young and clings in hopeless threads to the new cement.

He stops us in the middle of the quad and says, "It's time we got married." I laugh, because it's such a surprising idea, and his face turns

grave and inward-looking. He always appears most reflective when en-
raged. "My family believes in traditional values. Always has. If this is
just a joke to you, you can forget it all." He strides away. I call after him
but he doesn't turn.

I think he'll call that night, or the next. It seems impossible everything
could change so quickly, just because I laughed. I think we'll make it up
as fast as we fell out. But days pass and he doesn't call. I've been locked
out in the cold.

A week later I see Irving at a distance, walking on a lawn with a young
woman, one of his students. His dark head is bent toward her golden
one. She is blond, small, has my coloring and my slight build. I don't call
out to them, I have at least that much sense. And I feel what he wants me
to feel, the spike of jealousy, of ownership.

I feel very alone, like all those sad times when Jack wouldn't speak
to me. It's clear that I push people away. What is wrong with me, that I
can't accept Irving's love? I cry and think heavily of the ways in which I
have failed. But I can't decide how to fix it.

One night I take my courage in my hands. I drink two wine coolers
and walk across campus to Irving's apartment. He doesn't answer my
knock for some time. I call in through the mail slot. Eventually he opens
the door in his robe, fairly drunk.

"I'm so sorry," I say. "I'll do better. I'll be your wife. I love you."

"Thank you," he says. His arms are so strong and enclosing. "I forgive you."

His sheets still hold the warmth of female flesh and a faint trace of
unknown perfume. I hold my breath and hide my grimace. It's wonderful to be forgiven by him, and anyway all that's surely over now. There's
no point in starting another argument and all over nothing.

IT TAKES ME years to understand that Irving's fury was all to do with
the bare bleak buildings, the linoleum corridors, the smell of soup in
the faculty lounge. Irving had been ostracized from the old red brick
and stone, the red leaves blowing in the fall gust, undergraduates in
blazers and crew scarves, singing the songs their fathers sang, the

words passed down, frictionless, on the tide of money. He feels his exile deeply.

I don't know that Irving's father is about to cut him off, and that to placate him, Irving needs to settle down with a wife. I don't realize that I owe him. That Sundial owes him. Irving has to be paid, for the humiliation of what had happened with Jack, for not having seen out his early promise, for being reduced to the status of adjunct professor at a dingy desert university, clinging to the hope of tenure.

I learn all these things from Irving later, over and over, in each argument we grind through. It is only when the children arrive that we find something new to fight about.

I love him, so I am willing to pay. And there is a little bitter kernel in me that is excited about returning to Sundial, with him on my arm, and seeing their faces. Seeing Jack's face.

WHEN I CALL to arrange the visit, Mia's voice cracks with eagerness. Falcon sounds old and glad. They think they're forgiven. I don't ask to speak to Jack. I haven't been to the house since I started college. I wanted a clean break, to forget them and become whoever I was meant to be. I wanted to thoroughly cover my old self with the veneer of normality, like plating a statue in gold.

IRVING AND I get out of the car and the desert evening hits us like a blow. The air is warm as tea but I can feel the cold creeping in underneath as the sun falls.

Irving gets the bags and I call out to the house but there's no reply. When I look at the time I realize they must be out on the back lot, taking the dogs for their evening run. I told them I was coming, but not what time. I told them I was bringing someone home, but not who.

The round walls of Sundial have been blasted by sandstorms, the rich adobe red faded to a tired tan. There are bird droppings all down the walls, and the bougainvillea and desert broom that used to line the beds under the windows are gone. Stray cholla cacti push up at intervals on the broad driveway like malign growths on old skin. It doesn't look like a home. It looks like a place old, crazy people live. I don't know if it has recently become this, or if I just never noticed before.

Irving gets back in the car, to take the white Chevy to the parking lot behind the house. "No," I say. "Leave it here, by the door." He looks at me with understanding, and leaves the car in the drive at the front of Sundial. I know it will be the first thing they all see when they come back. I wonder what Jack will feel. *She can't control me*, I tell myself. *This is my new life, my own life*. But my heart is beating like a kettledrum.

Even when we get indoors, Irving can't stop shivering. He's sensitive to cold, and has forgotten how frigid the desert nights can get. I give him a sweater I find lying on the kitchen table. It's an old one of Falcon's, a tan knitted thing with leather patches where the elbows have worn through.

I make us both a cocktail—Campari with soda. I don't want either of us getting pickled too early. I mix the drinks with supplies we brought with us, stashed in Irving's briefcase. There's only whiskey and beer to drink at Sundial, Mia doesn't like anything else. Then we sit in front of the picture window to watch the sunset. So that's how they first see Irving again—Mia, Falcon, and Jack—when they at last come in. Feet up, arm around me, wearing Falcon's sweater, tossing a cocktail olive into his open mouth.

I stand. I wonder if I'm going to have a cardiac arrest. Irving doesn't get up. He's nervous at the last moment, so he hides behind me, pinching my wrist hard between finger and thumb, as if he's trying to dig out my pulse. (It's these little details between people that sometimes seem to spell the future, when you look back on them.) My family's faces are pale ovals in the dim.

I say, "I'd like you to meet my fiancé, Irving Fitzgerald Cussen the third." I picked the word *fiancé*, and am careful to emphasize "the third." I know they'll hate it—so bourgeois, everything they say they stand against.

Falcon turns pink, right up to the tips of his ears. Mia just goes very still. Jack comes in last. She stands for a moment, silhouetted. Then she slowly and casually leans against the doorframe. I feel a rush of anger, but also of relief. I haven't hurt her after all. But now Jack begins to slowly slide down the wall, making a small high gasping sound. Then she's on the floor, all boneless and white, sort of like a puddle, not a person. I realize that she has fainted, which I have never seen anyone do in real life before. Irving exclaims, and Mia and Falcon turn and everyone is around Jack where she lies.

I feel a kind of hazy fury that she has somehow upstaged me, once again.

WE GET JACK onto the couch. Pawel comes in and fetches her cold water, and I fan her. She comes around and says she feels fine. No one argues. I notice that it is Pawel who takes her upstairs to lie down, who she leans on.

Mia goes to get dinner on, and when Jack comes back downstairs, Falcon asks if we all want to come see the cows, because he's going to put them away for the night. Jack trails behind us in silence. Everyone has decided to make the best of the situation, it seems, and there is to be no mention of the past.

THE COWS COME when Falcon whistles. They're three kind old Criollo, not fast, not easily spooked, accustomed to the heat. As we lead them to their shed I hear the dogs whuffing and scratching in their run. I notice that Falcon has a slight stoop that I don't recall from before I went away to college.

As we pass the dog pen a big shape detaches from the pack and comes to the wire. Our flashlights glint on his yellow eyes. Thirty-One has grown. Muscle shows through his coat, which is the color of the dusk that envelops us. He tracks us the length of the fence, silent.

Jack puts the tips of her slender fingers through the wire.

"Don't," I say, shocked. Childhood prohibitions run deep. But that was all before, when Sundial was whole and Jack and I were children. She's grown-up now, and can't be protected anymore.

Thirty-One bends to Jack's hand with his great muzzle, puts forth a long tongue to touch her knuckles gently. All I can think of, looking at him, is his teeth.

The jacaranda tree is in spring bloom. As we walk back toward the house the last of the pink dusk light shines through the vibrant purple flowers. I have the familiar growing sense that always fills me at Sundial: that this is the only real place on earth, and the rest of the world is a kind of dream.

MIA SHOWS US our room, which is a guest suite in one of the converted outbuildings where the grad students used to be housed. At first I'm ready to take offense—are they pushing us out, reducing Irving once more to a researcher? Then I think, *They don't want us sleeping together near Jack, upsetting her.* Then after that I realize that there is only one double bed in the main house, which belongs to Mia and Falcon. I never had call to notice it before. I am a little disappointed that the explanation proves so logical. I realize I've been holding my breath, poised for battle.

Pawel goes into the room with the bags, and Irving follows. Mia grabs my arm, holding me outside. "Rob," she says, quiet and desperate. "I know what it's like to think you're in love—"

"I'll see you at dinner," I say. I take Irving's face and kiss him while Mia stands silent in the doorway. When I look over, she's gone. I realize that I'm being unbearable, but I can't seem to stop.

AT DINNER JACK sits slumped and quiet while Mia and Falcon talk brightly. They quickly stop when Irving begins to speak, and listen to him in attentive quiet, both with their heads tipped to one side, their active listening posture. I keep waiting for them to roar at him, to berate us both. But they just sit there and listen like two tortured statues. Even when Irving says, "I see you've changed the rug, since last time I was here," Mia says nothing, though I see her flinch. Mia looks older than I remember. Her hair is streaked with broad swaths of gray.

I see now that I despise my family. They set themselves up as gods, but they're easily toppled. I'm lit by a mixture of euphoria and contempt, the intense meeting of two fronts, which so often brings on a storm.

As we finish our strawberries, I excuse myself from the table. I go upstairs, to the bathroom that's directly over the kitchen—I have some vague idea that I might hear them talking about me while I'm gone. The window opens wide, and I press my face to the screen to feel the touch of the desert. It's impossible that those people downstairs are the Falcon and Mia who loomed so tall over my childhood. Maybe they aren't. Maybe this is all some kind of elaborate trick, or government experiment.

On my way back I pass our old room. The door is closed, which never would have been allowed in my time. I can't resist. I wince at the familiar scratch as the knob turns and push the door gently ajar.

My first impression is of being outside existence, in a place where the order of things is disturbed. Everything looks pink and fleshy. There are flashes of light and I can't see the outlines of the room properly; the walls seem to have holes in them, squares of night sky. *For the ghost dogs to come through*, I think before I can stop myself. I am breathless, trapped by the close pinkness, the dizzying reflections. It's like being inside the gut of a reflective snake.

Slowly as I regain my bearings, I see that it's a clever arrangement of the pink star lamp, reflected in twenty or so small mirrors set up around the room. The effect is so disorienting, as good as an old-fashioned booby trap to repel intruders. Some mirrors, set at angles, produce that strange effect of being displaced squares of other places, like eyes looking in. On the washstand a corner of the moon peeps through the jacaranda tree; its blooms shiver, dead gray in the moonlight, refracted over and over again. Jack has made this room a jagged nightmare of time and place, spliced into one another.

I see then that both beds are made up identically. My old single is waiting for me.

I told Mia and Falcon I would be bringing someone home to Sundial. I had been vague. I wanted them to wonder what kind of a person I had become, what adult secrets I now keep deep within me. Maybe I succeeded too well. I have the uneasy suspicion that my family thought I was inventing my boyfriend.

I imagine sleeping in this room of fleshy pink and reflections, with Jack in the twin bed beside me, like another mirror image of myself and all the past. The very air seems to close in on me and I back out of the room, close the door, and run downstairs toward Irving's voice. He's describing in ringing tones his latest published paper. I have never been so grateful to him, for holding me safely in his arms at night, surrounding me with the everyday world, protecting me from the madness of my childhood, making sure I don't have to sleep with my strange sister in a mirrored womb where we can no longer tell where one of us ends, and the other begins.

"LET'S GET THE fire going," Mia says. She's drunk much more whiskey than I ever recall her doing in the past. And that unsettles me too, the strain leaking through her once effortless façade.

I am about to say "no thank you" and go to bed, to distance myself even further from the person they used to know. But instead I hear myself say, "I'd like that."

Irving has never been included in the Sacrifice fires before, they are just for family. I can see the little flicker of triumph in him. And I feel it, too. They have to accept who I am now; it's their turn to adjust themselves to me.

The fire is a good idea. Facial expressions are concealed by the flickering light, and the loaded silence doesn't seem as oppressive against the background of the desert night, the friendly snap and rustle of flame. We relax somewhat. Falcon passes the bottle around, and I notice again how quickly the level drops. I'm glad of it, of the artificial glow it gives me, resembling courage.

As we begin I wonder if Mia is going to tell her story of the handkerchief. I half expect it. But she stays still and pale with her eyes fixed on me. I'm the center of things now, just as I wanted. So I stand and take out what I've been keeping in my pocket. I didn't know why I'd brought it with me but it's the perfect end. It leaks sawdust in the dark air. I kept it safe at the back of my underwear drawer all these years, wrapped in plastic film. I couldn't bear to throw it away.

I throw the severed head of my old Jack doll into the center of the glowing wood. It catches and roars. "This represents my childhood," I say. "I'm throwing it in the fire, because I'm ready to move on from it now. I want to have children of my own." I realize with a wash of feeling that I mean it.

Irving looks at me, eyes shining in the firelight, and takes my hand. "That's what I want, too," he says. "Let's just do it. I don't want to wait." I think, *This is a forever moment*, even more than our engagement or bringing him home to Sundial. We're putting ourselves in harness together for life.

Jack doesn't say a word. She watches the Jack doll's head where it burns on the fire, crumbling into hot red.

Mia looks shaken, and then she comes around the fire and hugs me. Her arms are strong and for the first time in my life I feel her love to be something I can accept freely, without question. I had planned a mean kind of coup against them but somewhere along the way it has turned real. I smile into the distance, in what I hope is a mysterious, motherly way.

"Please," Mia whispers into my ear. "Don't do this."

"What?" I pull back and stare at her.

"Rob," Mia says.

I shake my head and hold out my hand to Irving. "I'm tired," I say coldly. "I think we'll say good night."

I am tired of these exhausting games. I started them, but I've lost control. *I just want everything to be normal*, I think, resentful. Why can't I ever have that?

IRVING AND I wander back along the sandy path to the annex. Outside of Mia and Falcon's company, a little of our former hilarity returns. We are still lit by whiskey and firelight and the enormity of the decision we've made.

A shadow steps forth from the dark. I scream and cling to Irving, terror blunted by the whiskey.

"You did a bad thing," Pawel says. "The doll's head. You hurt her."

"She doesn't care," I say.

Pawel shakes his head and my stomach lurches. For some reason I can't bear to disappoint Pawel.

"Hey," Irving says. "Is this because I didn't tip you for carrying the bags?" He fumbles in his pocket. "Five, OK? Don't get greedy." He holds out the bill. Pawel ignores him.

"This is a bad choice," Pawel says, and I know he doesn't just mean what happened at Sacrifice. Irving lets go of the money, and it flutters away on the breeze.

Pawel waits for my reply but I don't speak. I cling to Irving's arm. Pawel turns away and goes into the dark.

"You're gonna have to chase that five quicker than that," Irving calls after him.

IRVING AND I keep the lights off, open the drapes, and let the moon shine in. We have the kind of solemn sex people have in movies and books, and rarely do in real life. We've been kind of careless about protection recently, anyway. Maybe we've been working up to this. Now we will abandon it altogether. I doubt either of us gets much enjoyment out of the sex, but that is not the point, and afterward we whisper to one another that we think we've made a baby. I burn with hope. A child will be something entirely my own. Jack has always done everything first—it was only those four minutes but she's always been the oldest. Now I will be the first to do this life-changing thing. Not even Mia has had a baby, I realize. I will be the absolute first. Pleasure floods through me, tinged with guilt. But why should I feel guilt? It isn't my fault she can't have children. I feel different already, as if my balance has forever been altered to accommodate the new places within me.

"We could, you know," Irving says.

"What?"

"Start a family straightaway. We could move back here. You could stay at Sundial full-time taking care of the kids and I could commute to the university. Half the week here, half there."

"Maybe," I say. "What about me finishing college?"

"What about it? Stay home. Why should you work? We might not need the money, if . . . well, they're getting old, aren't they? They're going to need someone to help out some day. Your sister can't—she's nuts." He says "help out," but I know what he means is *take over.*

"She is not." I slap him lightly. "But it could be nice, couldn't it?"

"That's right, it could," he says, slightly mocking.

I plummet hard into sleep after that. The day has been exhausting, a reckoning of the most unexpected kind. My dreams are uneasy, liquor-infused, full of half-realized revelations. Some time in the night I reach out and think Irving isn't there. My heart is fit to break. But then his arm snakes around me and I realize he's been there all along.

THERE'S A KNOCK on our door before breakfast.

Jack looks very like a ghost. Her eyes are large black asterisks. There's some smudged, dark makeup around them, as if she hadn't taken it off before going to bed the night before, or even the night before that. She wears a pink T-shirt I recognize. She's had it since we were twelve. It rides up to show her stomach, which is pale and almost concave.

"Come talk to me."

Throughout the visit, some part of me has been waiting for her to claim me. We rotate around each other like this, like binary stars. And I feel bad, a little, about burning the Jack doll-head. Maybe we can spend a little sister time together.

"I better go," I say to Irving. "I won't be long—fifteen minutes? Do you mind?"

He shrugs, turns over, and puts the pillow over his head. "Whatever, if you have to." The sullenness of it feels hurtful in the light of our new understanding and our plans. I wonder whether he feels uncomfortable around Jack, whether her presence brings back memories of his ignominious exit from Sundial. I pull on sweats and shove my feet into sneakers. "Let's go."

Twenty-Three gleams black with muscle. There are some new, big dogs I don't recognize. They pool at the fence, tails wagging. Thirty-One stays back, doesn't move, head resting on his paws. But when Jack whistles he rises and weaves his way through the pack with ease. He leans against the chain-link, against her welcoming hand, yellow coyote eyes closed in love. Even now, after everything, I feel the stab of envy. *I'm going to have a baby, which is better than some dumb wild dog*, I tell myself, but in the gray early light it no longer seems real.

"They'll never forget what he did," Jack says, not looking at me. "Irving. But they'll never try to stop you, either. We are supposed to be what we are, right? No discipline, no forcing of the kids' personalities. 'Let it flow, man.'" Her impression of Falcon is uncanny. She has always possessed the small, cruel gift of mimicry.

"Shut up, Jack." I resent Mia and Falcon, don't I? Why do her words upset me?

"You don't know who you are, Rob. You don't know any better, I guess. But they should. They should stop you." Jack sounds friendly, but very tired. "You think they let you down back then but it's now they're really failing you."

Panic rises. "You're just jealous," I say, but the words feel as empty as blown dust. She looks at me with those too-big, too-black eyes.

"I see the wind, Rob, and I see how time is carried on it. And I see that this doesn't end well for you."

"Please," I say to her, "please don't be so weird."

Jack pulls an apple from her pocket. She takes two bites, one from the top near the stem, one from the underside, and passes it to me. It means *I'm sorry* in our old code.

I hold the apple for a moment; the lovely yellow and pink of the skin swims before my eyes, which are filled with tears. Then I take a bite from the middle, connecting hers. *I love you.*

We eat our mouthfuls of apple. I think about taking her hand but I don't.

"You abandoned me," I say at last. "Shut me out, kept secrets. I was all alone."

"You never would have left this place if I hadn't made you," she says with a little smile, which makes me feel like I have been cracked open. "Even now, you'd come back if they'd let you. You need to go and have a life. So go do that. But don't do it with Irving."

She pulls something out of the pocket of her deep smock. It's her old Rob corn dolly. The torn-up face is obscured with glued-on fragments of broken mirror. "You can't burn things out of existence just because you want to," Jack says. "This is what the future holds for you if you stay. See? You don't have a face. You just show back what you think people want to see."

I feel the creep of horror. There's something awful about the doll's face, now filled with shards of reflected sky. But I think, *No—I've fought so hard for things of my own, I won't let Jack ruin this for me.* "You're jealous, and you're high," I say. I feel the warm bath of certainty. I don't know when I became sure that Jack was on something. Saying it now is the first time the thought has coalesced properly in my mind. But it has the quality of long-held knowledge.

"Don't change the subject," she says, impatient.

"I'm in college. I know what high looks like."

"You got what you wanted, Rob. You came back and taught them a lesson. Isn't that enough, even for you? Don't do this, not with him. He's bad."

I take her face in my hands like I'm going to kiss her and I look deep into her black-scrawled eyes. "What are you taking? Where would you even get it, out here?"

She looks back at me and doesn't struggle. "Don't lose yourself. Don't be the mirror anymore."

"You have got to stop. We're engaged," I say.

"He said it was only because you wanted to," she says.

"When would he have said that? We've hardly seen you." As soon as the words are out of my mouth I realize that I should have said, *Irving would never say that, we're in love.*

"I saw him last night, after you passed out. He came to find me."

"Jack," I say. "Please, please don't do this." I don't know exactly what I'm pleading for, but fear has begun to stir like a worm.

Jack stares at me. Her mouth screws up like she tastes something bad. "We were together by the fire, Rob," she said.

"No," I say. "No."

"I asked him if he wanted to do it like we used to. He said he did so I let him."

The sounds of the world fall silent. "How could you?" My voice sounds tiny and far away, like something happening at the bottom of a well.

"I wanted to see what he would say. I thought maybe he'd changed since I last saw him. But he hasn't."

"You're lying," I say. "You say you drove me away from Sundial for my own good, but that's not true, either. You lost control of yourself a long time ago. You're the one who left, not me. And you need help. I advise you to get it."

I turn on my heel and go back toward Irving, toward my life.

"LET'S GO," I say, hurling the door open. "Let's go back to the city."

He sits up in bed looking mulish. "What the hell?"

"You were right," I say. "About my sister. All of them. They're nuts."

Irving's face softens. "OK, let's go. Whatever you want, Rob."

I hurl clothes into the suitcases. "Take them. I'll meet you at the car. I have to talk to Falcon."

Falcon is poking at some briars by the front door to the house, muttering to himself about garden shears. Once again I think how fussy he looks, how old.

"Jack is taking drugs," I say. "I think she has been for a long time— since before I went to college. She has a problem. Maybe you should have noticed that, in your own daughter. Or whatever we are to you."

Falcon says nothing, but he goes gray.

"You knew," I say.

"She gets help," he says. "We take her to meetings twice a week . . ."

"Apart from that, what? You just let her take that stuff?"

"We try. For a while we searched her room every morning. We never found anything. I figured she was getting it from the biker gang that took over the old Grainger place, down in the canyon, so I took her car keys. But even when she couldn't drive out to the canyon she kept getting it from somewhere. Mail order opiates maybe? It has to be her decision to stop."

"You have to try harder. Confiscate her mail. Lock her up."

"Oh, Rob. You know that wouldn't work."

I stare at him, trying to frame an answer, as Irving comes around the corner with the suitcases.

"You're not going?" Falcon's distress turns the bottom of his mouth down. I feel the familiar twang of anxiety. I have disappointed him again.

No, I tell myself. *He is the one who is disappointing.*

I get in beside Irving and slam the car door, shutting out the rest of Falcon's words, shutting out the desert, the past, my feelings. "Let's go."

As we pull away I see Mia come out of the house. Her mouth is formed into an *o*, and she springs after us as though she can catch the car. I watch her in the rearview mirror as she gasps and wipes sand from her mouth. Mia shrinks and shrinks and then she's gone and it's just road and the desert, rolling out behind us as far as the eye can see.

THE DRIVE BACK to Cielo is slow and hot. The wind is up and visibility poor. Sheets of dust ripple through the air. The AC in the Chevy is broken, but if we open a window, in seconds we will be covered in fine desert grit. I know from experience how it finds its way everywhere— into your ears, your panties, your hair, under your tongue. So we keep the windows closed and boil. Little cool puddles of sweat form in the hollows of the plastic seat beneath me.

I am filled with a heart-stopping anxiety, made worse by the suspicion that I am the architect of my own destruction.

I can't stop thinking about Jack, how she must have sat in this seat, exactly where I sit now, as she ran away from home with a man she barely knew. Was she scared, as the familiar land rolled away and was left behind? Did she change her mind? It was only a couple of years ago but it seems a lifetime. She had been very young, then, even younger than her age.

Irving should have taken better care of her than he did, I think. *He should have known better.* But here he is once more, driving away from Sundial with one of us in the passenger seat. Why can't he leave us alone? Jack's voice rings through my head: *I thought maybe he'd changed since I last saw him. But he hasn't.* How could I have imagined that I was ready to have a baby? It must have been Sundial and the desert wind getting into my brain again.

We pull up in front of my dorm. My roommate and two other girls I kind of recognize are sitting on the steps, fanning themselves in the heat and drinking deeply from cold cans of Tab. I can see the dew of condensation on the pink sides.

Irving ducks his head to play with the car radio. He doesn't want them to see his face while I get out of his car. I feel a spurt of anger. Why then did he pull up right in front of where I live? I slam the door and fetch my suitcase from the trunk. The girls stare. The scent of bourbon mingles with the soda, slippery-sweet.

I knock on the car window and make a wind-down motion with my hand. He leans over and the glass creaks down, releasing a parallelogram of boiling air. I lean into the hot interior and put my mouth right up to Irving's ear. "I had a little talk with my sister," I say. He doesn't look up but the ear turns an acute shade of crimson. He starts the engine without a word and I yank my head back out of the car window just in time as he drives off. I feel the wind of it on my cheek.

I stand there in his dust, clutching my suitcase. "Oh god," I say aloud. "He did it. She wasn't lying. Oh my god." Irving, gone from my side in the night. I thought I imagined it, but it was just what had happened. I feel the truth like a rip to the throat, although I must have known before, deep down, or I wouldn't have made him bring me back before I said anything. He would have left me in the desert. I know that now.

I struggle to breathe. *I shouldn't blame Jack*, I think. *She's sick.* But the feelings beat on my guts like hammers. Is there no end to which she will not go? I thought my return to Sundial, the show I put on with Irving, was for Falcon and Mia. I deceived myself. It was all for Jack's benefit, I realize. She's always my audience. And she will always beat me at any game.

And even through this, a tiny deep part of me still whispers that she did it all because she loves me.

My eyes water—from the heat and the grit, I think at first, because it doesn't feel like crying, the tears are something outside myself. I am sitting on the hot asphalt; I can't remember how I got down here. Something pink hovers before my smeary, burning gaze. My roommate holds out her Tab.

"First guy to hurt you," she says, "does you a huge favor."

"Some favor," I say, trying to imitate her light tone. I suspect that if I let my true feelings out, they will destroy me, eat me, burn me up like a spark to dry leaves. "Hope he never decides to *really* help me out." That makes her laugh. I take the can and drink deeply. The caffeine kicks like a horse. My heart flutters. The bourbon licks away at my brain, making me dizzy. Sharp cold Tab replaces the taste of old soda in my mouth. "Thanks," I say, remembering her name. "Thank you, Asia."

She puts an arm around me. "It's OK," she says. "Come on, let's get you up out of the road. Come up here." She pulls me gently onto the steps to sit among them. Several pairs of arms come around me. It's the nicest thing I've ever felt and it's too much—I put my head on my knees and weep. The worst of it, somehow, is that I know that I've done the right thing. Irving is a bad man. I'm better off without him. For some reason that makes it hurt more. I have nothing, now. No Irving, no Jack, no Sundial, no Falcon or Mia. I have thrown everything I love into the fire.

ARROWOOD

The ocean observation classroom was lit with sunlight. Desks and chairs threw long shadows like spiders. Sea light played across the ceiling. The room was empty. Callie sighed in bitter disappointment. She was thinking furiously about where to search next, when she heard footsteps approaching from the east. A scent drifted on the air: bergamot and cinnamon. Miss Grainger's perfume, so spicy and enticing. Heart pounding, Callie slipped into the old supply closet at the back of the classroom and pulled the door shut.

The spicy scent grew stronger, mixing with the moldy smell in the closet. The supply closet was full of old board erasers, and chalk dust tickled Callie's nose agonizingly. Footsteps passed the closet and Callie held her breath. She peered through the keyhole. She was scared but she knew she had to prove what Miss Grainger really was.

Miss Grainger was at the blackboard and began writing. Chalk squeaked. The symbols she drew shivered like worms of light. *Maybe it's a code,* thought Callie. Maybe the blackboard was a kind of communication device with whatever school Miss Grainger was spying for. She was probably telling them all about her triumph with the porridge this morning, which sent everyone crazy . . . Callie's blood boiled. She felt so angry, her breath was too fast . . .

Suddenly Miss Grainger stopped writing. Her nose twitched like that of a rat or a rabbit. She inhaled deeply. Then she crooked a finger, beckoning. "Come out," she said. "Whoever you are."

Callie felt her limbs move without her permission. She tried to grab on to shelves but it was like being pulled on a chain, out, out, toward Miss Grainger. The door to the supply closet flew open and Callie stood in front of her, blinking in the bright air.

"You," said Miss Grainger. "I should have known."

"I'm going to tell the headmistress," Callie said. "It's too late, you can't stop me. I've seen. I know what you are. A thief, and a poisoner. A spy, from another school—"

"No, you don't." Miss Grainger smiled as she took off her hat. Her chic bob was gone. Instead, a mane of copper flowed down her back. It was the same color as Callie's. "Did you not suspect that I am in fact your mother the witch?"

"No," Callie whispered. "You're not my mother. My mother's dead."

"That's what I made everyone think. I swallowed Miss Grainger, many years ago. She had outlived her usefulness as a friend."

"Are you going to . . . swallow me?" Callie was trying to be brave but her voice shook.

Miss Grainger looked at her with her head to one side, considering. Her eyes burned in her head like golden coins. How could Callie have ever thought her human?

"Nooooo," said Miss Grainger, drawing out the word. "I don't think I'll swallow you. It might be fun to have a daughter. Yes, in fact, it will. And daughters are powerful magic. That will be useful. Yes." She nodded, briskly. "You will come with me. You don't need this school. We'll go be witches together, flying over the shining sea, dancing in the moonlight."

Callie took a deep breath. "I can't leave Jack alone," she said. "I won't run out on her. Especially while she believes I'm a thief. Plus, she's just been made a prefect. She won't be able to handle the Elegant Upper Fourth all alone. They're always playing pranks on their prefects and Jack is sensitive."

"You refuse me," Miss Grainger said. Her tongue flickered gold over her lips.

"Get away from her," a voice said. Jack stood, white and trembling, in the doorway to the classroom. Callie's heart leaped—Jack had come! Then she saw the terrible danger they were both in.

"Hello," said Miss Grainger to Jack. "Let me smell you. Yes," she said, musing. "You could be my daughter. OK. I'll take you instead. And as for you," she said to Callie, "as a special favor, as we're family, I won't eat you."

"I don't want to be your daughter," Jack said. "Leave our school and never come back."

Miss Grainger stared at Jack. "Good," she said. "You've got the right stuff in you. You've got gold behind the eyes."

Then Miss Grainger disappeared with a sound like bone cracking. In her place stood a great golden dog. The dog leaped for Jack in a huge bound. There was a flash of light and Jack and the dog were both gone. Callie stood all alone in the sunlit classroom. She had failed, and Jack was gone forever.

ROB
T H E N

"You're not from Cali," Asia says confidently. She's tweezing my eyebrows.

"No," I say, flattered to be seen as different. "From Nebraska. I'm adopted." It's the first time I've said it out loud and for the first time it feels like something that might be a regular part of life, one day. Maybe I'll take a trip out there, and it'll feel like home. Maybe there are fireflies in Nebraska.

Asia's real name is Anne, but she picked a new one when she started college. I like it, her casual assumption that she can become a different person just like that. "What else is college for?" she said when I asked her about it. "School sucked. Why would I want to hold on to all that?" She wears a black velvet choker with every outfit and tweezes her own eyebrows into ghostly lines.

"That looks . . . OK," she says, uncertain.

I look in the mirror. My blond brows have disappeared into my skin, leaving me with the appearance of an adult baby.

"They'll grow back, Berta." Asia's worried I'll be mad. I hug her. When I introduced myself she assumed Rob was short for Roberta and I didn't correct her. I want a new name, too.

We hang out with her best girlfriends sometimes, Betty and Ariel. Those aren't their names, either. They're all amazed by my complete ignorance of popular culture and test me eagerly, bombarding me with unfamiliar names—actors, bands, football players.

I shake my head again and again. "The only actor I know is Robert Redford."

"I think my mom likes him," Asia says politely.

"Mine, too. Actually, that's who I was named after." It feels true as soon as I say it.

Betty laughs behind her hand and Asia frowns at her. "It's cool to be so against commercial, mass-produced culture," she says. "Berta is retro. That's cool." A warm bubble rises inside me when she says that, and I resolve that she must never find out that I'm not against anything, I'm just ignorant.

Every morning Asia draws my brows on with pencil, until they grow back in. I have never had a friend before.

I GET A job in the college library. It's quiet there as a rule, which I like, and it smells of old books. The scent is not too dissimilar, if you close your eyes and use your imagination, to the desert at sundown. I learn to cook hot dogs in boiling water. I get a cheap pay-as-you-go cell phone in a violent lime color called gecko green. I love it. I play with it for hours on end, typing just to watch the screen change. It costs two weeks' food money, a ridiculous extravagance since no one even has the number. I only give it to Asia. "You have got to stop texting me when I'm in class, Berta." She isn't mad at me, though. She's a really kind person.

I work and catch up on the papers I missed. I find studying easy. I lie in the sunshine on green grass and have conversations with people—people I don't even know.

I even go on a date with a thin bespectacled guy I meet at my Austen lecture. He takes me to the movies, and we kiss, mouths buttery from popcorn. I don't really want to at first, because the movie is so exciting. I've only been in a movie theater a couple of times before. Irving doesn't like movies and Mia and Falcon only occasionally took us to the drive-in to watch old classics, usually black-and-white.

This movie is nothing like those films. Explosions chase one another across a vivid screen, sweat gleams on muscle, guns of unreasonable size fire thousands of bullets. *Come with me if you want to live.* I start to feel tingly, like when I punched Jack, and then I find that the kissing is a good idea. After it finishes he wants to go and get pizza, but I suddenly feel terrible and throw up on the sidewalk outside the movie theater. He makes a quick exit. It's OK, it was enough. He says he'll call, but I don't expect him to and he never does. I spend an enjoyable evening calling him names with the girls. All of it seems to add up to a normal experience, just the kind I'm looking for.

It's not like I've never seen a cell phone before, or talked to people outside my family, or seen movies. I have. But not much. And it's different; all these things are mine now. I start to make the smallest, most tentative plans for the future. I like books and talking about them. I could even be a teacher, maybe. I try to picture it. An English teacher in a nice small town, with a boyfriend, maybe a carpenter or someone who works in a bank, who looks just a little like Robert Redford. I live in the real world now, I know better than to ask for the actual Robert Redford.

Whenever one of the girls comes to my room to tell me I have a phone call on the pay phone in the hall, I ask them to say I am out. I know it will be Mia. I don't feel like describing what happened between Irving and me, or apologizing for my rudeness to Falcon. As for Jack, the very thought of her is like a fatal, tectonic shift in the fabric of things. I can't tell who needs to forgive whom. Better to shut it all out. I've finally disentangled from them. Everything is new and I've started my life, at last.

I have my new secret, too. It burns in me like a light.

One day I drive to a coffee chain on the outskirts of town. I order a latte and the thin girl behind the counter writes the name I give her on the cup.

When the thin girl calls, "Callie? Latte for Callie?" I don't answer right away. I make her say it again so that I can savor the thrill of hearing it. I dump the coffee in the trash as I leave.

Callie. It's the right name.

NOVEMBER. SHE'LL BE a fall baby, born as the desert cools. She was already begun inside me, that night I made the Sacrifice. Maybe Callie was speaking through me when I said I wanted her. Maybe my body was trying to tell my mind what it knew. All I know now is that I'm so ready for her. I can't wait to meet her. I feel almost ravenous when I imagine holding the little body in my arms, looking into her eyes, feeling her fingers curling about my thumb, having her out in the world— this little creature that will be part of me forever, but fresh and new—a clean start.

I don't ask myself how I'm going to finish college and become a teacher while raising a child.

ASIA, BETTY, ARIEL, and I are running between the bathroom and the front hall. The plastic cups in our hands spill water everywhere. Back and forth. Everyone else is at the football game, as it's a Saturday, and we have to finish by the time they come back. The dirty linoleum of the hallway is already half covered by a tight matrix of white cups, brimming with copper-scented water from the faucet in the bathroom. When the front door opens it will send them flying in a swath. The only way to dismantle it is cup by cup, laboriously. Kick it and there will be a flood.

The four of us are giddy, picturing our dorm mates' dismay and bewilderment; the wet socks, the shrieks. We can't stop giggling. A couple of times the cups slip from our fingers, which are weak with laughter. They hit the floor and send up fountains of cold water, reeking of pennies. They're all a little drunk—I'm not, but I feel heady. I've never been part of a prank before and I feel almost wild with pleasure.

At last it's done, with minutes to spare before the girls are due back from the game. We admire our handiwork for a moment or two; the sea of white cups, each containing a disc of water, gleaming under the overhead fluorescents like a secret. Then we go to my room and open books, to make it look like we're studying. We plan to blame the neighboring boys' dorm, who are given to that kind of thing. We sit on my bed, racked with silent laughter, weeping into our textbooks, backs rigid with anticipation.

When we hear the sound of the front door, we all freeze, hands covering open mouths. The sloshing of water follows, and someone says in an odd dead voice, "Water." The others throw their heads back and laugh, but my heart stops, solid and cold. I know that voice, and it does not belong here. Sundial has found me. I should have known it would.

Jack stands in a circle of wet wreckage, head to one side, regarding the still unspilled cups as if they are difficult mathematics. Her hair has been cut, from the looks of it with a knife. I suppose she did it herself. She wears a long, gray poncho and dirty jeans ripped at the knees. There's a bruise on her cheek. She looks beautiful. I wade to her, carving a path through the cups. I don't even feel it as the water floods up ankles.

"What are you doing here?" I ask. Her eyes are very black, very large. I take her in my arms. She allows it. She is as still and passionless as wood.

"Water," she says, "is a mirror, too."

"Do Mia and Falcon know you're here? We should call them. Come."

The three girls in my room stare at the pair of us.

"You have a sister?" Ariel asks. "Wow. You guys look so alike. You didn't say you had a twin sister!"

"Family emergency," I say. "Could you give us a minute?" They file out, still staring. Suddenly, in Jack's presence, they seem very ordinary. I notice that Asia, who I thought so pretty, has buckteeth. Betty has oily, patchy skin. Ariel scratches her elbow as she goes and I realize, *She's always scratching herself somewhere.*

My friends stare over their shoulders at us until the last minute, when I close the door firmly behind them. Jack sits on the bed, stroking the comforter, which has a pattern of blue butterflies. "You didn't tell your friends about me," she says.

"I don't know them that well." I feel a stab of guilt at my easy dismissal, but Jack's arrival has changed things. Why were we even putting those cups of water out in the hallway anyway?

"How did you get here?" I ask Jack, meaning, *How can I get you back to Sundial?*

Jack smiles. We still understand one another. "I'll find my own way back, Rob."

I blush. "How did you get here?" I ask again.

"They took me to a doctor's appointment in the city," she says. "I climbed out of the bathroom window. It was easy."

"They're probably really worried about you."

She shrugs. "I'll call them as soon as we're done."

I don't like the sound of that. "Done with what?"

"I wanted to tell you myself—to see your face. I guess I figured then I'd know how to feel about it."

I sit down next to her. My heart's pounding in cold splashy beats. "Tell me what?"

"I'm pregnant," Jack says. "Going to have a little Jack. Hence the doctor's appointment."

"That's . . . are you sure?" I feel that dimming of the world and sound coming over me again. Four people in the room, not three, as I thought.

She nods.

I look at her thin face and black eyes and fear creeps over me. She's like a thing from underground that has crawled up to the surface. "You're too young."

"We're the same age. You thought you were old enough, before."

"That was before," I say. "I changed my mind."

"You don't think I can do it?"

"Why don't you leave that place, Jack, like I did? Get some kind of life of your own, away from Mia and Falcon."

"You're using all the right words," she says. "But not in the right order. Broken mirror. They own me. I have no life."

"They don't own you," I say, irritable. I remember suddenly how all-consuming and dramatic things get with her. We sit in silence for a second. "Well, at least I broke up with him already," I say. "It's Irving's, I'm guessing."

"I know what I want now, Rob." Jack looks at me with her terrible eyes, which are filling with tears. "I want to keep it."

I say nothing. I try to gather a thread of sense out of the thunderous feelings inside me. I try to ignore the bitter thoughts that seep in at the corners—Jack has caught up with me again.

"So, Rob, I figured you might have a car now," Jack says.

A terrible thought crosses my mind. "Did you . . . are you here because you need a *ride*?"

Jack shrugs and gets up. "OK. I can hitchhike. I do it all the time."

"Sit down." She knows I can't let her do that. "I'll figure something out."

Someone screams in the hall then, and the scent of pennies drifts to us in the air. I can't think what it is, at first. But everyone is coming home from the football game.

IN THE END I borrow Asia's car.

"Is your sister staying over tonight?" she asks brightly. "Slumber party?" Her face is shiny with an aloe vera face mask and her pajamas have bunnies on them. On Saturdays she likes to get into her PJs at about five and read books about babysitters' clubs. Sometimes I join her. It's fun.

"She can't stay," I say. "Her ride ditched her, she's freaking out, kind of."

"She's in trouble, isn't she? I feel it. I feel stuff like that, sometimes. Psychic stuff. She's very sad inside." I don't think you need to be psychic to see that Jack isn't well. Asia wears her concerned look, which makes her resemble a little cross-eyed mouse. It is very sweet and I feel a rush of love for her then, for her normality, her kindness.

"Yes," I say. "She's in trouble. I really need to get her home. I wondered if maybe . . ."

"Take my car," Asia says. "I hope she's OK."

I think longingly of reading babysitter books and drinking hot chocolate, tucked up in bed. "Thanks," I say. "You're the best."

Some of her aloe vera smears off on me as I hug her, but I don't mind. The homey smell follows me out into the night.

DRIVING THROUGH THE desert with Jack at my side, time seems to have slipped from its socket. By the faint dashboard light my sister's profile doesn't look so hungry. We could be seventeen again, on our way back from—where? We rarely left Sundial in those days.

I will try harder, I promise myself, stealing glances at Jack. *I will come out to the house and see her more. I'll help with the baby. We'll make our family work again.*

"You can't take drugs anymore," I say. "You know that."

"I know," she says. "But I'll keep doing it. I know that, too."

WHEN I CLIMB out of the car and slam the door, Mia comes running. She still wears dirty gloves; she must have been in the greenhouse. "How could you do that to us, Jack?" Her face is desolate. "To your father? He's out looking for you." Jack walks past her into the house without a word.

Mia puts both of her hands over her mouth, closes her eyes, and takes a deep breath. Only then does she look at me. "Hi, Rob, I tried to call you. A lot."

"I know."

"You alone?"

"Yes," I say. "That didn't work out—with Irving. You were right."

Mia nods. "That's good." And I love her, in that second, for not saying anything more. She pushes the heavy oak door of Sundial. It swings wide and the familiar scent of cedar drifts into the air. "You coming in?" Mia asks, eyebrows raised.

"No," I said. But I don't move.

I look at Asia's car, and think about how kind she is, and all those things she's done for me that seem so small but mean so much. I think about her friendship. I didn't know something so fun and good existed. I also think about all the things I've done myself, to carve out independence, in recent months. A phone, a date. Not much but it's all mine. I think about those plans to be an English teacher, and maybe have a nice boyfriend who looks a little like Robert Redford. I think about Callie, who is the biggest adventure I will ever have, I know that.

I look into the shadowed entrance of Sundial and remember the monster that lives inside Jack, its dark stony voice in the night. As long as I am near her, I will never have a life of my own. I will be my own ghost. Or worse. Jack is a lit match, sending everything she touches up into flame. If I stay, I might not survive it. I might burn.

I remember how Jack always comforted me when we were little. She even invented a mother for me because she thought I should have one. She would have given her life for me, and I for her, when we were young. Even now she's still my heart, beating outside my body.

I don't hear Mia close the door behind me, because I'm running, running across the round hall, along the corridor, and up the stairs. I shove open the door to our room. Jack is standing by her bed, eyes trained on the doorway. She has been waiting for me. I throw my arms around her and she hugs me back with her thin ones. "I'm staying, Cassidy," I say into her ear. Her tears run down my neck, into the hollow of my collarbone. She's shaking. "Are you OK? Are you sick?" Passionate love roars through me and with it comes fear.

"It's just relief," she says. "I wasn't sure if you'd ever be back."

"So you came to get me."

She nods, mouth awry with tears. "I can't do this without you, Sundance. Oh god." She covers her mouth and retches.

I help her to the bathroom. "Pregnancy," she says grimly. "Might not need to hurl, just need to sit still awhile. It's cooler in here, too." We sit on the tile floor, arms around each other, until Jack's head starts to nod. I help her back to bed and wait until she drops off again.

I lock the bathroom door behind me. I vomit, voiding myself until I am clean of the past, and everything. I will discover in the ensuing days that our morning sickness comes at the same time each day. Jack rests afterward. It makes keeping the secret easier.

THE FIRST THING I do in the morning is clean our room and take down Jack's horrible mirrors. I throw them in a big black trash bag and pull down the dark construction paper she taped over the windows. Jack lies on the bed and watches. Her skin looks like parchment in the sudden light.

"I can't sleep with all this junk around." I'm annoyed by the note of apology in my voice.

Jack shrugs. "I don't need it anymore. You're back."

The pink star lamp has a burn on the underside of its little pink lampshade, but I can't bear to throw it out. Jack will need it tonight. She will need all the help she can get in the coming months. I make a mental note to myself to drive out and get a new shade tomorrow.

There's some other disturbing stuff. A small skull, which appears to be from a deer or a young calf. It has shiny raven feathers poked into its eye sockets. There's a copy of *Sense and Sensibility* with all the *R*'s, *O*'s, and *B*'s neatly circled in red ballpoint pen. There's a mannequin foot in a single sneaker, covered in some sticky, sweet-smelling substance. I sniff it, fearful. Molasses. When I pick it up, a torrent of black ants pour out of the broken ankle. I toss it into the trash bag with a shudder.

"What the hell is all this?" I ask.

"Magic," Jack says.

"You have got to stop being so weird."

"It worked."

At last it's all gone, and the room looks somewhat normal again. "OK," I say.

"Can we go see the dogs now?" Jack asks, playing with a strand of her hair.

"You go if you want. I'm not done." I pull out a drawer and begin hunting methodically through her underwear.

"What are you doing?"

"You could just tell me where it is," I say. "That would speed things up."

She chews on the end of her hair in silence. Her mouth is pursed up; it looks like a tiny little heart.

She doesn't tell me but I find it in the end, taped to the underside of her chest of drawers. I dump the white powder out of the little bag into the trash. Most of it lands on the mannequin foot. The ants go crazy. I think Jack's going to make a stink about it but she just watches me with those huge squirrel eyes, mouth tight as a tack.

JACK AND I are lying out by the dog run. By late April the desert is already furnace-hot, and Jack seems to throw up whenever she moves so we've taken to sitting out back, where Pawel set up an old beach umbrella for us. We wear big sunglasses, drink iced tea, wearing Falcon's old striped pajamas. It's fun. Sometimes it's like the last two years never happened.

The dogs lie in the shade of the thorn trees, panting. "Where's Kelvin?" I ask suddenly.

"He died," Jack says. Is there a little pleasure in her voice?

I feel a stab of sadness about Kelvin. He was a good, good dog. His smile, his sweeping plume of a tail. "Well, he was old," I say firmly, to make myself feel better.

"Yeah," Jack says. "Sure." There's definitely something in her voice, a dark little spike. I look at her warily. Her eyes have regained once more that intense shade of pale blue, are no longer swallowed by a monstrous pupil. Each morning I search our room and find nothing.

Jack doesn't seem to realize it yet, but my job isn't to be nice to her. My role is to be the person she hates, who denies her what she wants, because there's no one else who will do it. I'm going to protect her and her baby, and she might not thank me for years but in the end she will understand. Or maybe she won't. I can weather all this because I hold my own precious thing deep in my heart—my flinty shining secret. Sometimes I think Jack knows. I catch her watching me, face shadowed.

"Give me the thing." Jack has become obsessed with my ChapStick. I pass it to her. It smells saccharine and tastes vaguely like citrus. The tube has a picture of a hippo on the side, above the words *Pinkopotamus Lemonade*. The ChapStick is one of the three things I had with me when I left my dorm three weeks ago. It seems right to share with Jack and at the same time a familiar bubble of resentment rises. It's typical that she wants half of everything I have, no matter how little that is.

I consider myself lucky that Jack settled on the ChapStick and not the car or the little green cell phone. The phone had started cheeping angrily the morning after my departure. *Family emergency here*, I texted Asia. *Sry. Will bring car back as soon as can.* Then I turned the phone off and put it at the back of a drawer with the car keys.

"You need lotion," I say to Jack. "You'll burn."

"What do you care? Sunburn won't hurt the baby."

I feel myself flush. I thought I had been so subtle, getting her to eat fruit and have one more glass of milk, reminding her about her vitamins, making sure she naps in the afternoons. I've been saying stuff like, "Your body has been through so much," or "Relax. Take some you time." I should have known she'd understand what I was doing.

All I say now is, "I'll get the sunscreen."

"There's some on Mia's dresser." Jack slides down on her sun lounger and hitches her dark glasses up her nose.

There's no sunscreen on Mia's dresser so I wander into our room. I idly begin going through the tubes on Jack's bedside table. I open up a bright blue mascara and apply it, mouth open, in the little mirror over Jack's bed The bright blue is great. It makes my eyes look very green. My elbow catches the little pink lamp, which falls to the floor with a *clunk* but thank god, does not break. I feel a surge of guilt. I completely forgot to go out and get a new shade for it.

When I bend to pick it up I find the hollow center of the ceramic base is filled with tinfoil and a plastic bag containing white powder. The mouth of the bag is tied closed with a bowline knot.

Mia burns the plastic bag in the firepit. We do it quickly, without ceremony. Even from this distance, we hear Jack screaming and pounding on the bedroom door. She is locked in. I should have realized the first trove I found was a decoy, but I was deceived as she intended. Jack knows how to fool me, better than anyone.

PAWEL GETS IT from the people out in the arroyo by the old Grainger place. Who would want to live near there? But those people don't care about what happened in a place once.

He cries as Falcon kicks him out. I listen, glad. When he comes to the door with his stuff I am waiting. I want to make sure he goes.

"Fuck you," I say. "Get away from us."

"I understand her," Pawel says. "You don't know who she is."

"I hope you die screaming, alone in a ditch," I say, "with your guts hanging out. I hope the vultures start eating your insides while you're still alive."

He stops crying, now, and when he looks at me I see a new person behind his eyes, not the one I grew up with.

"Maybe you do understand her a little, after all." He heads out toward the highway. It's nearly dark but I don't care. I hope he has to walk all night before he finds a ride. I hope he never finds one, and the desert takes him.

IN THE EVENING I go to see her. She has stopped beating on the door of the bedroom and I hope maybe she has exhausted herself. Still my heart is in my mouth as I turn the key to our bedroom door. To my surprise Jack is lying in bed, her battered paperback of *Sense and Sensibility* beside her. The covers are pulled up to her chin.

"Hey," I say, uncertain. "What part are you on?" I pick up *Sense and Sensibility* from where it lies facedown on the bed. All the *R*'s, *O*'s, and *B*'s on the page have been blacked out. There are traces of red at the edge of the marker scribbles, where the letters were once circled. Jack has undone the magic that brought me home. Despite myself I feel a cold finger trace down my spine. It's nonsense, obviously. But it's horrible seeing yourself crossed out of existence.

"You know, we read this in my English class," I say. She doesn't answer. "It's all about sisters." I shake the book and flip the pages, just in case. Nothing falls out. "I wish I didn't have to spy on you. I hate it. Please, Jack. We only just made up." I kneel by her and take her hand in mine. She puts her arms around me gently, as if remembering how to do it. I breathe her. When we were little she always smelled like grapefruit, and I can still catch traces of that odor in her skin, her hair. It brings tears to my eyes.

Jack puts a hand around my throat and flips me off the bed onto the floor. She is kneeling on my chest. Her strength is incredible. She beats me in the ribs, the stomach, the belly. I hit back at her but she has me in a fast grip. I feel myself receding. I cry and beg, through pounding blows, for her to stop. But she doesn't. The pain comes, and I know I'm losing her. "Stop," I gasp, breathless. "Please, Jack, the baby." She doesn't stop until the bleeding starts. I crawl to the door, gasping.

"Mia!" I scream. "I need to go to the hospital!" One time seems to overlay the other. Is it Jack bleeding on the floor or me? Mia is in the doorway, rushing toward me but everything is slow and all the sound has gone. I can hear myself screaming, *Callie, Callie, Callie*. Something bad is happening inside me.

It happens quickly. Callie is gone.

I DIG SLOWLY, painfully. I put her to rest beneath the sundial. My little Callie. There's nothing to put to rest, really, but I bury the clothes I was wearing, including my favorite T-shirt—and I put the Pinkopotamus ChapStick in with her. I have nothing else to give.

Earth falls, covering the little bundle. I lay the stone back in its place, atop the disturbed earth. When it's done I put a weary hand in the small of my aching back. I seem to be held together with cobweb. Each part of me wants to fly apart.

When I look up Jack is leaning on a rock, watching me.

"Did you know I was pregnant?" I ask her.

"No," she says. "Would it have been in December, like mine?"

"Earlier. November, I think." I would have been first, for once. Maybe that's what she didn't like. Jack shivers in the warm sun, slowly approaches the semicircle of stones. Her shadow throws a thin dark spoke across me, the stone, the grave. Today is Callie's death day. She'll never have a birthday. Suddenly I don't care why Jack does things, or what she knew.

"Get away," I say. "You don't deserve to be near her."

"You don't know it was a *her*."

Everything goes very still inside me. I get up and dust my hands off. I go up close to Jack and look into her face. There's some movement behind the blankness. Some glimpse of feeling. But it's far too late for that. I bring my fist back, slowly, giving her plenty of time to pull away. She just watches me. As my fist meets her face with a crack I see something in her eyes. For a moment it looks like gratitude. "Get out of here," I say. She goes. My hand, my knuckles, sing with pain. I wonder if they're broken. It doesn't matter.

I look at the grave, licking my lips to catch the last synthetic sweet-ness of the ChapStick. They still sell that flavor and sometimes at the mall or in a changing room or a restaurant I'll catch the cloying scent of pink lemonade; it never fails to transport me back to Sundial with the smell of sun on fresh-dug earth.

"Maybe it would have happened anyway," I whisper, as if the desert could answer. "Would it have happened anyway?"

I kept my pregnancy from Jack—I wanted a secret. I could have pre-vented this. *She wouldn't have done it if she'd known,* I tell myself. *Would she?* I don't know which answer is worse.

Wind howls across the plain, sand scores my face, clinging to the tears. I scrub my tongue with my fingers and then with gritty sand. But the scent and taste is everywhere, seems to fill my nostrils, I am coughing, choking on it, the warm synthetic sweetness of flat soda.

I THINK ABOUT killing Jack in the days that follow. I picture holding a pillow over her face, or slipping a knife across her throat. I imagine wrapping wire around her neck and tugging until she stops breathing. But I can't kill Jack of course, not without killing her child, too.

Instead, I stand over her twice a day as she takes her buprenorphine.

I go to the study and take out a copy of *Catch-22*. With a red pen I scratch out the letters *P, A, W, E,* and *L,* and *J, A, C,* and *K* on every page, for as long as I can stand it, before my hand gives in to cramp.

It isn't magic of course, there is no such thing. But I will take any way I can, to hurt.

I have to stop here. I need a moment.

CALLIE

MOM GOES INTO the kitchen. "Stay here, Callie," she says. "I need a moment." I am OK to stay here in the living room, because her face is like paper with holes in it. Scary.

When we're alone, Pale Callie says, *Um, I think your Mom is escalating. I think she killed her sister.*

Maybe. I don't know what to think. This story is sad, sad, sad face.

When I'm sad I get hungry so I look through Mom's purse, which is on the table in the round hall. She sometimes has cinnamon candy in there. It's a big purse, and it has a bunch of stuff in it. Mom's copy of *Pride and Prejudice*, which she reads over and over and over. Kleenex, keys, wallet, phone, bottle of aspirin. The last one makes my stomach lurch, reminds me of another bottle of pills. Annie's little mouth. I look at the phone. There are fourteen missed calls, all from Dad. I read her last few texts.

You're a bully and a liar. Stop threatening me.

                                      You've crossed the line, Rob.

So you keep saying.

Is she crazy? Pale Callie asks. *That's just going to make him even madder.*
Yes. I'm worried, though I don't admit that to Pale Callie.
It's almost like that's what she wants.
They're always fighting, I say.
This is different, Pale Callie says. *You know it's different. Look out.* Pale

Callie is putting her head through Mom's lipstick again and again, trying to make it rub off. And I swear, her dead mouth looks just a little pinker.

There is a good smell coming from the kitchen. Cookies. Hungry face! Mom often bakes when she's upset.

I take *Pride and Prejudice* out of her purse. You can hardly read the title; the cover is all creased and beat-up. I eat cinnamon candy and flip through. It's partly curiosity and partly because Pale Callie and I have a rule to keep an eye on Mom and her unstable secret habits. And there is something here, actually. Some of the letters are blacked out in ballpoint. It makes the page look like some kind of alien code or something. Is it code? I am pretty good at puzzles. I stare at the letters, trying to think. Only certain letters are blacked out. *I, G, R, N, V.* It takes me a couple tries but I work out what those letters spell. IRVING. It doesn't feel like a code suddenly, but like bad magic, and I'm afraid.

Cookie scent fills the air. I think of witches and ovens. I think of those stories Mom writes. I take the controller out of my pocket. I know what it is, now, and what it does. Or did, anyway. I press the button that looks like saltwater taffy.

"Hunt," I whisper. "Come here. Hunt." I imagine them out there, somewhere in the moonlight. It would be good to have your own pack of dogs! I need something to protect me. For a moment the world seems to hold its breath. I can almost hear meaty panting, smell the dog stink.

Something stirs in the doorway and I scream. It's Mom. She stares at the thing in my hands.

"Give that to me." Her voice is mean and croaky. "Callie, give it to me now."

She comes and tries to take the controller from me. I scream and hit her hands. I want it. It feels like protection, even though it's broken. Her eyes get bigger and bigger and her arms are tight like she's going to squeeze me to death. I can't think of how to stop her so I panic and do Dad's thing with the hair, even though I hate it. She pushes me and it's horrible. Red angry face!

I run to my room and slam the door. I feel better now, with the door shut. I think I would do OK in prison, because I like small enclosed spaces and being alone. I don't seem to feel bad about things in the way regular people do. Plus, I am very healthy. Healthy as a horse, my mother always says, giving me that look, like maybe she thinks she's wrong. Annie likes stories about princesses and girl stuff. She is little for her age and she is always getting sick. She wouldn't last a minute in one of those places. Juvenile correctional centers or whatever. They're like schools, but bad ones where you don't learn anything. You have to remember about being an animal in those places. I have read up on it.

I read up on things because knowledge is a weapon. You can use it to keep yourself safe. So I like to read about people who kill things, so that I can understand what they feel and why they do it, but I also need to understand what might happen to them. I know that if you kill animals, there is a good chance that you will escalate and maybe start to kill people. Pale Callie always makes fun of me because I like the word *escalate*. It sounds like a beautiful kind of frilled lizard, or maybe a move in ice dancing. But *escalation* is not great news, obviously. So the next question is, what happens to the people who escalate? I took out all the books from the library about people who have escalated. I thought there might be some answers in them.

The answer seems to be that if they're smart, nothing happens to the people who escalate. They don't get caught. If they do get caught, some of them kill themselves. Myself, I don't see the point of that. If I went to kid prison, I'd be OK as long as I had some paper and pencils for drawing, and didn't have to share a room. In fact sometimes it's quite a calming thought. Yes, I would be pretty happy in a little plain room on my own, with my thoughts and Pale Callie. She would come, too. I don't think she has a choice. She goes everywhere I go.

Wow, interesting stuff, says Pale Callie. She can be very sarcastic.

They're my own private thoughts.

Pale Callie becomes a freezing mist with eyes, which she knows I hate. She folds about me until I shiver.

Stop, I say. *Don't. Blue cold face!*

Look out the window, she says.

And I can just see it, in the distance, behind the white picket fence. The hole, six feet by four feet.

Why hasn't she filled that in?

I don't know, I say. *Maybe she was tired. Maybe it got dark. I don't know! It's a big hole!*

It's a grave, waiting, Pale Callie says. *Not long now. I think you're going to have to run.*

"Sweetie?" Mom is outside. "I'm sorry I scared you. Please come down. Please."

Better do it, Pale Callie says. *Say sorry.*

I do it really well. I even squeeze her hand back a little as we go downstairs. The smells are so good down here that I even cheer up a little for real. A plate of warm cookies is on the coffee table, and a glass of milk. Usually Mom is trying to stop me eating.

There's something else on the table, too. It's a blue plastic box.

"Sit down, Callie." Mom pats the place beside her. I sit cautiously, at the far end of the couch. She passes me the cookies and I take one before I think. She hands me milk and puts the plate down on the table, next to the box. It's kind of dirty.

Her phone rings again. It's Dad, I can see his name on the display: IRVING followed by an *x*, like for a kiss.

Mom cancels the call.

Here's the thing about X; it means kiss but it also means cross out, cancel. Mom doesn't want Dad to know what we're doing. She is canceling his calls. Sometimes I feel like she wants to do that to me; she wants to cross me out from time and memory, so that I never existed.

"What's that?" I ask, pointing at the blue plastic case. "Bright blue."

"You'll know soon," she says. "Don't worry, Callie. It won't be much longer."

ROB

I'M HUNTING FOR the oven gloves. I've already burned my fingers through the dishcloth I used to check the cookies. I'm shaking. I'm trying to tell it honestly. I'm trying to give her the truth. It feels like bleeding.

I can hear her next door, talking quietly to herself.

The scent of cookies fills the house. Cinnamon, bergamot. I put a tablespoon of Earl Grey tea in the dough. It adds an extra little something.

"Hunt," Callie says clearly and I nearly drop the tray. Quickly I put it down on the counter. I run next door to the living room. Callie is holding something up to the lamplight, looking at it closely with her big green eyes.

It's Mia's old controller. The buttons. Green for come here. Red for stay. And the little red-and-green one that looks like hard candy or a bee drawn badly with an Etch A Sketch.

"Come here," Callie whispers. "Hunt." She presses the buttons.

"Give that to me." My voice shakes. "Where did you find that?"

Callie looks up sharply. Her face is moonlike, blank. She holds the controller protectively away from me. "No."

"Right now," I say. "I mean it." Her face just goes even blanker. Callie comes toward me and relief washes through me. This won't be a pitched battle. Maybe that fragile trust we've been building will hold after all.

I open my arms with relief. Callie walks into my embrace but she doesn't put her arms around me in return. Instead she reaches for the base of my neck where the fine hair has escaped the ponytail. She takes a pinch of it between her forefinger and thumb. Just as I realize what's about to happen, she tugs, hard and vicious.

Red closes over me, tears come to my eyes. I can't breathe. "Get off!" I shout and push her. "Get off!" She staggers back. For a moment she looks at me with her still gaze and then she runs. Upstairs, I hear her door slam.

I stand gasping for breath. The room swims around me. Another lesson from Irving. What else has Callie learned? But I am most horrified at myself. Three times, now, I have touched my daughter in anger.

Part of my text exchange with Irving shines from the screen, a malevolent green.

Don't leave me. I'm sorry. I didn't mean what I said.

You've gone too far to go back, Rob.

Please don't leave me.

I put the phone down, feeling cold. I go to the bathroom and spit. I brush my teeth till my gums bleed. But still the sweet, tinny warm taste of soda clings to my mouth, my tongue, my teeth.

I PUT MY mouth to the keyhole. "I'm sorry," I say. "Callie, I shouldn't have done that. But that thing is not a toy. You've got to let me look at it, make sure it's safe. If I'm completely sure it's not dangerous, you can keep playing with it. OK? Please come out, sweetheart."

The door opens a crack. "No more pushing. No more yelling."

"No, definitely not." I squeeze her hand. There is just the ghost of a squeeze in return.

"Come downstairs," I say and she does. She's still obedient. That's good. As we go I slip the key to her bedroom into my pocket. I'll need it later.

DOWNSTAIRS, I OPEN up the back of the controller. The circuitry is decayed; fraying copper wires spool out all over. This thing can't have worked in years. So I give it back to Callie. She hugs it to her and looks at me with eyes that still hold a trace of accusation. Then she looks at the coffee table.

I follow Callie's gaze to where it rests on the blue plastic box I dug up from the dog graveyard. I put it in the center of the table. It feels suddenly like the world's most tragic show-and-tell. But she needs to connect what I'm saying to her to the present. She needs to understand.

"Mom," she whispers. "What's in the box? Bright blue."

"Don't worry, Callie. It won't be much longer."

As I watch, I swear the box gives a tiny twitch. Like there's a small rodent inside it or maybe a nest of maggots, writhing. I hope I know what I'm doing.

ROB
THEN

JACK IS GROWING big. Still, she refuses to visit a doctor. "I don't need it," she says. "I'm having it here at home. Women have been doing this on their own for thousands of years."

"And dying," Mia says grimly, wiping sweat from her top lip. The days are growing hotter. I can hear the rubber soles of my sneakers melt with a hiss on the stone paths.

"We can only hope," I say.

I GO TO the big mall off Route 40. I buy tiny socks, diapers, hats, shirts, bottles, toys, and a mobile to hang above the crib. I buy formula and blankets and lotion and a bath. I fill the flatbed, the back seat, and the passenger seat of Mia's truck. The stuff is crammed flat against the windows. For Jack's little baby. I know Jack hasn't thought about a name. She calls the baby *it*.

I forget the prenatal vitamins, so on the way back I pull off the highway into Bone.

"Hey, stop right there," the pharmacist in the drugstore says and I duck in guilty reflex. He's mild-looking, balding, a dad type, except for one thing. His eyes are such a pale blue that they look white. I wonder if the desert can get into your eyes. He says, firm and not unkind, "You know you're not allowed to come up to the counter. Ten steps back, and you call out what you need."

"Oh, hey," I say, wondering for a second whether I'll pretend. But I can't think of anyone more unpleasant to be than Jack. No fun in that at all. "Actually, I think you've mistaken me for my sister."

He looks at me closely. "The voice is different," he says. "And, ah! The eyes. I see that now. But most of all the manner. Where you been?"

"College," I say. "But I'm back." Then I say, "My sister's gone away for a while, actually. Visiting relatives out east in Nebraska."

"Hm." He neatly folds down the top of the white paper bag containing the prenatal vitamins. "She does strike me as someone in need of a change." He nods at the truck, parked out front. "Been doing a little shopping I see. So congratulations are in order?" He smiles, holding out the bag.

I smile back. "Due December," I say, passing a protective, loving hand over my stomach. "Thank goodness. It'll be cooler, then." For a moment, the ache that lives deep in me abates. I feel her there again, my Callie.

"Well, I'd never have guessed. Showing late; that means it's a boy."

"It's a girl," I say, smiling. Flirting a little, full of that sense of safety that pregnant women carry with them.

"Ah," he says. "Time will tell. When does the other one get back?"

"She's not sure," I say. "She's thinking of moving out there, actually. It's where we're from originally, you know. Nebraska."

"Well, she left you with us," he says. "A replacement."

"We have our differences."

"Oh sure. But—" He gestures at all of me. "It's like a magic trick."

I curtsy, which is an odd thing to do I guess but seems natural in the moment. I feel his pale eyes on my back as I go out into the heat.

I drive the rest of the way out to Sundial humming. The desert is so beautiful this time of year. Shimmering, white-hot. I wonder if Jack will stay in Nebraska. She might move there—for the snow, and the green. Or maybe she'll come home to have her baby. Callie should be born at Sundial.

My hands tighten on the wheel. Misery flows back into me, echoes through my empty spaces, the place where she was, my little Callie. Howling like the wind in the hollowness of my body. I hear my own hoarse whisper, over the engine. "Get a grip, Rob." The golden land blurs and I slow and pull the truck over. I weep, cheek pressed to the hot steering wheel, hating the return to myself. That was the most wonder-ful five minutes I've had in months. Already I miss the warm, beating red love I felt at having her inside me again. I saw things through the crack, a new world. To have all that withdrawn is terrible punishment.

But it's a cheap trick, I won't do it again. The loss is too much, after.

Or maybe I could pick up colored contacts next time I go to town.

THE DOGS PANT in the center of the pen, held by Mia, controller in hand. When she releases them they trot and crowd up against the wire, friendly. A couple of them ignore the food to make their hellos. Jack bends, gives her fingers to their pink tongues. Twelve, a cock-eared mongrel, goes down on his forelegs and grins at her. He's a burly little dog, a terrier cross. Jack gives a little smile back. The only thing that gets a smile out of Jack these days is the dogs. Eighteen is a German shepherd with almond eyes. She pads quietly around the pack, as if making sure all is well. Her ears are pricked and her gaze stays on Mia. Twenty-Five is a husky–Great Dane cross. And of course, in the distance, Twenty-Three lies brooding in her pen. Her coat gleams like jet in the sun.

I count the dogs again, as they mill around the pen. There are ten bob-bing heads, ten waving tails. Weren't there eleven yesterday?

Forty whines and puts a paw through the chain-link. She wants Mia to pet her. She's a tiny mutt with a springy topknot that stands up like a shock of dead grass.

Mia lets herself into Twenty-Three's pen and stands, frowning at the controller. She won't let us into the pen anymore, even to help with feed-ing. I smile at the familiar crease between her eyebrows. Some things remain the same, after all.

"Here." I give Jack the orange I brought, and a thermos. She takes both, listless. She peels the orange and eats one segment before throwing the rest into the brush. When she sips on the thermos she grimaces and spits a jet of bright green. It lands in the dust beside the trank gun.

"What the hell is this? It tastes like feet."

"Spinach and this stuff called kale. It's really big in the city, you know, tons of vitamins . . ." *And folate for the baby,* I want to add, but I don't want to push her. I spend a lot of time tricking Jack into eating well.

Jack upends the thermos and the juice pours out onto the ground. It does kind of smell like feet.

Her eyes go blank at some sight behind me. "Grab the trank," she says.

At first, I think Twenty-Three and Mia are dancing. The rottweiler is on her hind legs, paws locked about Mia, mouth eagerly straining toward her face. Mia has her hands wrapped about the dog's neck. A long string of drool gleams in the afternoon sun. *Did Mia put a dance button on the controller?*

I pick up the gun, but time seems to have slowed down, everything is underwater—as I watch, Twenty-Three's jaws graze Mia's throat, and Mia's hands go white at the effort of holding her back. Twenty-Three makes high yelps—not angry, but afraid. Her head swivels, ducking something invisible we can't see, and she howls.

"Rob, shoot her," Mia calls, but I can't seem to move.

"Rob," Jack says.

Mia tries to shove the heavy paws off her shoulders, but Twenty-Three lunges again. Mia gets a chokehold on the dog and Twenty-Three makes a high keening noise. Her lips and gums are pulled all the way back, her teeth look like vast stalactites. They stagger about the yard in their desperate waltz. *Mia finally got her to hunt,* I think. I am frozen, clutching the gun, my throat closed with that sickly sweet taste. Mia wrestles the sharp jaws from her fragile throat, again and again.

"Give it." Jack grabs the gun from me and shoots Twenty-Three twice in the slab of muscle on her hindquarters. She reloads and shoots her again in the neck. Twenty-Three howls, her maimed tail tucked between her legs, and that long, liquid growl pours from her again. The pink tails of the darts dance perkily as Mia takes advantage of the dog's pain to thrust her away and run for the gate. I don't know how long I have been screaming, but I don't stop for a long time.

"WHAT THE HELL is going on?" My voice is strangled, my heartbeat rapid and splashy.

Twenty-Three is sprawled on the dusty ground in the isolation pen, a dark tarry mark in the dim light. Her tongue sticks out a little from her teeth. She breathes heavily and peacefully. Thunderheads are boiling in the distance. I think we're going to have a storm.

"Please control yourself, Rob." Falcon rarely moves from his chair these days, but he came out when he heard my screams. "You know as well as I do that there will always be setbacks in live testing like this. The failures are as instructive as the successes. Mia has safety procedures in place."

"I don't think they're working," I say. "Explain please, now."

"The click has failed in Twenty-Three," Mia says tersely.

"But that can't happen," I say. "It changes them forever. How can it go wrong?"

Mia takes a syringe from the yellow case at her side. "We don't know. We think . . . we think maybe the click doesn't stop cutting. It starts pasting the wrong material back into the code." Mia pauses. "It seems to prevent her from processing fear correctly. The prefrontal cortex, the amygdala, and the hippocampus all light up like Manhattan at night." She nods at Twenty-Three. "She didn't see me, when she attacked me. She was experiencing something very traumatic. A memory—something imagined. She curls her tail between her legs, trying to hide it. I think she's remembering what happened to it. Who did it to her."

"Psychosis," I say.

"In a sense. She reacted hyperaggressively, but it's self-defense, in her mind."

"How can you know that?"

"I've been around dogs, and this dog in particular for many years. I know fear when I see it."

"She should be shot," I say.

"That's not an option, Rob."

I am filled with rage at Mia's unreasoning love for this ugly, dangerous dog. She puts her hand on the latch of the gate. "You're not going in there?"

"I have to give her this. We've got a work-around, another minor edit to the MAOA-L. I really think we've got it right, this time—"

"This time? How many times have you tried to fix this?"

"I think it started when she killed Kelvin," Mia says bluntly. "But I didn't get it at first. Dogs will do that in the wild, sometimes, when a member of the pack gets old and begins to hold the others back." Mia turns quickly and goes into the pen. Her flesh looks so vulnerable, her skin so fragile. "It's OK, Rob, she's out. She won't wake up for hours." Mia lifts the rottweiler's ear and blows into it. "See? Jack kind of overdid it with the darts."

The syringe goes in, the millions of little scissors, too small to be seen with the naked eye. Mia comes out of the pen and goes to wash her hands under the spigot.

"There's something else, isn't there?" I ask. I've gotten really good at telling when people are holding something back around here.

"Rob . . ."

"Just tell me."

"She started to eat Kelvin," Mia says. "While he was still alive."

WE FEED THE dogs without opening the gates now, throwing chunks over the chain-link. The dusty ground on the other side is stained with blood.

"It's not good for them," Mia says, shaking her head. "They need exercise."

"You can't let them out," I say. "Don't be insane."

The coyote emerges from behind the kennel. The pack parts for him like a crowd parting for a parade or a king. He takes no notice of Mia. He eats in big sucking gulps.

"He's been digging back there," Mia says. "I've seen it. Holes all along the length of the back fence. He's smart. He thinks he's out of sight behind the shed." She sees my face. "He can't get out," she says. "The wire is sunk into a concrete bed, five feet down. We built it like a fortress, Rob."

I SCREW THE suppressor onto the .22. That should take care of the noise. It will only take one, I promise myself. Even that ugly dog doesn't deserve to suffer. But someone has to do something.

When I get to Twenty-Three's pen, I drape a piece of meat on the wire. She comes up and grabs it. She seems kind of normal today. Maybe I'm being too hasty? But I think of her, dancing with Mia, and I shiver.

I take aim at her left eye.

"Rob!" someone screams from the house. Mia. I shake my head and steady my aim. She's irrational about these goddamned dogs. Twenty-Three wanders, shaking her head, worrying the meat. I track her with the sight.

Something stirs behind me. "Don't, Rob. Whatever you do." Mia's fast when she wants to be.

"Sorry, Mia, someone has to."

Twenty-Three has stopped moving, is gazing at me steadily with her black button eyes. This is my chance.

"Bye," I whisper and take off the safety.

"Stop, Rob, stop; she might be pregnant!" Mia sounds terrified. What's the big deal about a pregnant dog? Surely the last thing we need around here is more dogs.

"Sorry, Mia," I say, and take aim again. But now I hesitate. I think of puppies and things taken away too soon, and this gives Mia just enough time. I see a flash of her strained face as the blow comes down.

THEIR FACES SWIM before me. Falcon, Mia, Jack. I have ice on my head. Everything is pulsing, hot and black. The kitchen seems to be pitching like a ship.

"Let me go," I say, but it comes out weak. I try to get up and Mia supports me as I stagger. "Careful, Rob," she says. "Here." She pushes me gently into a chair and wraps my hands around a glass of iced tea. I almost spit it out, there's so much sugar in it, but she guides the glass to my mouth again. "Drink."

"What the hell did you hit me for?" I want to sound commanding but it comes out tearful.

"That dog is really important," Mia says. "I wanted to tell you before but Jack didn't . . ."

"What? That you want to do some messed-up experiments on a

pregnant dog?" I turn to Jack, who sits silent and pale in the corner, staring into space. "What is it?"

She shrugs. "I kept telling you to get away from here," she says. "You don't need another reason to stay."

"We're well past that," Mia said. Her voice is tight. It's like she's had a frog lodged in her throat all these years, and she's now coughing it up. "It's time." She takes a breath and visibly steadies herself. I am scared, because I have never seen Mia like this. She looks like her heart is breaking.

"We think you were four when you were found. But there was no way to be sure. You were small for your age, malnourished. When they found the cages in the cellar—well, we think you spent most of your time in there. There were five cages. There had been other children there, too. You were the only ones left, by the time they found the place.

"There were two bodies in the house. A man and a woman. I don't want to call them parents. The man had overdosed. The woman had been strangled with a length of wire wrapped around her neck. It seemed that the man had killed her before overdosing, either intentionally or by accident. There wasn't much of an investigation, because it was clear what had happened. If such a thing as monsters exist, it was those two.

"I had never seen children so damaged. Until that day you chose your names, Rob, neither of you spoke. Your eyes couldn't handle light for a long time. You had never seen anything but the dark, and the cage. Your muscles were underdeveloped and atrophied. I don't think you'd ever been outside. It was exactly a year, two months, and a day before you could take a walk in the daylight. I wrote it in my diary. It was even longer before you spoke. Before you could dress and wash yourselves. Years of gradually coaxing you into clothes, persuading you to sleep in your beds, not under them. And there was the other kind of damage. Show her, Jack."

Jack lifts her hair. On her thin white neck is the star-shaped scar.

"You've always had that," I say. "It's nothing to do with me."

"You put a screwdriver in my neck," she says. "Blood everywhere."

"It wasn't your fault, Rob." Mia is almost crying. "You didn't understand that you were free. You had fought so hard." Mia rubs a hand over her eyes. "The first time you tried to kill me," she says, "I woke with a piece of wire wrapped tight around my neck. You were holding the ends in your fists, pulling it tighter. I got loose, because I wasn't incapacitated by drugs or alcohol. You didn't speak but I saw what was in your eyes. The police assumed that those two killed one another, but I knew better. You did what you had to do, to get free. I don't blame you—never have. Those people deserved to die for what they did. But you wouldn't always be five and I wouldn't always be there to protect you."

"I don't believe you," I say. "That's not right. I'm the good one." I push through them all blindly and find my way out of the kitchen, into the open air. I can't breathe right. Sunset is painting the mountains red. Red, red blood. The desert knows who I am.

It must be a lie, it must. But something stirs in my memory, horrible tendrils, like maggots or worms. Wire in my hands. Darkness, a cage.

I feel Mia behind me. She puts a hand on my shoulder. I shake her off.

"You don't have to hear it if you don't want to, Rob."

But of course I do. I march past her back into the kitchen. "Just finish it," I say.

"We knew we had to do something. It wasn't an easy decision to make. But what options did we have? People were starting to take notice of your . . . tendencies. Falcon thought of it. We could make a tiny edit to the MAOA-L, just tweak it a little—"

"Oh god," I say. "Oh my god."

"We're the bad dogs," Jack says. "See?"

"It was safe," Mia says.

"In chimpanzees," Jack says. She laughs, a terrible sound. "Neat, huh? Nice to know some thought went into it."

"That's not true, Jack." Falcon sounds wounded. "We had already had great success with our first human volunteer."

"You were so bright," Mia says. "I could see it, even from the very beginning. I knew, I just knew that with the right care and education, you could both do incredible things. We couldn't abandon you to the state. We would never be so cruel."

"Cruel," says Jack. "Huh."

"But it worked!" Mia's voice cracks. "The click. You were normal young women. But then Jack started to display signs . . ."

"Jack," I say, helpless. "You should have told me."

She looks at me and shakes her head and I know what she means. There are some things that are too big to tell.

I take her and hold her as tightly as I can in my arms. I'm trying really hard not to cry but I do, anyway. Jack lets me hold her but I feel her absence. She's gone, has been gone for how many years? I think of hummingbirds. Her heart left her body and I didn't notice.

"You got snot in my hair," Jack says.

"I know," I say. "Sorry." I stroke her head, snot and all.

"Why did it stick with me," I ask, "and not with her?"

"We don't know."

Greedy little scissors, snipping away inside Jack, eating away at her. *Click click click.* I understand now, why Mia stayed out here, watching over us, taking our insults and our spite with a bowed head. She gave us her youth, her life. We are her penance.

"Don't you look at me like that." Mia is suddenly savage, intent in a way I have never seen her. She leans in, we are face-to-face, noses almost touching. "You would do the same, Rob, to save your child." I wonder if it is in fact us she wanted to save. Or a little sister, long ago abandoned. Peppermint. A handkerchief.

"The dogs," I say. "Why the dogs—"

"Just be grateful they didn't put little bowler hats on us," says Jack.

"We had to know what would happen to you later," Mia says. "We had to have some kind of control group. It was my idea to replicate the Langley experiments—with the remote control. It was all so outdated. But it hid what we were doing from outsiders, which was observing the pack, and the click—for you."

Memory and the past are spinning around me in circles, helixes, breaking. Nothing is as I had thought it was.

"All that stuff with the controller and their brains," I say. "That was just a—distraction?" I think of kind Kelvin, torn to pieces by Twenty-Three. I think of the coyote puppy staggering in circles, driven on and on by Mia's commands. I think of all the dogs who didn't make it, who died of sepsis and electrode insertion that went wrong.

I rest the gun gently against the kitchen table and bend over. I retch, but nothing comes up. "You used to think there were ghost dogs here," I say to Jack. "Maybe you were right. I'd haunt this place, if I were them. I'd want revenge."

"I swore I'd never leave here," Mia says. Can she be asking for forgiveness? "I swore I'd make sure you were OK." Her eyes are huge with her urgent need for me to understand. It makes me want to hurt her.

"Jack isn't OK," I say.

"She's getting better—"

Jack raises her eyebrows. "Liars go on pyres," she says, thoughtful.

"Please," I say to her. "Not that again." Though a pyre seems like an excellent solution right now. I would happily watch Mia and Falcon burn, their skin cook and crackle, their eyeballs burst, their lips shrivel in the flame, until only their empty grins are left . . .

"Rob," Mia says and I come to with a start. My hands are on the stock of the gun. *Choo choo.*

"We haven't given up. We're trying to reverse it," Mia says. "We'll make the perfect notch in the sequence—"

"We're going," I say. I hold my hand out to Jack. "I have a car. Come on." *But where?*

"I'm a bad dog. I can't leave Sundial in case I—you know—bite someone. Falcon explained that to me, the day I ran away." Jack's voice is dreamy. "Hey, Rob, I'm glad you don't remember those early things. What they did to us. What you did to them. Those were tough times and you're not very resilient, as a person."

Mia says sadly, "She won't, Rob. She can't. For the baby."

"What do you mean?" But I have an idea. I'm afraid.

"Sometimes you change genes for one generation," Mia says. "Other kinds of alterations . . . can be passed on. It's called germline editing, it's somewhat ethically . . . that doesn't matter. The point is, she has to stay."

"Are you for real?" I lift the gun. "I'm going to put that dog out of its misery then I'm getting in the car and you're coming with me, Jack."

Jack takes the gun from me. "You can't shoot the dog, dumbass. Think. Why do you think Mia wants to get her pregnant? We have to see if the puppies are *bad*."

Horror washes through my brain, making it blank.

"Everything we've done, we did because we love you." Falcon's voice is sincere. He believes what he's saying. His eyes are warm. He looks at me without guilt. It's like I've never seen him before.

"Tell me," I say. "Do you have a record of the tests on us through the years? All the data? The MRI scans? The blood samples?"

He is silent.

"I thought so," I say. "You couldn't resist. But it's one or the other. Either you loved us, or we were a study. You can't have it both ways." I take a deep breath. I won't cry, not now, not in front of them. "Let me guess," I say. "You didn't intend to, but then we just turned up, in need of help, in need of exactly the experimental treatment you could provide. Such good fortune. Maybe you can't admit it to yourselves. But you scouted for us just like you scouted for stray dogs."

"That's not true," Mia says. I see that she is shaking, from top to toe, like a windblown sapling. "You can't believe that, Rob." I watch her tremble. Her brow is damp, her cheeks cavernous, her lips are pale against her teeth. I wonder if this is it—the moment Mia breaks at last. I feel only a cold flicker of interest at the thought.

"I tried to make you leave," Jack says sadly.

"But as soon as I did you came to get me."

She looks at the ground, shakes her head, as though it's all beyond her control.

I could drag Jack by the arm to the little car, drive into the night. I might even make it. But I think of her black eyes, her grin, her monstrous voice. Can I care for Jack, help her give birth, then look after her and the baby? I feel the defeat all through my body. My shoulders slump.

"OK," I say. "You win." What will her baby be?

I TAKE THE little green phone out of the drawer. I walk out toward the desert, stumbling in the dusk. The vanishing sun glows behind the mountains. I thought maybe the battery might be out, but the screen lights up like a friend. I dial.

"Where the fuck are you, Rob?" Asia's voice is thin and acid with rage. "Where the fuck is my car? It's been *two months*."

"Asia," I say. "I'm so sorry." I'm doing that ugly sob thing before I can stop myself. The weeping comes in painful spasms.

"Bring it the fuck back fucking now."

"I can't leave. It's all so messed up. I'm scared."

She takes a deep breath. "I found the pregnancy test in your drawer, Rob."

"Oh, Asia . . ." I clear my throat of the bitter bile that's gathered there. "Yes, I'm pregnant."

"Oh, wow. Are you OK?"

"Not really."

"Are you being . . . have you been kidnapped?"

"No." I can't think how to even begin to describe my situation.

"Are you, like, in a cult? Your family sounded so—eccentric, I always wondered a little about them . . ."

I hang up. I shouldn't have done that. It's no good. No one else can help, I see that now. Sundial has me. It feels inevitable somehow, like something long fated. I tried to make my own life in the big world but it was too hard. The pack wouldn't accept me.

But that little glow flares again, deep within me. Telling Asia that I was pregnant brought Callie back to life, for a moment.

JACK IS SITTING on the floor of our bedroom. Her face is wan. She looks really sick. "Poor old Rob," she says. "Poor old Rob got kept in the dark again. Poor old Rob didn't know any of the secrets . . ."

"You look bad," I say.

"Don't pity me," she says. "Just because you're the good dog doesn't mean you're not a dog all the same."

"Why didn't you tell me?" My anger shimmers on the air before me. I'm holding her hard by her thin shoulders, I realize.

She says, "One of us deserved a chance."

I let her go and sit on the floor. I am suddenly tired, like a puppet whose strings have been cut.

"It's strange," she says. "The not knowing. I feel happy, but am I happy? I feel anger. Is it real? Or is it a tiny hole in the ladder, a little gap that's been cut away?" She makes scissors with her fingers, mimes cutting, clicking her tongue on the roof of her mouth with each imaginary snip. "Click, click, click. Pawel knew first when I started slipping. I told him about seeing the dead dogs. I thought they were ghosts. Pawel saw things that weren't there, too. It's something the click does. Emotional memories are processed incorrectly—they become hallucinations, maybe? Anyway Pawel helped me."

"Pawel got you addicted to drugs." Hatred burns in my throat.

"It stops me hurting people," Jack says. "Pawel discovered that trick. He was the first person Mia and Falcon did it to. Their volunteer. He's famous in Poland, did you know that? He killed his entire family one Christmas. Mother, father, grandmother. And an aunt, I think. His wife and four children. Tied them up and took them out, one by one, over the course of the week. He went to jail for a very long time, but even a long time ends eventually. It was, like, back in the sixties."

I think of Pawel's constant tears, his endless grief, the tattooed line of chess pieces on his arm. Maybe the click can be a punishment even when it works. It makes room for regret.

"They shouldn't have sent him away," Jack says. "He was only trying to help. Sundial is his home. The click stopped working for him years ago but he kept it secret. Better than I did, anyway. We found different outlets. He hurt animals. I was scared I'd hurt you."

"Did he kill Nimue?" I ask, suddenly. "Did he take the jackrabbit's eyes?"

"You're really asking me about cows and rabbits right now?" Jack smiles that thin smile, with no happiness in it. I think of Nimue with her big kind eyes, how she loved her poll scratched, how kindly she stood still when I milked her. It's suddenly too much. I slap Jack hard across the face.

Jack rocks back gently, looking at me with interest. She touches the tender pink place on her cheek. "Maybe the click never lasts forever," she says. "Maybe it's only a matter of time. How about you, Rob? You're acting pretty out of character, these days. Hitting people, trying to shoot dogs. How are you feeling?" Jack smiles with her bloodless lips. "Are you a bad dog, too?"

ROB

I LOOK AT Callie where she sits across from me. "They didn't tell me everything," I say. "Not even then. Scientists and secrets. Jack told me, though. She left me a message. I found it in the end." Sundial breathes around us. We're nearly there, at the point of no return.

I take the note out of my pocket. Jack's buried message—Snoopy's secret. The paper is damp and soft along the folds. But my sister's writing is still clear, blue ballpoint. *What's with you?* I asked—no, screamed—at Jack. *Why are you like this?* I hit her, that day.

Every fairy tale tells you: knowing someone's true name gives you power over them. No one ever talks about how it might go the other way around. It might give something a hold over you.

I won't let Callie read the letter. It is not for children.

I take a deep breath. "We're not from Nebraska, as it turns out," I say. "Not at all."

JACK
T H E N

Sundance,

I've written this letter lots of times. I don't know if I should give this to you. The truth doesn't always set you free.

Lina and Burt first named it, not the newspapers. No one seems to remember that now. In Bone people thought it was a joke, maybe, about how many dogs they had. Lina and Burt would say, "Time to get home to the puppy farm." "When we first settled at the puppy farm." Stuff like that. But there were no puppies at that place. It was us.

At first, there were other kids, too. Some were Lina's and some were street kids they picked up in cities. Which were we? I don't know. Why did Lina and Burt even want kids, to raise them in cages? There are only bad answers to that. Sometimes cars came and people, and they looked at the kids in the cages. Sometimes the cars took kids away. I used to wonder, which is worse? To be picked to go in the car, or not? But we didn't get picked. We bit when people touched us.

There was never enough food or water but we shared. We fought the others for food—Burt thought that was funny. What else? I recall the yard out back, where racks of hides stood drying in the sun. Something hanging from a hook in a barn, wrapped in cheesecloth. Like you would hang a ham, I guess, but it wasn't a ham. Turning, turning in the barred sunlight.

Pawel got some of it right, in those stories.

Lina and Burt stopped sleeping at night. I think they were making their own meth at this point. They stopped feeding us. There were *fewer and fewer kids. One jumped in the well, trying to get away, I remember that.*

In the end we were the last ones left. There was an old teddy bear in the bottom of one cage. It had no eyes. You wanted it so bad—we'd never had a teddy bear. But I couldn't reach it.

Burt died. An overdose. Lina left him on the floor. Her eyes were red and staring. She hadn't slept in days and she kept talking to people who weren't there. We knew we didn't have long. When she came to open the cage, you took her around the throat with the wire. You thought she was going to eat us. Maybe she was.

Coming out into the sun was like walking into an explosion. We had never seen anything so bright and hot. We hadn't had food or water in days but the well stank and when I lifted the hood, clouds of flies swilled out. I could smell a coyote nearby.

We walked into the desert. We couldn't see; our eyes were bad. But there was silver, gleaming in the distance. Fences. I guess they looked like cages, and that was all we knew, so we went toward them.

Mia found us at the edge of the west run. We were red and burned by the sun. Our skin had never seen it. We got sick. For a long time, I think.

A truck driver found the puppy farm a couple of days later. The police came. They found the other children where Lina and Burt had put them. None of them had made it. People never guessed that two of us got away. Maybe we didn't get away, not really. Kids are mirrors, reflecting back everything that happens to them. You've got to make sure they're surrounded by good things. Remember that, Sundance, if you have kids one day.

Falcon and Mia figured out what we were. They saved us—whatever else they did. Try and remember that, Rob. I do. You couldn't get out of the puppy farm, in your head. You tried to kill Mia with a piece of wire, and me with a screwdriver. So they gave us the click. They made you a good dog. I was glad that you would be safe. Even then I knew what happens to bad dogs.

You didn't seem to remember it, when we got better. I've tried to give you other memories, in place of the bad. A mother. I believed it, almost, some of the time. Falcon, Mia, and Pawel hid it in their own way. You really love Pawel's dumb story about rescuing the dogs.

They're afraid that a grad student here or someone in town will let it slip to you—what the puppy farm really was. Or you'll see an old newspaper lying around, or something. It hasn't happened yet. Secrets have a way of staying hidden out here. They're sure one day you'll find out.

I think you're determined not to. You've spent every day since it happened pushing it further down into the dark. That's good.

When the click started to go wrong with me Falcon told me I could never leave Sundial. I agreed. I said I'd always protect you and the best way to do it was to make you go. I know you won't go without me. I'll have to tell you as much of the truth as it takes for you to hate me.

It's still there, you know. From the stone garden, you can see it in the west, in the foothills of the Cottonwoods. Those roads don't have names or numbers. Here's something funny. People set up a camp there. They sell Pawel what we need to get by—to keep the bad click under control. Isn't that funny. A circle, a full turn of the dial.

Lina and Burt, they were known as, around here, but their names were Jacqueline and Robert Grainger. I know you keep that in there somewhere, no matter how hard you try to forget, because you named us for them—Rob and Jack.

Keep your chin high, Sundance.

Cassidy

ROB

IMPRESSIONS TICK THROUGH my mind. Shining wire, tight about a mottled, blackened throat. The taste of days-old warm soda, sickly sweet. When they gave us a can, we shared it, I remember that now, trading sip for sip so that it would last for days. The scent of rot and unwashed bodies. For a moment, I am looking through the rusty bars of a cage, the kind you put a dog in. Another little hand in mine, holding tight.

The heat baking our heads, throats dusty with thirst. A voice. A hand on my head. Mia, a dark shape against the light. Water, a cool round room, with a wheel of light on the floor, like a circus ring.

Are these memories real? The mind is a liar.

But I think of Miss Grainger, stalking through Arrowood with her burning eyes. Our names. Rob and Jack. Maybe these memories have always lurked in the deep places of my mind, ready to wake, squirming like maggots.

How did Mia and Falcon explain our sudden presence? But people leave one another alone, out here. That's why they come to the Mojave.

I have to focus. My daughter doesn't have a chance unless I give her one. I put Jack's letter next to the blue case in the center of the table. I am a teacher, after all. I know about visual aids.

"These two things define you," I tell Callie. "They are the history of us, ending in you. Everyone has one story that explains them completely. You are very special, because you have two. They used to be mine, and I passed them down to you. This box, and the puppy farm."

She squirms. Her eyes flicker to the side, as if someone to her left just said something in her ear. Who is she listening to?

"I am a murderer," I tell Callie. "Finding that out messed me up. More than I even realized at the time. So I promise, I will never let that happen to you. You are what you are, but I can save you from that."

She looks at me with those shallow green eyes and for a second I think, *She knows what I'm going to do.* But how could she?

"Are you OK?" I ask. "Do you understand what I've told you?"

"The puppy farm is famous, so it's almost like you're famous." Callie's tone is frightening, matter-of-fact.

After a moment I hold out my hand. "It's OK that you don't know what to feel. Let's get there together." She takes my hand lightly in her damp one and I try not to flinch. Her hands are always as clammy as toads.

I glance at my phone but the screen is dark. Irving has gone quiet.

ROB

T H E N

I TAKE TO spending much of the days sitting in front of Twenty-Three's pen. Twenty-Three seems fine, sometimes. Like Jack, she grows larger and rounder by the day. She casts about for scent and wags her maimed tail at Mia. Other times she hurls herself against the wire, eyes wide with fear, attacking invisible enemies, roaring until she's hoarse. I hate the sound of her, the stink of her, her squat musculature, her two sets of eyes. But I can't drag myself away. She is a mirror.

IN AUGUST, IN the height of the desert heat, Jack wakes up and won't speak, though it's more than that. She's gone behind the eyes.

I take care of the shell she leaves behind. I make her eat, I make her take her vitamins. I make her take a walk with me every day, out to the property line. At first I talk about the past, our memories. I stop doing that after a while, because so much of our childhood is lies. Only the stuff that happened between us two was real. And only some of it. Jack stares ahead and doesn't answer. She doesn't fight me, but there is a twitch to the side of her mouth, a flicker, that I don't like. It speaks of some great battle taking place within her. What is she wrestling with, and which part of her is winning?

THERE'S SOMETHING WRONG with Falcon, too. He has difficulty breathing, hasn't been able to leave his bed for some days. We're all falling apart, here. I can't stifle the feeling that Sundial is eating away at us like the click, and soon there will be nothing left but dust on the hot wind.

Mia wants to get someone out from Bone to see Falcon but he refuses. His eyes grow wild, showing how yellow the whites are. His heart flutters and his breath becomes dangerously labored. In the end she decides it's best not to upset him. It's probably a bug or a flu. Scientists and doctors are terrible patients.

I take Falcon canned soup and buttered toast at noon. I feel a strange contrast of feelings when I look into his face. Here is the man I loved more than anything, for so many years. I remember that love vividly, how it felt, the intensity of my desire to earn his approval, the painful pulse of need. But when I look for it now, it's no longer there. Where it once was is only emptiness.

"Rob." Even his voice is weak, a faint version of him.

"Yes."

"Will you sit with me?"

I consider. It's cool in here, with the fan, and I don't really want to go down and help Mia peel potatoes. "OK."

Falcon lies, eyes clouded with sickness and the past. "My father was in the war," he says. "I don't know what he was like before he went, but by the time I came along he was changed, my mother said. Or maybe she didn't want to believe he was always like that." His handsome face is anxious. A strand of silver hair falls over his tanned brow. He looks very old these days. He's smaller too, or I've grown.

"I was afraid of my father," Falcon says. "And I hated him, too. The fear was bad but the anger was worse. I never wanted you to feel that fear or that anger. We tried, Rob. We really tried." He looks at me, pleading, an old man asking for absolution.

"Your soup is getting cold," I say.

Falcon struggles to eat, hand trembling. So I take the spoon and feed him patiently, sip by slow sip. Afterward I wipe his mouth. Maybe Falcon will die soon. Even this thought brings nothing but a mild twitch of interest.

———

"I THINK THIS will work," Mia says. We're in the dog lab. The syringe with its distinctive bright yellow label lies in its bright yellow case.

"It had better," I say. "I might kill you if you're wrong again." It just slips out. I am so worn out that I can't feel anything about it, except maybe that it would be fitting.

Mia goes pale. "This is right. I know it. It will make the click repair the damage it has done."

Twenty-Three is sedated while Mia plunges the needle into her. The dog spends so much time unconscious that I begin to worry it will affect the results. As we walk back to the house, I steal a glance at Mia. Her eyes flick away as soon as they meet mine, but too late. I have seen what's in them. Mia is afraid of me.

"When the click goes wrong there's fear, at first," I say. "But I think even you know that in the end, it eats them alive. Everything they are."

Mia doesn't argue. "That's what fear does," she says, weary.

THE POINTED STAR lamp casts its pink glow. It used to be so comforting, but now everything makes me think of blood.

In the other bed Jack lies staring at the ceiling. I brush her hair every night, and put her in the old T-shirt and boxers she uses as pajamas, pulling them up gently over her bulging belly. I even brush her teeth for her. "Spit," I say and she spits, obedient. She is aware of the world around her and what I'm doing. She just doesn't care.

I take the book out from under my pillow. I searched the house for it for several days. I didn't think that Jack would have destroyed it. I found it under a stack of *National Geographics* in a disused bedroom. I picture Jack, in better times, sneaking off to read on her own, sinking into the healthy jolly world of Bingley Hall. The needle of sorrow slides in. I miss my sister.

"Shall I read?"

She doesn't give any sign of having heard me. I start to read.

I WAKE TO see Jack standing at the window of our room, staring into the night. In her hand is a knife with a long shining blade. I thought I'd got all the carving knives from the kitchen, but I must have missed one. Or maybe she has had it stashed away for a long time, since before I even came back. The point hovers over Jack's belly. Her face is bathed in moonlight. "You don't get to take her," she whispers. "Anything but that."

I come up quietly behind her, and wrap my forearm about her neck, while grabbing the knife with my other hand. She screams and I wrestle her to the bed, careful to jostle the baby as little as possible. I tie her to the bed with cable ties. We use them to muzzle the vicious dogs. I have had these ready, hidden under my mattress, for some time. I seem to be the only one who is capable of thinking ahead these days.

THE NEXT DAY, Twenty-Three ambles over to the fence, wagging her damaged tail. She grins at Mia, as if none of it ever happened, as if she didn't crack Kelvin's bones between her teeth like twigs.

"I think it really worked this time," Mia says. "Now we just have to see how the little ones do."

Neither of us says what surely we must both be thinking. It's worked for now. How long until this click begins to get greedy too—before it begins to snip away again, replacing old DNA? The only way we'll know is when it fails. When Twenty-Three kills someone.

"Come with me," Mia says. She takes me into the lab, and unlocks a cabinet covered in red biohazard signs. Cold white smoke billows out. There is only one thing in the freezer, a plastic case. Instead of the usual yellow, it's bright, shocking blue.

"This is the last one," Mia says. "It's for the puppies. The last one I ever have to make. I hope they never need it. They might be fine. But I'm thinking ahead."

Mia doesn't need to explain. She's making sure I know about the click in case something happens to her. I wonder who she thinks is most likely to kill her—Twenty-Three, Jack, or me?

———

"It worked," I tell Jack. "Twenty-Three is a good dog again." I cut the cable ties that bind her to the bedposts. I don't keep her like that all the time, of course, just when I'm out of the room. Jack lies unmoving, spread-eagled like a star, staring up at the ceiling.

I say again, "It worked, Jack. It's going to be OK." I sit beside her. I am so tired. I feel her arms around me, tentative, and I brace myself for attack. But she just holds me very gently as I cry.

Twenty-Three goes into labor in September. Early in the day she starts panting heavily. I shriek for Mia, who shoots her with the dart gun. We wait for the anesthesia to work and then Mia and I carry her between us into the lab. The cesarean goes smoothly, without incident.

There are five puppies like squirming black sausages. We put them to feed on Twenty-Three's sleeping form. Then we go behind the glass and wait. I think of her great jaws on their baby necks. But we have to know how she'll act around them. We have to know what they're like. We can't give Jack another version of the click until the dogs are grown. So I have to stay here, for as long as it takes.

Twenty-Three wakes slowly as if from deep dreams. When she sees the puppies she makes a high sound in her throat, and licks them each carefully. They mew and squirm. Twenty-Three lies down again, exhausted.

The puppies grow. They learn to walk. They growl like little lions and play-fight. We wean them on minced chuck and milk replacer. They're very cute but we don't give them names or numbers. The nights grow cooler and Twenty-Three sleeps in her shed, her babies nestled warm around her, whining, legs paddling as they chase someone, something, through their dreams.

I allow myself to hope.

When Jack goes into labor I feel it, too.

The day is chilly. I go to the greenhouse to pick tomatoes and chilies for dinner. My mind is elsewhere. But it's a task that suits a languid pace, a distracted state. My absent mind registers the satisfying snap as the fruit leaves the stem, the soft whisper as it lands in the basket on my arm. Jack wanders by from the direction of the dog pens. "Chili for supper," I call, bent over a tomato, trying to sound cheerful. Then a cold feeling runs down my spine like sweat.

"How did you get untied?" I don't expect an answer—when she speaks, that cold finger strokes me once again.

"I chewed through those plastic things." Jack's voice is cracked with disuse. "Had stuff to do."

"You're talking!" Anything's better than that dead silence. "Wait, you chewed through the cable ties?"

In this moment something shocks me upright, like a distant crash or a gunshot. There is a splash on my sandaled foot. When I look down, my toes are covered in something red and shining. My hand is squeezed like a vise around the tomato. The seeds and flesh are dripping slowly over my closed fist, landing in gory plops on the cement floor. Then I feel it, the pain. It's happening now.

I say, "Get inside, Jack."

THE ROUND HALL is filled with light; it streams through the glass roof, falls on Jack where she stands, clutching her rippling belly. She must have been hiding it from us for hours. Mia holds her by the elbow. She walks her.

"I told you to go to a doctor!" I scream at Jack. "We need to go to the hospital right now!"

"No hospital." Jack groans and pushes me away with a feeble hand. "What, are you going to tie me to the bed for this, too?"

"You're an idiot," I shout, before I am seized in strong arms and lifted away.

"Not now, Rob," Mia says. "Go to the kitchen. When you've calmed down, you can come back, but not until then." Mia's look is not without understanding. I lash out at and punish those I fear for. Those I love. Maybe we all do.

In the end it happens while my back is turned. I'm getting some lavender oil from the kitchen, which Mia says will soothe Jack, although Jack seems beyond that.

"I can't find it," I say, fretful. Behind me in the round hall there is a cry. When I turn, she has already slipped into being. I run to them.

The moment Jack's daughter opens her eyes I am in love. She waves little fists, as if raging at the world. "Good girl," I tell her. "Good girl. There are so many reasons to be angry."

Mia tries to put the baby into Jack's arms. Jack lies unmoving, staring ahead.

"You're tired," Mia says. "Everything in good time." But I can see she thinks that Jack's time is running out.

Jack feeds the little nameless baby. Mia holds her to the breast because Jack won't. I think of Twenty-Three, passed out on the gurney, the little black sausages feeding busily at her vast body.

"You want to hold her?" Mia asks. I take the little bundle from Mia. I look at the baby and the baby looks at me with her squashed tomato face and dark hair. It's wonderful. Love surges through me. Mia smiles.

"What are you going to call her?" I ask.

"What am I going to call her?" Jack whispers. Her eyes are glassy marbles. "What am I going to call her, Rob?"

"Callie," I say. "It's going to be OK," I tell the baby, certain. I edge slowly toward the front hall. The car is parked under the salt cedars, with a full tank of gas. There are diapers, formula, baby clothes, wipes, bottles in the trunk. I'm ready.

"Where are you going?" asks Mia, smiling but not looking, busy with sutures. "Maybe let Jack hold her baby now, Rob."

"Yeah, Rob, what are you doing?" Jack speaks softly.

"I'm taking her," I say. I stand firm now, and look Jack in the eye, suddenly filled with courage. "It's the right thing to do."

Mia raises her head. "Don't, Rob," she says.

"Why not? She'll be safer with me than she will with Jack. I'll give her a good home."

"It's not safe," Mia says. "We don't know enough . . ."

"Better than staying here."

"I know something about abandoning a sister, Rob. You think it won't cost you, but it will."

"It's not just Jack I'm saving Callie from—it's you, too."

"She's been planning this all along," Jack says seriously to Mia. It's still there, the twin thing. "Callie." She smiles and behind the white mask I see a glimpse of my sister. "Pretty name. But you can't take her. I won't let you, Rob."

Mia trembles. She puts the needle down carefully. "All done," she says to Jack. She strides up to me and slaps me hard in the face. Sprinkles of bright light dance before my eyes. The baby startles in my arms. I hold her tight. "Have some common sense!" I have never heard Mia yell before. *It's happening,* I think vaguely. *We've broken her at last.* Strangely, it brings me no pleasure.

"I've taken everything you've thrown at me." Mia is very close to my face. I feel every word on my cheek. "The pair of you—all those years you froze me out, all those little looks and comments and every petty little meanness. Each time I felt like I might die out here, with no life and no one to talk to, I pulled myself together again. I have given you two every breath. No mother could have done more. And you know what? You're both monsters. That's not of my doing." Mia's body sags. "I'm done," she says. "You win, Rob. Take the baby. Abandon each other. I don't care."

"Mia," I say. I don't know what to do so I reach out and touch her back with one hand.

"Rob," Jack says.

"I'm sorry," I say to Mia, stroking her.

She shakes her head and doesn't look up. "I was so happy when we found you two. But it didn't turn out anything like I thought."

"I know," I say. "Jack is fighting so many battles inside—don't blame her. But there's no excuse for me. All I can say is, forgive me, Mia." The baby makes a noise and Mia looks at her and then at me with a gleam.

"She's great," she says. "Maybe it'll all be OK."

"Rob," Jack says again, and there's something in her voice that makes my heart stop. Jack is staring past me. "There's a dog in the house," she says.

Twenty-Three stands in the open screen door, bright-eyed, surveying us. There is blood on her loose jowls. *Puppies*, I think, and even now there is a moment of sadness like a sweet pull on my heart. Then fear comes in a sweeping tide. Twenty-Three's head moves again in that ducking motion and she yelps. I realize that she's trying to avoid blows from some invisible thing in the air.

Mia lunges for the kitchen where she keeps her gun. But she won't make it. Twenty-Three rises into the air in a graceful arc to meet Mia, and her jaws close on Mia's throat. She shakes her to and fro. Mia goes limp, becomes a Mia-doll.

I grip the baby tightly to me and drag Jack toward the stairs. She staggers against me, heavy. Blood runs down her legs, leaving a spattered trail on the floor. I stumble, waiting for hot breath on my neck, for teeth to puncture my flesh, but nothing comes. Somehow the baby is OK. She starts crying. I throw Jack's arm over my shoulders and we make it all the way up the stairs, along the gallery, and almost all the way to our bedroom before Twenty-Three grows tired of throwing Mia around. I slam the bedroom door behind us. The dog is coming fast. Her weight makes a crack on the stairs with each leaping stride.

The click and skitter of claws comes closer, closer. We hold one another and I close my eyes. But the claws pass us, and there is sound from an adjoining room. I know which room.

"Falcon," I whisper. "I left Falcon's bedroom door open, Jack. I left it . . ."

The sounds are soft, indistinct. Every so often there is a little high growl.

"How did she get out?" I am whispering to myself, really, because I don't expect an answer. "But she got better, Mia fixed her . . ."

"She's been in a safe place with food and water," Jack says. "That's not a test. I felt the baby coming, and I knew I had to make a real test. She had to feel fear, pain. Like in life."

"What did you do?" But I know.

"She was sleeping by the fence. I grabbed her by the tail and pulled it through the chain-link. I did what her owner used to do to her. I hurt her. I had to make her afraid. It started for me inside the MRI machine.

Remember? I'm afraid of being trapped in the dark because that's how they kept us. Her tail is her darkness.

"I let her go and she started crying and running in circles. The puppies followed her, clinging to her legs. I tranked her and unlatched the gate to the pen. Left her sleeping like a big slug." She takes my hand, pleading. "I didn't want to be right, Sundance." Her eyes are vast with pain. Dark rusty blood pools beneath her. Her nightgown is soaked in it. Her hair is lank with sweat.

"Why would you do a thing like that?" I can't breathe; the air seems to have turned into a solid mass.

"I had to," Jack says. "It was the only way to really test. If she woke up OK and didn't come after us, she could be a good dog, even with the fear, and so could we. But the dark came out in her—we're bad. Or we will be. It's already happened for me. It will happen to you and the baby. Maybe not today, but when the fear gets too much, it will happen. We should be ended. Trust me, Sundance, it's better this way. You don't want to live like this." Her grip tightens on me; her hand is a claw, nails digging in.

My voice is barely a breath. "You've done a terrible thing, Jack." The words aren't big enough to describe what she's done. No words could be. I pull my arm free and she whimpers. The worst thing is, Jack is here, now, after months of being gone. It's her eyes, her voice. Jack did this, not the click.

I put the baby down carefully on the bed. I crack the mirror on a corner of the dressing table and take a shard. How many years of bad luck are we on now? I wrap a sock around the end and hold it like a knife. It's unwieldy, slippery; I'm as liable to hurt myself as the dog.

I shove the chest of drawers in front of the door, squealing across the floor. It's waist high, heavy.

The cell phone. I haul the top drawer out, wiggling it, cursing its every drag and stick. It never opened smoothly. I had asked Pawel to fix it but of course that didn't happen. I throw socks and panties and bras out in a flurry, until there's nothing left but the bare cedar drawer. It's not there.

"I took it outside," a dead voice says, "and threw it in the cacti." When I turn, Jack is smiling.

I take her by the shoulders. Her eyes are full of stars. She is luminous, grinning, gone. "Please," I say. "Come back to me. I need you, Jack, or the dog will break in here and tear us all to pieces. I'm going to die. You're going to die. Your baby will die. It will be slow and painful. Please, please help. I'm begging you to come back." The sounds in the next room are growing less frequent, softer. I can't think about what's happening in there.

"Liars with bad desires," she says. "Liars burn rubber tires."

I hit her across the face with a crack. She just smiles again. It's not her fault, I know. She's being gnawed away from within. I start knotting bedclothes together. If I can get down to the sliding doors on the deck, maybe I can shut Twenty-Three in the house. Then what? The thought of getting both Jack and the baby down two stories on a rope of knotted laundry is terrifying. My car, Mia's truck? Keys are in the kitchen, I think. Maybe I can run to the highway, flag someone passing, get help. Maybe I can sneak in another way, get to the phone in the hall? But I don't want to leave Jack alone with the baby. *Fine*, I decide, *I take the baby with me*—

What stops these thoughts is the silence. A peculiar quiet has fallen. You wouldn't think you could hear death through walls and doors. But you can. Falcon is gone.

Maybe she'll be tired now. Maybe she'll sleep.

There comes the *click, click, click* of claws on wood. A snout is pressed to the gap under the door. A friendly whuff of breath. She found the blood trail to our door. Twenty-Three howls, a miserable sound.

I think quickly. Then I haul Jack upright. "Get up here," I say. I guide her up onto my bed, then boost her up onto the big wardrobe. I take Callie from the bed and lift her gently into Jack's arms. Then I push the single bed away from the wardrobe, screech it across the floor, and wedge it against the dresser, barricading the door.

"Don't move," I say to Jack. "OK? Stay up there with the baby, no matter what. And hold the baby tight, OK?"

She looks down at me, expressionless. But she doesn't move so that's good. They're eight feet up. Will it be enough?

I take up the shard of mirror and face the door. The snuffling moves up and down, taking in our scent. Twenty-Three whines and paws at the door. "Bad dog!" I shout. "Go seek!" She barks—no—she bays, long and high like a hound. Then she hurls her weight against the wood. The cedar makes a cracking protest and stays sound. But the doors at Sundial are thin, light. They're meant to let cool air flow through the house. They're not meant to resist 140 pounds of muscle and bone.

She hits the door again with a killing blow. Is she hitting it with her head? Above the dresser, the varnished surface of the door cracks as the wood buckles inward. Twenty-Three leaps at the door, hurling herself against the top half of the door. At the next blow, pale splinters appear in the wood. Another blow, and a long vertical crack opens. I see a black shining nose, an eye. She worries her head back and forth until it fits through the door. I can't look at her snout, her jaws. They are slick, coated with stuff my mind will not accept. She is writhing and her shoulders are through now. Every part of me wants to run but there's nowhere to run. I lunge forward and stab at her eye with the mirror shard. Her head flips quick as a snake and her jaws just graze my wrist. I recoil and the piece of mirror goes spinning out of my hand, to land somewhere behind me.

I didn't think a dog could scream but that's what she does now, and bursts through the door, shattering the top half into splinters as she goes. I leap back, thinking maybe I can get up on the wardrobe with Jack, but of course I have moved the bed, and now it's too high, hopelessly out of reach. Twenty-Three leaps down into the bedroom, jumps and skitters, barking and snapping at the air. What is she seeing? Who? The person who maimed her tail, long ago? For a moment I wonder if I can get out, past her, but I have barely had the thought when her head flicks up, ears erect. *Click, click, click* go her claws as she stalks toward the wardrobe. I back away from her slowly, my mind racing uselessly through options. Too far from the window, and my makeshift rope lies useless on the floor. I'd probably be too injured by the two-story fall to run once I hit the ground. My back meets the great oak wardrobe. I have reached the end of my retreat. I feel behind me for the handle. I don't know how I can tell she's preparing to spring. Something changes in her eyes, her gait, her stance. I know it with old instinct, the ancient exchange between hunter and hunted.

I reach behind and open the wardrobe door. I slip inside and pull it closed behind me, just in time. Twenty-Three hits the old oak with a grunt. The wardrobe shivers a little but stays steady. My fear was that she would topple it, and then reach Jack and the baby. But it seems to be holding for now.

Even so this is a last resort. The oak is probably sturdier than the bedroom door, but not much. Twenty-Three will make short work of it.

"Jack," I call. I knock on the wood above me. I hear her shifting. "The dog is going to come in here to get me. I'm going to tell you exactly what to do, so listen. When she comes for me, you take the baby and jump down. You've got to be quick. There's a big hole in the top of the bedroom door now. You can fit through. Don't try to move the dresser and the bed, it will take too long. When you're out, you run downstairs to the kitchen and take Mia's car keys from the hook by the phone. Then you go outside, and shut the glass door behind you. Get in the car and drive. Don't stop. Don't look back."

There is no reply.

"Did you hear me?" I can't tell what Jack is thinking and I have no idea if she'll do what I say. I have to hope. "Don't forget to take the baby. OK? Don't forget." I am crying now, tears coming so fast I have to lick them away. I have been trying not to let them into my voice.

It's going to be bad. It's going to hurt. I'm scared. I don't want to die.

Above, the baby starts crying, long thin wails of endless sorrow. As if in response the dog roars again and the wardrobe door makes that cracking sound that I am coming to know well. Not long now.

Hey, Sundance, Jack says in my ear. *Don't let Mia git you with the choo choo.* I start at the feel of a warm hand on mine.

But Jack is gone. This is just my exhausted mind, firing its last rockets into the sky. It's comforting all the same. It's enough. I whisper my sister's name over and over. I can't hear the words because the dog is baying again; the sound feels so close, as if she's by my ear, opening her jaws . . .

Crack. Light in the dark. The cupboard door gives, shatters. I smell blood. Falcon's blood. The light is blocked by her great shape. It's time. I close my eyes. I smell her. The dog's hot carrion breath fills the dark cupboard. She comes.

There's a sound, a *whump*. Is this it? Maybe death was easier than I feared it would be. But I'm still alive, I think. The baby is still crying. Through my eyelids, I see light.

Sundance.

Her voice is right there, right in my ear, alert and young. I gasp and open my eyes. The shattered wardrobe door is open, swinging slightly. The room looks empty. I slowly come out, braced for the lunge, the breath, the quick jaws. But nothing happens.

"Jack?" I whisper. No answer comes. A little hand waves helpless from the top of the wardrobe, and I leap up and take Callie in my arms. Where is Jack? Both she and the dog seem to have vanished into thin air. A quiet gurgling sound from my right. I look around the side of the wardrobe.

They are there, wrapped in a quiet embrace. Twenty-Three is sprawled on top of Jack, teeth in her throat. Red is spurting from Jack's artery. It falls in slick torrents down over her shoulders, her chest, her arms and hands; a pool spreads across the floor. One of Jack's fingers lifts, twitches. Her eyes are on me. She sees me. Her other hand holds the shard of mirror. It is buried in Twenty-Three's exposed brain. Jack somehow knocked off the putty seal that covers the skull. The dog is gone.

I roll her black weight off Jack. I put my hands on the wounds, trying to stop the blood. But it ripples up hot through my fingers. Twenty-Three tore her apart. "I'll go call for help," I say. "Hold on. You're going to be OK."

I try to get up but she grabs my hand and won't let go. I hold the baby to my chest and slip down gently beside Jack, put my arm around her. "Cassidy," I say. She has been trying to save me, all my life. She managed it in the end. "You'll be OK."

She tries to say something. The word is lost, drowned in blood. It's a terrible sound. It sounds like *liar*. She tries again. This time it sounds more like *dance*.

"Don't try to talk." I stroke her hair. We lie like that, the three of us. Desert light falls over distant mountains, the land grows dim, spread out like a dirty coyote pelt under the sky. Jack breathes shallowly, warm against me. I think I knew that one of us would die here. Maybe we both will. As dark slides over us I wonder if this has happened.

Memory and worlds flash by, all the times Jack and I clung to each other like this. We grow smaller and smaller and younger, until we're back there, in the dark, looking through the rusty bars of a cage, the taste of old soda in our mouths. We go back to the beginning, when we had only each other. We have come all the way around the dial, because this is how it ends, too. Us, together.

She reaches up and touches my face. I feel the track of blood she leaves across my cheek. Warm, then cold. Jack's eyes are on the baby, who looks back at her with a slanted, dark-blue, newborn gaze.

"You did something beautiful with your time," I tell Jack. She smiles, or maybe it's pain.

"I'll be OK," I tell her. "You can go."

I can almost see it as it happens: see her rising from the bloody ruin of her body, edged in silver light against the coming night, her edges humming like a swarm of flies. I almost see it when she turns and walks away, through the wall, out into the wide dark desert. I think of my own little Callie, gone too soon. I hope Jack finds her, somehow. It comforts me to imagine it—my sister holding her, a faint silver baby limned with light. And I need comfort, now.

I give Jack a kiss on her cold cheek. Then I cover her gently with a sheet. I can't follow her out into the night after all. The baby stirs and mews.

I move the bed and the dresser away from the door. I am so weary I could die. But there are things to do. I am tempted to kick Twenty-Three's unmoving corpse on my way out. I stop myself. This wasn't her fault.

I don't look left or right as I go through the house. I don't look at the rusty pawprints that mar the shining cedar floors. I don't look at the ragged thing slumped against the wall of the round hall. Even so it seems to follow me, hanging like a storm on the edge of my vision.

I MAKE FORMULA and try to feed the baby, standing at the kitchen window in the dawn. She cries and cries. Formula dribbles out of her screaming mouth. I try to comfort her. But what comfort is there for either of us? *Please don't remember any of this. Don't let it take hold in the dark places of your mind.* What will become of her?

Of course I know. "You're Callie now," I say aloud. "You are my daughter and I will never let anyone hurt you." The baby looks at me with little eyes. It's a knowing look, and unease stirs within me. But she's just a child. She's my child, and I will protect her from everything from now on.

I BURY JACK by the sundial, under the rose, where once I thought my mother lay. Now it's a real grave. She's near my little lost one. Callie murmurs from her bassinet as I dig. I wonder, does she feel her half-sister, her cousin nearby, under the earth? Two Callies; one living, one dead.

I OPEN THE gate in the west run, leading to open desert. Then I go to the dog pen.

I stare through the wire at the nine remaining dogs. They lie idly in the shadows, panting in the growing heat. The shotgun is heavy in my hand. Callie is in the log shed, in her bassinet. I locked the door. I hope she's OK. I hope I live to go and fetch her, after this.

I go to the gate on the west side. I hesitate with my hand on it. I wonder what it feels like. What Jack felt. The long canines puncturing your flesh. I remember that they haven't been fed today. But this is my decision. No more making things into what they are not, or punishing them for what they are.

The dogs look at me, expectant. They're waiting for Mia. "Go on," I say. "You're on your own, now." I press the button that means "go seek" on the controller. It doesn't have any visible effect, but when I open the gate they move toward it, ears pricked. I keep the gun at my shoulder the whole time.

One by one they trot past me out of the enclosure. The coyote comes last. He pauses by me for a moment, yellow eyes rest on my face. His nostrils flare and he makes a tentative movement toward me.

"No," I say. "Time to make your own decisions."

The dogs scent the air and cast about, looking for Mia. Some of them sniff along the fence, straining toward the house. They smell blood. But I press the *seek* button again, and they reorient. Eventually, they trot away toward the open gate. They go out into the desert and are gone into the distance.

I THINK OF them sometimes; those dogs, wandering year after year through the wild, looking for a dead woman. Of course that's not what happened, really. They all died of age or exposure or thirst or hunger, or got eaten by something bigger. But at least they got to make their own way.

Even so, every time I come here I leave meat all along the perimeter. I don't know if it's an offering or appeasement. The meat is always gone within an hour or so. I don't watch out to see what takes it—if any of the dogs still live, they've earned their privacy.

I DRAG FALCON and Mia out to the empty dog pen. It's hard. They're heavy. How can they be so heavy? Falcon's feet thump on every step down. I lay them gently on the earth. Their bodies, the empty pens, the gates swinging open—they tell a story. Falcon and Mia were attacked by the dogs they experimented on.

I put Twenty-Three beside them. Her tongue lolls as I drag her. Her teeth still have blood on them.

It takes hours to bleach the house. I scrub blood from the surfaces. I remove all the evidence of childbirth. If I can direct attention away from the house, I might stand a chance.

One last task before I rest. I have to put the click beneath the earth. I pick the dog graveyard to bury it. A few feet away, Callie lies in her bassinet in the shade of the tree. She talks quietly to herself of secret things.

This is not just a burial. There is something in the ground here that I need. I want the message Jack left buried here that day under the dead dog, in the Snoopy lunch box. I hope this is the right spot. My spade hits something with a crack. It's a rib cage. But there's nothing in it, no metal heart. I push it aside with the blade of the shovel.

I dig on, but I can't find the metal lunch box anywhere. "Come on," I whisper, as though the earth could answer. "Where is it?"

In the end, I give up. The pages my dead sister wrote have gone into the earth, vanished just like her. Maybe it was disturbed by scavengers. Maybe Jack dug it up again one lonely night. It seems like the last in a long series of blows. I don't even wipe the tears away anymore. I just let them fall. "Whatever it was," I say to her, "it's your secret forever now."

In the hole I lay the bright blue case containing Mia's last version of the click, which she designed for Twenty-Three's puppies. The last, the only click left. I fetched it from the cabinet. It seemed to stir in my hands as I carried it. As though something alive and intent was inside. I raise the spade high for a killing blow. Bury it whole or destroy it?

"I bet it doesn't even work," I say aloud. "Wouldn't that be rich? If we went through all this for nothing. Who knows? Maybe the pinkopotamus knows." I'm losing it. I can feel sanity slipping gently from my grasp like a piece of silk.

I shovel earth over the blue case. I want it out of my sight. I could destroy it, but I won't. I don't know what the future holds for me or Callie. I do know that, whatever Callie needs, I will give it to her. Even the click? I shovel on and on, sweating and shivering. Will I be forced to dig it up one distant day while my daughter stands by muttering about liars and pyres?

It's done. I stand, weary as death. A shadow falls over the freshly filled grave. Someone stands behind me, looming against the sun.

Irving says, "What the hell happened?" He is pale and a handkerchief is pressed to his mouth.

"The dogs got out," I say. There are no words to describe what actually happened here.

"Why haven't you called the police?" But I don't need to answer, because he has seen Callie where she lies in the rippling shade. Irving goes to her softly, picks her up gently from the bassinet, holds her aloft. Her little bare legs look so vulnerable. "She's mine," he says. It is not a question. "Hello," he says to her. "Hello." Callie touches his nose with a hand. Pride blazes on his face, sun-bright. I see in this moment that I will never be rid of him. He will never leave Callie. If I want her, I have to have him, too.

It was Asia, of course. After we spoke she called everyone who might know where I was. Eventually she thought of Irving and found him in the faculty directory. She was upset, and it took him some time to understand what she was saying. She told him I was pregnant, being kept prisoner by my cult of a family. So Irving came to claim what was his. Callie.

I know Asia only wanted to help. Everyone and their insatiable desire to help.

IRVING AND I are on the deck, in the shade of the old beach umbrella. Callie lies contented in Irving's lap. With his free hand he holds the handkerchief delicately over his nose. The air already holds the scent of death.

I don't sit, I stand facing him like a disobedient pupil. I thought about it and decided that was what he would like best. I am swaying, nauseous with heat and exhaustion.

"She's not yours," he says. "That much is clear. You haven't just given birth."

"She's mine in every way that matters," I say.

"I'm not letting her go," he says. "I'm taking her. If you fight me, I'll fight back. I'll get a court order. The things I know about this place, and about you, would fill a book."

"I'm her mother," I say.

"But you're not. You're her aunt. Your baby died, you say. But did she, or did you do something? Where's the body? This could get very bad for you." He takes out his cell phone. "I'm calling the cops. Should have done it earlier. That's my civic duty."

Black swarms across my vision. I breathe deeply. *Just a little longer*, I tell myself. I have to play it right. "Wouldn't it be better for her to have a family?" I ask. "Who's going to take care of her when you're teaching?"

"I'll get a housekeeper," he says, but I see the beginnings of doubt. I have a feeling Irving's daddy has been threatening to cut him off from those oil fields again.

"It would be better if she had a mother," I say. "If she could grow up with more traditional values."

"What do you have in mind?"

"I think we should get married." The more bonds I can tie around him, the better. "Your family will like that."

Uncertainty crosses his face. "I thought you believed those lies your sister told about me."

"She was sick," I say. "We both know that." I don't point out to Irving that if Jack were lying, Callie's not his daughter. I save that ammunition for the future. I'm going to need it in years to come.

"Please," I say, because he likes me to plead. "We both want the best for her. It makes sense. And I'll be a really good wife." I can almost see cogs turning behind his eyes.

"So, we stay together for the kids," he says, mocking.

"Yes. She'll be ours. A normal childhood. With Little League and prom and friends and hanging out at the mall, and maybe a pony." *No dogs*, I think with a shiver. Everything goes slippery. As I look his face is melting. "Irving, I think I'm going to faint."

I feel his arms around me. "OK," he says. It's soothing. "You're OK. I'll take care of it." And despite everything I know about him, god help me, it feels so good to have someone say that, to lift some of the weight from my back. It feels good to be held and told it will all be OK. Above all it feels good to believe it, if only for a moment.

"Well," he says. "I guess we're engaged." His voice is puzzled and I laugh a little through the tears.

"Thank you," I say. Children change things. Maybe, if he and I pretend hard enough, it will become real between us.

"We have to go back to Cielo," I say.

Before we go, I slide open all the window screens, and fling the heavy front door wide. Wind whistles through Sundial.

I GET THE call when I'm out on the little balcony of Irving's apartment. It's shaded from the late, sunlit afternoon. Callie is sleeping beside me. I hate to let her out of my sight.

I'm holding a posy of honeysuckle and orange lilies and their scent drifts around me as the voice talks. We've been visiting florists this morning, getting ideas for wedding flowers. It will be small, but Irving wants a wedding. The posy is already wilting in the heat.

The mailman found Falcon and Mia when he went out back, to get a signature for a package. It's been some months, they can't say exactly how long; the desert has mummified the bodies. The evidence is there, however. Dog attack.

Callie wakes as I disconnect the call. I leave the bouquet on the table and go to her. She settles quickly. I stare at her perfect face, touch her perfect cheek with a light finger. She stirs.

"Sorry, baby," I say to her. "Sorry."

A rapid sound makes me turn. A hummingbird hovers over the honeysuckle posy, dipping its beak into the pale trumpet of the blossom.

TWO POLICE OFFICERS come to Cielo to talk to me. One looks like a kind goblin. The other is dark-haired, handsome.

Irving and I sit side by side, his arm clamped around my waist. His shirt is very white, he drops his father's name several times. He's enjoying it, I realize. I am rigid with fear.

The officers are consoling. I've got a new baby, I'm just about to get married and move to our new house—this is terrible news.

"I only saw them a couple of months ago," I say. "I can't believe it. We haven't spoken much recently, but they're eccentric."

The officers nod. They've heard about the eccentricity. They've seen the labs.

"The house is a mess," the dark-haired officer says. "You got lots of animal intrusion. Some predator used it as a den—mountain lion or coyote. Evidence of some smaller mammals—squirrels, maybe raccoons. All the doors were left open."

As they leave, the cop who looks like a kind goblin pauses. "Those experiments they did," he says. "I've got dogs. Hell of a thing to do to an animal." He shakes his head and they go.

I LAY MIA to rest next to Falcon, near the house, under the jacaranda tree. They lived and died at Sundial—now they'll lie here forever. I can't tell whether this is revenge or forgiveness on my part. I order big headstones from Ojai.

Sometimes I wonder why I keep Sundial—it's steeped in my family's blood. But that's why I can never give it up.

IN BONE THEY say Jack's in Nebraska. She was trouble, according to everyone in town, and no one worries too much about that kind of girl. But I think of her often, keeping my little daughter company, near the sundial.

ROB

I STOP. I don't want Callie to know the next part. The slow betrayal, which happened inch by inch. As the days and months went by, I discovered the endless grinding horror of being afraid of the man I married. And, later, of my daughter.

"So I'm not yours." Callie is openmouthed. It could be incomprehension or wonder on her smooth, inexpressive face. Does she understand what I have told her? We have to understand one another, because I am done pretending.

"Never say that. You are my daughter." And it's true. I love Callie. I should have left Irving long ago. But I thought normal was armor. I thought it would protect my children.

"Mom, you should text Dad," Callie whispers, as if Irving can hear us. "He's been texting, Mom. You know you should answer."

"Have you been in my purse?" I control my voice. I don't want to spook her now.

Strangely, of all the ghosts that crowd around us, it's Mia's voice I hear now. I can almost see her, holding the syringe, face serious.

You would do the same, Rob, to save your child.

I repeat my reasons to myself. The decision tree. How much of a life will Callie have? She can never get better. How will she make her way in this world? I look at her expressionless face and her flat green eyes and I see, perhaps for the first time, what lies there. Innocence. She's staring at the two unburied things that sit on the table, fresh from Sundial's red earth. The blue case, and the torn notebook pages, which are the story of our names, the story of a place I don't remember, except at the darkest edges of myself. The puppy farm. She never had a chance, my daughter.

I swore I'd keep them both safe and I will.

Everyone has one story that explains them completely. I thought I knew what mine was. I was wrong—I am in it, here and now. This will be the choice that defines me. The decision tree unfolds before my eyes, the terrible fruit at the end of each branch.

I pat my jeans pocket, to make sure the key to Callie's room is still in there. All set. I take a deep breath. "Hey, shall we go count the stars from your window, sweetheart? I need to see something beautiful."

CALLIE

MOM'S STORY WORKED in a way, because I understand now. I get Pale Callie's song. It's me she's going to *stick a needle in*—change me into a different daughter. The blue case sits between us. It shines a little in the last of the light, as if to say, *Hey, I'm not that bad.*

"I fought so hard for you, Callie," she says. "And I will keep fighting. I won't let you become what she was." Mom's biting her lip like Annie does. She looks really young. She touches her eye as if adjusting her contact lens—but that's not right, she doesn't wear them. She's all sad, sad face, her eyes gleaming wet. For a second it almost fools me. I want to give her a hug. *It's OK, Momushka.* But then her eyes flicker again toward the blue case.

"Hey, shall we go count the stars from your window, sweetheart?" says Mom, or Not-Mom.

I get up and we go up the stairs like it's no big deal. My heart is pounding.

"Get the lights, hon," she says, hovering by the door to my room. Her hand is in her pocket. She's got the key to my room in there, I know.

I go in. As I flick on the lights, she slams the door shut behind me. But I am ready for her and I shove back hard. The door hits her head with a crack and she stumbles. I grab the key out of her hand and shove her into my room. Then I slam the door and lock her in. Good thing she had a couple of glasses of wine earlier.

I race downstairs, toward the door, and the dark. As we pass the living room, Pale Callie whispers, *Grab it.*

I snatch up the click from the table and run, Pale Callie yelling *go, go, go,* in my ear. The front door has that sticky latch. I can hear Mom pounding on the door upstairs.

Cold desert dusk wraps about me. Behind, I hear Mom shout, "Callie? Callie, let me out!"

The wind is up, it blows sand everywhere. I crouch behind a stand of cacti. The light is the color of a bruise, of storm clouds. Overhead are cold, early stars. If I wasn't so scared, I'd be happy. It's beautiful. I throw the key hard, into the dark.

Which one of them is she, Jack or Rob? Pale Callie says in my ear. *You ever think of that? Maybe it was all lies.*

I nod, because I had thought of that.

I tuck the blue plastic case into my sweater sleeve and start to pick my way through the dark, creeping slowly and silently around the back of the house. I can hear Mom, or Not-Mom, faintly screaming my name from inside. She sounds crazy. She *is* crazy.

I need to hide until daylight comes then I can make my way to the highway, to find a phone and a ride. I'll probably be abducted by a psychopath. Can't be worse than the one I'm running from. Maybe the labs? Then my heart stops at the thought of meeting whatever ghosts live there. Dogs with no tops to their heads. Plus, the labs are chained and padlocked.

Why didn't I steal Mom's cell phone when I had the chance? Stupid. It's getting cold out here.

Something rears up suddenly against the dusk. I gasp, but it's just the big jacaranda tree, branches spreading against the sky. Strange to think it was here, under this tree, that my mom first met my dad, years ago. Whichever mom that is.

Dad tried to warn me about her but I wouldn't listen. Dumb, dumb.

I can't hear her calling anymore. Is that footsteps? Mom's coming. Or is it the wind? She can't have got out yet, surely. My heart's beating so loud, surely she can hear it. I hop up into the crook of the tree trunk, wincing at how much noise that makes. I hold my breath for a moment, listening, but I hear only night sounds so maybe it was the wind. Then I climb, as quietly as I can, into the high branches. It's nice up here. There's a very gentle sway, as the branches give to the wind. I feel close to the sky.

Yes, stay here, Pale Callie says. *It's not time yet.*

Great, thanks for all your help. Pale Callie's not the only one who can be salty.

I climb up farther until I find a place where the branches make a kind of seat-shape. I lean back cautiously. They hold me, strong and solid. The plastic case digs into my arm. I slip it out. The sleeve of my sweater will be all stretched now, I hate that.

Open it, Pale Callie says.

Time to throw the click away. Break it on the tree trunk, let it trickle down into the dirt of Sundial and be gone forever.

I open the blue plastic case slowly. It's scary, but I do kind of want to see it, the way you want to look at venomous snakes and sharks, and things that want to hurt you.

The syringe lies, held in its plastic bed. The needle gleams wicked in the falling light.

It's empty. There's nothing in the reservoir. Gingerly I take out the hypodermic. I stare at it and shake it gently, to make sure it's not a trick of the light. Definitely empty. Does Mom know? Was there even anything here? Something is happening and it's not what I thought.

Now there comes a faint sound of an engine in the distance. Two little pinpricks appear on the far-off highway. As I watch, they swell and become twin stars. Headlights. The car's coming from the direction of Cielo. I know who it must be. Sure enough, it turns down the drive to Sundial.

I put the click back in the case and shove it back into my sleeve. Even empty, the hypodermic is my only weapon. I slide down the tree, skinning my hands.

Pale Callie becomes a small silver beetle clinging to my earlobe.

No, she says, *don't go that way.*

I don't listen. If I can get to the car before Mom hears it . . .

I stumble past the great shape of Sundial, lights streaming from cracks in the blinds and shutters. I run toward the headlights, toward safety, barking my shins on unseen objects. Where is Mom? My breath is coming really fast. I almost fall into the middle of the drive, waving my arms. I am surrounded by blinding light. Too late, I realize how fast the car is coming.

Behind there is the pounding of running feet. Something else runs out of the dark and seizes me in its arms. It pulls me out of the path of the car, which slaloms across the drive, tires screeching.

"You could have been killed," Mom says tightly in my ear. "What did you think you were doing?"

I struggle in her grip as the car stops. We shade our eyes in the white glare of the headlights.

A tall figure gets out.

"Dad? Dad!" I am so happy to see him.

"Irving," Mom says.

"Didn't expect me?" Dad sounds pleased.

I feel Mom shake her head. "You should have let me lock you in your room," she whispers in my ear. "Good thing those bedsheets are strong." I should have remembered that Mom has already thought a lot about how to escape from that room.

"Come here, Callie," Dad says.

"Stay here, please, Callie," Mom says. Her voice is level but I hear fear in it. Her arms tighten around me.

"I've come for my daughter."

"She's not going anywhere with you," Mom says.

Dad relaxes, leaning against the car. "You're not fit to look after her. Callie, hon?"

I know what he wants me to say. "I'm scared of Mom," I whisper. "She shook me. And she wants to stick a needle in me."

"Please, Callie . . ." I can hear Mom's tears. "Callie . . ."

"Let me go, Mom," I whisper, and to my surprise, she does.

Dad says, "Hop in back and put your seat belt on for me, will you, Callie?"

I look in the back seat of the car. It's empty. My heart goes cold.

"Dad," I say. "Isn't Annie with you?"

"No, sweetie. We'll see her soon."

"But where is she?" The cold pumps out from my heart, all through my body. Fear.

"She's with Hannah. Mrs. Goodwin. Don't worry, sweetie. Everything's OK."

"Where are Mr. Goodwin and the boys?" I say to Dad.

Dad flicks me an impatient glance. I can tell he's getting tired of the questions. "Camping. Mrs. Goodwin will take care of her." To Mom he says,

"Annie was so happy to see Hannah. Her own mother abandoned her while she was sick. She's traumatized. Did you know that your youngest daughter wouldn't even go over to Hannah's house without taking that pink night-light? She's terrified. It's unnatural."

"Dad!" I scream. "Dad, you shouldn't have left Annie with Hannah!"

"Calm down, OK, sweetheart?" Dad and I are buds, of course we are. But that's the tone he uses when he pulls hair. "For the last time, Rob," Dad says. "She's coming with me." He turns to me. "Get in the car, Callie." There's that sticky voice again, I hate that voice, and I hesitate. "Now, bud," he says.

He comes toward us and Mom steps in front of me. "No," she says.

They are two black figures blazing against the headlights, like their edges are on fire. Dad reaches for her, and she leans toward him and their black shadows touch. I think, *Oh, they're kissing,* which is unexpected, but then I see that Dad has her by the hair. He does something with his other hand very quickly and there is a crunch sound. Mom bends double. Her hand is on her face and something dark runs through her fingers.

"Callie." Mom sounds calm, but there's something blocked about her voice, like she has a really bad cold. When she spits on the ground it splashes red. "Go back to the house. I'll be just a second."

Dad draws back his fist again. Mom puts out a hand, like she's saying *no thank you* to another bread roll. His fist comes and her head recoils like a pool ball hit by the cue. Her neck goes limp. *Run, run,* I want to scream but my mouth won't work, it just makes fishy open and closed motions, and she's down in the dirt, lit weird by the headlights; I can see every shadow, like they're all deep holes. Dad kicks Mom in the middle and she jerks. He stands above her looking very tall. How come I never noticed how tall he is?

I put my hands in my pocket and pull out the controller. I push the buttons, stabbing with my fingers.

Come here.

Hunt.

Come here.

I know it's useless. What did I expect? Ghost dogs to rescue us? It's as much good as hitting the dirt with a fist. But it's all I've got. Dad and

Mom are a monstrous shape; she shakes to and fro, arms floppy and limp. SCREAMING FACE.

"Callie," she says, "Callie," and Dad is drawing back a foot and I can see that his kick will land on her head. Mom is just lying there and I want to scream at her and hit her myself because why won't she get up, why won't she run?

I run at Dad and hit him. He makes an *oof* sound, then his fist comes. When it lands in my side I fly up into the purple air and land with a crunch. Glitter explodes. When it clears, Mom is crouching over me, shielding me with her body. "Leave her alone," she says to Dad. The words are mushy. Blood.

"You hit our daughter, Rob." Dad sounds so shocked. "Callie, come to me. Mom's not stable right now."

I don't understand, because Dad hit me, not Mom. Didn't he?

Pale Callie whispers, *It's time, now, Warm Callie. Run.*

I roll out from under Mom and run, away from the house, the drive, toward the desert, through the ruined sheds and cacti, stumbling on the rocky ground. Pale Callie streaks ahead of me, lighting my way in a bolt of silver.

Follow my light, Pale Callie says. *Keep going toward the west fence.* Sagebrush makes spider shapes against the coming night. The last of the sun is a burning red sliver on the Cottonwood Mountains.

Someone calling, behind. I look back. It's Mom, struggling across the ground. "Callie!" she calls.

There's a roar of engine and the stars of Dad's headlights glow brighter. They start to bob. Dad is driving across the scrub, bouncing and roaring. He drives Mom ahead of him like a sheep. But then he passes her, leaves her behind in the dark, and the headlights are coming for me.

Come on. Pale Callie darts ahead.

The fence rears in front of me, black diamonds against the dark blue dusk. I slam up against it, panting. *What now, Pale Callie?* I am scared. *Why are we here?*

It's time, now.

I look around but there's nowhere left to go. I am walled in by the wire fence and a thick grove of arrow weed. The camphor scent is sickening on the night. Approaching headlights rake the ground. Dad and Mom are coming fast. *You tricked me,* I say to Pale Callie. *You've led me into a trap! You want me to be pale!*

Pale Callie doesn't answer. She dives in and out of the fence. I think she's enjoying the feel of the wire going through her. I am crying now. The white headlights are coming closer, the engine is like a monster. Will Dad stop or will he drive through us?

Light pours over the ground in a flood. I shade my eyes as Dad roars to a halt. He gets out and opens the back door. "So dangerous, all this running around at night," he says. "Time to go, bud. In you get."

I feel the big tender place where his fist landed. I feel the other side, where I hit the hard ground. "Dad, I don't want to," I whisper. "You hit me."

"Callie, don't make stuff up," he says, impatient. He comes toward me and picks me up with ease. Dad rowed crew at Princeton. His body seems as big as a house. He smells clean. His grip is tight, too tight, and I wriggle. His arm clamps down on my tender side, squeezing. It hurts.

Mom stumbles into the flooded white light of the beams. The blood on her looks black like paint. There's something wrong with her leg. She comes at us and grabs on to Dad's belt. He kicks her. She makes an *ugh* sound and it's almost like I can hear the important things inside her break. I smell the fear on her skin. Dad shoves her down again but she hangs on. Mom reaches out one hand to me, palm open.

"Callie," she mouths, through bloody lips.

If I give it to her, it means I've made my choice.

Which one of them do I pick, Pale Callie?

Pale Callie expands, looms over the land and sky, vast as the stars. *Stick a needle in his eye.* Her voice is from everywhere.

I wriggle the click from my sleeve and toss it down to Mom. She wraps her arms around Dad's legs and we're falling. Dad screams like an eagle. We both hit the ground. His arms loosen and I roll out from his grip. Dad turns over and Mom crawls up his fallen body, toward his face like a lizard climbing a tree.

The sound of his knuckles on her cheekbone is like gunshot. *Crack.* Mom shakes but she gets herself up again. "Look away, Callie," she calls. She holds the needle, shining, high above her head. Then she brings it down and Dad screams.

"Cover your eyes," Mom says. "Keep them covered, sweetheart."

But I can't. Dad crawls toward Mom on the ground like a maggot. Silver in his eye. She crawls away from him but she's slow. He reaches. His hand closes around Mom's ankle.

It's behind you, Pale Callie says. *Go backward.*

I don't need telling twice. I back away from the horrible crawling thing. The ground gives way behind me and I fall. There's a hole, a depression in the hard ground. Some animal has been scrabbling here. I see why. The outlines of a skeleton can be seen beneath a thin layer of dirt. The end of one femur and the skull are exposed. Vines wind in and out of the eye sockets like little snakes. I'm pretty good on bones, so I know it's a cow even before I see the bell gleaming in the moonlight.

Pick it up, Pale Callie says. *You can do it.*

I pick up the cow femur.

Now give it to her, Pale Callie says. *It's time.* She shines bright, brighter than the headlights; we cast stark shadows on the sandy desert floor.

"Mom!" I call and throw it. The bone lands by her with a *thump* and she looks at it in surprise. Dad reaches up toward her. Blood runs down his face.

I cover my ears with my hands. The last thing I see before I close my eyes is Mom, kneeling in the moonlight, bone raised high above her head with both hands.

AFTER A TIME, when the air feels quiet, I open my eyes. Mom is lying beside me, eyes closed. I think she's passed out, but she's breathing, which is good.

I don't look at what lies there, in the white light of the beams.

BIG. RED. X.

Stuck a needle in his eye, Pale Callie says, pleased. But I'm very, very screaming ghost face. I can't handle any of the things that just happened. Chills race up and down my body. Something wet and hot hurtles up in me and I gag.

Pale Callie is upset that I'm upset. She becomes a cool silver and gold mist. She sits around my temples like a crown. It's actually very soothing and my heart stops splashing quite so hard. The world stops dancing and shaking at the corners of my eyes.

I always thought you weren't real, I say to her. *Like an imaginary friend. When Mom told me about the click I thought, OK, that makes sense, I inherited a brain glitch. What are you, Pale Callie?*

You know.

Nothing in the world makes sense anymore and everything I thought was wrong. I say the thing that's in my heart even though it makes no sense. *I think—I think you're my sister.*

That's right, she says, in wonder.

My side hurts, Pale Callie.

I know, she says. *But you keep going.*

I'm so happy you're here.

She gives a long sigh and stretches out all over me, holds me in her silver-and-gold embrace. *Me too.*

I feel her outlines begin to fade. *But this is as far as I go,* she says. *I did it right in the end, didn't I? I helped. I get confused, sometimes, about mice and mooses . . .*

You did great, I tell her. *You lit the way for me. You found the bone to hit him with.*

Mooses and mices and Morocco, and Mauritius and Monaco. She fades, until she's just a scatter of silver on the air. Her voice grows fainter until it's just a whisper. *Manacles and manatees and morose . . .*

Wait, Pale Callie, wait! Then I yell, "Wait!" because I need her. We've always been together.

Oh good, she says very, very faintly. *They're here.* And then even the silver pinpricks fade on the night, and the only sound is the wind. She's gone. I am so sad; it's too hard; I only just figured out what she was.

"Callie?" Mom's awake. Her eyes are fixed on a place beyond me, in the dark beyond the beams of Dad's car. Something moves there, at the edge of the light. "Oh my god," she says. "They're here."

ROB

HE COMES INTO the light like he belongs, which he does. This has been his home for many years. He's old, gray, fur thin in patches. But the dental cement cap on his head is intact. Even without it, I'd know him anywhere. As if hearing my thoughts he turns and grins at me and I see a couple of teeth are missing in those powerful jaws. I am caught in his golden eyes. All the desert is in them. He is still a king.

"Stay still," I say quietly to Callie. "Not a muscle." I can't tell her to cover her eyes again, in case we have to run. I wish I could.

The others come forward now, melting out of the shadow of thick arrow weed. Somewhere in there is the place they've dug under the fence, I suppose. There are five or six. They have his yellow eyes, but they're not full coyote. One has a springy, jaunty little topknot. Another has a brown-and-tan coat like a German shepherd. The coyote pads over to Irving. For a moment he pauses. Then he lowers his head and grabs the cuff of Irving's pants in his powerful jaws. He tugs gently, testing.

Irving stirs. His fingers flutter. He makes a sound, as if tasting something bad. The coyote pauses, then tugs on Irving's pants cuff once more. It's almost polite. *Come play.* Irving's fingers flutter again, as if seeking a hand to hold.

I could grab my weapon of bone—it lies a couple of feet away from me, slick with blood. I could run at the dogs, yelling. It might work. I breathe deep and think of the decision tree. I think of Annie; her fragile limbs so easily bruised, her wide gaze, her faith that the world is a good place. When I look at Callie her eyes meet mine. My strange, clever daughter, so at odds with the world.

I don't move.

The other dogs come forward now. They gather around Irving and drag him toward the shadow of the saguaro. With a deep breath, I toss the bloodied femur after them. *Nimue.* Her bones have lain here all this time. I hope it was quick for her. I hope she didn't suffer. A little burly dog with big ears breaks from the rear of the pack, seizes the bone in strong jaws and drags it proudly into the dark.

None of this seems strange to them. I've taught these descendants of the Sundial pack that they'll be fed by me, here at the boundary fence.

"COME ON, SWEETHEART," I say to Callie. "We have things to do." I lift her gently to her feet. Her body, usually so stiff and resistant to my touch, is pliable. Have I done her more harm tonight than Irving ever could? No point in such thoughts. I made the choice. We must all live with it.

The driver's seat is still warm. The car is filled with Irving's too-clean scent and I shiver. His cell phone is on the dashboard. The battery and SIM card sit neatly in the cupholder.

"He didn't need to do that," Callie says. It's the first time she's spoken since it happened. "Switching the phone off is enough to stop the police tracking it."

"Smart girl," I say. "You're so smart, Callie."

Callie doesn't reply. We both understand what this means. That should make me feel better about what I did, I guess, but it doesn't.

We drive back over the rough land, jouncing. The undercarriage drags over rocks and brush. Something beneath us cracks, breaking. It doesn't matter. We go down the drive to the highway. Callie doesn't ask where we're going. Maybe she knows. The headlights look strange on the road ahead. We move like a spaceship or an underwater creature. I think I got a good blow to the head, too. Honesty rears, darker against the dark.

I pull the car off the road and guide it through the forest of tangled metal and crumbling brick. When we get to the big mine shaft, I stop and open the door. The beams are trained on the portal. When Callie realizes what I mean to do, she screams.

"No!" she says. "Not that one! That's where they live!"

And now she says it I can hear them down there, whining and yapping, bouncing eerie off the tunnel walls. Not all the pack went out to hunt to-night. Then it comes, echoing up through the night: the long, high song of a coyote puppy. Night music, desert music, chiming deep in the earth.

I close the door and drive on, veering to the left. We pull up by another shaft—it's wider, looks older. Deeper, I hope.

I turn off the engine. The headlights and the interior of the car stay lit. It's a safety feature. We get behind the car and push. It rolls down the scree, the light fades like a falling star. There's a crash. The sound is like the end of everything. The portal is eerily lit from below, as though by lava, or some demon from underneath the world.

Callie watches. "I'll be so lonely now," she says.

It feels like a knife in my heart. I stroke her head. "Oh," I say, "oh, oh my darling. I'll always be here for you. I'll be Mom and Dad both."

"That's not what I meant," she says. "I miss Callie." These words open up awful dark places, yawning before me. Have I broken my daughter's mind?

Nearby someone is crying quietly. It's me.

Callie's hand pats mine lightly. "It's OK, Mom," she says. "You had to. I know that."

I take a deep breath. I have to hold it together for her. I take her hands gently. "Come on." My voice is all high and squeaky. "Come away, sweet-heart."

For a moment longer, the headlights glow from deep in the earth. Then they go dark.

ARROWOOD

Callie bent low to the ground, running through the misty morning, following the footprints in the soft earth. They ended, as she'd hoped, at the door to the west tower, where the Uncouth Lower Ninth lived. They would still be sleeping after night classes, perfect prey for Miss Grainger and her golden eyes.

The door opened with a soft groan, and Callie slipped into the darkness of the stairwell. The air was warm with the breath of forty sleeping girls. Did she also hear the click of claws on stone, as if a big golden dog was stalking between the beds?

Her hands still had faint purple stains on them. She thought of what she'd had to do and frowned. But Arrowood had taught her that sometimes the right choice was the hard one.

"Always trying to be the hero."

Callie turned slowly. A dark figure walked out of the mist.

Callie ran to Jack and tried to hug her. "You're back," she whispered. "Now everything will be all right again."

Jack pushed her away. "Stop." Callie saw that her eyes had become gleaming golden coins.

"She changed you," she whispered.

"Yes," Jack said. "It's better this way. No more worrying about mandolin practice or school honor or merit badges or being prefect. Now Miss Grainger and I fly through the night sky. We creep into bedrooms and eat people's memories while they sleep. Memories taste like warm soda, Callie, did you know?"

"It doesn't have to be like that," Callie said.

"You think you're so smart," Jack said. "You burned purple dog sage to bring us. A trap. Your hands still stink of it. But you messed up. She's already up there, you know. All the girls in there are going to die and so are you."

From inside the tower there came a soft sound, like cloth tearing.

"You can't beat her," Jack said.

"You're right," Callie said. "I can't beat her, but we can—together."

"No," Jack said. She came closer and took Callie's shoulders in an iron grip. "I'm going to eat your memories now."

Quick as a flash, Callie whipped the straight razor from her sleeve. She slashed at Jack's eyes. Jack recoiled, gasping, flinging up protecting hands to her face. Too late. Callie flipped the eyes out of Jack's head. The golden coins fell glittering through the air and disappeared without a sound before they reached the damp grass.

Slowly, Jack took her hands away, and looked at Callie, blinking and bewildered. Her irises were back to their regular blue. "You're fast."

"My reflexes are excellent," Callie said. Mrs. Oolong the sports mistress had always told her so.

More soft sounds came from above, in the tower. A sigh, as something tore forever.

"We're too late," Jack said.

"We can save some of them," Callie said.

"You used them," Jack said.

"I had to lure her here with the purple dog sage so she'd bring you. And I had to distract her so I could fix you."

"You did a lot," Jack said, and Callie thought she was mad. But then Jack hugged her hard. "Can we really beat her?"

"I hope so. I'm her daughter—then she made you her daughter, remember? 'Daughters are powerful magic,' she told us. But we're sisters now, and they're powerful magic, too." Callie's straight razor fell open once more with a *click*. Jack's hand felt warm as she took Callie's free one.

"For Arrowood," Jack whispered.

"For Arrowood," Callie breathed.

Together, hand in hand, they crept up the turret stairs.

ROB

WE WALK BACK along the highway toward Sundial. I look at my hands in the moonlight. They're slick with blood and dirt.

I shouldn't be surprised that Irving came out here to kill me. That's what I intended, after all. My sister told me what to do. As soon as I read her letter, I knew I could never give Callie the click. Jack showed me another way. *Kids are mirrors, reflecting back everything that happens to them. You've got to make sure they're surrounded by good things. Remember that, Sundance.*

Irving was not a good thing. I couldn't stand to see what Callie had begun to reflect back—him.

I knew how to make Irving come. Answer the cell phone once in seventeen times. Incessant, irksome little gestures of defiance and capitulation. A constant push and pull, push and pull, ignoring him, letting the cord grow slack and then tautening it again. I had already learned everything I needed to know about how to do that—from him, and our marriage. How infuriated Irving got when he wasn't at the center. How much pain to show him, so that he couldn't resist coming to take a closer look. I knew I could work him to a fever pitch, bring the maggots out in him, make him come here to end it. Those last couple of messages, in particular, were a delicate balancing act.

Irving wrote: *Don't think you're leaving me. I'm going to leave you. Hannah can give me so much more.*

I replied: *I hope you'll be happy.* After some more thought I sent: *She'll make you take your shoes off when you come inside. You know how she insists on it.* Irving hated that.

No one can make me do anything. They'd been arguing, I could tell. Maybe Hannah had discovered the terrible bargain she'd made.

The truth is, I typed, *you're scared to be without a woman.* I think this was true.

Careful, Rob. Or I'll take the girls and go back east.

Hannah would never agree to separate me from my girls.

I'll go alone then. You've never understood me, Rob.

I gave it a minute, then I sent: *Fuck you.*

It was an hour before he answered. He was always good at keeping me in suspense. *No need for that language. It's done. Maybe we can have a civilized talk when you get back.*

I'm a better wife than her.

That last message wasn't delivered. I knew the phone must have been switched off. I was pretty sure he was on his way. I had come to understand, over the years, how much and how dearly my husband loved to surprise me.

I had it all planned out. I was trying to grab Callie and lock her safely in her room when she ran. When Irving arrived I would wake the maggots inside him. I knew they'd be close to the surface. He would chase me across the night land, this land I know so well, to the grave I had dug for him behind the picket fence, among the dead dogs.

I emptied out the click—depressed the plunger and watched the purple liquid trickle down the drain. I planned to stop Irving's heart with a needle full of air. A pulmonary embolism, it's called. I got the idea from something Callie said. She stumbled over the word at breakfast—*em-bol-ism. Emblamism? No, embolism.*

It felt right to do it with the syringe that had once contained the click. It was an act of faith, too. Getting rid of the contents was my guarantee that I would never, never use it on my daughter.

I knew it would be OK if I got close enough. Strangely, I wanted him to have a chance—a fair fight between us, for once.

I shudder as I recall the resistance, the needle sliding into his eye. I feel again the give of his skull under my blows. I'm a murderer, again. It's the fate that's been waiting for me all those years, maybe. Everything comes around the dial in the end. I did it for my daughters. And for those who lie here, beneath the desert sand. The decision tree always brings you to the right place, even if it's one you don't want to go. But I got stuff badly wrong. I wish Callie hadn't run. I was trying to scare her. I did my job too well. I wish beyond anything that she hadn't seen it. I wish he hadn't hurt her.

So this is it—the story that defines me. My leg hurts, my eyes swim. It's cold out here. Funny if after all we've been through, the desert took me in the end.

There are things to think about. What to say. Build the story, brick by brick. But it will be OK. I know it will. The desert knows how to keep a secret. Irving was planning to go back east. He'd been fighting with Hannah and decided to abandon us both—his messages say so. If, as I suspect, Irving has already revealed the maggots to her, Hannah will believe it, too.

IN THE DOG graveyard, I fill in the grave I meant for Irving. I am tired as death. Callie crouches beside me, holding the flashlight. I don't suggest she go inside or leave. She stays close to my side without being told. We need each other. We're in this together.

"Do you think your sister is still here, somewhere?" Callie asks, looking around at Sundial, stretching into the dark. "Do you ever see her?"

"No," I say. I touch Callie's arm gently, for comfort. Hers or mine? "Jack is gone." It feels true for the first time.

"I pressed the button and the dogs came," Callie whispers. "They hunted."

"They come here all the time, sweetheart. You hear me? The controller is old, broken. It doesn't work. This is not your fault."

When it's finished I lean on the shovel. For a moment the night seems to hold the scent of blood, the heat of a desert day, long ago. For a moment I see a bassinet by the graveside, my little Callie's fists waving. I always loved her hands, as a baby. So clever and nimble. She was always grabbing mine, as if desperate for closeness. How could I have forgotten that?

As if hearing my thought, Callie reaches out to me. She does it stiffly, unaccustomed to asking for affection. I take her in my arms and kiss her hair, leaving blood on her head. I'll lose that tooth. It doesn't matter.

"I love you," I tell her. I hold her tight, careful of her bruised sides. Somehow, I did it. I have saved both of my daughters.

"The click was gone," Callie says in her squeezed little voice. "The hypodermic was empty."

"I threw it away," I say. "We don't need the click. We're going to be just fine. You and Annie are both safe." I squeeze her hand. "Callie, you can tell me. Was it Dad who did that to the animals? It's OK, he can't hurt you now."

"It wasn't me," she says, and the world sways. Relief sweeps through me. I hadn't realized how tightly wound I've been over the past few days. Maybe the past decade. Sleep will be welcome.

"Mom, we have to go get Annie, right away." There's an adult look in her eyes. Something is not right. This should be the end of this particular story. But it's not, I see now. A terrible thought sweeps through me, a wing of shadow over my mind.

CALLIE

MOM TOUCHES MY cheek and kisses my head with her broken mouth. Now there's blood in my hair. I think of how she tried to protect me. Moms are like the desert, too. Sometimes you can't stop them.

I have to trust her. I have to give her the biggest secret, the one that rules my life. So I take a deep breath. "Mom, we have to go get Annie right away."

"What do you mean?" But there's knowledge in her voice already; she's trying not to, but she knows. It's like the darkness has made her clearer and I can hear everything she feels. It occurs to me that love is as bad as pain sometimes, which is a very interesting thought but there is no time for it now. I have to make her understand.

"We have to go get her, Mom." I tug her by the hand. She stumbles. In the moonlight I can see one of her eyes has closed up into a little horizontal line like a serious mouth.

"Hold up, Callie. I . . . I'm not feeling so good."

"No!" I scream. "Now, now, now! Annie can't be left alone with Mrs. Goodwin."

"What?" Adults are very slow sometimes. But she is starting to get it. I feel the understanding run through her like sickness. She gasps and sags a little. I feel sorry for her. I wish I didn't have to do this, but I do.

"Annie didn't eat the diabetes medicine," I say. "It's in the lamp. The star lamp. Dad said Annie took the lamp with her when she went to Mrs. Goodwin's . . ."

We run toward the house. Yellow light spills out of the open front door over the step, over the wooden sign. NO DOGS IN THE HOUSE. I jump in the back and Mom falls into the front seat of her car with a groan. She fumbles with the keys, fingers trembling.

"Aren't you going to lock the door?"

"Leave it, it's just a house," Mom says, impatient. "Thank god," she says as the engine growls into life. Dirt flies from the tires as we pull away with a lurch. Even in all my fear about Annie, I still turn to take one last look at Sundial, where somewhere Pale Callie lies peaceful in the earth. I never thought to wonder how she could come with me, even though I don't have her bones. It's because I am her bones. She's in me. Or she was. I won't see her again, I know that.

You're supposed to protect your little sister. That was one of the first things I ever learned. Mom drummed it into me. And Annie is so little and cute. I knew she would never make it in one of those places where they put bad kids. So when I found her with Dumpster Puppy that day, I made her swear never to tell, and I kept it secret, too. Poor Dumpster Puppy. I told her to finish quickly because he had been through enough. I could see that.

I try to stop Annie but she can't be stopped. She is who she is.

I've always been able to help pale things. They're not scared of me the way they're scared of most people. I don't expect them to be anything other than what they are. My first memory is of looking at a little flower, dried and dead on the curb. I can't remember where or when it was. I must have been very little. But I saw the little silver flower ghost of it detaching, and fading away, into nothing. I found that if I kept the bones and stalks of things they stayed with me and I could care for them. So when Annie's done I take the bones. If the dead things want to go, they can go. If they want to stick around and be pale, I keep them company, make them my friends so that they're not sad. It's all I can do.

Parents think kids don't notice when they fight but we do. Annie and I were lying in the shade of the pink lamp, listening to them hiss at one another like snakes. Sometimes after lights-out I sneak into her room, because she doesn't like the nighttime. I think bad thoughts come to her then. I think she has too much time to think about who she is, at night. Annie's hand was in mine. It was early fall and hot; the windows were open. Occasionally a beetle or a moth would hit the bug screen with a *thunk*.

"Mom and Dad are going to get a divorce," Annie said.

"No, they're not," I said.

"They are. Daddy is making the bad monkey with Hannah next door."

"Call her Mrs. Goodwin. Anyway that's not true."

"I saw them. They thought I was at Maria's house but that was canceled. Daddy never checks the calendar."

"Shh," I say. "Try not to worry about it." I knew all about Dad and Mrs. Goodwin next door. "It's just how it goes." He would make the bad monkey with someone new for a couple of months and then it would end and everything would go back to normal. At least until the next time.

"God wants her to die," Annie said. "You could put her bones on your wall. That would be cool."

"You can't do that, Annie. I'm serious. You'll get caught. And what happens then?"

"Kid prison. I know, Callie. You're so annoying. I would make it seem like she did it herself. Grown-ups do that."

She reached out with a finger and stroked her pink star lamp. "There's a hiding place in here, Callie, did you know? It would be best to do it when Mom isn't home." She sounded thoughtful. "She's always watching over me because I'm her favorite."

"Come on," I said, to distract her. "Let's make up a story about princesses. You like that."

It's no good trying to argue Annie out of things. It makes her angry and you really don't want that. I tried several times to get the star lamp away from her, but that didn't work. Mom kept giving it back.

For a while it seemed like Annie had forgotten about it. She stepped up her activities, which made her happy. A stray kitten, a gopher, a couple of squirrels. She sneaks out of the house to wander the neighborhood, looking for sick or injured animals. Some people around here use a kind of pesticide on their yards that makes the small animals slow and shaky. I read up on it. I helped her hide the bodies whenever I could. I took the bones, to stop them being lonely.

"They were going to die anyway," Annie always says. "I just sent them to God a little sooner."

I think Annie got the chicken pox when she got into Mrs. Goodwin's house somehow, trying to carry out her plan. I guess something went wrong that time.

When I found her with her mittens off I taped them back on. "You'll scratch yourself, Annie. It will leave a scar forever. You won't like that." I was a little exasperated. She knew she wasn't supposed to take the mittens off. "Plus, Mom will go crazy and she'll probably blame me."

So Annie even tricked me into helping her frame me. I didn't understand what she'd done until Mom found the bottle cap in my special hiding place in the floor. I hadn't realized Annie even *knew* about my hiding place.

I snuck into her room much later. "Annie," I whispered. "You're making it look like I stole Dad's medicine. You're making it look like I poisoned you. Plus, now she thinks I did that to the animals."

She said, "Don't you think it's smart, Callie? I even ate some blue Tic Tacs to throw up, so it looks like you made me take the pills. But really I'm saving them for Hannah." She was smart. She had planned carefully.

"Mrs. Goodwin. Come on, Annie. Don't say silly things. You don't mean it."

"I mean it," she said.

"I have to tell Mom," I said. I tried to think about how I would punish her for this. I couldn't think what would fit the situation. Everything had suddenly got much more serious and I really wanted a grown-up to tell me what to do.

"If you tell, I'll give Mom the medicine instead. Anyway, she'll never believe you."

I weighed up my options and decided that maybe it was better if I let Mom keep thinking I did it, even the stuff with the animals. That would give Annie time to cool down. Sometimes she does cool down if you leave her alone. I thought that so long as she was sick and in bed, and a grown-up was home and Mrs. Goodwin was next door with Mr. Goodwin and the boys, Annie couldn't do much. Now I think maybe I chose the wrong option.

Screaming face.

MOM DRIVES FASTER than I have ever seen. "How could I not know?" she says over and over. "How?" Dumpster Puppy has become very small and is hiding up my sleeve. I wondered if he had gone with Pale Callie but he hobbled up, three-legged, as we got in the car. His bone is buried there, so I guess part of him will always be at Sundial.

"I'm scared we'll be too late," I say. "I'm scared she's already given the medicine to Hannah." I am almost sure we'll be too late.

"Mrs. Goodwin," Mom corrects me automatically. She blinks hard, as if contacts were bothering her. "And we'll get there in time. She won't do it. Annie doesn't understand what she's doing. She's smart, she's a smart girl . . ." Mom keeps contradicting herself like this. Everything she says cancels out the last thing.

I think about what I saw in Pale Callie's light. Two figures, struggling. Flesh on flesh. I shut my mind quickly. *BIG RED X*.

"Mom?"

"Yes, Callie?"

"I really did have *the best time* at Sundial. It was good, just you and me."

She gives a little sobbing laugh. "You are the weirdest kid," she says. "Just like your mother." Her eyes are large and gleaming. She wipes her hand across her cheek. "I did, too."

"What happens to her if we're too late?" I ask. "To Annie."

"We protect her," she says. Her mouth is an invisible line.

"How?"

"I don't know. I'll think of something."

Mom's right. If we don't protect Annie, she'll end up in kid prison and I will miss her so much. I can already feel the pain of separation. She might die if they put her in prison. She'll definitely cry in there. When I even think about Annie crying my own eyes sting and my heart feels fit to break. Prison for Annie is not an option.

We'll have to keep protecting her as long as she lives. I can't stop thinking about how long a person lives. Mom will die one day and then it will just be me. How many years will I have to worry about Annie and keep her safe all by myself and stop her hurting people? I'm so tired already and I'm only twelve. A little part of me is thinking about the click. That part of me wishes Mom hadn't gotten rid of it. Maybe it could have helped Annie. So I guess I'm a bad person, because I should accept her how she is.

I don't know what to hope for, anymore. All I know is that whatever happens, Annie is the clock that will measure my life from now on.

We roar into Cielo after two a.m. Mom trembles, her hands sweat and slip a little on the wheel as she takes the corner. Her breath saws in and out. Both of us are straining forward against our seat belts, as if we could make the car go faster that way.

Our street is dark. People keep early hours around here; it's a good neighborhood. There is only one light burning at the end of the block. In an upstairs bedroom of Hannah's house, the little pink lamp shines out just like a real star, set to guide us home.

ACKNOWLEDGMENTS

I AM PROFOUNDLY thankful for the good-hearted, wonderful, hilarious Ed McDonald. You understood this book from the very beginning and championed it as it came to life. You throw the best surprise parties, make the best jokes, and write the best books. I am so lucky to have you in my life.

To my wonderful agent, Jenny Savill, I can only say once more a most heartfelt *thank you*—you are as kind as you are brilliant. Michael Dean, many, many thanks for your tireless work and care in bringing my books to film. To Andrew Nurnberg and everyone at Andrew Nurnberg Associates, especially Barbara Barbieri, Rory Clarke, Lucy Flynn, Juliana Galvis, Halina Koscia, and Sabine Pfannenstiel, thank you. I am so appreciative of everything you do.

I remain deeply grateful to my amazing US agent, Robin Straus. So much of this exciting journey is thanks to you. You and Danielle Matta have done such a fantastic job of bringing my books to the US.

To my talented UK editor, Miranda Jewess, thank you for putting such enormous care and thought into this book. You're a powerhouse—not at all a fussy biscuit. I am very fortunate to work with you. Drew Jerrison and Niamh Murray, you are both incredible. To Graeme Hall and Hayley Shepherd, thank you for your keen editorial eyes—and thank you to all the wonderful team at Viper and Profile. I'm very grateful to Andrew Franklin, for giving my books such great support.

Many thanks go to my equally wonderful US editor, Kelly O'Connor Lonesome, you have worked day and night for *Sundial*, and I can't sing your praises highly enough. Anneliese Merz and Alexis Saarela, I am so appreciative of all you have done to help this book find an audience—I don't know when you sleep. Thank you to Devi Pillai, Michael Dudding, Jordan Hanley, Sarah Pannenberg, Kristin Temple, and the rest of the fantastic team at Tor Nightfire and Tom Doherty Associates. I feel very fortunate to be published by you.

The beautiful, dramatic cover art for *Sundial* was created by Corey Brickley and Katie Klimowicz in the US and Steve Panton in the UK. Each cover captures the spirit of the book in a very different, striking way.

All my love and gratitude go as ever to my mother, Isabelle, and my father, Christopher, for all their help from the very beginning. To my dear sister, Antonia Ward, and to Sam Enoch, thank you so much for always being there with support, cheerleading, beautiful flowers, and sage advice. It means everything. Lovely Wolf and River remain a constant source of joy.

For long talks, support, and kindnesses too numerous to mention, my thanks to Emily Cavendish, Kate Burdette, Oriana Elia, Andrew Fingret, Lydia Leonard, Craig Leyenaar, Andy Morwood, Natasha Pulley, Alice Slater, Dea Vanagan, Holly Watt, Belinda Stewart-Wilson, Rachel Winterbottom, and Anna Wood.